YEAR·OF·THE·SCARAB·TRILOGY
BOOK ONE

BY ANDREW BATES

AUTHOR	ANDREW BATES
COVER ARTIST	TOM FLEMING
SERIES EDITOR	CARL BOWEN
COPY EDITOR	MELISSA THORPE
GRAPHIC ARTIST	RON THOMPSON
ART DIRECTOR	RICHARD THOMAS

Copyright ©2001 by White Wolf, Inc.
All rights reserved.
Printed in Canada

No part of this book may reproduced or transmitted in any form or by any means, electronic or mechanical — Including photocopy, recording, internet posting, electronic bulletin board — or any other information storage and retrieval system, except for the purpose of reviews, without permission of the publisher.

White wolf is committed to reducing waste in publishing. For this reason, we do not permit our covers to be "stripped" for returns, but instead require that the whole book be returned, allowing us to resell it.

All persons, places, and organizations in the book — except those clearly in the public domain — Are fictitious, and any resemblance that may seem to exist to actual persons, places, or organizations living, dead, or defunct is purely coincidental. The mention of or reference to any companies or products in these pages is not challenge to the trademarks or copyrights concerned.

White Wolf Publishing
735 Park North Boulevard, Suite 128
Clarkston, GA 30021
www.white-wolf.com

YEAR·OF·THE·SCARAB·TRILOGY
BOOK ONE
HERALDS OF THE STORM

TABLE OF CONTENTS

PART I: ANSWERING THE CALL	7
PART II: THE HATE MACHINE	121
PART III: DRAWING BACK THE VEIL	185
PART IV: LIFE AND DEATH	245

ANDREW BATES

Oblivion screamed its triumph through the ether. Freed from shackles that had chained it too long, terror tore through the shadowlands, destruction its only goal. The force of its passage shredded realms of spirit and emotion. Its might tore asunder souls living and dead.

The maelstrom ravaged existence a heartbeat away from reality. But the living felt only echoes. Most in the waking world sensed the rape of the shadowlands as that nameless dread you can't quite put a finger on. Someone walking over your grave. Chills down your spine.

Others felt the full impact of oblivion's rage. Some took shelter from the tempest. Some worked to harness the storm for their own dark intent. And some stood firm against the things the maelstrom drove forth with its soul-rending winds.

ANDREW BATES

PART I:
ANSWERING THE CALL

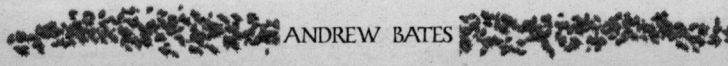

ONE

Thea Ghandour knew that the tales of things that go bump in the night weren't just stories. She knew there were monsters in the world. She and a half-dozen others had been hunting the bastards for months. They practically had it down to a science: keep an eye open for strangeness, track the creature back to its lair, then swoop in armed to the teeth and blow the freak to Kingdom Come.

They had no idea what they were getting into.

• • •

"Colder'n a witch's tit out here," Parker grumbled over the headset.

Thea smiled. "You know from first-hand experience?" He was right, though. Siberia was supposed to be this great frozen wasteland. *Try Chicago in the winter, Ivan.*

They were outside an estate by Lake Cosman, about a mile from the Alexian Brothers Medical Center. On the way in, Jake said it was a nice coincidence having a hospital so nearby in case we needed it. Carl said he wouldn't be surprised if the vampire had the whole complex in his back pocket, using it as his own personal blood bank. Jake looked startled, then nodded.

Cold? Hell yes! Being fifteen miles in from Lake Michigan didn't slow that arctic wind down much. Having Lake Cosman a stone's throw away didn't help, either. And for that extra special touch, it was an hour before sunrise without a cloud in the sky. That's when you get what the pocket-protector-and-lab-coat set call "radiational cooling." Thea thought Parker's description was more apt.

Welcome to February in Illinois.

"Stop the chatter," Romeo's whisper from the earpiece dropped the temperature another ten degrees. Feeling like a kid caught passing a note in class, Thea shot a glance at where Romeo hunkered nearby against the stone wall. He was right, though. They were being professional about this — body armor, winter camouflage, radios, synchronized watches, the whole bit — but Thea admitted they weren't actual *professionals*. Well, everyone except Romeo.

Samuel "Romeo" Zheng. The two of them joined the group at the same time, about seven months ago, but Thea didn't know much more about him than anyone else. From what Thea had been able to gather, he might have been a cop in Hong Kong. That or part of one of the tongs or triads or whatever they called their version of the Mob. All Thea had nailed down was that he knew a lot about the law and how to break it without getting caught. The group called him "Romeo" after Dean made a joke about how Zheng resembled Jet Li from some action flick from a couple years back. Romeo made like it bothered him, but Thea thought he secretly liked it.

He might have looked like the wiry Hong Kong action star, but as far as Thea had seen he didn't know much in the way of martial arts. She remembered when they'd met — the night she was first exposed to the things they now hunted — and how even with only basic self-defense training she'd had better moves than Romeo. She'd figured it couldn't hurt to learn all she could after that night. Thea was no Zen master, but she could kick Romeo's ass. She thought he secretly liked that, too.

Their little group didn't have a leader per se, but Romeo claimed the role of designated hard ass. Thea heard that Parker had the gig before Romeo came along. Parker Moston did okay, but he was really just a big corn-fed lug playing at being John Wayne. Romeo just stepped in and, next thing you know, he was the guy planning their nighttime adventures. Romeo kept them all in line when they were "in the shit," as Parker loved to call it. The Asian made sure their Kevlar was buckled on right and that they pointed their small arms — automatic pistols, submachine guns, bullpup-configuration shotguns; take your pick — at the enemy, not each other.

And saw that they weren't gabbing on their little radio headsets when they were about to go after a vampire. After all, who's to say Count Fangula didn't have a nifty little radio nest monitoring for just this sort of thing? Thea considered that if she were an undead creature of the night she'd spare no expense in making sure her immortal existence was as protected as possible. Which was also why they were sneaking up on the fucker's house during the ass-end of night, armed with enough firepower to take over a middling-size third world nation.

Romeo looked back at her, like he knew what Thea was thinking. *Shit. Maybe he did!* Thea and her fellow hunters all had strange abilities, like the kid in that *Sixth Sense* movie. No one knew where the powers ultimately came from, but they all seemed to have triggered the first time they encountered monsters. Helped a lot in the hunt, but Thea wouldn't exactly call them a blessing. Anyway, they each had their edges; did Romeo have some kind of telepathy along with his? If so, he'd picked up her little fantasies about grabbing that wiry Asian bod of his—

Hey, Romeo, Thea thought. *What say we take a quickie here in the bushes? Jake can stand guard.*

His expression didn't change. Instead, he flipped his headset's lip mic back up and motioned for her to do the same. Then he flicked open the dull primer sprayed three-step ladder he carried to help him peek over the top of the wall. A second later he'd slipped over the side to scope things out further.

Well, that was something anyway. Unless he *did* hear her and was just a damn good poker player. *Nah*, Thea thought. *A roll in the hay with Yours Truly is not something to sneeze at.*

HERALDS OF THE STORM

An equally mortifying idea occurred to her: What if someone else in their little gang could read thoughts? Embarrassing on a whole different level.

Then Thea's blood went cold.

What if the *vampire* could? What if he was "listening" to her — to all of them — right now? Radio silence wouldn't mean a fucking thing if a nasty could pick up their thoughts like satellite TV.

Thea waved Jake after Romeo while she forced herself to calm down. She got like this every time they went after supernatural shit. Her thoughts ran a mile a minute under normal circumstances. Whenever they were on the job, though, her mind shifted to sixth and hit the nitro. She was fine once the action started, knowing instinctively what to do and when to do it. But leading up to the main event was a real bitch. Thea didn't know how much of that was just her — attacking an undead predator was bound to make anyone tense, right? — and how much of it was the vibes she felt ever since she first encountered this strangeness. Either way, she had to deal with panic attacks at the worst times.

Jake went over soon as Romeo's gloved hand scraped the stone on the other side in their agreed-upon signal. By the time the scratching came again Thea had her shit back together.

•••

No turning back now, Thea thought as she hunkered down between Romeo and Jake. Quick look around, get the lay of the land. Thea had a pair of night-vision goggles — everyone did except Romeo, who didn't need them. She seldom bothered with them herself, though. Thea was a touch color-blind and for some reason that artificial green played hell with her eyesight. She made due with good, old-fashioned peering into the dark.

The place looked pretty nice, actually. No cover to speak of near the wall; the closest tree was about ten yards in. It had a lot of pals once you got there, though. Naked trees and some shrubs filled the interior to obscure a view of the house itself. The best Thea could make out from there was that it was big and had an unusual profile. It might've had a couple outbuildings, too. Some landscaping to make it all work together. Unfortunately, that landscaping included placing lights every twenty yards along the wall. They'd come over midway between two lights. A thin layer of old snow covered the ground, but with a new moon and their winter camouflage Thea thought they were safe from a casual glance. Still, exposed was exposed any way you sliced it. Thea was just a tad puzzled why they weren't busting ass for the trees. The whispered argument between Romeo and Jake answered that one.

The two were crouched over a body. Since it was still an actual body instead of a pile of dust and she hadn't heard a God-awful scuffle, Thea figured it was a human Romeo had encountered when he first came over the wall. The undead typically put up more of a fight before they went down. That being the case, she had a guess what Romeo and Jake's argument was about. The two represented opposing schools of thought on how to handle monsters. Romeo thought all nasties should be destroyed utterly. Jake felt that it was simplistic to assume that all these creatures were irrevocably evil. When the verdict was in, though, they generally agreed what had to be done. Take the vampire they were after now. It was involved in all sorts of dark shit. Using one of the many under-funded orphanages in the Chicago area for everything from slave labor to kiddie porn — that was all they'd needed to know. The guy was begging for a stake even if he wasn't undead. They hadn't figured out why a vampire would bother with such pursuits to begin with, but that wasn't as important as shutting him down.

Most often it wasn't a simple case of taking down a solitary nasty working all by his lonesome, though. Turns out a lot of the bastards had living folks helping them out. The vampires, at least. Your zombie and skeleton types didn't seem to do much in the way of mortal lackeys. Thea didn't

know what the bloodsuckers used as hiring incentives — probably had good dental, but the retirement plan? — but they typically had a few Renfields on the payroll. Thea had only ever seen the goons acting as gofers. That was how they'd first stumbled across the vampire they were after now, "Augustus Klein" (an alias if she'd ever heard one).

Whatever their role, normal people made the hunters' mission less clear-cut. Destroying a *monster* was one thing, killing a *person* quite another. Thus far Thea's gang had avoided that moral quandary by the simple expedient of avoiding the living and distracting or subduing them when that wasn't possible. The goons only had to be out of the way for a little while, after all. Take out the fang and his stooges couldn't do much after but start looking through the classifieds. Thea figured it was only a matter of time until they couldn't dodge the issue, though. Nice of Romeo to prove her right.

It was obvious Jake wasn't too happy with Romeo having asserted his point of view on the thug lying there. Thea wasn't thrilled either. She could understand silencing the guard so he wouldn't give them away, but did that have to mean killing the guy? But it was not the time for debate.

At least their lip mics were up so their tiff wasn't being transmitted. Thea slipped up and smacked Romeo on the shoulder then glared at the both of them. Romeo and Jake looked at her, surprised and pissed. But at least they shut up. *So busy trying to see who has the bigger dick, they forget all about the vampire lurking not two hundred yards away.* Thea grimaced, irritated with men and their single-mindedness.

Romeo was all business in a second, picking up the dead guard like a sack of dog food and hustling for the tree line. Jake followed, chin thrust forward in anger.

Jake Washington. On the surface a typical middle-class black kid from Boston, budding intellectual and computer geek. You didn't have to scratch too far beneath that to see he was just as odd as Romeo, if not more so. The story went that Jake got snuggly with a vampire a couple years ago.

ANDREW BATES

Then she tore his legs off when one of his pals tried to stake her. The pal didn't get off as easy as Jake did.

After that, Jake dropped out of sight from hunter-net, the half-assed computer network monster hunters used. Many of the loose brotherhood of hunters first found one another through the Internet. It had proved helpful at sharing information on habits of the undead, tactics in hunting them, and coordinating hunts. Despite the efforts of the hunters who'd first established the network, it was open to infiltration from wackos and from the nasties themselves. Thea seldom logged on to hunter-net; she got enough fevered ravings and pointless argument face to face without indulging in the electronic variety. It wasn't all useless crap, though. Jake had been one of hunter-net's most visible, and most reliable, contributors before his accident. Afterward, he emerged only now and then to post stuff. Then, about nine months ago, he was back on the scene... *walking*. Somehow his legs were completely restored. He's made his way around the country since then, helping other hunter gangs. He'd been with Thea's group since just before Christmas.

Thea had to admit Jake was a great help, but she had trouble swallowing his whole story. She admitted that monsters existed (not that she was thrilled with the situation). She accepted that certain people who joined the hunt had some kind of weird psychic powers or something (not that she was too comfortable giving those talents an official label). But regenerating your legs? Thea secretly suspected Jake had only had them injured, maybe some kind of spinal damage that kept him from walking for a while. So he built this story to give him a reputation, right? She could dig it. Even if the kid did have an overactive imagination, there was no denying he'd gone through some heavy shit. Yet despite devoting his life to the hunt for years, longer than any of the rest of them in the Van Helsing brigade, he still had an optimistic view of their collective mission. The kid believed there was virtue in everyone, the good guys would win, there was a happily ever after, blah blah blah. Choose your cliché. Goofy as the attitude was at times, it was a refreshing change of pace from the constant gloom and doom from the rest of the crew.

It looked like Jake set aside his anger at Romeo by the time the trio got under cover. Thea knew there would be trouble later, but for now they were back in action. Romeo took a moment to stash the corpse behind a tree, then they wove their way toward the house.

The place was situated left of center from the middle of the estate. The trees formed a crescent, with the house and related buildings in the points. Further landscaping made sure there were about ten yards between the tree line and the house proper. Well-placed lights cast a soft glow around the perimeter. Tasteful, and bright enough to reveal anyone sneaking from the woods to the complex.

Quite a complex it was, too. The main house was a rambling affair designed by Frank Lloyd Wright. If the hunters hadn't already known that from the blueprints they'd tracked down, the low-slung wood-and-stone design and seemingly random exposed beams gave it away. A two-car garage peeked out from the other side, the direction Parker and the others were supposed to be coming from. It was clear the garage was added later, and not just because it wasn't on the blueprints. It looked like the architect tried aping Wright's style and ended up with something closer to a kid's treehouse in design.

A separate glass structure stood about fifty feet away from the rear of the house. That wasn't on the blueprints, either. They'd had a bitch of a time getting those plans to begin with — a testament to how well nasties covered their tracks. Nary a hint that there'd been any more construction since the house itself was built back in the '50s. Which meant Augustus Klein was putting stuff up without the knowledge of the local zoning boards or that he'd made sure there was no paper trail. Either way, Thea was sure some hefty influence was being thrown around.

The hunters' plan was to move in as close as was safe (relatively speaking) just before dawn. At daybreak they'd make for the vampire as he headed for the safety of his coffin or equivalent enclosed anti-solar relaxation site. Then they'd try to hurt him enough to get the stake in and drag him outside for the sun to finish him off.

Problem being that they didn't know exactly where his lair *was*.

Thea had hoped the blueprints would give them some indication. They were less than helpful, though. The place didn't even have a basement. New buildings, though. Ah, now that was what a savvy journalist like Thea called "a lead."

Parker's crew would check out the garage, so Thea gave the glass building a once over. At first she thought it was a greenhouse, but a closer look revealed that the panes enclosed an Olympic-sized swimming pool. The arched roof kept the snow from piling up in the winter and a number of panels could be cranked open in clement weather. Not surprisingly, they were closed now. A small stone building was attached to the pool house — some kind of pump house or changing room, she suspected. The whole thing was more tastefully done than the garage. Thea's first thought was that it must be nice to splash around in a heated pool while it snowed outside. Then she figured that it must cost a staggering amount of money to heat the place. Then she realized that someone who could afford this joint probably didn't worry about things like the heating bill on a glassed-in pool.

Enough pondering the lifestyles of the rich and undead. A glance at Romeo and Jake showed they were as interested in the pool house as Thea was. She raised her eyebrows and shot a look thataway. Romeo nodded and Jake grinned. They had a bet with Parker's team as to who would find the lair first. They would need to check to be certain, of course, but Thea was pretty sure the pool house was it. Time for her to do a little razzle-dazzle.

Ever since Thea first ran into one of the walking dead — an experience she still shuddered to remember — she'd been gifted with a kind of supernatural radar. If she focused,

Thea could often sense whether a given course of action was advisable, or even if something or someone was harmless or dangerous. At times it could even pick out weaknesses in a target. It was, at best, an instinctive response tied solely to the supernatural. She couldn't use it to pick the winning lottery numbers or find Mr. Right. Plus, Thea had always preferred hard evidence; she was uncomfortable relying on this "sixth sense" if her mundane talents could get the job done. She admitted it came in handy in situations like this, though.

In fact, she should've had it up since they came over the wall. They might have been able to avoid that guard entirely. *Too late for regrets now*, she told herself, knowing it would still eat at her conscience.

Calling up her sixth sense was like doing one of those visual puzzles, trying to see the sailboat hidden in the random dots. You direct all your attention at it, but if you really squint you won't see anything. Instead, you don't look at any one particular thing. It's more like you're looking *through* it, as if you can see what's on the other side. That explanation didn't make sense, Thea knew, but that was the best she could describe it. The pool house got a bit hazy yet sharper.

And, sure enough, there was the sailboat.

To be thorough, Thea scanned the rest of the grounds. Certain areas, mainly inside the house, were important. Big mojo in the house, actually — maybe even overlapping sensations? Hard to tell, but probably just nerves. She figured she was just picking up their blood-sucking pal inside. Another look around confirmed that the pool house was the sweet spot. Their target may be in the house, but Thea felt sure the pool was where he went to ground. Probably in or under that stone pump house.

Thea pointed at the house and grimaced, making fangs with her index fingers. Then a jerk of the hand toward the pool followed by swimming motions. *Queen of pantomime, that's me*, she thought.

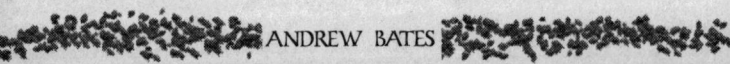

ANDREW BATES

Jake's eyes lit up and he nodded in appreciation. Romeo got it a second later. He gave the pool house a critical once over, figuring their next step. A slight exhale betrayed his exasperation. Following the direction of his finger, Thea saw the video camera on the far peak of the pool house. Once that one was pointed out, it wasn't too hard to find the others. Fuck. Thea's instincts told her they were safe at the moment, but it was dumb luck they hadn't been spotted already.

Something had to be done about those cameras. They could try rushing Klein when he left the main building for the pool house, but Thea didn't think that would work. Sure, they had weapons with names that got men grunting with excitement — Browning automatic pistols and MP-5 sub-machineguns with 9mm Glaser Safety Slugs and Spas-12 semi-automatic shotguns. Even with that kind of firepower it took sustained use to bring down a vampire. It was like shooting a side of beef; given enough time and ammo you were bound to turn it into hamburger. But your typical undead differed from a side of beef in that it usually didn't hold still long enough to get a good return on your investment of lead. And being in the open, the vampire simply had too many directions in which he could run. Thea knew they had to get him in an enclosed space first, the house or the pool, to wear him down enough to stake him.

They were too far away, hiding in the trees as they were. At best they'd pepper Klein with bullets before he ran back inside or off into the copse. Either way it'd turn into a chase scene. Not good, since he'd probably pull some sneaky shit and pick the hunters off one by one or just give them the slip and head for a backup hidey hole. Plus, there were bound to be more guards who weren't going to stand by and let Thea and her pals mob up on their boss.

Instead they could wait until after the monster made it to his coffin. No one wanted to take on a vampire in his lair, though. Soon after Thea joined the crew they fought a zombie in its crib. It was one of the nastier walking dead they called "hidden," named that since such things looked alive enough to hide among the living with no one the wiser. The hunters went in figuring it'd be like shooting fish in a barrel. Nowhere to run, right? Just one of it and a half-dozen monster hunters. Piece of cake. They took the hidden down, but the thing took two hunters with it and Thea rode a hospital bed for the next month with a story about being assaulted by a couple gang-bangers. If *that* wasn't enough to make the group gun shy, Jake claimed your average vampire took self-preservation seriously enough to install boobytraps to take care of the curious. Any passageway to the vampire's lair was more than likely rigged to high heaven.

Thea felt a surge of pre-fight panic and put a stranglehold on it. There were seven of them against one vampire. They were well-armed and as well trained as a bunch of weekend monster hunters could be. And Thea wasn't the only one with Jedi mind tricks. They'd gotten this far without mishap; if they stayed cool and worked together, they would be fine.

•••

Romeo flashed the UV light clipped to his vest and made a bunch of hand motions when Jake signaled that he'd seen Parker's response through his night-vision goggles. Jake made sure his headset mic was out of the way before he whispered in Thea's ear, "Romeo thinks our best bet is to get inside the house and find the security room."

Thea nodded. Dangerous, but it made sense. Get control of the cameras and they should be able to confirm where the vampire's lair was and lay an ambush. Plus, it'd be easier to pinpoint any non-monsters around, thereby reducing the chance of normal folks ending up dead.

They took turns sprinting the few yards from the tree line to the shadows under the camera mounted by the patio door. Thea expected the fingers-down-the-blackboard sensation that told her of immediate danger, but nothing happened. Either they timed things just right or whoever was watching the monitors wasn't very good at his job. After

Parker's team met them, Romeo tried the door. It was unlocked. In the stillness of the predawn winter the patio door sliding open on its track sounded like a tank rumbling down the street. The tension was unbearable. Thea was damned if the men were going to out-Rambo her, though, so she bit her lip and followed Romeo and Parker inside. Jake came after while Dean, Carl, and Lilly waited outside to cover the exit.

They were in a kitchen. What a vampire needed with a kitchen this huge Thea couldn't imagine. Sure was nice, though. Jake poked her in the back to move along; Romeo and Parker were heading down a hallway, weapons at the ready.

A dining room opened off the kitchen in the other direction and flowed into a sunken living room beyond. Aside from furniture, both were empty. The hallway ran past a foyer that led to the front door (nobody there either). The hall continued on another five yards before taking a left. A closed door stood opposite the foyer and Thea saw another just before the turn in the hall. After waving Parker to watch the hall and Jake to keep an eye on the front, Romeo stepped up to the first door. Thea came up next to him. She was supposed to sense for trouble before he opened the door. This routine didn't always work but it was better than just charging right in.

Romeo leaned cautiously against the door to listen then jerked his head away, a tight smile creasing his features. *Metal*, he mouthed. That meant fire-resistant, probably armored. Thea wondered if every door in the place was the same way or if they'd hit the jackpot first time 'round. She supposed they'd find out soon enough.

She gave him a nod. Romeo crouched and took a deep breath. Then a turn of the knob and he was inside the room. Thea did a fake around the doorjamb, just like in the movies. When trouble didn't leap out at her, she followed Romeo inside. Jackpot, all right. They were in a small security room. A dozen monitors lined the far wall, with a computer, two

phones, a fax machine, and other electronic appliances here and there. A gun rack holding six bullpup shotguns hung next to the door. Two uncomfortable looking swivel chairs comprised the only furniture. One was empty; the other held a guard who faced them.

Romeo stood with his silenced Browning pointed at the man's head. The guard was middle-aged but quite fit. He was dressed in paramilitary fashion and slouched in the chair, legs sprawled and arms dangling awkwardly over the sides. His head lolled to one side with bulging eyes and slack jaw. The guard looked faintly surprised, but not from their sudden entrance. It was pretty clear why no alert had been sounded: The guy was dead.

She shot a questioning glance at Romeo. He shrugged. All the hunters but Carl had weird tricks; one of Romeo's was the ability to see the true nature of the supernatural. Every hunter could see through the disguise of normalcy a rotting corpse could wrap around itself, but quite a few undead — most vampires and the better-preserved zombies — looked unremarkable even when a hunter used the second sight. Pale and often with spooky stares, but you get that with everyone from fashion models to heroin addicts. Romeo, though; he had the knack of picking up on the little things, the *tells* as gamblers would say, that revealed the undead for what they were. It also allowed Romeo to see in the dark, which Thea found more disturbing for some reason. Romeo's perception augmented Thea's own sight well; whatever she might miss he'd pick up, and vice versa. Thea took Romeo's shrug to mean the guard wasn't a monster playing possum, that he really was dead. Good, old-fashioned, lie-there-and-decompose dead.

Even so, Romeo wasn't the type to take any chances. Stepping closer to the body, he pulled down his lip mic. "This is Romeo. We are off radio silence, but speak only when necessary." He removed a glove, then trained the pistol on the guard's temple while he felt for a pulse. "The guard in the security room is dead. Jake, join us. The rest of you get under cover."

Thea moved to one side to give Jake some space in the cramped room. What, did this used to be the hall closet or something? She bumped a small table and set the mug of steaming coffee to sloshing. "Romeo," she said, "this guy hasn't been dead very long."

He motioned for Jake to shut and lock the door. "I know; the body is still warm."

"So's his coffee."

Romeo put his glove back on and looked down at the guard. "I am more interested in knowing *how* he died than *when*."

"Yeah, it is a little convenient," Jake said. He gave the room a once over, then focused on the body. "Doesn't look like he's been shot or drained of blood, right?"

"Correct," Romeo replied, his accent giving an exotic delivery to his words. "No sign of a struggle, his color is good — for a dead man. A heart attack, perhaps."

Thea left this to Holmes and Watson and looked at the screens. The cameras covered the grounds thoroughly but didn't monitor inside the house. They were well-positioned; in fact, she saw their teams would have been visible on screen as soon as they came over the wall. It took them, what? Ten minutes to get all the way in here? She imagined a body wouldn't cool much in such a short time, but what about the coffee? She'd drunk enough in her day to know it wouldn't still be steaming after this long.

Romeo made a command decision before she could voice her concern. "We do not have time for this. We are here without raising an alarm; that is what matters. It is almost sunrise. We must be ready for Klein."

Jake nodded slowly. Thea saw he was as disturbed by this convenience as she was. Romeo was right, though. Wasting time on... what the hell? "What's that in the pool?"

They looked at the screen she indicated. The view showed the pool and a portion of a hot tub to one side. It looked like there was a rectangle inscribed on the bottom of the pool.

"That's weird." Jake adjusted his glasses and leaned over the guard's body for a closer look. "Hard to tell with the scale and the water and everything. That the panel for chlorine or whatever?"

"Doesn't make any sense that it'd be in the deepest part of the pool, though. And it's pretty big." Thea frowned. "Those things are usually at the water line, right? Or outside the pool entirely."

Jake smiled. "Don't ask me. We never had one, and I didn't get down to the municipal pool much when I was little." He noticed what he was leaning over and straightened up with a slight shudder. "What do you think, Romeo?"

Romeo frowned. "That camera is positioned to monitor any approaches to the panel. These others are also. Here, here, and here."

Thea felt her intuition kick in the same time her brain puzzled it out. "That's Klein's lair! It probably has a watertight seal and I'll bet it's not the main entrance — it'd fill with water every time you opened it and you'd have to have pumps or whatever to clear that out. Plus imagine how strong you'd have to be to close it up again." Her eyes were afire with the epiphany. "It's an escape hatch, maybe. He goes in through, what? A ladder in the pump room? But if there's trouble, he can pop that panel and get out while whomever's after him is stuck below!"

Jake smacked his lips as he considered. "Maybe. Seems a little complicated, but if you're immortal I suppose you might take some extreme steps." He rubbed one thigh distractedly.

Carl's voice came over the headset. "Hey, guys? It's cold out here, the sun's coming up in a few and I'm getting really nervous."

"We hear you, Carl," Thea replied after tugging down her own mic. "I don't know how he gets in and out, but I'm sure the pool's the hot spot. That's where we need to be." She looked at Romeo and Jake, daring them to dispute her claim.

Romeo shot a glance to the guard, the monitors, then Thea. He nodded. "Carl and Lilly take positions here. The rest to the pool house. I will check the area. Quickly."

That was Romeo's way of getting Carl and Lilly out of harm's way. They weren't fighters; this way, they could watch the monitors and keep the rest of the group up to speed. Jake wasn't a fighter, either — he only carried a pistol at Romeo's insistence — but his special abilities made him handy during conflict.

Romeo grabbed the guard's navy pea coat and stocking cap from the back door hook as they left. Thea figured he hoped to pass as just another guard if anyone spotted him as he checked the back yard. They moved into position, Thea and Jake going into the pool house while Parker and Dean took spots in the shadows outside. Romeo slipped like a shadow around the back yard.

Thea didn't trust how easy it had been to get this far unopposed. She was pretty sure her sixth sense would've buzzed a warning if they were walking into a trap, but that didn't help her relax any. There was definitely something strange going on. She only hoped she wasn't misreading the whole situation. She didn't need any more blood on her hands.

• • •

"What the hell?" Jake muttered to Thea as they checked the pump room, the stone building attached to the pool house. He'd been certain there was a secret passage from there to the chamber under the pool, but they'd found nothing aside from pool cleaning gear including necessary pump and filtering equipment, some pool toys, and a backup generator. The last item looked like it could power the whole estate for a week, considering its size and the plastic fuel cans stacked in an alcove next to it.

"Maybe he dives right into the water and swims through the panel." Jake said, wandering over to the pool. "Not a bad idea, actually. If the lair's already flooded, there wouldn't be as much pressure when he opened and closed the panel. And it's not like he has to breathe. He'd get soggy, but he'd be almost impossible to light up while he was in there. Not to mention hard to reach." He grinned. "Yeah, damn clever."

"You may be right," Romeo said as he entered the enclosure. He carried a crowbar he'd grabbed from the garage in case they needed to force a secret panel. He gestured with the tool for Jake to follow him into the small stone building where Thea heard them rummaging around. They emerged carrying gas cans, the contents of which they upended into the pool. A rainbow hued slick soon covered the pool's surface.

Thea kept a weather eye out. It was getting damn close to sunrise and still no sign of the vampire. She was sure the thing was somewhere in the house. She was starting to doubt they'd found the lair, though. He might have gone to ground inside already. The pool might be a red herring. Too late to do anything about it, though. It was best to wait till sunrise. If the bloodsucker didn't come out, they'd search the house. Which would probably get very messy, since Thea was sure they couldn't continue to avoid guards and whatever traps were set around the place.

"Hey, guys?" Carl's voice whispered over the headsets suddenly. "This guard was dead when you found him, right?"

"Yep," Thea replied.

There was a pause. "And you would've told us if you'd noticed that someone shoved something sharp through the back of his skull?"

"What?!"

"Lilly and I were checking him out, trying to figure out how he might've died. We leaned him forward and saw a little blood on the back of his neck. There's a small hole at the base of his skull. That's not normally how vampires do it, is it? Looks more like someone stuck him with an icepick."

Thea wondered how Carl would know what that'd look like. "Just one hole?" She asked. "You sure it's—"

Then Dean's voice cut in with a panicked whisper. "He's coming!"

An instant later, the patio door slid open. From her spot behind a pair of deck chairs Thea saw Dean in the shadows by the side kitchen window; Parker was around the other side by the garage. Romeo was in the pump room, but Jake was in plain sight, preparing to empty the last gas can into the pool!

Augustus Klein strode toward the pool house, the security lights catching him in sharp relief as he emerged from the house's shadow. Thea and Jake had snapped some photos with Jake's digital camera when they'd tracked him in the city days before. Then the monster had a look Thea described as "movie star poseur": some species of pricey khaki slacks, staggeringly expensive leather boots, tight silk T-shirt, and dyed leather jacket. Now he wore only a tattered pair of canvas shorts, the rest of his sinewy form covered with a surprising amount of hair. His lower jaw jutted forward belligerently and he walked hunched forward with a fluid gait.

His feral attitude was accentuated when the vampire paused halfway across the frozen ground between the house from the pool. He shifted his gaze about suspiciously, then lowered even further into a crouch. His eyes took on a reddish gleam and his nose sniffed the still predawn air. Before, the thing might've just been some hairy guy heading for a morning swim. Now, though, the creature looked every part the monster in human form.

Thea almost attacked, sure he was about to come after Jake. Then she realized that although Klein sensed something was amiss, he hadn't sensed anything. Jake had the knack of being able to remain unnoticed by monsters, even when he was in plain sight — he simply stood still and acted

like he wasn't there. And although the mix of chlorine and gasoline burned her nose, she'd noticed coming in that the pool house door had a tight seal. Even if the vampire had a superior sense of smell, he probably couldn't pick up anything outside.

Registering the reek of gas, Thea realized what a dumb idea it had been to pour the gas out before Klein showed up. Sure, they didn't want him using the pool as an escape — for all they knew, that hatch led to extensive underground tunnels. But he'd have to be a moron not to cut and run soon as he opened the pool house door and smelled the gasoline. She grimaced. Just have to hope they could catch him in a crossfire in the doorway.

If he even came in the pool house, that is. The vampire was rooted to the same spot, trying to nail down what was bothering him.

Come on, Thea thought. *Everything's fine, just get in here.* The vampire didn't agree, though. Thea wondered if he was picking up on the gasoline or if it was just a more general sense of unease. Klein glanced above the tree line where pale hints of dawn grew ever stronger. Then he took a hesitant step backward and shot a look at the house, toward where the security room was located. *Shit.* That's all they needed, the hairy bastard going back inside and checking with security. Which was now Carl and Lilly, who were sure as hell not going to open the door for this thing. Which meant the vampire would cut and run or try to get through. Either way, things would get very messy very quickly.

Thea wished Romeo would give the signal. If they struck now, they could catch Klein in the open. Far from perfect, but better than chasing him down hallways. *Let's go, Romeo*, she urged silently. Any second now Thea figured the Asian ex-cop/ex-gangster/ex-whatever would come charging out of the pump room, just like his adopted namesake. She was partially right, anyway.

Romeo stepped casually through the door, his back to Klein, then paused to look back inside the pump room as if in puzzlement. His MP-5 hung neglected from its shoulder strap and he held the crowbar by his leg, hidden from the vampire's view. Romeo had the stocking cap pulled low on his head and had the pea coat's collar pulled up. . Facing away from the front of the pool house as he was, Romeo could've been almost anybody... including, say, the guard who used to own the cap and coat.

Klein noticed Romeo immediately and took two tremendous strides that brought him a foot from the pool house door. The vampire stared intently, but his unnerving crimson gaze and his sniffing nose seemed to give him no more information than before. Thea was close enough to see the fiercely focused eyes trained directly on Romeo's back. Still alert but focused on Romeo, Klein raised his hand to the door latch. For his part, Romeo acted like he hadn't noticed Klein and took a step back into the pump room as if he'd forgotten something inside.

The vampire opened the pool house door, his features twisted in irritation. "Stanson!" he growled, his voice choked with a bestial energy, "what are—" Then, paused halfway through the doorway, the vampire sniffed the air. Thea's heart sank. Just as she'd suspected, he'd caught scent of the gas blanketing the pool. Thea was close enough to see the monster's expression shift abruptly to surprise, then to mounting rage... and a hint of something else. Fear?

Thea took a breath to call for the attack, assuming Klein would retreat to the house. Before she could make a sound, a rumbling snarl of fury erupted from the vampire. Apparently Klein's outrage at facing an intruder in his lair outweighed the fear of the potential danger the gas posed. His face warped into something completely inhuman as he lunged toward Romeo, fangs distending with hideous exaggeration from his mouth, eyes blazing like twin pits of hell. Wicked claws sprouted from the monster's hands and feet, his every step gouging the tile surrounding the pool.

Vampires were different beasts from zombies and other walking dead. They were the top dogs of the undead world, she knew. Strong, fast, clever, all-around deadly; perhaps the greatest predators ever to walk the earth. But this transformation was so fast and monstrous that Thea was taken aback.

The rest of the team didn't hesitate but the results were mixed. Parker and Dean charged the front of the pool house, blazing away in hopes of nailing the bloodsucker before it got to Jake and Romeo. Rounds slammed into the clear panels, spider web cracks multiplying by the score in seconds, but the glass didn't shatter. "Fuckin' A!" Parker yelled in frustration. "Bullet-proof!"

Jake, still unnoticed, remained a statue until Klein was almost on top of him. Then the kid threw the gas can at the thing's head. The quick, aggressive action brought Jake into the monster's view, but the gamble paid off. The vampire literally jerked with surprise and skittered away, slashing reflexively at the gas can. Its claws tore into the molded plastic and deflected the twisted remains into the pool, but not before dousing the creature's arm with the last of its contents.

Romeo leapt from the pool house at the same moment. He channeled another of his bizarre powers as he lunged, transforming the crowbar into a white-hot brand through sheer force of will. Like every other talent hunters shared, Thea had no idea how Romeo did it, but she was impressed and disturbed every time she saw it. The crowbar spat and crackled with barely contained energy, but Romeo wasn't bothered by it in the least. Grinning savagely at the vampire, who was trying to decide which of his two targets to disembowel first, Romeo plunged the crowbar into the pool.

A deep *whoosh* filled the pool house as the gas ignited, the water's surface becoming an inferno. Thea felt the air sucked from her lungs and the temperature skyrocketed in a matter of seconds.

The vampire's eyes almost bugged out of his head at sight of the flames. His mouth impossibly opened even further and unleashed an ear-splitting shriek. Thea figured this was as good a time as any to make her move. She rose from behind the deck chairs and let loose at the monster with a burst from the MP-5.

Thea hit the bastard from behind, spinning him around with the impact. Blood flowing freely from a half dozen ugly wounds on his right side, Klein faced back toward her and the door through which Dean was entering.

Thea saw from Klein's eyes that whatever humanity he might have had was gone. Augustus Klein was an *it* now, a beast of pure rage and death given physical form. It was violent instinct and destruction with but one goal: survival at all costs. Thea suddenly knew she had to be outside. It wasn't fear she felt. The calm of the battle was upon her. She understood with perfect clarity that the vampire would escape unless she could be outside the pool house.

She and the creature moved at the same time, both heading for the door. Although Thea had a good five yards on the vampire, she didn't possess the preternatural reflexes of the undead. The thing took a single leap that halved its distance to the door, then grabbed one of the support beams that crisscrossed the roof. It swung around on the beam, crouching to brace its feet on the metal before pushing off. The vampire's lunge sent it straight for the doorway where Dean stood. The thickset hunter had a wild grin on his face as he raised his MP-5 to fire.

Thea was still three paces from the door with Jake and Romeo some distance behind her when the vampire hit. Dean Sankowski was a huge man who worked as a nurse. He was the team's rock, neither a leader nor a follower but the calm center that held everything together. The vampire tore into him like an axe through a piñata.

Dean slammed into the ground at the force of the vampire's impact, his head cracking against the ceramic tile. The vampire shredded the dazed man's camouflage jacket and flak vest while its feet ripped into his unprotected thighs. It grabbed Dean by the shoulders as if to tear him in two. Then Thea saw the monster's head dart downward.

Thea turned her forward momentum into a slide, skidding the last couple of feet on her back. She braced her hands on the tile and shoved, flashing her legs in a powerful scissors kick at the vampire's head. She connected with the monster's fangs bare inches from Dean's throat. Felt like she'd kicked a tree stump, but the bloodsucker's head rocked back from the impact.

Thea continued her motion, tucking her legs and rolling backward to end up in a crouch facing the vampire. The monster shook its head, roaring in outrage as it turned its attention on Thea. The force of its fury was palpable.

"Get off him, you rabid asshole!" Parker yelled from the doorway as he planted the Spas-12's barrel in the vampire's chest. The blast ripped through its torso and sent the monster skidding to the pool's edge. Its right arm remained attached by only a few strands of muscle and sinew, and the muzzle blast ignited the gas soaked into its skin. The scream the vampire unleashed was louder than the shotgun's thunder.

Thea felt equal parts terror and triumph. Although far from defeated, the vampire wasn't the threat it had been seconds ago. She had to move before it got the chance to escape, though. "Don't let it through the door!" she yelled, her voice dim to her own ears after the sounds of gunfire and inhuman cries.

Still shrieking, the vampire was on its feet in a flash. The flesh of its torso knitted as they watched, but the fire along its arm and chest ate into its body just as quickly. The thing was in a frenzy of agony, but it hadn't lost all its cunning. With the burning pool and Romeo and Jake behind it while Thea and Parker covered the door in front of it, the vampire sprinted for the pool house wall. It moved so fast that Parker's second shot missed it entirely. Trailing acrid smoke and screams, the creature slammed into glass already weakened by earlier gunshots. The pane popped from its frame and the monster lunged for the frozen ground like it was diving into water.

Amazed, Thea saw the creature sink into the earth! She shoved aside her surprise at this new trick and sprinted after the vampire, pulling a wooden stake from her belt as she ran. Now she knew why she'd wanted to be outside: It was good as gone if it succeeded in diving completely underground. Still half deaf from the gunfire and screams, she had no problem tuning out the rest of the team's shouts as they ran after her.

The vampire had plunged into the earth at an angle; its head and the right side of its body were already completely submerged along with part of its torso. Only a flicker of flame remained on its upper back. Thea saw that its chest would be out of reach completely within another second or two.

Rearing up with both hands wrapped around the stake, Thea drove the wood down with every ounce of strength she possessed. She felt the tattoo on her left hand grow hot — *what the hell?!* — and the stake hit home. Thea felt virtually no resistance as the stake tore through the vampire's back and pierced its heart.

The monster stopped moving almost instantly, its downward course halted and its limbs frozen in place. It looked like a statue partially buried in the ground.

Thea fell back a few steps, suddenly exhausted. As if through a haze she noticed Jake kneeling over Dean with Carl sprinting toward them carrying a first aid kit he'd grabbed from the security room. Romeo and Parker rushed to the vampire, ready to lay into it with crowbar and shotgun. Just then, the first rays of dawn cleared the treetops and touched the vampire's upflung legs. The monster went up in a blaze so intense Romeo and Dean were driven back a good six feet.

Thea staggered over to the side of the pool house and threw up.

• • •

Draining as the fight was, they had barely a chance to rest. The nasty was dust, but the ruckus was bound to have alerted the remaining guards. And if the gunshots hadn't alerted the neighbors, the oily smoke roiling out of the pool house was bound to.

Dean was fucked up but Jake and Carl got him stable enough to move. Parker shouldered him in a fireman's carry and the group hustled for the wall. Thea found it hard to stay focused as she came down from the adrenaline rush. Seemed like the rest of the gang was getting similarly ragged. Except, of course, for Romeo.

Their luck continued to hold all the way back to the Chevy Suburban. No guards popped up, and the hunters had made sure to park out of sight of the neighbors. The toughest part was getting Dean over the wall without aggravating his injuries.

Lilly dashed forward to where the Suburban was parked amid a small cluster of pines. She fumbled her keys, unlocking the side door first so they could load in Dean. The vehicle came standard with three padded bench seats behind the driver's cabin; they'd long ago removed the rearmost seat so they had a spot for their gear. That normally left enough room for the seven of them, but with Dean laid out in the front bench the rest of the team had to make do as best they could. Lilly took the wheel and big Parker grabbed shotgun. Thea, Jake, Romeo, and Carl were still jockeying for position in the rear bench seat when Lilly roared onto the road.

Five voices yelled for her to slow down! "C'mon, Lil," Carl said, "take it easy. Jostle Dean as little as possible, eh?"

Parker nodded. "Yeah, and you know how suspicious a big blue Chevy's gonna look speeding away from the sound of gunshots?"

"It's a big place; I'll betcha the sound didn't even carry past the walls," Lilly snapped back. She did slow to a more reasonable speed, though. "The neighbors are all probably still sleeping."

That's about when the vampire's house blew up.

TWO

Thea flicked the lighter's flame over the bong while she took a series of short, quick puffs. She leaned back in the hot water and set the small pipe, fashioned in the shape of a dolphin, on the little bench next to the tub. Exhaling the pungent smoke became a sigh of contentment. Nothing more relaxing after fighting the minions of hell than smoking a bowl, relaxing in a mineral bath, and sipping some wine. Well, except for a few hours of sex followed by pot, bath, and wine.

Thea tented her eyebrows in mild frustration. It'd been a few months since she'd had *that* opportunity. Her current lifestyle didn't allow for much in the way of relationships. Her last serious relationship, a semi-serious DJ and musician named Archie, showed definite promise — animal magnetism and he could actually carry on a conversation. But their schedules were so erratic that it ultimately went nowhere. And now, adding monster hunting to her freelance journalism career — there's an odd pairing for the old résumé — she had even less free time. Nights of clubbing and the couple blind dates her friends set up fizzled. Thea was often on guard, checking passing strangers and even her date for evidence they might be one of the walking dead. It didn't exactly put one in the mood to get it on.

It was getting harder to socialize with people who didn't know the truth of the world in which they lived. Thea still went out, still had fun with her roommate Margie and other friends, but a part of her was always on watch now. She could never completely relax, even with the help of drugs and home spa treatments.

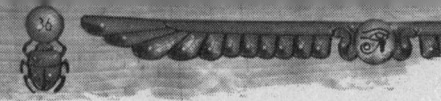

She kept a distance from her hunter pals also. They shared a great dark secret, but that very secret made Thea keep the rest of her life hidden from them. Partly because she wanted to keep a distinction between the two aspects of her life. Thea saw how people like Parker and Romeo and Jake let the hunt — or, as she imagined they thought of it, The Hunt — take over their lives. Hell, Romeo and Jake didn't even have *jobs*. They spent all their time tracking nasties. She knew what they did was important; she felt the rightness of it. But she wasn't going to give up her entire life for some crusade.

Thea's distance from the rest of the gang was also a matter of self-preservation. She had no delusions about their competence. It wasn't like they could go to some monster hunting boot camp to learn the ins and outs of the trade. They generally succeeded more through luck than skill. Thea wasn't exactly an investigative reporter — most of her work consisted of fluff pieces on ways to jazz up a relationship or the life cycle of a cheese curd — but she was bright and observant. She knew they weren't operating in a vacuum. The undead weren't wandering around graveyards slobbering for *braaaainsss*, just waiting to be picked off. Not all of them, anyway. They lurked behind the scenes, scheming and manipulating. Toward what end, none of the hunters Thea talked to really knew for certain. There was no doubt that many of these critters were wired into some serious influence and resources. If stories were true, some creatures had been around for centuries. You didn't survive that long without establishing a serious power base.

Still, it didn't make rots invincible, as she and the rest of the Van Helsing brigade had shown from the number of monsters they had taken down in the past few months. But activity like that didn't go unnoticed. All the undead in the greater Chicagoland area had to be on guard. The nasties knew something was thinning their ranks, and those with functioning brains were probably starting to track the hunters down just like she and her pals were hunting them. If someone really wanted to find them, they wouldn't be that hard to track down.

Take their vaunted "secret hideout" — a delinquent convenience store on the fringe of the River North area, within spitting distance of the Magnificent Mile. Parker Moston's uncle owned it, along with a half-dozen gun stores and army surplus shops scattered around the Midwest from which they got most of their equipment. Parker claimed his uncle didn't know, didn't *want* to know, anything about why they were using the place. But Thea reasoned that old Uncle Ray knew enough to make life difficult. He got them semi-automatic weapons and conversion kits and surplus military body armor and communications gear. Maybe the guy thought they were just a bunch of survivalist nuts who used the shop until they finished their Armageddon bunker on some farm outside of Black Earth. Maybe Parker had secretly spilled the beans to his uncle; who could say?

Regardless, anyone with motive and means could access the information needed to see all the hardware and other relevant gear moving through Uncle Ray's stores. Favors and bribes were commonly exchanged in Chicago business and politics; a couple phone calls would do the trick, Thea figured. From there it was just a hop, skip, and jump to Thea and her buddies. Not that Parker was the weak link of the group. He got on her nerves, but he always came through when they needed him. No, each of them had likely left a trail that anyone with proper incentive could follow. They were regular people with real lives; only someone who vanished from the landscape of society could hope to stay under the radar.

Even those who took serious precautions faced the danger of discovery. After all, look at Augustus Klein. He was a vampire, and if his underwater lair trick was any indication, a pretty savvy one at that. Yet with just a few weeks' worth of surveillance and some well-placed bribes, they'd nailed down his routine, gotten blueprints to his estate and taken him down. Didn't mean they were more skilled than

Klein was, though. Their raid could easily have gone sour any number of times — the cynical part of her thought that it *should* have gone sour, all things being equal. But in the end, it came down to who was luckier.

She sipped some wine and added a little more hot water to the tub. Thea knew she was suspicious — okay, paranoid — by nature. She had a fucked up home life and some shitty relationships to thank for that. Getting dragged into this hunting gig merely accentuated it. Even so, she hadn't always worried about the hunters becoming the hunted. As they kept pursuing the undead, she saw how cunning the monsters could be. At first she, like most in their little group, assumed the rots would be like the mindless shambling things you saw in cheesy horror flicks. Some were, but her gang ran into those less and less. Maybe they were all getting picked off; maybe they were slowly getting smarter. For all Thea knew, there might be a whole life cycle to the walking dead. Start out as a mindless zombie, learn to think again, become allergic to the sun and need blood to survive, and hello, immortality!

Bizarre theory, but no more fucked up than the rest of what she found herself involved in.

Whatever their origins, Thea couldn't dispute their existence. The undead were out there, God only knew why, and Thea was afraid it was only a matter of time before they figured out where *she* was. Considering the strangeness of their pre-dawn raid on Klein's joint, she wondered if they didn't *already* know.

Her thoughts kept returning to the morning's attack, so Thea stopped trying to relax and turned her attention more closely on the subject. Three things bothered her about the raid. Well, four, if you count Dean getting mauled:

Thing 1: The dead guard. The one that Romeo didn't kill, that is. Finding the guy already croaked when they entered the security room was disturbing. Some freak aneurysm was hard to swallow but not inconceivable. An otherwise healthy guy dropping dead 'cause his brain popped was tame compared to some of the stories Dean had related from his years nursing at Cook County Hospital.

But the guy was *killed*; an icepick through the brain, if Carl was right. And there was the timing of it. Poor bastard bought it at most only a minute or so before they got inside the house, if the steaming coffee was any indication.

So….

Thing 2: Who offed the guard? It couldn't have been any of her hunter pals. Was it another guard, pissed because he had to patrol outside while this guy got to sit in the security room all nice and toasty? Just happened to decide his working buddy deserved six inches of steel in his gray matter the very morning a squad of amateur assassins sneaked onto the grounds to take out his undead boss?

Thea's thoughts went on a tangent as she pondered if killing something that was already dead could be termed "assassination." Or even "kill," for that matter. There was a puzzler for you. She wondered if the undead were in touch enough to have a good word for that in their vocabulary. "Unkill?" She'd have to ask one when she had a chance. *Yeah, right*, Thea chuckled, reaching for the bong. *Dialogue with the dead. Sign me up.*

So was a disgruntled employee too much to swallow? At the moment, yes. How about the hairy fucker she'd staked, then? Thea rubbed distractedly at the tattoo on the back of her left hand as she considered. It just didn't make any sense. If he was Klein's breakfast he should've been pale from having his blood drained. Plus, vampires had fangs, right? That's normally a matching set of holes. This guy had only the one, which Carl said was nice and circular. Fangs sinking in weren't generally that neat. Unless this vampire had some thing about only sucking blood through straws? That was just too stupid to consider.

Even if Klein did kill the guard, why do it in the security room and not replace him? The vamp couldn't possibly have had only two guards on the entire property. Not with

the obvious wealth at his disposal. It just didn't make sense that a bad guy took out one of his buddies like that.

Which segued nicely to...

Thing 3: The explosion. Thea wouldn't have been surprised if Parker had gone in with a couple grenades. Yet he never had a chance to set up a booby trap. Besides, the explosion was Hollywood big. The Suburban rocked under the shock wave and got peppered by debris as they hightailed it out of there. Thea thought maybe the burning pool set off the generator, but it couldn't possibly have blown that huge or have lit up the main house. It ran on gas, but it was an electrical generator. It wasn't as if the flames could've run through pipes into the house. And the pool was a good fifty feet away from the mansion proper. Thea just didn't see flames jumping the distance and hitting something volatile enough to raze the place.

It's possible the vampire had the joint wired to go in case anything happened to him. Maybe he had to ready a timer in his lair each morning or everything would go boom. Or perhaps a guard saw his boss get taken down and carried out one last order before hightailing it back to Goons R Us.

Thea shook her head. Possible, but it sounded really weak to her. Someone more than likely planted explosives.

Thea realized she was pounding away at these other avenues because she didn't want to admit what that meant. She groaned in frustration. Despite bath, herb and vino, Thea was still tense.

Fucking vampires, she thought, and reached for her cell phone.

•••

"What the hell do you mean, 'someone got there before us'?" Parker Moston demanded.

"Think about it. Romeo's showed us how to sneak around and stuff, but we're not ninjas." Thea pinched the bridge of her nose between thumb and forefinger while she

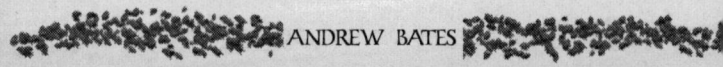

considered using even smaller words so Parker would understand her.

It was just over twelve hours since their raid on the estate. Thea had called them all to meet in the convenience store on North Sedgwick. The Stop n Go had been closed for a year or so. From the bits and pieces Thea had gathered from Parker, his uncle wasn't about to waste any money starting it or any other business up here. He intentionally left it fallow, confident that sooner or later someone would want to throw up a building there. Then he'd unload the property for ten times the amount he paid.

The current place certainly wasn't worth much. The building sagged in on itself like it was too tired to even collapse properly. Weeds grew in a cracked asphalt parking lot that was barely big enough for one car to turn around in. The interior was a mess. They'd swept most of the debris outside, but the place retained the phantom order of years of chips, candy, and pre-processed cheese snacks. When it got particularly hot inside, the bitter stench from what Thea conditionally termed the bathroom wafted in. Black spray paint covered the windows that made up the front wall, hiding them from casual view and making the interior pretty grim. Half the fluorescent bulbs had burned out, casting a wan light over everything. They'd shoved the shelves against the front and side walls, clearing out the center for a combination meeting area/training space. The only real concession they'd made to comfort was a half dozen space heaters scattered around.

Jake and Lilly sat on a couple of the castoff chairs they'd scrounged up when they'd first started their Extra Double Secret Monster Hunters' Club. Parker leaned his knuckles on the checkout counter. Romeo slouched against the decrepit cooler, subtly outside their rough circle.

They'd all long since changed out of their combat gear. Thea wore hiking boots, a favorite pair of old cargo pants, a long-sleeved Polartec thermal top and a well-worn Air Force T-shirt she swiped long ago from an old boyfriend. She'd

left her shoulder-length hair pulled back into the pair of pigtails she'd done prior to soaking in the bath. Along with the gloves she wore to combat the chill seeping past the heaters and her loose-limbed way of moving, Thea had a spunky little girl look to her. Jake was wearing boots, jeans, and a cable-knit sweater. With his glasses and serious expression, Thea could mentally triple the kid's age to get the spitting image of one of her old college professors. Lilly had on cross trainers, sweat pants and a T-shirt. She kept her obnoxious lime green parka zipped and her mittened hands placed primly in her lap. Parker wore metal-tipped cowboy boots (he claimed the tips were silver), jeans, and a Chicago Bears sweatshirt under a navy turtleneck. He always wore clothes with team logos emblazoned somewhere on them. Romeo wore his standard black — Doc Martens, slacks, sweater. Thea didn't think he wore black to look cool; he seldom seemed to put any thought into how he was dressed, in fact. She saw he still wore the navy pea coat and stocking cap, though. Perhaps he considered them spoils of war.

Dean was still in the hospital with Carl keeping an eye on him. They'd all been lucky that, if anyone had to have been hurt, it'd been Dean. He worked at Cook County, and the doctors and nurses were not unlike cops and firemen — they took care of their own and were willing to overlook a lot in the process. Lilly had driven straight there from the vampire's estate and offloaded Dean. They claimed a wolf attacked him when they were playing paintball. While the ER crew gave the rest of the group appraising looks, they hadn't pushed it. Turned out that although Dean had some nasty gashes on his chest and legs, he would be okay. Not in any shape to sit in a stank abandoned building and puzzle out a mystery, though.

Thea started pacing again as she continued. "Don't any of you think it was just a little too easy getting in and out of there? The way that place was set up, there should've been guards all over the place."

"Maybe there were," Parker countered. "Maybe they just weren't very good at their jobs. Plus, we're the soldiers of God. We have the Lord on our side."

Parker's overconfidence worried Thea more than his "soldiers of God" spiel. He could be right; their ability to sense the supernatural *could* be divinely inspired. Thea didn't believe so; in her view, it was instinct. Humanity's genetic response to a predator. She figured the human race carried a recessive gene that triggered psychic powers, just like porcupines developed their spiny quills to protect their soft little bods from things that wanted to eat them. All this talk about messengers or angels "choosing them to take up the hunt" was just the mind's way of rationalizing it. A psychological placebo.

Thea was willing to admit she was wrong if she got enough evidence to the contrary. What troubled her was that half their gang thought just because they were "divinely inspired" that God would protect them. That kind of sloppy thinking was bound to lead to disaster sooner or later. Only Romeo and Jake seemed to agree that caution was warranted at all times — about the only thing the two did agree on. Still, that one thing was a big reason why she insisted on being teamed with them whenever possible.

She cleared her throat, gathering her mental forces for another sortie. "Okay, Parker. Even if we grant that the fang hired a bunch of nearsighted morons, it still doesn't explain the guy in the security room or the estate blowing to hell after we left. I think someone got in there before we did, took out the guard, and set a bunch of explosives." She shrugged. "It may not have had anything to do with us — although I don't believe that — but there's no disputing the evidence."

Thea didn't mention the steaming coffee. It was disturbing enough to think that someone had slipped into the vampire's estate ahead of them. But if the coffee was still that hot by the time they got into the security room, that meant it'd been poured from the thermos within a minute before they got inside. To what purpose? She didn't think the guard's killer hung around enjoying a cup of joe and sprinted when he caught sight of them on the monitors. Thea was certain the killer *did* linger, but only to watch their advance. The coffee was poured deliberately, to make sure they knew someone had been there.

Parker snorted. "You watch too much of that *X-Files* crap, Thea. Not everything is a conspiracy. Those psychos worked for a fucking *vampire*, for Chrissakes! So one of 'em turned on another one. Just meant we were even more slick pulling this thing off." He crossed his arms high on his chest.

"I don't know, Parker," Jake said. "She has a good point. And we weren't *that* slick. Otherwise we would've avoided that other guard by the wall." Though he looked at Parker, it was clear that last comment was directed at Romeo.

Of course, Romeo took the bait. "You would rather that man had alerted our enemy?"

"No, but you didn't have to *kill* the guy."

Romeo tilted his head as if considering Jake's point. "This is war, and we fight an enemy we know little about. We must be hard. If we are soft, we are lost."

"Oh, great," Jake replied, throwing up his hands. "More haiku wisdom from Sun Tzu." Shifting in his chair to face Romeo directly, Jake continued, "Look, I agree it's not much of a moral quandary whether or not to destroy something that's pure evil. I have no problem with what we did this morning to that rot. But that doesn't mean its followers are beyond redemption. I bet a lot of them are just average guys doing their jobs."

Lilly looked askance at Jake. "You really think those guards didn't know what kind of thing they were working for?"

"Well, no," Jake admitted. "But I also don't think they were helping Klein sacrifice kids to Satan or whatever. All I'm saying is it's not our place to judge them. And it's especially not our place to execute them."

The sides of Romeo's jaw bulged as he clenched his teeth. "You say such things, knowing the monsters and those who work for them do not hesitate to execute any who cross them? They are like the triads or your Mafia, ruling from the shadows, using fear and death to cow decent people. The living who become their lackeys know what they do. They deal with the devil, whatever their claims. Just because their hearts still beat does not make them any less evil than the monsters themselves. They know nothing of mercy—"

"So *we* should show *them* no mercy in return? Descend to their level? Become just like them?!"

"The only way to defeat such an enemy is to destroy every trace of it, so there is no chance for it to rise up ever again!" Romeo spat, stepping forward to point a blunt finger in Jake's face. "You are naive if you do not see the atrocities they are capable of."

Jake stared, wide-eyed, at Romeo. "You're saying *I'm* naive? Where the hell do you get off—" He was suddenly standing, angrier than Thea had ever seen in the three months since they'd met. "—Jesus! One of those things *tore my fucking legs off!* Do you have any idea how that *feels?!*"

"One of those things butchered my family while I watched, helpless. Do you have any idea how *that* feels, boy?" Romeo faced Jake without expression but his voice trembled with anguish and fury. "If only my wife and children could be restored as easily as you have regained your legs."

Thea saw Jake's face turn gray. He swayed, blinking rapidly a couple times. His legs seemed to lose their strength and he sat heavily in his chair.

Silence smothered the room. Thea felt she should say something, but how do you come back from a capper like that? The chirp of her cell phone startled everyone, but Thea scrambled for it like an addict after a fix. Thank God! She welcomed anything that would distract them from the current ugly scene.

"This is Thea."

"Well hello, Thea." She didn't recognize the voice. "How's your friend holding up?"

"Excuse me?"

"The fat guy. He took quite a hit this morning."

Everything went dim for a second. Thea took two shaky steps backward, barely feeling her butt hit the checkout counter. Gripping the stained Formica with her off hand, she pressed the Motorola more tightly to her ear. "Who is this? How did you get this number?"

A chuckle that contained not the slightest warmth. "I'm a resourceful guy. But then, I bet you already knew that. As for who I am, I think you already know that, too. You just don't know you know."

"Listen, I'm not playing games here—"

"No? Then what do you call that amateur shit you pulled this morning?"

"I don't have any idea—"

"—what I'm talking about?" Another chuckle. "You ever notice how people say that when they know and are just *acting* like they don't? Me, when I really don't know what someone's saying, I say, 'What the fuck are you talking about?'"

"Okay, then. What—"

"You know what, babe? I don't like games, either. So—"

"No?" Thea cut in. "Then quit interrupting me, shithead! I don't know what the hell you're talking about and I'm full up on my psycho quota right now."

She jerked the phone away from her head and glared at it as she punched END. Taking a deep breath, Thea found she was shaking, and not with anger. She looked around at the others. "I fucking told you so," she said.

• • •

Thea knew the voice was lying about playing games. Otherwise why call her and act all smug and mysterious? She ended the call as much to show she wasn't going to follow his rules as to get a minute to collect her thoughts.

Thea had been a journalist long enough to know that the best way to get the story from a subject was to get him off balance and keep him there. She was damned if she was going to let this guy do that to her.

Not surprisingly, Parker didn't much see the logic of it.

"He knows who we are and what we did, Thea!" he thundered, slamming his fist on the counter. "What the hell were you thinking hanging up on him?"

"Relax, Parker. He called once; he'll call back."

"And what's to stop him from just calling the cops and telling them we blew up some guy's house?" Parker ran beefy fingers through his close-cropped hair. "Or maybe he's a bloodsucker, too. It's sundown; the rest of the undead fuckers in this town are up and running around by now. I'm sure their buddy getting lit up was the first thing they heard about when they got out of their coffins."

"If that is what he wanted to do, he would have done so already," Romeo said. He stood by the door as if he might leave at any time. Thea imagined the dust-up with Jake still bothered him, but she could read nothing on his face. "This man wants something from us. He will not contact anyone else until he has it, or until he is certain we will not give it to him."

"What, like money? He's gonna blackmail us?"

Romeo shrugged. "It is possible."

"Maybe you're right," Lilly piped in. "But I don't want to take any chances. What we do is pretty dangerous — but deal with this, too? I think we should find out who he is and what he wants right away."

Jake had yet to chime in. Thea looked at the kid. He hadn't moved much in the past few minutes; she couldn't tell if he was still blown away by his spat with Romeo or if he was considering the call. "Jake? What do you think? Do I star-sixty-nine this asshole or do we wait for him to—"

Thea jumped when her Motorola chirped again.

"Damn. This guy has killer timing," she muttered. "Couldn't stay away, huh?" she said into the phone.

"No, actually," Thea's roommate Margie replied. "But I'm guessing you thought I was somebody else."

Thea muttered a curse. "Hi, Margie." Everyone lost interest immediately. "Yeah, I did. What's up?"

"Just wanted to pass a weird one along in case it's that stalker."

Thea intentionally distanced herself from her friends as she grew more involved in the hunt. She couldn't imagine how to broach the topic with them — commenting casually "Hey, last week I blew away a zombie in Grant Park" didn't seem a good idea — and it seemed the safer course to maintain some space were anything to happen. Thea remained close with Margie, though. They'd been roommates since college five years ago. Some people found it odd that they got along so well, as different as they were. Thea grew up a rebellious tomboy in defiance of her mom's often smothering attempts to raise her alone. Margie was always a proper daughter to her proper third-generation Polish immigrant parents. Though a staunch follower of correct social attitudes, Margie had a sense of humor about herself that kept her from being prissy. Each being a single child first established their connection, and the contrasts between them actually acted as a glue to cement the relationship. They hadn't seen much of one another lately, though.

Thea never had a steady schedule since a given story might send her out at any hour of the day or night. Factor in monster hunting and any semblance of regular habits went out the window. Margie Woleski was doing graduate work in engineering at the University of Illinois at Chicago. She'd spend long hours in the lab, come home and crash for a few hours, then head back early. Even so, they used to find the time to hang out — whether splurging for tea at the Drake or club hopping along Rush Street. Thea realized with a start that she and Margie hadn't been on the town in a good six months. Since a few weeks or so after Thea had joined the hunt, in fact.

Since the two were such close friends, Thea knew right off that she'd have difficulty keeping her new circumstance — that minor thing about knowing the dead walk the earth and all — a secret. So Thea told Margie that she thought someone might be stalking her. The supposed stalker provided a simple rationale for learning self-defense and basic firearm training. (Thea also parlayed it into a series of articles on how women can protect themselves in today's world without sacrificing their freedom.) She hoped it would make Margie more cautious herself and more inclined to pass along any strangeness she observed. Her roommate's mention of the phantom stalker, right on the heels of the mysterious caller, put Thea on guard again. For a panicked moment she envisioned some monster breaking into the apartment and forcing Margie to call.

"What is it, Margie? You okay?"

"Almost had a heart attack hearing a man's voice on the answering machine, but I'm fine now." A laugh over the line. "Thought for a second it might've been that cute professor's assistant I keep bumping into in lab. But no, it was for you."

"Who was it? He leave a name or number?" *Was* it the stranger from a few minutes ago?

"No, that's why I figured I'd pass it along. You always said you wanted to know anything odd right away. It's nothing bad, I don't think, but it does qualify as strange." Some faint clunking as Margie shifted the phone. "Here, I'll play the message for you."

A faint beep, then, "—nother one of these answering machines?! Christ—" Then the click of disconnection.

Margie came back on. "Like I said, goofy. Mean anything to you?"

The voice came across distant on the answering machine's cheap digital recording, but Thea recognized it immediately. It was her game playing pal, all right. "Yeah;

yeah it does, Margie. Thanks. Might be a guy who's trying to get me for some dumb story or other. When did he call?"

"Uh…" Thea heard the answering machine's artificial voice in the background as Margie paused to check. "Says 6:09 P.M. Not too long ago."

It was almost seven now. The caller evidently tried her at home before moving on to her cell number. "Thanks, Margie. Nothing to worry about. Save that message though, will you?"

"Sure thing. Hey, I was going to make some stir fry before heading back to campus. You going to be home any time soon?"

"I think I'll be another couple hours maybe. Sorry."

"That's okay."

Recalling how little they saw one another any more, Thea said, "Hey, Margie, want to do the Drake tomorrow? Take a break from all that studying, what do you say?"

Another giggle. "Yeah, I think I could do that. Long as you promise not to run off after another hot story and leave me with the bill."

Thea smiled. "I keep telling you, I ran off after a hot *guy*. I only said 'story' so I wouldn't sound shallow."

They said their good-byes and Thea ended the call. It felt good to relax and joke with a friend. She was definitely spending too much time dealing with monsters. A leisurely afternoon with Margie was just the break Thea needed.

"My roommate," she said to the gang, pointing at her phone in clarification. "She played me a message from our machine. Sounded like the guy who just called me."

"That's strange," Lilly said. "I wonder why he called your home first?"

"Or why he's only called you," Parker added. "If he claims to know we were all in on something, I mean."

"Maybe he did try to call us all," Jake suggested. "We might all have messages on our machines. And Thea's the only one with a cell phone, so it makes sense that he reached her here."

"Which I don't exactly hand out to everyone I meet," Thea said.

"What?"

"My cell number. Kinda makes you wonder how he got it."

Jake shrugged. "That's not too difficult, but it does take a little effort."

"So," Romeo said, rubbing his chin with the thumb of his left hand, "there is least one person skilled at observation, infiltration, assassination, and demolitions."

"Oh, yeah; could be a 'they,'" Lilly said. "I hadn't thought of that." The rest of the group nodded. It offered a whole new level of complications, but they couldn't afford to discount it.

Romeo continued, "Right now, we know only one other thing: He, or they, wants something from us. But we do not know what." He looked over at Thea. "We must learn this. Until then, we are not safe."

"Were we ever?" Thea wondered.

• • •

After another half-hour's worth of discussion — well, okay; *arguing* — with little productive results, they agreed that they were best off contacting the caller and trying to meet. Considering what they were involved in, they couldn't afford to ignore him. If he turned out to be some crank from the hospital, fine. But if he was an extortionist or one of the undead, they'd deal with him accordingly. Thea noticed Jake and Lilly squirm a bit at that. She wasn't too pleased with a gray area like "deal with him accordingly," but she figured they could nail down their options once they had a better idea of who this yahoo was. Everyone was tense enough already; no need to add to it with talk of murdering a living person. Or persons.

Damn; when did my life turn into a Tarantino movie? Thea wondered.

When Thea checked her phone's memory to call the guy back, she found he'd blocked his number. They were back to the waiting game.

"Why don't we, you know, *track* him?" Lilly asked. "Like we do the monsters?"

Romeo and Jake shook their heads. The kid spoke first. "We could if we had more to go on, maybe. But we don't even know where to start. At least with the rots we're generally following up on a hot trail. See a monster, track it to its lair, right?" Lilly nodded. "We've never even seen this guy. We don't know his habits, where he's from, nothing.

"In addition, if he's a normal guy we can't use our edges. Those talents are our biggest advantage against the enemy, but most of them don't work for spit against everyday folks."

"That's not true!" Lilly disputed. "Romeo and Parker, they can make those, um, flaming swords, right? I've seen them cut through doors and stuff."

Thea wondered how Lilly Belva had lasted this long. It wasn't that she was dumb, just almost impossibly naive. Which in some ways Thea found worse. At least if you're dumb you learn from mistakes sooner or later — even an idiot would figure out putting his hand on a hot stove was a bad idea after the second time around. But the naive, the obtuse; they never learned. You could keep pulling the same trick on folks like that time and again and they'd never wise up. Lilly was the type of person who never caught sarcasm or irony. She couldn't differentiate between an actor and the role he played. She believed Clinton when he said "I never inhaled." Thea had thought more than once about suggesting to the others that they give Lilly the boot. Blind to the obvious though she might be, Lilly was at least helpful in the hunt. She could stop monsters with a word — or The Word, like "The Word of God," as Lilly referred to it. It did little more than stop a critter's immediate effort, mind you, but it was usually long enough for the rest of them to swoop in and clean up. At other times, though, Thea had to wonder if that knack was worth the rest of it.

About the only other thing Lilly had going for her was her looks. Even those were fading fast. Thea bet Lilly was quite the perky cheerleader in high school. That was a good twenty years ago (Lilly said fifteen), though, and her figure was looking more pudgy than perky. If she ran a bit, did some exercises, the gal could hold onto pretty a while longer. As it was, though, Lilly was on the fast track to frumpy middle age.

Thea knew she was being shallow, there. She chose to blame society for that one — magazines with vapid airbrushed waifs and movies with artificially enhanced knock-outs. Beauty is only skin deep, in the eye of the beholder, whatever. She admitted that Lilly's appearance didn't seem to bother Carl. A friendly, outdoorsy type, was Carl Navatt. No winner in the brains department himself, Carl was nonetheless a shrewd judge of character and had a decent amount of common sense. Carl and Lilly were good for each other, often acting with a single focus. Thea had learned the two had been together for years, even worked together at Home Depot. When they first joined the group, Thea had been surprised that Carl didn't have powers like the rest of the hunters. Lilly had "answered the call," as they referred to it, but Carl didn't get tapped. That didn't stop him from saddling up right alongside his lady, though. Thea knew it was for the best. Very little actually flustered Lilly, a nice change of pace from the high strung routine everyone else except Dean followed. But when Carl wasn't around, Lilly got a little scattered and gave off an undercurrent of nervousness.

Which is what she was doing now. Jake caught Thea's exasperated look and smiled slightly. Speaking as if to a child, Jake said, "Well, yes, Lilly. Some of these abilities work on anything. But those usually focus on combat. Far as I can tell, I can't hide from normal folks, right? And while Parker and Romeo can cleave through about anything with their… swords… that tracking ability of theirs only works on the rots."

"What about her?" Lilly asked, pointing an accusing finger at Thea. "She can tell stuff, things that don't have nothing to do with monsters sometimes."

"Well, yeah," Thea agreed, reining in her irritation. "But it's not very reliable and half the time I don't even know what I'm looking for. It's not like I can just sit here and think 'Lead me to the guy!' and some spooky arrow will appear and show me the way." She half expected a flash of insight — or even a dramatic knock on the door — just to prove her wrong, but the fates were playing it cool.

"Okay, so we can't track him supernaturally," Parker said. "What about doing it the old-fashioned way?"

"We just got done saying we didn't know where to find the guy, Parker," Thea snapped. She knew the combination of tension and being up since 3 A.M. were taking their toll, but she couldn't help it.

"Settle down and let me make my point, okay? I'm saying we go back to the vamp's estate, do a little checking around, see if anyone saw something strange, y'know?"

"What?! Return to the scene of the crime? Are you fucking nuts, Parker? First off, it's bound to be crawling with cops, having blown sky high and all. Secondly, if the guy was good enough to slip in and out of there without any of the guards seeing, he was probably able to sneak past the neighbors, too. And thirdly, do you *really* think it's a good idea to show our faces around there on the chance that one of the neighbors spotted us running away carrying weapons and all?"

Parker stood, face beet red and linebacker's body trembling with anger. "Listen, I'm tired of your know-it-all attitude. Your stupid 'spider sense' doesn't make you omniscient, and anyway we're just brainstorming, here. So get off your fucking pedestal or get the hell out!"

"Wow, you get a raise recently?" Thea sneered. "Using a lot of three dollar words there."

Parker lunged forward. "*That's it!* I don't care if you're a woman, I'm mopping the floor with you!"

"Who writes your dialogue?" Thea stepped away from the counter, grabbed the back of a chair and spun it around on the floor between her and Parker. Knees bent slightly in a relaxed fighting stance, she said, "Bring it on, corn-fed.'"

A dark figure appeared between them. "That is enough," Romeo said softly. "You are being childish. Parker is right." Thea barked a short laugh, but Romeo's cold glare kept her from saying anything more. "I do not mean we should expose ourselves to identification. He is correct that we do not need our... special talents... to investigate. I am sure the man who called is watching us. We must be alert and watch for him in return. If we are observant and careful, we shall find him."

Thea and Parker continued glaring at one another for a few long seconds. Thea finally laughed and broke eye contact. "Yeah, fine. I'm tired and I'm cranky. Do whatever other planning you want. I'm going to get some sleep."

"That's a good idea," Jake said, giving Thea and Parker puzzled looks. "Why don't we all do that. We can talk more about this tomorrow. Maybe get some input from Carl and Dean."

Thea didn't feel like doing a goodbye scene. She just grabbed her coat and headed for the door, tossing a "Sounds great" over one shoulder.

The frigid night air was like a blow to the face. She scrambled into her ski jacket, its Thermalining warming her immediately. The cold effectively cooled down her mood, though. Starting the trek to the El station on West Chicago Avenue, Thea wondered what got into her. Parker Moston was a big chauvinistic jerk, but he had a kind of asshole charm to him. Much as they sniped at each other, they normally got along okay. Still, the occasional blow-up was to be expected in any group, especially in extreme situations. And this certainly qualified as extreme.

Thea stopped suddenly, certain someone was nearby. Spinning around, she expected to see Jake or Romeo or maybe even Parker following her to apologize. The Stop n Go sat, dark and silent, a half-block away. Nobody had left yet, and looking around, she didn't see anyone else on the street. An icy gust of wind chose that instant to snap down the road, tumbling wrappers and cans in the urban equivalent of fallen leaves.

This stuff is really getting to me, she thought. *Just get me home with the rest of that wine and forget about everything for a few hours.*

Hunching her shoulders against the cold, Thea hurried on.

•••

Thea had missed initial coverage of the estate explosion, so she caught a follow up report Sunday morning. Investigators were now willing to declare the cause of the blast. Explosives weren't mentioned; instead, the authorities claimed that the house blew when the furnace ruptured. They would continue to investigate, but were confident no foul play was involved. So far three victims of the fire were found, including one tentatively identified as the estate's owner, Augustus Klein.

Thea laughed humorlessly, marveling at the load of crap she was watching. Any lingering thoughts of looking to the authorities or the media for help with the hunt dissipated. The information being suppressed was staggering, and Thea had no confidence in the police being that efficient about it. Immediate facts on the explosion aside, it was clear the news was in on the snow job considering the fluff piece they ran on Klein. European investor, new to the city, expected to bring much industry, tragic loss. Cut to commercial. Thea's gang had a head start on the guy thanks to their talents, but discovering he was trafficking in kiddie porn, child slavery, and snuff hadn't been very difficult. That had been all the evidence they'd needed to start sharpening their stakes, but Thea prided herself on being thorough. Further digging over a few weeks showed Klein wasn't above dabbling in everything from video pirating to drugs to terrorism. Yeah, he brought all sorts of industry to Chicago, all right.

An honest media should have discovered a hint of this — enough shadowy dealings to warrant more in-depth investigation, at least. Flipping through the *Tribune* and *Sun-Times* while she waited for Margie to finish in the bathroom, Thea merely saw more of the same angle from TV. The farthest it seemed they were willing to go was to admit that Klein "was involved in a number of business endeavors and kept his personal life very private." *Hard-hitting journalism at its very best*, Thea scoffed in disgust.

Thea kept hoping their efforts would result in others taking a closer look at what went on in the fringes of society. Although none of them was foolish enough to stand up and yell, "Monsters walk among us!" they tried leaving evidence suggesting as much when the opportunity presented itself. But nothing ever broke. Just like with Klein's extremely public demise, anything out of the ordinary was hushed up, made to look as mundane as possible. The fact that some nasties out there had the fourth estate in their back pocket was a big reason why Thea stayed freelance.

If they could just find the ones behind it all, they'd have a chance of blowing everything wide open. Of really putting the nasties on the run. *Start calling 'em the running dead*, she thought, a smile quirking the corners of her mouth. So far it hadn't even come within a thousand miles of being easy, though. Whomever or whatever controlled Chicago was very well hidden, and it would take more than some part time Nancy Drew action to flush them into the open. Thea wasn't surprised, of course. Even the mindless zombies were damn powerful, and the ones that had half a brain could bring some potent abilities to bear. And she was sure she'd seen only the barest fraction of what the undead could do. Thea had no trouble imagining creatures operating from the shadows, exerting great influence over the living.

The one thing that kept her clinging to hope was at the heart of that idea: the monsters directed things *from the shadows*. They stayed out of public view for a reason. Powerful they may be, but they weren't omnipotent. They had weaknesses, and Thea was learning to sense them... and exploit them.

• • •

Thea felt relaxed and in a good mood for the first time in a while. She'd spent most of the afternoon doing girl stuff with Margie — tea at the Drake Hotel followed by a couple hours spent popping into galleries and shops along North Michigan Avenue.

They'd both decided to dress up a little for the outing. Comfortable as jeans and old sweaters were, the brilliantly clear winter's day called for something more ladylike. Margie wore black pumps and gray slacks with a red cashmere sweater that brought out the color in her fair skin and accentuated her full features. She topped it off with her black fur-trimmed overcoat, at one point explaining to a glaring salesperson at Neiman Marcus that the fur was indeed fake. Thea opted for tan flats (she was too much of a tomboy to bother with heels), a long patterned sheath skirt her mother got on a recent trip to the Mediterranean, and a white sweater. With her loose curls pulled back and pinned in place with a pair of chopsticks and the sweater's high collar reaching up to her jawline, Thea's dusky features stood out dramatically.

Warm as the sweater was, Thea chanced not taking a coat. The day was clear and still and the sun provided a surprising amount of warmth for a mid-winter day. They were only outside long enough at any given time that the chill was merely bracing. Thea didn't even bother with her leather gloves, leaving them lying on top of the Browning Hi-Power she carried in her small, low-slung leather backpack.

Acutely aware at first of the hideout just blocks away where she spent so much time of late, Thea soon chased all thoughts of monsters from her mind. The afternoon was just the pick-me-up Margie needed, too. She admitted to feeling pretty ragged from the pressure of her lab work. Stepping away, even for a short time, did wonders to clear her head.

They were relaxing over coffee and making up histories of the guys who passed by the window when Thea's cell phone rang. She almost didn't answer it, but figured what the hell; it could be something as mundane as some magazine offering her work. Hearing Jake's voice on the line shot that theory to hell. Still, he didn't sound concerned, just his normal serious self.

"Hey, Thea. Dean's been released."

Thea sipped her latte. "Oh yeah? How's he doing?"

"Pretty good, I guess. Stay off his feet for a while and all that, but no complications." A pause. "We were planning on heading by his place to talk some things over. You up for it?"

"Well… what time?"

"Say four? It shouldn't take too long, what with Dean needing his rest and all."

She checked her watch — a stainless-steel Vitesse with a slide-rule function, tachometer, telemeter, and pulsemeter, built to withstand up to ten atmospheres of pressure. The fact that it told time seemed almost incidental. Thea was a sucker for gadgets. She refused to think of her attraction to such things as an addiction, despite what her credit card balance suggested. Her watch, cell phone, laptop, palmtop — each was something she didn't exactly *need*. But she found it all very cool.

It was 2:30 currently, and she imagined Margie would need to get back to the lab soon. And, frustrating as last night's meeting was, she knew the gang needed to work some things out. They seldom all got together like this due to real life scheduling conflicts — work, families; little things like that. Klein had been a big job, though, and it was best that they all dealt with the fallout, at least initially. Hopefully having Dean and Carl around this time would keep things calm. "Okay, that's do-able."

A moment of silence on the line, then Jake said, "You haven't heard back from, well... you know. Have you?"

"Nope." *In fact, I'd let that whole thing slip right out of my brain until you called.* "How about you? Any messages?"

"No. Well, Lilly said she had a hang-up on her machine, but that's it."

He went alphabetically. The thought bloomed full-fledged in her mind. *Belva, Ghandour... if he hadn't reached me on my cell, Parker Moston would've been next.* Thea hoped that, should the stranger have it in for them, he wouldn't use the same method to knock them off.

"Right. I'll see you in a bit, then." She hit END and slipped the phone back in her bag. Margie was slurping at her mochaccino and raised her eyebrows inquiringly. "Fellow journalist," Thea explained. "Wants to talk about maybe working on something together."

"Hey, that's cool. It's been a week or so since you did that thing for the *Reader*, right?"

"Yep." And she hadn't lined anything else up because she'd been too busy trailing Augustus Klein. Freelancing made for a flexible lifestyle, but it played hell on her credit balance. "We'll see if anything comes of it."

Thea hated lying to Margie, but what was she supposed to say?

THREE

Thea had the cab drop her at the corner so she could enjoy the last of the daylight while she strolled down the block toward Dean Sankowski's apartment. The taxi from Michigan Avenue to Greektown wasn't terribly expensive, but a few bucks here and there added up quickly. She'd begun pondering the problem of work thanks to her fib to Margie. It wouldn't do to keep running up her cards. She sure as hell wasn't going to crawl to her mom for money anymore. Time to get a good-paying gig; maybe even bite the bullet and get full-time work for a while. Or maybe take some time off from the hunt and figure out what the hell she was doing with her life.

Gee, there's a thought. Plan for the future.

She looked down at her Visor and checked the address displayed on the palmtop's screen. Thea had never been to Dean's before. After Jake hooked up with them, he suggested they share addresses and phone numbers in case of trouble. Although forthcoming with her numbers, Thea had given everyone the address of the building across the street from her Wicker Park apartment. She knew she should trust these people — she put her life in their hands more than once, after all. But there was *trust* and then there was *self-preservation*. She saw her home as the one safe place in the world to which she could retreat. She didn't like the idea that a half-dozen people whose sanity was at least marginally in question (she grudgingly placed herself under that heading) and who were involved in vigilante activities could drop by any time they wanted. Plus it wasn't impossible to assume that nasties might capture one of them at some point,

or that the critters would be clever enough to follow one of them home and break in. Either way, there was a chance of the monsters they hunted finding out where Thea lived. No thanks.

Hence the house across the way. It was one of many large stone mansions in the area, and was long ago split into multiple apartments. It had caught fire shortly after Halloween, the upper stories almost completely gutted and the bottom severely damaged. Aside from basic cleanup, though, no other work was done to the place, the residents (hopefully smart enough to have renter's insurance) forced to find new apartments elsewhere. Thea had learned the owner decided to wait on repairs so that workers wouldn't have to battle the harsh Chicago winter. Thea suspected he planned on razing it come spring and building something else — a winter spent protected from the elements by only plastic sheeting certainly wouldn't help the place. Not that she much cared.

She figured using it as her address with the others gave her nine months at least before warm weather hit and the landlord got his shit together enough to have the place renovated or something new built. Once it was habitable, she'd give the others a different address. In the meantime, it served as a simple enough warning system. Thea was always very cautious when she returned home, focused on discerning any supernatural forces that might be following her to make sure nothing saw her enter her real apartment. Anyone skulking around the rest of the time would find a wreck that no one had lived in for a while. They might reason she lived nearby, but good luck figuring out which building. She imagined one of the team would take it upon himself to check up on everyone else sooner or later and discover what she'd done. Thea was content to wait until that happened before she said anything. No reason to make something out of nothing.

Lost in thought, Thea staggered when tremendous, gut-wrenching fear washed over her. She almost dropped her

Visor when she whirled around. She sprinted back toward the corner before cogent thought kicked in, such as it was. *Have to get away. Find that taxi, or get another. Get to safety. Run. Just run!*

She was a good piece down the next block when her skirt tripped her up. It reached to mid-calf and hugged her hips. The side slit went just above her knee to help give a range of motion (and show a little leg), but it certainly wasn't built for running. Thea stumbled, grabbing onto a tree by the sidewalk to keep her from falling. *What was I thinking, wearing this thing? Should've gone home and changed first. Home! Gotta get there, get safe—*

The stumble must have cleared her mind somewhat. When the fear welled up again, another part of her questioned the suddenness and degree of panic. She wasn't some chick in a slasher movie who ran squealing until the killer hacked her up in gory yet imaginative fashion. She was the type to stand there blasting away as the thing walked up and tore her head off. *Stupid, but not a coward, right?* She smiled, the grim joke helping center her further.

Something wasn't right, that much was clear. Terror making a jackhammer of her heart, Thea straightened and faced back down the street. Strangely, her belly felt warm, like she'd just taken a shot of whiskey. Still trying to marshal her fear, Thea rubbed at her midsection through her sweater. *The tattoo.* Fellow hunters had developed a kind of rough symbology; the tat around her navel of the double circle with four radiating spokes represented "protected." She'd combined it with elements of Egyptian hieroglyphs culled from one of the books her mother had brought with her from the homeland. She'd done the same type of motif on the back of her left hand, on her right shoulder, and above her right ankle. Nothing garish, and the iconography blended rather well.

This was the second time in as many days that she'd felt warmth radiating from one of these tattoos. Her fear lessened further with the puzzle this presented. Maybe a

subconscious response to certain stimuli, just like her more overt powers? Perhaps, but the pseudoscientific contemplation could wait for later. Thea had shaken enough of her panic to sense she was being manipulated. She didn't see anyone on the street so it didn't appear that she was in immediate danger. In fact, she didn't see any movement anywhere.

It was time to take control of the situation. Thea released a shaky breath and tried to focus. Although hunters manifested different strange abilities, all shared what they called the second sight: the ability to see past many of the illusions the undead wove. Most zombies, no matter how horrific or decayed they actually looked, had an aura that made them appear normal to mortals. Once properly focused, a hunter could see past the supernatural camouflage. Thea's talent of sensing things of importance was a heightened expression of this, as was Romeo's knack for noticing the undead who looked normal even beneath their veils. The second sight also provided the ability to resist mental influences some monsters projected. It came in damn handy when a rot was trying to make you shoot your best buddy instead of him.

The only problem was you had to focus to do it. It didn't take too much effort, but it wasn't something you could do all the time. The mental equivalent of staring hard at something; you had to relax, had to blink sometime. So if you blundered into a nasty without your guard up, you were just like any other shmoe: fucked.

Just like I am now, if I can't get a handle on this.

Another cleansing breath, then Thea sharpened her focus like she did when performing a kata. Everything shifted of a sudden, shapes and colors not any different but nonetheless fundamentally changed. And the fear vanished like dandelion spores blown on a gust of wind. *Fucking monsters*, she thought. Anger welled up, replacing the panic that had existed a second ago. *Got a surprise for you, whoever you are.*

She slipped her pack from her shoulders, taking one last look at Dean's address before shoving the palmtop in the bag. After a glance around the deserted neighborhood, she took out the Browning Hi-Power and checked the clip and safety before putting it in the backpack's unzipped exterior pocket. She decided to stay unarmed for now, and not because the gun wouldn't be useful. In general, unless you got a lucky shot, nailing a walking corpse with a pistol didn't do much except get it to notice you. The Browning could be useful, mainly due to the Glaser Safety Slugs it held. A Glaser is a "frangible round" — designed to make very nasty holes in flesh while greatly reducing the chance of ricochet, hard target penetration, and other collateral damage. The hollow-point tip is a little bowl filled with tiny metal beads suspended in liquid Teflon. It tears into soft targets easily, the scores of beads making a puree of the poor bastard's insides. Yet it disintegrates completely on impact in a single sheet of wallboard at anything past point-blank. All this meant Glasers normally chewed up zombies pretty well.

Thea was simply more comfortable with unarmed combat. It was quieter and could be used to subdue instead of kill (at least in the case of the living). Plus, she was still jittery enough that she wanted to avoid shooting one of her pals if they popped around a corner. Having the pistol within easy reach was at least added comfort.

Thea focused again to summon her sixth sense, noting as she did so that the warmth in her stomach had dissipated. She was sure whatever thing had scared her before was trying to keep everyone away. Each person in the neighborhood was likely sitting behind locked doors, TV turned up loud to distract from the nameless dread that caressed the soul. That should give Thea the element of surprise, but first she had to find her target.

A few minutes later she stood before the address on the palmtop. *Something* was in Dean's place. She knew it as sure as she could see the building in front of her. It was like many others in the neighborhood: a four story walk up built following the infamous Chicago fire, lots of stone and little wood, with each level its own apartment. Dean shared a place with his lover on the second floor. Thea saw lights on but the shades were drawn, giving no sign of disturbance from the outside. A last look outside showed Lilly and Carl's Chevy Suburban on the street but not Parker's Toyota 4Runner. Romeo and Jake didn't have cars that she knew of, so she had no idea if they were here yet. She hoped so. With Dean wounded and only Lilly to protect him — she knew Carl, not being gifted with their talents, could do little more than gibber in a corner under the influence of this fear effect — things would get ugly fast.

Thea barely felt the increasing cold as the sun set. That it wasn't yet dark meant the invader was more than likely not a vampire, though. Good; those fuckers were damn tough to beat. They'd gotten lucky with Klein the other morning, the way he'd panicked on seeing the fire. Even so, she did not feel up to taking on a fang one-on-one. *Probably a ghost or a zombie*, she thought as she entered the front door. Making her way cautiously to the second floor, the stairs of the old apartment house creaking unavoidably under her weight, Thea hoped it was the zombie. She couldn't do much against a ghost. A hunter's second sight typically didn't bring the sneaky bastards into view. Her own senses were more acute, but even she couldn't perceive the unseen like Romeo could. And even if she could see a ghost, she couldn't touch it. Be like fighting a cloud of steam.

Thea realized she was stalling. She didn't want to go up there alone. Regular fear this time, not the preternaturally produced variety. *Come on; they could be dying up there.* She paused on the small landing between floors to tear the slit in her skirt all the way to her hip. She hated doing it, but she needed her legs free to move. *Sew the damn thing back up after you've beat the shit out of the monsters.*

She crept up the last few stairs, already flushed by the heat pumping through the building after being outside for so long. *Wipe the sweat off; don't want to be blinking it away when a nasty jumps you.* The second floor had an open hall that ran the length of the building, with stairs on the opposite end leading to the third floor. The banister she gripped tightly extended left to the wall, giving a clear view of the half landing and stairs to the ground floor that she'd just walked up. There was only one door, just to her right. More properly, there was only one door*way*. The door itself had been dashed in as if by a battering ram. The force of entry had torn the door partially off its hinges and hammered the locking plate and part of the jamb completely free from the wall.

Thea didn't recognize the man she stepped over in the entryway, carefully avoiding the pooling blood. From his shocked look and the way he lay on his back with his chest caved in from a hammerblow as powerful as the one that opened the door, Thea felt safe assuming he wasn't one of the attackers. Dean's lover — Wayne, she thought his name was. Poor bastard was probably dead before he hit the floor. Then she heard the faintest hint of noise and caught the stench of something long dead.

An entryway opened on a kitchen immediately to the left. *A good place for somebody to ambush from*, she thought, just as danger screamed along her nerve endings. Thea flung herself backward as a shambler lunged from the kitchen doorway. It was your prototypical movie zombie, moved with a shambling gait (hence the nickname) and about as bright as a pocketbook. As if to compensate, it was shockingly strong and hard to take down. About the only way to drop a shambler permanently was to turn its brain to pulp or tear out its heart; otherwise you could beat on it for a year and a day and it'd keep on coming.

The monster grunted deep in the back of its throat as it swung at her. Thea noticed, almost in passing, that the flesh of its fingers had rotted away to expose its finger bones as claws. She'd seen that kind of thing before, and she knew how much damage those claws could do. Not to mention if

it got a good hold of her; one squeeze and her insides would be goo. *Never give you the chance, asshole!* Thea slammed her back into the opposite wall, her backpack crushing painfully against her shoulder blades. Bracing her arms against the plaster, she crouched slightly and lashed her leg up. The creature gave little thought to defensive measures and left itself wide open. Thea's heel smashed into the monster's jaw, shoving the mandible into the rotted skull and rocking the shambler back through the apartment doorway.

The zombie didn't even pause to shake off the kick and came at her again. Thea saw her shot had torn much of the thing's front neck tendon and showed hints of the spinal column. Thea grabbed the railing on the landing with her right hand, keeping her left braced against the wall. She swung up both legs this time and caught the zombie in a scissors lock. Using her leverage, Thea swiveled her hips and wrenched the creature's head around and down. She heard snapping and popping, but the skull was on there more solidly than she'd thought. One of the thing's arms struck her as it fell but did little more than tear a chunk of her loose sweater away. The thing hit the hall floor, its head twisted unnaturally to face away from her over its own right shoulder.

Despite a broken neck, the shambler wasn't done yet. Without even clear sight of her, it lunged where Thea stood in the corner formed by the banister and the wall. Thea's sixth sense intuited the attack and she leapt over the zombie as it came in low, performed a sloppy forward roll and came to her feet in a crouch. Swiveling on the balls of her feet, she spun around to face her attacker.

The shambler had smashed its fist through the wall — the *brick exterior* wall, Thea realized with a sudden drop to her stomach. Its head rolled toward her as it tried to get free, its crushed features giving a bizarre impression of embarrassment. Thea moved in, linking her fists in a forearm smash on the zombie's back to drive it to the floor. Its trapped arm snapped and the other swung low at her, catching her in the left thigh with enough force that Thea rebounded off the opposite wall.

Thea's leg went numb almost instantly, but it didn't feel broken. She gave a grunt of her own and went for the thing again before it could get back to its feet. She jumped on its back, slamming it to the ground again, then grabbed the rotting tatters of its shirt — some heavy metal tour T-shirt, she noted distractedly — and shoved the zombie forward so its head was caught between two banister rails. The shambler struggled mightily beneath her, almost launching her completely over the rail onto the stairs below. Thea barely caught herself on the banister. She was in a poor spot, on top of this thing with no real leverage and nothing but the half landing ten feet below her. Then inspiration struck.

As the monster readied itself for another upward lunge, Thea leaned over the banister and, balanced precariously with her belly on the rail and her upper body dangling over the drop, grabbed its head in both hands. She felt the back of her left hand flare hot and twisted with all the force she could muster. There was a wet tearing sound as the shambler's skull tore free from its body in a spray of gore.

Using the momentum of her pull, Thea swung her legs down hard on the near side of the banister. She popped upright and staggered back clumsily over the still-twitching shambler corpse, the head a gruesome trophy clutched in her hands. Thea dropped the skull with a cry of disgust and reached out to gain her balance. Her momentum and her weak leg worked against her, though. Thea brushed the far wall and tripped over her own feet to slam on her ass at the base of the third floor stairs.

She watched the zombie twitch a couple more times, then lay still. The head looked with seeming curiosity at a spot high on the wall. Directing her own gaze down, Thea saw her sweater was torn and sprayed with decayed zombie bits. Her left leg was starting to throb like hell, too. But she was still alive and in one piece and it was dead. For good.

Thea wanted to take a minute to catch her breath, but she still had to see how her friends had fared. A second surge of adrenaline propelled Thea to her feet as she remembered something else about shamblers. Aside from being dumb and strong, they seldom traveled alone. Although she hoped Dean and the others might have taken care of this thing's pals, she expected the worst. Even if that shambler was the only one left mobile, the fact that it was still up and about didn't bode well for her friends — *teammates, anyway*, Thea automatically corrected herself.

She walked gingerly toward the apartment. Her leg hurt like hell, but that was better than the numbness. No more zombies jumped from the kitchen doorway so she looked down the entry hall. It continued forward for fifteen feet and opened on a space to the left. The exterior wall was to her right, so Thea walked with her back facing it. Bloody footprints and smears along the wall dragged drunkenly down the hallway — more than one set, she saw. That confirmed the shambler came with at least one friend.

Edging along the wall, the living room came into view. It might have been tastefully appointed at one time, but the nasties had redecorated the place in gore. The television further to her right was knocked off the low entertainment stand, smashing an aquarium in the corner. One fish still twitched faintly in the puddle. An armchair had been tossed entirely across the room to shatter glass shelving by a door halfway along the wall opposite where Thea had entered. Pictures, pottery, and plants from the shelf were strewn about, turning the floor into a minefield of broken glass and earthenware. A couch sat against the far wall, strangely untouched by the chaos.

Another shambler lay facedown on the floor about halfway across the room, its upper body savaged by bullet holes. Thea saw it was once a woman. All that remained of its head was a fist-sized gob of pulped flesh and bone. Glancing along the wall separating the kitchen and living room, Thea saw more bullet holes and wads of rancid flesh in the near section of wall between the entry hall where she stood and an archway leading back into the kitchen. The creature had been caught in a fusillade of Glaser rounds, probably fired from an MP-5. Thea imagined it provided cover for the other one, since the wreckage and blood spatters continued through the opposite doorway. There may have only been the two shamblers, but you never knew for sure. That gore trail could've been from the one she took care of on the landing, or there could be a third laying in wait. Thea was acutely aware of her breathing, the blood thundering through her veins, the oily roll of her eyes as they moved in their sockets. She'd never gone into a situation like this alone, and the tension was unbearable.

Trying to decide the safest way to cross the floor, Thea noticed a leg sticking out from underneath the armchair. Her eyes widened with dismay as she recognized Lilly's cross trainer. The woman had evidently held the first zombie with "The Word," but must not have been able to freeze both of them. Lilly had to focus pretty intently to use her talent. She'd have made a convenient target when a second rot threw the chair.

Thea thought about Dean and Carl and immediately got a sense of them in the far room. She edged along the bullet-riddled wall, moving toward the couch to avoid the worst of the wreckage.

Danger bloomed in the base of Thea's skull as she passed across the empty kitchen doorway. Thea tucked and spun as something snatched at her. A hand tore at her sweater and slid to grab her backpack. Thea relaxed her arms and twisted further, continuing her initial motion to slip out of the pack. In her surprise, Thea staggered forward as she turned and ended up on her ass for the second time in as many minutes, though this time in front of the living room couch. Pure luck she didn't fall on a jagged shard of pottery, but Thea was in no position to appreciate her good fortune.

Standing in the kitchen archway was a stocky middle-aged man. He looked like a phys ed teacher despite the off-the-rack suit he wore. A gentle smile with a hint of the mischievous brought dimples to his cheeks, the sudden youthful look contrasting with the fine wrinkles around his eyes. His attitude as he looked at Thea was one of mild reprove.

Thea was baffled, wondering who the hell this dude was. He clearly wasn't a shambler. Then Thea noticed his eyes. Despite his animated features and the empathy he radiated, the man's eyes were as lifeless and cold as a shark's. Thea's second sight would have revealed any decay visible on the man, evidence of death normally veiled from mortal eyes as in the case of her headless friend in the hall. Aside from his dead eyes, though, the man looked completely fit. Focusing further, Thea sensed this bastard was the locus of the horror in the neighborhood. Thea felt certain she faced one of the hidden.

The hidden were zombies who could pass for living. To all intents and purposes, they looked like anyone else. Even the second sight was virtually useless in sensing them, much as with vampires. In fact, it took hunters some time to distinguish between the two types of walking dead (and some folks still argued the topic on hunter-net). Only someone like Romeo could typically notice a hidden. These überzombies apparently did not possess the same degree of power that vampires did, but they made up for it by not having to drink blood or avoid the sun. They were nasty pieces of work, all right, a single one often a match for a half-dozen hunters. Thea was lucky; she never would've sensed the guy in time to dodge if he hadn't been radiating that wave of fear. *If you call this lucky, sprawled in front of the damn thing.* If she hadn't been so focused on Dean and the rest, Thea imagined she'd have sensed the rot before she stepped in the living room.

No sense whining now, though. Thea had to do something, and fast. Like beat some zombie ass.

"Interesting," the man said. Thea was surprised; aside from screams and howls and other noises associated with violence and death, she'd never heard a zombie speak. "You do not feel the fear either. But I sense your own within you. Like water for my parched soul." The man's smile expanded, losing all semblance of gentleness. "You restore me and, in so doing, spell your own doom."

One part of Thea's mind wondered what it was about being evil that made you talk like you were reciting movie dialogue. The rest of her brain rapidly weighed her options. Thea had to drop this hidden, and it was going to be tough without her Browning. They'd put the heavy duty firepower they'd used on the estate raid in a hollowed out space under the Stop n Go's floor, but Thea was sure Carl kept his shotgun in the Suburban. If she could just get out front, she'd give this thing some 12-gauge slugs to wash down with his damn "fear water."

Thea's biggest problem was getting up. The hidden didn't look very fast, but that didn't mean a damn thing. Thea needed a distraction, something to give her time to get up to speed. The pottery shard by her hand suggested itself nicely. *Okay, throw the pot and hope that there's still enough of a person in there that he flinches. Then down the stairs and—*

There was a flicker as a black-clad figure moved up silently behind the zombie. Relief flooded through Thea. *Romeo! You grumpy bastard, I could kiss you!*

The hidden paused, frustration creasing his brow. "Your fear! I've lost its taste. Why…?" The creature turned then, stepping to one side of the doorway as he looked for an intruder.

It wasn't Romeo. Thea didn't recognize the man in the dark tailored suit who came into view when the zombie moved. The main impression was dark and grim, like in old paintings of Puritans. Thea's focus shifted almost instantly to the pair of large automatic pistols he held. He faced the stocky hidden coolly, almost familiarly, not even sparing Thea a glance.

The zombie showed obvious surprise at seeing the figure. "You! But—"

At the same moment, the stranger raised his pistols with blinding speed and placed both at the hidden's throat. The automatic in his left hand angled up under the jaw, while the one in his right hand pointed downward in a diagonal through the torso. The concussion of the big weapons firing was a double cannon blast that rang through the apartment. The pair of .45 caliber bullets vaporized the zombie's neck, their momentum hardly slowed. One punched through plaster as the contents of the creature's head sprayed across the ceiling. The other ripped through his internal organs and shattered his spine before embedding itself in the floor.

Thea watched in amazement, showered with carnage as the undead collapsed beside her. Her head echoed with the pistols' thunder and the air stank of decaying flesh and cordite.

The stranger negligently dropped the still smoking pistols to the floor. He looked critically at the haze of blood covering his fine leather gloves, his expression deepening to a frown as he viewed the specks of gore scattered across his arms and torso.

Shocked, it took Thea a second to find her voice. "…" was all she could get out at first. Then, after clearing her throat, "Who…?"

Eyes as dark as a mineshaft locked Thea in their gaze. "Hmm?" He seemed irritated, as if she was disturbing him from something important. Then he blinked, a cold smile pulling at one corner of his mouth. "Oh, right," he said, "forgot we haven't met formally.

"I'm Maxwell Carpenter."

• • •

"You're the man from the phone," Thea said. It was a declaration, not a question.

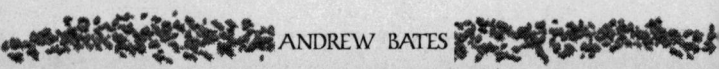

The man nodded, still preoccupied with the splatters on his clothes. Thea thought he got off easy; a good dry cleaning would put him back in business. Her own clothing was stained beyond recovery, and her face and hair felt caked with bodily fluids. The carnage she'd been exposed to in the past few minutes was so overwhelming that her senses shut down reflexively. She barely noticed the stench, and as long as she didn't focus on the massacred zombie corpses and the disturbing sight of Lilly's foot she could maintain control of her gagging. The dark figure standing before her was more than enough of a mystery to keep her occupied.

Thea scrutinized the stranger closely as she regained her feet. Maxwell Carpenter was maybe an inch or two over six feet, but his physical presence was of someone much larger. He was lean, almost gaunt, and clean-shaven with short dark hair and heavy brows. She found it difficult to nail down his age. She'd normally have placed him in his early 40s, but he seemed much older. Not decrepit or anything. More... seasoned. Experienced. She realized her earlier comparison to a Puritan was off the mark. He looked more like a figure from the Old West; hard features, piercing gaze, the whole bit. With that image in mind, his pale skin and relatively unlined features seemed incongruous. Actually, a gunslinger wasn't quite right. Carpenter moved with fluid grace yet also a subtle, strange awkwardness. It was a dissonance she couldn't reconcile, but she nonetheless found it natural on him. Thea realized Carpenter reminded her of Christopher Walken: cool, suave, unpredictable. Attractive yet disturbing, alluring yet downright spooky.

His look was vintage Prohibition. Carpenter wore a charcoal, double-breasted pinstripe suit under his overcoat, a colorful tie, and patent leather wingtips. The ensemble was cut in a style reminiscent of the '30s yet with a modern sensibility. The blood spatters seemed even more outrageous as a result of being on such finely tailored clothing.

Thea was bemused to realize she was thinking about this guy by his last name. Perhaps a reflection of his entrance. The mysterious tough guys of film and literature were typically last name only sorts. Even so, she just couldn't see calling him "Max" or even "Maxwell."

Of course, what to call him was of minor importance compared with what he was doing there. Favoring her injured leg as she stepped gingerly around the hidden's corpse (and being careful not to look down at the mess) to pick up her backpack, Thea figured it couldn't hurt to ask. "So, uh, what are you doing here?"

Carpenter paused from wiping at his face with a handkerchief that had started out crisp and blindingly white. He gave her another inscrutable look and said, "I was following you."

Makes sense. Just because he saved your life doesn't make him a good guy, though. Thea pulled the Browning and pointed it at his chest. "Pardon me if that doesn't make me feel any better, mister."

A blink-and-you-missed-it smile, and Carpenter went back to cleaning himself up. He was as fastidious as a cat. "Pays to be cautious. But don't you want to check on your friends before you give me the third degree?"

Thea started, guilt making her blush involuntarily. "I was just about to suggest that. Why don't you lead the way." She wasn't foolish enough to throw off her aim by waving the pistol toward the bedroom. He seemed bright enough to figure it out on his own.

"No problem. You might want to tell them we're coming so they don't ruin my wardrobe any further." The smile again. "If they're still alive, that is."

His cool routine was starting to get on her nerves. "Just start walking, buddy." Louder, "Dean? Carl? It's Thea. The nasties are down; I'm coming in behind... a guy. Don't shoot." She hoped they heard her. She hoped they were *alive* to hear her.

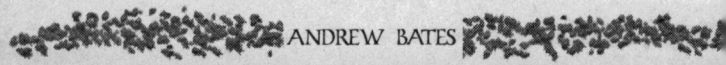

Carpenter strode into the bedroom, still brushing futilely at his clothes. Thea stepped in behind and felt her heart sink as her gorge rose.

A cherry wood chest of doors immediately to her left was pockmarked from gunfire and covered with shattered glass from the pictures that had once hung on the wall. A king sized sleigh bed that had previously rested against the left wall was upended. Its frame was broken, the mattresses tented against the far wall and partially obscuring a door that led to the back porch. There were two more doors along the right hand wall. The far one led to a bathroom while the near doorway accessed a closet. Each door was smashed to kindling, bloody handprints on the remains bearing the mark of a rampaging zombie.

Thea noticed all of this distractedly. Her attention was held, albeit unwillingly, by the spectacle of Carl Navatt. He'd been torn almost completely in two. The shambler had anchored one hand where Carl's neck met his shoulder while pulling with the other on Carl's arm. Carl's neck had been wrenched, pulled savagely up and out while his left shoulder was torn in the other direction, separating the entire shoulder joint and even part of his rib cage from the torso. His spine was visible, a good six inches of it below his neck torn free. Vertebrae were scattered around the room, the pieces looking like someone had chewed on them.

A patch of skin on Carl's head was peeled back, hair and flesh dangling from the skull which had been cracked open like a coconut. Portions of gray matter leaked out, but the majority of Carl's brain was missing. Off hand it wasn't clear where it might be amid the grotesquerie of the rest of the room, but seeing the gnawed vertebrae Thea suspected she knew. The zombie had also reached into the rude opening in Carl's body and pulled out the majority of his insides. Carl's intestines were strewn about like hideous holiday tinsel, indeterminate gobbets of other organs thrown at the wall and tossed to the floor. Thea realized the jellyfish looking thing she'd almost stepped on was one of his lungs.

It was too much to take in. Thea felt the world going black. *Where's Dean?* she thought just before the dresser struck her on the forehead.

FOUR

Thea woke with the dry heaves and a bitch of a headache. She felt too awful at first to even register that she was in an unfamiliar place. Anywhere was preferable to the dank horror of her nightmares. Brushing sweat-dampened hair from her forehead, she carefully straightened from the fetal position. Crisp sheets rustled as she moved and intermittent beeps in the background gave her enough of a thumbnail sketch to recognize she was in a hospital. She noticed a dull ache on the inside of her right forearm. Opening her eyes triggered instant vertigo, so Thea felt with her left hand for the IV stuck in her arm. A few more minutes of deep breathing seemed to help, so she chanced opening one eye. It was dark and blurry, but at least the ceiling wasn't moving around. The shades were drawn and the door closed, casting a nebulous timelost feeling over the room. She eased open her other eye and spent a while marveling at the sensation of her vision dimming in time to the throbbing in her forehead.

She didn't know how long she laid there, conscious but certainly not alert. Many bad things lurked on the periphery of her mind, things Thea didn't think she was ready to face. Floating in limbo was more than enough to occupy her for the foreseeable future.

A millennia later, she sensed movement. Thea let whatever it was move into her peripheral vision. "Path of least resistance" was her new mantra. Why turn her head? Either it would come where she could see it or it wouldn't. No sense getting all hot and bothered about it, that was certain.

A figure in white, a nurse. The large woman checked Thea's condition with a gentle, confident demeanor that reminded her of someone. *Like a medical Oprah Winfrey. Nurse Oprah. Oprah Nightingale.* Thea chuckled mildly, the sensation triggering a coughing fit that burned her raw throat. The nurse did some "There, there" and had a glass of water with a straw ready when Thea's coughing settled down.

"Thank you," Thea croaked after she'd taken a few sips. Those few words didn't tear the heavens asunder, so she decided to try a few more. "Where am I?"

"You're in Cook County, dear," the nurse said. "You've been here since Sunday night."

Thea felt a tremor at the edges of her vision, but her curiosity had been aroused. The beast was not one to lie back quietly once waked. "And what... when is it now?"

"It's Tuesday afternoon."

Her head throbbed fiercely for a moment. When the pain faded to the background again, Thea felt better than she'd expected. "How did I get here?"

"In an ambulance, I expect!" Nurse Oprah smiled at her little joke. "You had quite an ordeal, dear. Get some more rest and the doctor can explain everything, okay?"

"No, actually. It's not okay." She evidently surprised the nurse, since the woman was already turning to go. "I... I want some answers now." Thea found herself possessed by an urgent need to confirm everything that had happened. She already faced too many mysteries.

The nurse momentarily lost her gentle demeanor, giving Thea a frank, appraising look. "I don't know that you're quite up to that right now. You were in a serious accident. The slightest excitement would take a lot out of you, and right now you need to think only about getting back on your feet." She smiled understandingly. "Just you trust me, dear, I know what I'm talking about."

Thea opened her mouth to push the issue, but a wave of dizziness chose that moment to attack. Willing to admit the nurse may have a point but not willing to give up so easily, Thea took note of the flowers at her bedside and asked, "Is there anyone here who might want to know I'm out of my coma?"

The nurse exhaled heavily at Thea's sarcasm. "You've actually awakened a number of times, Miss Ghandour—" she said the name with a flat Midwestern twang, *Gaan-door*. "But yes, you do have people waiting. I'll make you a deal. I can give you two minutes with just one visitor." Nurse Oprah made the peace sign to clarify the time. "Then you have to rest and wait to see Doctor Breckin in the morning. Okay?"

Thea nodded. She wondered who was waiting and got a sudden flash of a black-clad figure. Something more seemed hidden behind the image, but terror and darkness threatened to drag her down if she regarded it too closely. Thea corralled her wayward thoughts as best she could.

Nurse Oprah shepherded in Margie a minute or so later. "Here you go, dear. Remember, two minutes and then rest!"

Thea rolled her eyes at Margie as the nurse left. "Hey. Where's Mom, anyway?"

Though she obviously wanted to know how her friend was doing, Margie followed Thea's lead. "Work. She was here all Sunday night and most of Monday. You woke up a few times but were pretty out of it. The doctor said you were stable and it was best to just let you rest. I told her I'd be happy to stay till they could come back."

Thea nodded, wincing slightly at the throb it triggered in her head. She wasn't surprised. Her mother was always eminently practical. She couldn't accomplish anything productive by sitting in the waiting area, so why not go back to work? Thea would have been disappointed if Margie hadn't been there, though. "Glad you stuck around, Margie."

"No problem. My lab work can wait a day or so."

Yeah, right. "Well, before you ask, I feel fine. Just a nasty headache."

"That's great! The doctor said it wasn't anything to be too concerned about, but you never can tell with head injuries."

They both paused. Thea wondered what Margie knew about why she was in the hospital, and suspected Margie was wondering how to ask for more information.

As if on cue, Jake Washington slipped into the room. He gave one last look down the hall and came over to the bed. "Hi," he said, looking awkwardly between Thea and Margie. "Well. You seem to be none the worse for wear."

"Wish I could say the same for—" Thea realized Margie was watching them with some curiosity and mild confusion. "—Uh, hey, I take it you two haven't met?" Thea felt equal parts relief and frustration at Jake's appearance. Margie wouldn't push any questions with a stranger around. Of course, that same stranger would give rise to a whole new set of questions Thea would have to deal with later. *The fun never ends.*

Her visitors shook their heads. "I didn't even know he was waiting to see you till the nurse told me you were awake," Margie said.

"Same here. Sat across from each other for a good couple hours, even."

"Well, let me correct that," Thea said. She felt nothing good could come of introducing her best friend to someone she hunted monsters with, but she didn't see any way around it. "Margie Woleski, meet Jake Washington. Jake, this is my friend Margie."

They shook hands across the bed, Thea adding, "Jake and I've been, um, working together on some research. Off and on. For a story."

Margie gave her a look. She clearly didn't buy it. "Well, how about that," she said. "Working on a big scoop, are you?"

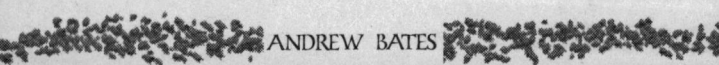

"You could say that," Jake replied. "It's still pretty hush-hush though."

A thousand questions roiled inside Thea, and she was sure she wasn't the only one feeling that way. Before they could see who broke first, though, Nurse Oprah's voice cracked the air. "Didn't I say just one person?" She tromped in like a drill sergeant and pointed an accusing finger at Jake. "Young man, you should know better." Her features softened but her voice was still stern as she told Thea, "It's nice to have such concerned friends, but you really must rest now."

Jake blushed and almost scurried out the door. Margie whispered, "Geez, Thea. What is he? Sixteen? Shame on you!" before following after.

The nurse admonished Thea another minute or two while she made sure everything was in order and her patient wanted for nothing. Having learned nothing from her friends, Thea tried again to get something out of Nurse Oprah. "Listen… what hap — Uh, did they… bring in anyone else? With me, I mean."

Nurse Oprah patted Thea gently on the shoulder. "Of course. You should be proud of what you did. That other lady will be fine, and of course old Dean. That boy's had the worst luck the past few days."

"What?" Thea was thoroughly baffled. "Other… you mean Lilly? Lilly Belva? And Dean is alive, too?"

"That's right, dear. It's awful those other folks didn't make it, but don't you go feeling guilty. It was a bad fire. I'd say you were lucky to get the two of them out alive."

•••

The next day was filled with follow up tests and counseling, visits from labcoats and needles and, finally, her mother and Margie to take her home. Medical science declared her rattled but otherwise none the worse for wear. Seventy-two hours after the horrors she witnessed in Dean Sankowski's apartment, Thea looked forward to returning home.

She wasn't ready to leave quite yet, though. Thea demanded she visit Lilly and Dean first. They were both reportedly in stable condition, but Lilly had been kept sedated since her arrival. She kept screaming about Hell and how God had failed her in her time of need. Dean was apparently in surprisingly good shape and his co-workers were happy to let the woman who saved his life spend a few minutes with him.

Dean Sankowski worked as a nurse at Cook County for half his life, since he was in his mid-20s. Thea was surprised when she'd learned that. It wasn't common for a man to become a nurse back then, after all. Dean laughingly admitted he faced a number of challenges regarding his masculinity and sexual orientation. Even his family and friends in nearby Aurora found it a little odd. But Dean explained he'd always wanted to be a doctor. He liked helping people. He discovered he didn't have what it took to be a physician, though. He lacked the temperament to absorb the minutiae of biology, physiology, disease, toxins, medicine, and the like. Nurses, Dean saw, played just an important role in health care, and were often more involved in a patient's mental well-being than the doctor was. He still struggled with some of the more technical aspects of nursing, but Dean knew almost immediately that it was the right choice.

Snide comments and sniping from the home town gang when he went to visit didn't bother him, Dean said. Part of it was his easy-going personality, but it was likely also because he was gay. Most of it was easy to laugh off, but things like "Nurse Fag" were a little harder to take. Dean chose to give the derision the silent treatment, focusing on the irony of it all to maintain his good humor. He'd kept his homosexuality a secret for years until he realized he was doing himself and other homosexuals a disservice with his silence. He said the shock on his childhood pals' faces when he came out was well worth it. Dean knew he was still a joke to many of them, but considering they muddled through hollow, menial lives while he helped people every day, what did he care about their opinions? Awakening to the existence of the supernatural and joining the hunt — being "blessed," he called it — had amplified his calm and contentment further. Dean knew it was his duty to help the innocent and to aid the victimized, whether in the hospital or on the dark streets of Chicago.

Dean was propped up in bed when Thea entered the private room, his heavy frame barely contained in the scrubs he wore instead of the standard hospital gown. He set aside a small packet when Thea came in and waved her over for a hug. She embraced him gently, afraid to aggravate the wounds he'd received from the vampire and whatever he'd suffered the other night. He held her tight, though, pulling her close for almost a minute. They were both teary-eyed when they broke the clinch.

"You look good," she said. He did, too. She figured he'd be flat on his back drugged to the roots of his hair and hooked to all manner of machinery. Aside from being a little pale and looking a few pounds lighter, he was the same old Dean as always.

He smiled. "Thanks. You too. That bandage gives you an air of mystery; bet it'll make the guys go crazy." Thea chuckled, reflexively touching the white square affixed to her temple. Aside from a lingering headache she felt like the same person. The same couldn't be said for her clothes, though. They were torn and covered with soot when she was brought in, and her backpack was missing; lost in the fire, she was told. She'd asked after the skirt, hoping to repair it, but apparently an orderly had taken the clothing to the incinerator. Margie had brought Thea the Timberland boots, jeans, old sweatshirt and ski jacket she now wore.

There was a moment of silence that threatened to stop all conversation before it could even get started. "I'm sorry, Dean," Thea finally blurted just as Dean opened his mouth to say some inanity. He and Lilly had lost the people they loved. Thea couldn't imagine how that felt, but neither could she avoid the topic. "If only I'd gotten there are little sooner…."

He was already shaking his head. "Don't, Thea. We can't have regrets for what we do. That'd destroy us more surely than *they* ever could." He sighed heavily, wiping the tears from his eyes. "It hurts like a sonovabitch, Wayne being gone, but you can't think it's your fault. If anything, it's mine for… well; you know." They shared a humorless smile.

"Yeah, we're 'blessed' all right." Thea sniffed and wiped her nose. "And I have to tell you, Dean, I'm a little scared, too. I mean," she looked around the room, "they got right in your *home*! You know?"

"I know. We got sloppy." He grimaced, but not from any physical pain. "All I can think is they were watching the hospital looking for strange injuries, or maybe they can sense us like we can them. Anyway, they must've followed us when Wayne… when we came home. Carl helped get me back, so when he showed up again with Lilly for the meeting they must've decided it was the right time. If they'd waited longer, they might've got all of us, y'know?"

Thea nodded. She didn't say that if the whole Van Helsing brigade had been there three zombies probably wouldn't have stood a chance, even with the element of surprise. Things were plenty grim already without bringing that up.

"So has anyone else come by?"

Dean shook his head. "I heard Jake tried to see me when I was asleep. I called around yesterday and told everyone to keep a low profile. Try not to be seen together, right? Especially not here if they're watching the place."

"Good idea." A pause. "Listen, Dean, I hate to ask, but… do you remember anything? Like about how we got out?"

Dean gave her a sharp look. "What d'you mean? I thought you dragged us out of the fire before the building went up."

"I don't remember any fire, Dean. Two of those things jumped me when I came in and... well, that's all I remember." Something else nagged her, death and salvation intertwined. Something veiled in shadows that the light of memory couldn't pierce. "That's it, till I woke up here."

"So maybe a fire started while you were fighting them off?"

"Two rots, Dean? I'm hell on wheels and all, but come on. And I don't remember seeing you in there."

He shook his head. "I don't know, Thea. It was pretty traumatic; maybe you just blocked it out." He glanced over at the packet he'd set on the nightstand. They were snapshots, but he'd laid them upside down so Thea couldn't tell what of. "I wish I could help."

"I know, I know. Something just doesn't fit. I feel like somebody used a paper puncher and knocked out a piece of my memory." She sighed. "And another thing."

"What's that?"

"The cops come talk to you about the fire at all?"

"No; why?"

"Well, just seems to me like they would. Suspicious circumstances and all, what with the gunshots, too. Not to mention it happened the day after *another* fire..." Thea let the thought trail off.

"Oh, well, that's just it." Dean pointed a meaty finger at the TV. "I caught some reports and asked folks around here. They said there was an electrical short that ignited some oily rags in the basement. The handyman's gonna have his ass handed to him in civil court." He ran his hands through prematurely graying hair. "They didn't say anything about gunshots. Maybe nobody heard 'em.

"And far as the other thing's concerned, aside from two fires there's nothing to link 'em. Different areas, different causes... this kind of thing happens all the time in a big city."

Thea frowned. "You don't actually think no one heard an MP-5 on full auto, do you, Dean? Plus, if I dragged you and Lilly out of a fire, how come none of us have any burns? Or suffer from smoke inhalation? I mean, my throat's a little raw, but nowhere near as bad as I'd expect. And how come nobody around here seems to find that the least bit odd?"

"Jeez, Thea, I don't know! What d'you want me to say?" He shifted his significant bulk as if trying to get more comfortable. "This whole thing is nuts. Has been for a long time. Hell, we all know there's more going on behind the scenes than just the nasties. We've figured for a while that the cops cover strange things up, right? This is just another one of 'em."

"Yeah, except those other cover ups never had any survivors we knew of. And why would *they* cover up something about *us*?"

They looked at one another for a few seconds, then Dean dropped his gaze to the packet again. "I don't know, Thea," he said finally. "How could I? Maybe they think *any* publicity is bad. But yeah, something's foul. Just one more stinking thing to add to the pile." He laughed bitterly a moment later.

"What?"

"Just thinking back to what I said before, about being 'blessed.'"

Thea just nodded, waiting.

"Well, I bet you're curious how come I look so good after getting all tore up twice in as many days."

"I was beginning to wonder."

Dean looked at her again, pain evident in his eyes. "Those claw marks are almost completely healed." He pulled the shirt away from his ample belly and peeled back one of the bandages. Thea saw the trailing end of a couple ugly red marks. The wounds were certainly vicious, but it looked like Dean had been healing for weeks, not days. "And they thought my back was broken when I came in, but now it only looks like a slipped disk." He gave her a twisted grin and tears ran freely down his face. "I think I've been given another blessing. Saint Dean, that's me!"

Thea could think of nothing else to say. She patted Dean gently on the shoulder and left him with his photographs.

• • •

Thea's mother, Newa, insisted Thea stay at her Gold Coast condo while she recovered. In reply, Thea demanded her mom take her directly from the hospital to her Wicker Park apartment. Thea knew she'd go nuts with her mother's constant monitoring and silent reproving. After one of their painfully polite arguments, they reached a compromise. Thea and Margie would join the elder Ms Ghandour for an early dinner, then Newa would take them back to Wicker Park.

It was an old ploy. Thea knew her mother would spend the evening, from the ride there and on through dinner, wearing her down. As the Director of Marketing at Panflex, a major producer of antibiotics for the pharmaceutical giant Magadon, Newa Ghandour was an old hand at such manipulation.

Truth be told, Thea was grateful to spend time with her mom. Although a stern, constantly poised woman, Newa Ghandour was also a caring and reasonable parent. Thea knew it must have been hard raising her alone, especially having eloped from Egypt with an American serviceman spouting promises of a grand new life in the States, only to leave her in the lurch when she became pregnant. Thea knew a big reason Newa had not returned to Egypt was because she had been unwilling to face the shame of being pregnant and without a husband. Staying alone in a strange land had revealed reserves of strength within Newa Ghandour. Thea's mom had triumphed over many adversities, overcoming barriers of culture, gender and religion to create for herself a career and a place within the community.

It didn't make for the greatest upbringing, though. Newa wasn't a harsh or unloving parent, but she proved to be more comfortable brainstorming new sales avenues than spending quality time with her daughter. Thea had grown up rebellious, on the lookout for new excitements that would shock and dismay her mother. She'd settled down quite a bit in the past few years, a genuine interest in journalism giving her direction. Plus, Thea found an outlet for her more extreme tendencies in the hunt itself.

Despite the many mistakes and outright stupid things she'd done growing up, Thea didn't regret much of it. It had given her insight into the unpredictability of life and the opportunities that remain hidden if you stick to the straight and narrow.

The one thing that did bother her tied directly back to her relationship with her mother. Though half-Egyptian and technically Muslim, Thea had very little understanding of or connection to her heritage. Part of her rebellious youth had been to dismiss any of her mom's attempts to teach her about the five pillars of Islam. In Thea's young mind, she was American and Islam was some strange musty religion old guys in robes and beards practiced. She already felt like enough of an outcast without adding that to the mix.

Thea now knew that her views of Islam were presumptive to say the least. And it wasn't exactly a cult faith; there were millions of practicing Muslims in the United States alone. She also knew this was the wound that cut deepest with her mother; Newa could understand rebellion — she'd left a traditional home and established a very different lifestyle in a foreign land. But Thea knew her mother felt that Thea's dismissal of Islam was a dismissal of God. It saddened Newa, but she had long since given up trying to force her daughter to see the error of her ways. The elder Ghandour practiced her faith without ostentation; it was simply another part of her life as was Panflex, golfing, cooking, and charity work.

Thea had noticed her mother's backing off, and it had allowed her the perspective to see she was still rebelling to an extent. Additionally, awakening to the existence of the supernatural had given Thea new cause to consider the concept of God. Yet the gulf between mother and daughter was still too wide, habits too strongly ingrained, for some movie of the week reconciliation. Each woman was too willful to be the first to actually admit to past errors, and Thea still carried resentment from feeling as if she'd been relegated to a supporting role through much of her mother's life.

Thea loved her mother and knew that Newa loved her in return, but at the moment it wasn't enough to overcome the long-standing disagreements between them. And certainly the aftermath of this "accident" was not the time to start mending bridges, as far as Thea was concerned. She had enough on her mind as it was.

Instead, Thea made a point to enjoy the evening for what it was: a chance to spend time with her mother and best friend, and to enjoy what was sure to be an amazing meal. Newa Ghandour was quite the gourmand, skilled at making virtually any cultural cuisine you could name. This certainly included the array of Egyptian meals — gebna, kebab, baba ghanough, koshary, and the like. Newa enjoyed exploring other cultures' culinary accomplishments, and could make anything from baked ziti to lobster bisque. Thea and Margie spent the ride over trying to guess the meal Newa had prepared.

It turned out to be shrimp creole with cornbread and beer. Thea wasn't allowed beer since her mom was concerned it might react badly with the medication. Thea pointed out futilely that the only medication the hospital had given her was *aspirin*, for Heaven's sake. Unless Mom was talking about Thea's birth control pills, but she didn't have to worry about *that* since her daughter had stopped taking them since they played hell with her complexion and besides she couldn't remember the last time she'd even needed them! This brought a scandalized look to Newa's face and a muttered entreaty that her daughter might someday learn restraint, *insha'Allah*. Having fired the evening's opening salvo, Thea dug into the meal with gusto.

Three hours later, Newa ferried Thea and Margie to Wicker Park. By the end of the meal, Thea's mom had only halfheartedly urged her to stay. It was clear from Thea's not-so-subtle hints that spending a week would be less than relaxing right now. And she showed enough of her normal energy that Newa accepted that Thea had weathered her recent experience well.

It was all a front, of course. Thea spent the evening secretly worrying. The blank spot in her memory bothered her greatly. She knew victims of trauma often blocked out the event, but she was certain she wasn't the type to do that. Thea had always had trouble fooling herself. Most people go through life creating convenient justifications for what they do, purposefully forgetting or twisting events in their memories to make life easier on themselves. Thea was saddled with an acute self-awareness. She'd long ago discovered that no matter what lines she fed herself, she was always very clear on the reasons why she did things — or that she didn't have a damn good reason for something and was just trumping up a rationale. This had made her quite good at puzzling out others' motivations. And while she didn't have a photographic memory, she proved good at recalling details of behavior and environment, a boon in her journalism career. Falling into the hunt had, if anything, sharpened Thea's self-awareness even further. The insight that she could project on her surroundings was frequently cast internally as well, often despite her efforts to the contrary.

She was troubled that her uncanny memory was failing her now. Had she seen something so horrible that her mind was trying to protect her? She couldn't imagine what might be worse than the things she'd seen since the first night she was forced to face the nightmares that existed in the world.

Perhaps the head injury had rattled something loose. She knew that the human brain remained a great mystery to modern science. Half the time doctors looked at head injuries, shrugged, and made a guess. It was possible Thea had simply suffered physiological damage that wiped her memory banks' recollections of Sunday night. Possible. But it didn't *feel* right. She felt certain the memory was there; she just couldn't get at it for some reason.

That left another option. An alternative that made less sense than the previous two, but that nonetheless felt closest to the truth.

Someone, or some*thing*, had made her forget.

• • •

Newa Ghandour pulled the Lexus smoothly to the curb. The engine idled as Thea and Margie said goodnight and got ready to dash for the door. It was past 10 P.M. and a bitter wind whipped through the neighborhood while stinging snow whirled through the air in hazy clumps. The first day of spring was barely a month away; looked like the weather planned to get in as much as it could before then.

Thea gave her mother a peck on the cheek and was halfway out the door when she felt Newa's hand on her arm. She looked back in surprise; Newa Ghandour was not much of one for physical contact. Even more surprising was the worry that peeked out from Newa's dark eyes. She broke the gaze almost instantly, raising her hand to slip a rich black lock of hair behind her ear.

"What is, Mom?" Thea asked, struggling to hold the half-open door against a sudden gust. "I'm freezing here."

Newa cleared her throat and look at Thea again, her composure restored. Her normally cultured, clipped tones quavered slightly when she said, "Be careful, Thea. I do worry for you."

Thea looked at her mother in surprise. "I will, Mom," she said. Then she was standing in the frozen grass by the curb, watching the Lexus vanish amid the swirl of powder that swept across the road.

"Hey!" Margie yelled from the doorway. "I'm not dragging your ass back to the hospital if you get frostbite!"

Thea ran inside and smacked Margie on her behind to hustle her up the stairs. "Hurry it up! Hot bath and a big hookah await! Doctor's orders!"

Margie laughed, digging in her purse for her keys. "So what was that at the car? Your mom try one last time to drag you off?"

"No. It was a little weird, actually. She just said she was worried."

"Wow; really?" Margie said. She looked back down at Thea as she turned on the landing. "For your mom, that's like breaking down and sobbing."

Thea laughed; Margie was certainly right about that. Then she saw a dark figure standing by the door to their apartment. Thea was up the last few steps and crouched defensively before Margie before she even realized she'd moved.

"Jesus, Thea; what—?" Thea noticed peripherally as Margie, still a few steps down, leaned around Thea to look down the hall. "Who's that?"

"It's Romeo," Thea replied, recognizing the wiry Asian. He still wore the pea coat, though he'd added a hooded sweatshirt underneath it. She tried to calm herself down, feeling almost lightheaded from the adrenaline rush. "He's a… friend of Jake's."

"Of Jake's?" Margie echoed, moving next to her and watching Romeo approach.

Thea flushed. "Well, and mine too, I guess." To Romeo, she said, "It's pretty late. What's so important you had to track me down and hang around outside my apartment half the night?"

He wasn't the least put off by her abrupt attitude, though Margie obviously was. Romeo looked coolly at Thea, then at her friend as he said, "I believe you know. It is important that we talk."

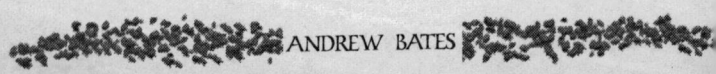

Margie shot Thea a look that clearly said, *Love triangle, eh? Just what have you been up to?* Aloud, she said, "Romeo, is it? I'm Margie. Why don't we all go inside? I could use some hot cider."

Thea wasn't thrilled about letting Romeo inside her apartment. But then, considering his shady background, he could have broken in and waited for her on the couch. No sense playing coy at this stage of things.

Thea and Margie's apartment had the cluttered, lived-in look that was typical of two young women more focused on careers than on homemaking. The style was Modern Eclectic and the women contributed equally to the decor. The mismatched floral print couch and loveseat covered in a half ton of throw pillows commanded a majority of the narrow living room. A small TV and a VCR sat on a handmade table along the wall by the door, looking embarrassed next to a new DVD player. A handful of videotapes and DVDs littered the floor next to the table, leaving the small metal storage rack on the adjoining wall free to collect dust. A compact stereo system was buried under CDs on an end table next to the love seat. Plants hung from hangers and crouched on speakers and shelves. During the day, they soaked up sunlight through the large pair of windows over the couch on the right hand wall which faced the street. Large unframed prints covering everything from Impressionist to Post-Modern (not to mention some unfortunate stains) hung on the walls. An antique coffee table stood timidly in the center of the room, covered with various magazines, coasters, and random nicknacks. The kitchen stood to the left of the living room and was separated from it by an open counter. Three stools — two leopard print and one cracked red leather — stood next to the counter in a sloppy row like poorly trained soldiers. A coffee maker, bread maker, and microwave fought for room on one half of the narrow countertop while bowls and glassware camped out on the other half (Margie wasn't renowned for her ability to clean up after herself). The hall extended to the left of the front door past the kitchen. Doors down the way opened successively on a closet, the bathroom (as large as either bedroom and a major reason they got the place), Margie's room and Thea's room.

"No messages," Margie said brightly as she checked the machine by the door. She breezed into the apartment, tossing her purse and keys on the countertop and waving a hand toward the living room. "Have a seat. I'm making cider — *with* applejack, thank you very much. Who wants one?"

She was doing her "I'm just a girl; I don't notice anything" routine. That meant Margie was irritated at Thea for not filling her in on what was obviously some kind of juicy story relating to the strange ethnic men suddenly popping up in her life. Thea knew she could look forward to quite possibly days of this until she finally broke down. Then Thea would be subject to an interrogation unlike anything seen outside of a Vietnamese POW camp.

"I'll help, Margie. Romeo, why don't you have a seat?" About the only gratifying aspect to the situation was that Samuel Zheng looked decidedly uncomfortable standing in the living room.

"I think it might be better if we spoke elsewhere," he replied. "I… would not want to disturb your friend."

"Oh, don't worry about me," Margie said, waving a hand in the midst of preparations over the stove. "After I fix all this up I'll be off in my room, checking on equations. A regular little bookworm, I am."

Thea's eyes shot daggers at Margie's back. *Laying it on a bit thick, aren't you?* Romeo obviously wanted to talk about the past few days. Thea had figured that if anyone would go to the trouble to find out where she really lived, it would be him. She'd imagined he'd hold off revealing his knowledge for a situation that warranted it, so he must have felt that current circumstances fit the bill. And the choice of shoving Margie in her room with her Walkman or slogging through a mounting snowstorm to shiver in their Hunters' Hideaway was an easy one to make. "Really, it's okay, Romeo." She made sure to catch his attention and glare pointedly before shifting her eyes to Margie and shaking her head slightly.

Romeo nodded. "I should call the others, then."

Oh, fuck. He wanted a meeting of the whole damn club? "Romeo—"

He looked at Thea, his features inscrutable as always. "It is important that we all talk, even if they must come to your home to do so."

Thea slumped against the counter. She wasn't in shape for this. Too much going on of late; she'd just wanted to relax in the bath for one damn night. *Not unreasonable, is it?* Men and their fucking take-charge attitudes. "Fine, fine. Call them. The sooner we deal with this the sooner I can get some sleep."

Margie put a hand on her shoulder as Romeo dialed the cordless. Thea looked up at her roommate. Margie said nothing but her concern was evident. She'd put aside the game playing, aware that she was on the periphery of something more serious than some ménage a trois.

Thea patted Margie's hand. "It's okay, really. And I'll explain everything as soon as I can."

"Good enough," Margie said. The worry didn't leave her eyes, though.

•••

Thea curled up on the loveseat sipping hot cider and looked around at her fellow partners in crime. Jake warmed his hands around a mug of cider as he sat on the near end of the couch. He wore the standard winter outfit: jeans, heavy boots, turtleneck and sweater; his parka was slung over the back of the couch with mittens and stocking cap sticking out of one pocket. He still wore his scarf to combat the storm's lingering chill. Parker sprawled on the other end of the couch, grudgingly drinking cider since the women didn't have any beer on hand. He was wearing his winter camouflage, of all things. Thea suspected he even had a flak vest on beneath his bulky camo jacket. Romeo had claimed the red leather barstool. Having passed on refreshments, he perched with arms crossed, returning Thea's gaze. Margie was as good as her word, hidden away in her room with schoolwork.

She shifted her glance back to Parker. Thea knew she shouldn't, but she couldn't help herself. "Thanks for taking time out from your survivalists' workshop to join us, Parker."

He rose to the bait immediately. "Fuckin' A, Thea," he snapped as he jerked forward, almost spilling his drink on himself, "this isn't a game."

"You think I don't know that?" she shot back. After all, where did these people get off inviting themselves into her home? Didn't they all have enough to worry about, what with monsters out there fucking up everyone's lives? And why them — why *her* — anyway? Why did she get tapped to be... well, what the hell was she? A holy crusader? A herald of cosmic justice? One of humanity's antibodies? Just another deluded wacko? She pointed to the bandage on her forehead. "You think I got this putting on makeup, asshole?"

"Hey!" Jake's voice cut across Parker's response before it had cleared his throat. "Can't you two *not* tear into each other for once? This is *important*."

Romeo nodded, scratching distractedly at his cheek. "Jake is right."

"Yeah, yeah. I know." Thea sighed. She slumped against the back of the loveseat while Parker nodded, resting his elbows on his knees and frowning into his mug. "Sorry, guys. Feels like I've been going non-stop since Friday night," she explained. "No, the week before that. Planning everything out and all. And with what happened to Carl and to Dean's boyfriend... it's a lot to deal with."

"We know, Thea," Jake said. "That's why we need to talk. We think there's more going on here than meets the eye, and we need to figure out what it is."

Thea snorted. *No shit.* "Okay, then. What've you got?"

Romeo shifted, creaking the worn leather. "I think we all agree that you were correct the other day, that someone was inside the estate before us. What you told us about the phone call you received leaves little doubt." He looked at her with hawk's eyes. "I think I know who the person is."

Thea's vision grayed momentarily, a dark figure seeming to flicker across her sight. "Who?" she croaked through a suddenly dry mouth.

"I do not know his name, but I have seen him." A pause. "He carried you and the others from Dean's apartment shortly before it caught fire."

"What?! So I *didn't* drag Dean and Lilly out of a burning building!" The three men shook their heads. "Did you all see this guy?"

"No," Jake said. "Romeo told us what happened, though." He motioned for the Asian man to continue.

"I arrived at Dean's apartment as the sun set. Walking from the train," Romeo explained. "At the corner of the street where Dean lived, I was… filled with terror. My only thought was to find safety, to hide quietly until the danger passed. I was almost to the train stop before I could control my fear."

Thea nodded, remembering. Romeo came in on the El, Chicago's elevated train, about the same time she'd arrived by taxi. If not for the fear effect, they'd probably have reached Dean's place together. It sounded like Romeo had run farther than she had before regaining his self-control. Which meant… she realized he was still speaking, saying what she was thinking.

"…I returned, it was too late. I did not know at the time, of course. I approached the apartment cautiously. Otherwise I think that man would have seen me. He moved like one used to danger, quickly but not rushed." Romeo's eyes unfocused slightly at the memory, and Thea thought she caught a hint of grudging respect in his voice. "He carried you in his arms and laid you on the sidewalk. After looking around, he went back inside and returned with Dean and Lilly. Then he once more went inside. He did not come out again that I could see, and then I saw flames in the building.

"I could wait no longer. I ran to the sidewalk and saw that you were all unconscious. Dean and Lilly did not look good. I was worried they would not survive. You were bleeding from your head," he pointed at her bandage. "Blood covered you, in fact. I feared at first... I soon realized most of the blood was not your own." He cleared his throat. "I tried going inside to look for others, or for the man, but the fire was too hot. The building burned very quickly."

"Wait. I never saw the news; just didn't have the stomach for it. Were there people in the other apartments?"

Jake nodded, looking a bit queasy. He set down the dregs of his cider and exhaled heavily. "They found nine people in the building. You three were the only ones who made it out."

"Well, three of those nine were crispy zombies, at least." *And the rest were innocent people.* "I'd bet anything our mysterious stranger wasn't one of the remaining victims, though."

"I agree," Romeo said.

Something was trying to break free in Thea's subconscious. "What did the guy look like?"

"Tall, but not too tall. Very thin. A white man. He wore a dark suit. He had the look of a killer."

Almost got it.... "And he didn't come back out?"

Romeo shook his head. "Not that I saw. But I was not as vigilant as I should have been. He could have left when I looked to your safety. And then the fire, the flames... I think he left through the back when the fire started. I did look at the snow, but many tracks covered the ground."

Thea nodded. *Misdirection. Get us out the front, start the blaze and run away in the confusion.*

"That is not all, though," Romeo added. "I said that I did not know who he was. But I do know *what* he was."

Of course. Romeo's sight! When he knew to look, Romeo could pick up the little things that gave human-looking monsters away as, well, monsters. Thea's memories rattled their chains even more noisily. "Don't leave us in suspense, tough guy. Let's hear it."

"He was not alive. He was one of the dead who walk. The stranger was one of the hidden."

Thea felt something tear loose in her mind. Memories flooded back with harsh clarity. She gave a strangled cry and hunched forward, dropping her mug to the hardwood floor as she clutched her skull. The full horror of that night slammed into her head all at once — the smell of decay, beheading a monster with her bare hands, the thing grabbing at her, Lilly crushed beneath the chair, Carl unspeakably violated, a creature coming for her…

…And the grim stranger with the depthless eyes.

"Carpenter!" Thea yelled, jerking upright. The suddenness of her movement startled the men, who'd been rushing forward to help her. "His name is Maxwell Carpenter! He just… appeared… when one of the zombies was coming after me. Took it out with a couple of pistols!" The hole in her mind was filling in rapidly. "We went to check the bedroom and I saw what they'd done to Carl—" Thea remembered the blur of the dresser zooming toward her, everything going dark for a short time, then, strangely, a disturbing green haze flickering fitfully in her mind.

"I… you know, I think he did something to make me forget he'd been there. After I knocked myself silly on the furniture." Thea shook her head as if to knock the last piece loose. "Doesn't make sense, I know, but it feels right."

"Sonofabitch!" Jake blurted. His eyes were bright with recollection. "That name, I remember that name! Carpenter… he snuck onto hunter-net about a year, year-and-a-half ago. He posed as a fellow hunter, giving us all sorts of secrets about ghosts and zombies and vampires and stuff. Jesus!"

Parker was nodding slowly as Jake spoke. "I think I remember that. Got a whole bunch of people nervous, afraid the nasties had totally corrupted the network, right?"

"Well, he wasn't the only one," Jake said. Words spilled out rapidly in his excitement. "A bunch of rots sneaked onto the network — probably still do, I'll bet. One of the reasons I'm a lot more cautious about what I read on there."

"So what happened with this Carpenter guy?" Thea asked.

Jake prodded his memory. "Uh… well, to start with he pissed a bunch of folks off with his smug attitude. Then said he had all this dirt on what we were hunting and offered it up. Since then, a lot of it's turned out to be pretty accurate."

"They finally figured out what he really was, though," Parker continued. "Somebody, I think it was the chick who runs the South Side hunters—"

"—Lupe!" Jake cut in. Guadalupe Droin ran a loose group of hunters that stuck mostly to the South Side. Chicago was big enough that the two groups usually operated separately. They kept in touch, sharing updates and the like, but they got together only when something really big was going down. Which was fine by Thea. She and Lupe hadn't gotten along at all. "Yeah, her and somebody else on the 'net; Witness, I think—"

"Dude, c'mon!" Parker smacked the kid lightly on the shoulder. "Doesn't matter who right now, eh?" He picked up the thread himself. "So her and maybe somebody else found out this Carpenter was some Mob guy in the '30s." He paused, brow furrowed in thought. "Something about the name's familiar. Not quite right, though… There were a lot of mobsters running around during Prohibition. Hell, I dunno. Maybe could check one of my books later. Anyway, he got killed back then, but he'd turned up again."

"He came back from the dead? What for?"

Jake and Parker looked at each other, both trying to remember more detail. Romeo watched along with Thea.

He'd been a hunter for quite some time, Thea knew, but he'd never bothered with hunter-net. "I'm not sure," Jake said finally. "Far as I can remember, he was still pissed at whomever had killed him." Jake chuckled. "Understandable, I guess. Anyway, I think it was some other Mafia family or something. Lupe said she was onto him, I remember. Never figured out what he was doing on the 'net to begin with, though. And he was booted off before we got decent answers."

"By Witness?" Thea asked. The individual known only as "witness1" ran the hunter online network. He (or she) was fairly hands-off in maintaining it, but a zombie raiding the 'net certainly called for intervention if anything did.

"I don't think so. As I recall, he got dumped in mid-transmission. Never came back on."

"That wasn't all, though," Parker said. "Didn't Lupe say she'd seen him after that?"

"Something like that, yeah."

"But nothing after her sighting? Till now, I mean." Jake and Parker shook their heads. "And she's still running around the South Side hunting nasties." They nodded.

Thea looked at them, then up at Romeo. She knew what they were thinking, but damned if she was going to make a road trip to talk to that chick during a blizzard. "Fellas, we all know what the next step is, but it's not going to happen tonight. I'm just too ragged right now and the weather's shaping up to be a real bitch."

Romeo furrowed his brow in disagreement but Jake nodded grudgingly. "No, Thea's right. We've figured out some important stuff tonight and I'll bet Lupe'll be a big help finding this Maxwell Carpenter." He shrugged, pointing a thumb toward the windows. "But it is getting ugly out, and we need to get in touch with her before we can actually meet. Right?"

Romeo obviously wasn't happy about it, but he was outnumbered. "Very well. Contact her, Jake. I will see what else I can learn in the meantime. This man... this *crea-*

ture… has tried to manipulate hunters in the past. It is clear he is doing so again. And so far he has the upper hand, for we do not know what he plans."

"Yeah, but we know who he is now," Thea said. "And he doesn't know that. Which gives *us* the edge."

FIVE

It was late by the time the guys left and the snowstorm was still going strong. Jake promised he'd contact everyone after he'd heard back from Lupe. Parker, a trivia buff on all things Chicago, said he'd dig through his library and see if he could find anything else out about a mobster named Maxwell Carpenter. Romeo didn't say anything, but Thea caught him looking out at the storm a lot near the end of things. She bet he was just crazy enough to try and track down the undead pal during the middle of the night in a blizzard.

Thea almost slipped off to bed then, but she felt Margie deserved at least some kind of explanation about what was happening. Exhausted mentally and physically, Thea wasn't sure she was up to a heart to heart with her best friend. If she didn't do it now, though, she wasn't sure she'd have the nerve to bring it up later. A light rap on Margie's door got no response, so Thea turned the handle and peeked in.

Margie was sprawled on her bed, swaddled in flannel pajamas and a huge down comforter. A reading lamp burned on the nightstand, reflecting off of Margie's glasses and the pages of a textbook and scattered photocopies. Her laptop had slipped off her legs and sat askew, its abstract screen saver flickering intermittent explosions of color. Thea wasn't sure how long she'd been asleep. Margie looked too peaceful to disturb, though, and just watching her lying there brought sleep swelling up to overwhelm Thea. She gently tapped the computer's rollerball and saved the open program that popped up before shutting down the laptop and setting it on the nightstand. Margie seldom moved when she slept, so Thea left her glasses alone and just clicked off the light.

Five minutes later, Thea was in her own bed and just as dead to the world.

•••

She'd have slept through the day if the phone hadn't awakened her late the next morning. It was Jake. Guadalupe Droin would meet with them. She drove a cab, so it was normally easy for her to meet just about anywhere. They'd agreed upon Union Station around 2 P.M. Jake said she refused to come by the gang's North Orleans Street hideaway. Thea suspected the chick just liked to throw her weight around, being one of the more seasoned hunters about. Still, it made sense to meet in a public place, considering recent events.

Thea stumbled into the kitchen in search of life-giving caffeine. Margie had long ago left for UIC, but she'd kept a half-pot of coffee warming. A Post-It was stuck to the coffee mug on the counter, with a sentence scrawled in Margie's jagged hand: *Hey, you. Can't duck me forever! We need to talk! — Me.*

Margie had a memory like an elephant. Thea knew she was fooling herself if she thought her friend would let go of such an obvious mystery as Thea having mysterious meetings with three strange men. Not today, though.

Thea slogged through drifts to the El around one o'clock. The blizzard had done a job on the city. Much of Chicago was snowed in, the plows having worked valiantly all night but with only the major arteries reliable to any degree. Like any good Midwesterner she gave herself plenty of time to account for any setbacks from last night's storm. It took quite a while to mush through the snow, but things went much more smoothly once she got to the neighborhood El. Thea finally reached Union Station and, after a few minutes of wandering the mammoth facility, found her way to the concourse. The place was built during World War I and refurbished in the early 1990s. The overall structure was quite a sight, its exterior designed with massive stone columns beneath a series of rectangular windows. The waiting area's vaulted ceiling was accented with steel trusses to form a striking interior space. Unfortunately, the whole place looked pretty seedy from years of sustained use. After a minute or two of searching, she found Parker and Jake on a bench with Dean, of all people.

Jake explained he'd called Dean to relate the basics, and he'd insisted on coming along. Thea knew he'd been healing rapidly, but she was nonetheless surprised to see him up and about, especially on such a shitty day. Although pale, Dean looked as though he felt fine. Physically, anyway. He talked with the same easy smile and gentle laugh as always, but Thea could see the haunted look in his eyes.

She was about as surprised to see Parker there. Of the remaining team, half had steady jobs. Lilly was still in the hospital, though, and Dean was formally on sick leave for obvious reasons. Parker managed one of his uncle's gun shops. It wasn't exactly a huge responsibility, but he had to trade favors with the help to take time off. He'd racked up quite a few favors in the past few weeks; Thea wondered when Uncle Ray would say something about it.

Jake and Romeo didn't work regular hours, but neither had much trouble taking care of financial matters. Jake had insurance money from his accident a few years back. Thea never figured out how Romeo kept himself in beer and Skittles. Not that he was a big spender, mind. He wore the same clothes all the time — always clean, so she figured he had a few changes of the same outfit — and still lived in the same closet he'd taken her to on the night they met. Living frugally otherwise, though, he had the money to buy much of the armaments, ammunition, and equipment they used in the hunt. Yet another mystery to put in Romeo's file.

Jake was finishing giving Dean the expanded version of their recent discussions as Thea approached. Dean nodded but said nothing for about a minute, obviously mulling something over. Then, with a look at Thea she couldn't figure, he described his new healing talent. Dean claimed he could even apply this gift to other people.

"I took Lilly's hand to comfort her," Dean explained. "She wasn't conscious, but I've always thought human contact is vital to patients' well-being. As I sat there, I was filled with certainty that I could mend her broken legs and internal injuries. So I focused on her, on the pain she must feel. And this... *warmth* flowed through me and into her. I could feel her growing stronger, more whole."

"Jesus, Dean," Parker said, then laughed. "Sorry; didn't mean... So how is she?"

Dean Sankowski, the Second Coming, Thea thought. Her impending conversation with Margie still fresh in her mind, Thea had a new perspective on just how bizarre she and her fellow hunters were.

"Lilly isn't completely healed," Dean answered Parker, "but I think she's a lot farther along the road to recovery. Physically, anyway. She still seems caught mentally in the horror of what happened."

"How about you, Dean?" Jake asked gently. "How are you holding up?"

Dean shrugged. "I'm okay. It's hard, no denying that. But I had a lot of time to think lying in that hospital bed. I figured I could wallow in grief or make sure Wayne, and Carl, didn't die for nothing." He turned, pain in his eyes but the old Sankowski grin on his face. "So here I am."

"Do you... Where are you going to stay?" Thea wondered.

"I have some friends happy to put me up till I find a new place. I hadn't really worried about that, though." A flicker of pain crossed his face. "I spent part of yesterday and this morning, well, taking care of Wayne. The service is tomorrow. I know none of you knew him, but it would mean a lot to me if you could come."

They shuffled and nodded soberly, offering their condolences again. Jake said, "Does anyone know who's... what's happening with Carl? Since Lilly's still in the hospital and all?"

Dean nodded. "Carl's parents stopped by the hospital yesterday. They wanted to check on Lilly and hear what happened. We talked a little bit; they thought about holding off on a funeral till Lilly was feeling better, but the doctor doesn't know when that might be. I think they have something planned for Sunday, give her a little more time, you know."

"D'you think she might ever snap out of it?" Parker wondered. "The doctors say anything?"

"I didn't get a chance to speak to her attending, so this is just my layman's opinion," Dean said. "But hopefully as her body continues to mend and as time passes she'll regain some stability mentally. There's no telling how long that could take, though."

No one was sure what to say in response. Lilly had never seemed very strong-willed. What she went through would have been traumatic for any one of them. Thea knew she wasn't alone in imagining it might have been too much for Lilly to take.

The silence got uncomfortable, and they busied themselves with people watching until Guadalupe Droin sauntered up. She was a year or two younger than Thea and came from the opposite end of the financial spectrum. Thea's mom had worked hard to get scholarships and grants and cultivated professional connections from years in college and graduate school to ultimately join the ranks of the affluent. Lupe's parents started out in one of Chicago's many housing projects, working menial jobs and saving what money they could to build a future. Both families were dedicated to their children, but money established an unmistakable distinction. Thea thought Lupe felt anyone who was born to wealth and never knew adversity was ultimately

soft and of weak character. And Lupe figured that was pretty much right on the mark.

Lupe was attractive and carried herself with definite maturity and confidence. She wore jeans stuffed into military surplus boots, a couple-three sweatshirts and a big old fatigue jacket. A black bandana was tied to cover her head and keep her long dark brown hair back over her shoulders. Thea knew the jacket protected her from the winter chill, but more importantly had plenty of pockets for things like wooden stakes, cigarette lighters, and a handgun or two.

Lupe checked everybody out, giving Jake a friendly jab to the shoulder and Thea a cold stare. Everyone else fell in the middle as far as greetings were concerned. "So where's the little Asian tough guy?" she asked. The woman stood casually, but there was a constant watchfulness about her. The only thing soft about Lupe was her curves.

"I dunno," Jake said. "I haven't been able to reach him since we talked last night."

Lupe shrugged. "Well, his loss." She scratched distractedly at one cheek. "Gotta roll before long. So what you got?"

Jake hadn't related much over email; he was very cautious about that kind of thing nowadays. Just that they were following something serious and Lupe should have some useful input. He didn't worry about secrecy here, though. The very fact that they were in a large public place actually enhanced their privacy. No one could eavesdrop without being noticed and anyone trying to listen with high tech gadgetry would have a hard time cutting through the ambient noise. "You remember a hidden by the name of Carpenter? He—"

Lupe snorted, muttering a curse. "Sure, I remember that Goddamn rot. Snuck onto hunter-net and pissed off a whole bunch of people for shits and grins."

"That's the guy," Jake confirmed. "We were wondering what you could tell us about him. I dug through the 'net

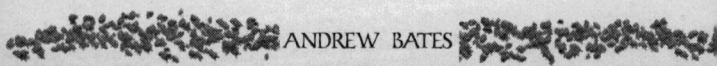

archives last night; we hoped you might've learned something more about him than what was posted there."

"You can bet that if I'd have tracked that shit down, the 'net would've heard about it the next goddamn day." She frowned, then shook her head as if trying to knock loose a misplaced memory. With a faint shrug, she said, "You know he was a legbreaker from the old, *old* school?" They nodded. "He came back to take out whoever was responsible for killing him, I figure. The big one was this Mob chick, Annabelle Sforza. I think they had a thing going, or maybe he just had a crush on her. Whatever, she was involved in him taking a dirt nap."

"Sforzas were part of the Mafia all right," Parker said. "I remember the name from some digging I did last night. Came over from Italy or something and started getting mixed up in the labor racket around the '30s and '40s." He paused. "You know, I'm sure I heard that name recently, too."

"Probably the old lady," Lupe suggested. "She died; papers ran a thing on it. Matriarch of business tycoon-something-or-other. Hinted she had Mob ties, but the papers never have any balls to come right out and say anything."

Parker frowned. "Yeah, that's probably it. I don't know, though. Seems like there's been something more recently. Speaking of names, I think I got something on our guy." He pulled out a wrinkled piece of paper for reference. "It's only a footnote, but I got something on a Dennis 'The Carpenter' Maxwell. Some Irish guy, part of Capone's mob in the Prohibition days."

"Yeah, that's his real name. He got the nickname 'Carpenter' from nailing peoples' hands to tables." Lupe shifted her stance, glancing around the concourse. "Anyway, those two were a thing, I guess. If I actually gave a shit about the guy, I'd wonder what the whole damn soap opera was about. Since I don't, all I know is that he had some serious hate boiling. You could tell from his posts. He was all clever and full of himself, but once I brought up that Sforza name he was all about 'bitch' this and 'payback' that."

"She was his anchor here, you figure?" Jake asked. Though it was clear that a lot remained to learn about the undead, they'd discovered some pretty useful stuff in large part thanks to Jake. For instance, many of the things that returned from the grave were tied to a certain person or place, like ghosts haunting a house. These anchors were something terribly important to them — obviously, if it was enough to bring them back from the dead — and kept them linked to the living world. Destroying the anchor cut the critter loose, but doing so had its own complications. Certainly if the anchor was a person, "destruction" meant one thing: "death." Thea had heard some hunters were zealous enough that the option didn't bother them. Thankfully, none of her group was exactly sanguine about killing an innocent person just to rid the world of a ghost.

"Yeah, that's what I think. But she died of natural causes. I… yeah, that's right. I took a fare to the funeral, if you can believe that. Messengers at work again, right?" The "Messengers" was one of a number of labels attributed to whatever force gifted hunters with their unusual abilities. Whether conscious entities or natural force, most hunters agreed that this influence aided them from use of second sight and edges to arranging for "coincidences" that brought them across the paths of monsters. "Carpenter or Maxwell or whatever you want to call him dumped off the 'net right about when the old lady kicked. When she bought it, his anchor here got cut. I think he held on long enough to say good-bye. I… yeah, I remember I decided to look 'round back of the funeral home, and the back door was off its hinges."

"But, what? You didn't go in after him?" Thea asked. "Why not?"

Lupe gave Thea a cool stare. "I'm tough, but I ain't stupid. Only a fool goes in after a heavy duty hidden with a heart full of hate boiling. Hit him one on one like that, when he's already trippin' in the red, and you're the one ends up getting your ass handed to you." Her brow furrowed as she dredged up the memory. "Besides, I don't know for sure if he was even still in there. Wouldn't look good if I slipped in there all armed and shit when the cops pull up. Look like yours truly trying some B&E, right?"

Thea almost believed it — Lupe was right about the danger of taking on a powerful nasty by yourself, at least. But something about the way the woman's gaze slipped away when she spoke, the way she notched up her attitude another level as if to defy any more questions about it… there was something more to the story. Recalling her own encounter with the stranger who'd called himself Maxwell Carpenter — notably the fact that she didn't remember *any* of it until the others helped jog the memory loose — Thea suspected she might know what it was.

Jake spoke before Thea could call her on it, though. "Lupe wrote a post about what happened. She said a couple of the symbols we use were written on the wall: 'hope' and 'corruption.'" He looked at Lupe. "You thought he was going to make peace with himself about what happened?"

Lupe stared through the crowd, jaw clenched defiantly. Then, after a moment, the muscles of her face relaxed and she dropped her gaze to her boots. "Look, I'm not an over the top crusader. Carpenter was a bastard and I'm sure he caused a shitload of pain in this life and the next. But those signs; yeah, I remember. I…" she brought her head back up, defiance and something else — compassion? doubt? — in her eyes. "He'd come to finish something, and with her already dead I didn't see the harm. I don't like blowing these things away, and letting him alone in there was just a different way of getting the job done."

It all made sense. Not every walking dead was evil (though Romeo would dispute that). Once a few months ago, Thea, Jake and Parker had come across a ghost of some forgotten ballplayer. He'd been called up to the majors as a pitcher for the Cubs, but he died in a car accident before

his first game. The frustration of missing his chance in The Show kept him lingering. Once they'd figured out what the spirit wanted, they'd broken into Wrigley Field and cheered him on as he pitched to them. It was surreal and heart-breaking at the same time — swinging at balls that weren't even there and hearing their thin voices being swallowed in the darkness of the old ballpark. But that's all the guy had wanted, an audience to watch him pitch. Once he got it, he just faded away. Thea wished all their encounters were as easily solved as her reverse *Touched by an Angel*.

So Thea could understand Lupe giving Carpenter the same chance at rest. But it still didn't sit quite right. It was obvious from Lupe's attitude that she hated the guy with a passion. And having seen him in action, Thea knew he was good at one thing and one thing only: killing. That kind of career path didn't make for a very nice guy. Lupe may walk around with an attitude the size of Rhode Island, but she was damn good at the hunt. She wasn't the type to let a threat like Carpenter walk.

Not unless he made her do it.

Something kept Thea from saying anything. She chalked it up to the headache that had returned while listening to Lupe's story and simply not feeling like getting into another argument. Rubbing her temple, Thea tried to focus on what the others were talking about.

"…So we think he's back," Jake said. "Or maybe never left. Either way, he called himself 'Carpenter' when he talked to Thea, and from how she described him the attitude matches, too."

Lupe gave a short laugh. "That's just fucking great. I hope you're not trying to lay the blame on me for this."

"Of course not!" Jake replied. "We were hoping you might be able to give us more information to help track him down."

"Exactly," Dean added. "If it is this Carpenter, he has the potential to be extremely dangerous. We need to find out what he's doing here."

"I hear ya. You check out his old stomping grounds? He'll be like any other walking dead. He's gonna head back to the places he knew when he was alive. They're more solid for him; like little anchors. Help keep him in the land of the living and all that."

Jake and Dean nodded, and Parker finally perked since they were getting to the hunt part of things. "We were planning on it," Jake said, "but we figured it'd save time if we got that information from you. Since you already did the research and all."

Lupe grinned, the smile softening her features. "Clever boy, ol' Jake. That I can do. Got a notebook in my cab where I keep stuff like that; a little trick I learned from the Doc." She looked at the clock hanging in the concourse. "And I should head out anyway. You wanna follow, I'll see what I wrote down back then."

They trooped toward the exit, taking it slow for Dean. He felt immeasurably better than he had a few days previously but still suffered from cracked ribs and a limp. Thea felt on display standing outside while Lupe dug for the notebook in her glovebox. Thea hoped they looked like they were negotiating a fare and not going through some kind of illicit transaction.

Lupe turned in the passenger seat, flipping through a tattered notebook. She muttered to herself as she searched, saying distractedly at one point, "I got this in a kind of code. Nothing major, but should be enough that it looks more like I'm tracking fares than rots, y'know?" After a minute or so, she nodded decisively and handed the pad to Jake. "About a third of the way down; here, see? After I dug through what articles I could find, I wrote down a couple neighborhoods to check out. Cruised them, but never found anything. Good a place to start as any, I'd say." Something struck Lupe then. "I think there's something else in here," she said as she dug through the glovebox again.

Thea looked over Jake's shoulder at the notebook. No specific addresses, just streets and neighborhoods, with a scattering of other names: Bonaparte, Canal, Cicero, Monroe, Roosevelt, Little Italy, Bonasera's, Greektown, MacGowan's, Union Row, even Gold Coast. A lot of it covered areas that the Van Helsing brigade patrolled now. Union Row was circled twice, the ballpoint leaving a deep depression in the cheap paper. The area was a hotbed of activity when the unions came into prominence, bringing together — clashing, one might say — different social classes, political interests, and mob influence in a roiling mess that never quite settled down. If Carpenter was an underworld thug, it made sense that he'd have done work around there. Especially if he was alive during Prohibition. The Mob had a blast back then, running booze and speakeasies and battling over turf as viciously as mutts over a particularly juicy bone. Capone may have been the top dog, but there were plenty of scraps for the rest to scuffle over.

Lupe popped out of the cab, a scrunched piece of paper in her hand. "Here, I got this when I was researching him; kept it when I made the rounds so I'd have a better chance of recognizing him." It was a photocopy of the *Chicago Tribune* from 1934 showing a grainy photograph of a large, almost brutish man being led out of a building by a pair of Chicago's finest. The caption at the bottom read "Dennis Maxwell, questioned in the disappearance of Walter D'Amato."

"What the hell, Lupe? This is a different guy!" Thea exclaimed. "The one I met was skinny and dark featured. Not this Russell Crowe looking guy." It was perfectly sensible if Carpenter was using a half-assed alias. That still didn't explain his dramatic change in physical appearance. Even if he'd dyed his hair and changed his diet, the body type was completely different. She said as much to the others. "If Romeo was here, he'd back me up."

Lupe looked ready to snap back, then a flicker passed behind her eyes. A forceful shake of her head and the fiery glare was back in place. "I don't know what to tell you. I never saw him aside from in this picture, but I know that's

the guy. He admitted to it, and what trail I did find matched up."

"You ever think that maybe he tricked you? That we're really talking about some other rot who wants us all to think he's this Maxwell guy?"

"What the fuck would be the point of that? Now, I mean?" Lupe shot back. "The bastard ain't stupid; he's got to know we all keep in touch. So why'd he call himself 'Maxwell Carpenter' to your face? Doesn't take much of a brain to match that up with 'Dennis Maxwell.' You leave out something from what you told everybody, honey?" Thea and Lupe glared at one another, ready to go at it. Dean and Jake stepped in at the same time, gently nudging the two women away from one another. Parker looked mildly disappointed.

"Okay, so we have another mystery," Jake admitted. "It might not be the same guy, but I'm guessing it is. Maybe the photo was mislabeled; happens all the time, right? Maybe he looks more like that than you remember, Thea. Sounded like things were pretty crazy that night and you did take a nasty shot to the head, didn't you?"

Thea nodded grudgingly. "Maybe so. But this asshole's already got us running around enough. I don't want to get dragged on some wild goose chase because she researched the wrong guy."

"Hey, *you* came to *me* for help, sister! I gave you what I know. If it ain't what you're looking for, ain't my problem." She looked ready to say something else, then shot a glance at Jake. "I got to go." She snatched her notebook, dismissing the photocopy Thea held and hopping into her taxi. The engine roared to life and the four hunters watched exhaust chase after the cab as it sped away.

"Well, then!" Dean said brightly, clapping his hands and rubbing them together. "That… helpful."

Thea socked him on the shoulder. "I'm sorry, guys, but she just pisses me off."

"Looks like the feeling's mutual," Parker said. "Maybe there's a little lezzie action going on in the old subconscious?"

"Parker, you are such a fucking moron sometimes, I don't know how you get dressed in the morning."

He grinned. "Play your cards right and I'll show ya sometime."

Jake looked up from the battered Palm Pilot he was using to enter the locations he'd memorized from Lupe's notebook. "Come on, you two," he said, sticking out his tongue in distaste.

"Yes, well. Sounds like we have a bit of mystery left to uncover," Dean added. "What say we get somewhere warm before we dig into this any further?"

Thea took a deep breath and tried to let go of her anger at Lupe and irritation at Parker. She'd be better served channeling it all into this Carpenter guy. Whether he was Dennis Maxwell or some other undead posing as a Mafia thug from sixty years ago — and how fucked up an idea was *that?* — there was no doubt he was playing some sort of game on them.

They were following Parker to his 4Runner when Thea heard a chirp from the pocket of her ski jacket. She fumbled open the flap and extracted her cell phone.

"Hello," a voice said, somehow able to cram friendliness, teasing, menace, and conceit into that one short word. *Holy shit, the man himself. Carpenter.* "You lose a little slant-eyed fella in the last day or so?"

Thea's body went cold. "What have you done to Romeo, asshole? If you do anything to hurt him, I'll—"

"Hey, settle down, baby. He's just fine. Resourceful, too. Tracked me down in a snowstorm, and I'm not an easy man to find when the weather's *nice.*"

"What do you want?"

That damn smug chuckle again. "I figure we've all run around enough. It's about time we had a sit down, don't you think?"

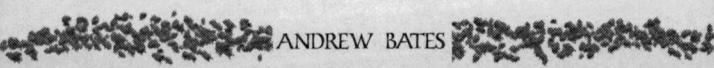

What was the deal with this guy? "And walk right into a trap? You think we're stupid?"

"You really want me to answer that?" A pause. "I'm on the up and up, really. Here, just ask your pal." Thea heard some faint voices, then shifting as the phone changed hands.

"Thea?" It was Romeo. *Holy shit.*

"Romeo, what the hell is going on?

"Do not worry. I am well. And I agree that it is time that we all met with this man." It sounded just like Romeo, but Thea sensed an urgency in his voice. Nothing approaching panic; more like he was trying to pass along a message. Before Thea could ask him anything more, though, Carpenter was back on the line.

"Look, baby, what can it hurt to come by? If nothing else, you don't like what you hear you can give me the same treatment as Klein." He gave her an address, then the connection was cut.

"That was Carpenter, and Romeo's with him," she said in response to curious looks. "Sounded like he's okay. Carpenter wants to meet; a place at 16th and Racine."

"Shit," Parker said. "You're fucking kidding me."

A look at the others' faces showed they were in agreement. Even if it was a trap, they were going in.

"At least there are four of us," Dean observed as they hustled for Parker's SUV. "We should be able to handle whatever one rot can throw our way."

Not much more than false bravado there, Thea knew. But what choice did they have? They had no way of knowing if Romeo was really okay. She piled into the backseat with Jake, stowing her Motorola back in her coat pocket. Then her hackles rose. Thea was certain she'd left her cell phone in her backpack.

The backpack she'd lost in the fire the night she met Maxwell Carpenter.

ANDREW BATES

PART II:
THE HATE MACHINE

SIX

Carpenter closed the compact cellular phone and turned it over a few times in his hands. "I'll always miss the '30s," he observed, "but I got to say you people have come up with some pretty amazing little gewgaws."

Just because Carpenter was a second-rate button man in the 1930s didn't mean he still *thought* like a second-rate button man from the 1930s. When he arose from the dead Carpenter had gotten with the times. Along with things like these tiny portable phones, he'd used everything from motion sensors to personal computers. Carpenter didn't know how it all worked, but he didn't need to. This stuff was virtually idiot proof.

Not that he was an idiot, by any stretch of the imagination. Carpenter had long dreamed of something more to his life than collecting, running booze, and leg breaking for the Mob. Of course, that's part of what ended up getting him killed. But he wasn't the type to dwell on past mistakes.

He was the type to make others pay for them.

Carpenter slipped the phone into a pocket of his crisply tailored suit coat. "By 'you people' I don't mean all you little yellow bastards, mind you. Wouldn't want to be accused of... what is it? 'Stereotyping'?" Carpenter strolled across the barren office, waving both hands in an all-encompassing gesture. "I mean, y'know; *modern* folks."

Nothing. The Chinese guy sat there impassively, only his eyes moving. No fun picking on a guy if he didn't react.

Carpenter shrugged mentally and looked through the safety glass he'd had installed.

The guy — what'd that curvy dame call him? Romeo? — had been that way, aside from the brief chat on the phone, ever since Carpenter brought him in at gunpoint a few hours ago. Hey, if the guy wanted to pout, Carpenter wasn't going to stop him. Romeo should've known he might get caught, sneaking around like that.

Carpenter wasn't a mind-reader — well, that wasn't exactly true, but it didn't work when somebody like this Romeo or one of his hunter pals had his guard up. Still, it wasn't too hard to imagine what the chink was thinking. He was trying to figure out Carpenter's angle. Old Romeo looked like a clever guy, but he'd need to do more than dress like a dockworker and scowl to get the lowdown on what Carpenter was up to.

After all, Maxwell Carpenter wasn't your average walking dead.

•••

Carpenter spent the time waiting for his guests to arrive thinking of revenge. It was the only thing that kept him going, the hate it stirred up the only thing that warmed his dead flesh.

Being a corpse was awful. He was always cold, even in the middle of summer. No matter how much clothing he piled on, no matter how high he turned the thermostat, Carpenter couldn't escape the chill in his bones. And that was only one of the problems with being dead. He had no need to do most all the little things that fill up your day — eat or sleep or take a shit or shave, that kind of thing.

At first he figured it was a great deal. He no longer had all the weaknesses of being mortal. Take shaving, for example. It was just a pain in the ass. You spent all that time and effort to scrape your face clean and then you had to do it all over again the next day. He didn't mind not going to the bathroom, either, though there was something to be said about a nice, long, gratifying dump.

He noticed the food thing first. He liked eating. Had started packing on the pounds before he went to the Great Beyond. So it was the first thing he did when he crawled out of the ground. He ate okay — chew, swallow, repeat; not much to it, really. But it tasted like ashes. Carpenter tried everything, from linguini to lobster, steak to sushi — he'd never even heard of that before, but by the end of his experimenting he was willing to try anything on the chance he'd actually *taste* it. It was like eating sawdust, every time. Same thing with drinking. At best he'd catch a phantom tingle from a shot of whiskey or a glass of wine. And he actually did have to shit after that — the stuff that stayed down to begin with, that is. He typically got nauseous after shoving the food down. Anyway, taking a crap was as much of a joke as the eating. The food came out all chewed up, but not digested. Clumps of rotting food, dropping out of his ass. Disgusting. At least taking a leak approached what it used to be like (though still nowhere near as satisfying).

A dead body had no sense of taste, you see. Didn't digest anything, either. And that was only part of it, he soon learned.

When he was a spook, Carpenter thought about sex just as much as eating. (Okay, maybe he thought about it more.) When the food thing fizzled, he looked for a woman. Prostitutes were as easy to find as they ever were. But when it came time to perform, nothing. He'd had that problem a couple times when he was alive, after he'd had too much to drink. That wasn't the deal this time, though. Just like his taste buds, his nerves were dead, too. Like the taste thing, he could tell he was touching something, but it was like wearing thick gloves or having a shot of novocaine. There was no tingle of caressing warm flesh, no charge from rubbing up against a woman's soft body. Carpenter bet he could've set off a dozen sticks of dynamite around his pecker and he would have barely felt it.

It wasn't just taste and touch. All his senses were effected. Smelling was like trying to sniff when your nose was stuffed with snot. Sounds came from a distance, echoing like he was underwater. A translucent film blurred his sight. It was as if he remained a step outside the living world, surrounded in a constant fog. He hadn't relied on normal senses for sixty years, though. Like any other ghost lurking behind the shroud that separated the living world from the dead, Carpenter hadn't had proper eyes to see with, ears to hear with… you get the idea. He was a thing of spirit. That's really all that spooks saw well: other spirits, whether living or dead. It was a disturbing way to see, but Carpenter was well used to it by now. And it had definite benefits.

The rest of the world might be a gray, murky mess, but any spiritual manifestations stood out like beacons in the night. One of the many clever accomplishments mortals had made since Carpenter's death was infrared sensing. The hotter the object, the more it stood out, right? Carpenter's deathsight was a lot like that. Spirits of all kinds showed up — living or dead, human or animal. It was easy to tell a lot of them apart; another ghost was bright but diffuse while a living person's soul was more concentrated, anchored to the flesh. With a bit of practice, Carpenter could tell the relative health, even disposition, of those around him. A shining, almost painfully bright aura was someone in the best of health. One riddled with dark splotches and pulsing irregularly belonged to someone not long for the world. It held true across the line dividing living and dead, even if a "healthy spirit" had nothing to do with its physiological condition.

Carpenter retained this deathsight after he returned to a form of flesh, and he was very skilled at sensing the nuances of spiritual states. His deathsight combined with his lackluster normal vision was easily up to the task of identifying someone at a glance or even in a crowd. This preternatural radar could see through walls and pinpoint weaknesses with uncanny accuracy. And given his current pursuit, that kind of thing came in damn handy. But what he wouldn't give to look in a woman's eyes and not see the

blackness of death staring back at him, or to taste the rich tang of a good marinara sauce.

Carpenter hated being dead, but he coped. And the anger and frustration he felt at his condition was just more fuel for the old hate machine.

Emotion was what kept him going. He didn't need food, but he desperately needed *sustenance*. Carpenter sucked up emotions like vampires drank blood. It charged him up, a fire in his belly that gave him the strength to maintain his hold on this prison of flesh. Strong emotions, too, of a particular flavor. Hate and anger were his favorites, with despair a nice treat when he could get it. Sucking up those feelings was like tapping into a power line. He kept his own passion up at all times, idling the motor so the engine wouldn't quit. But he really needed others' emotions to get a serious charge. Luckily, Carpenter was damn good at pissing people off. Give him a minute and a total stranger would get so riled up he'd have enough hate to exist on for a day. And, to Carpenter's perverse delight, the better someone knew him the greater their passion toward him. Apathy was not something anyone who knew the man felt toward Maxwell Carpenter.

If he didn't keep up a steady diet of these emotions, Carpenter would be swept away by the spirit storms that raged through the spirit world. And he was damned if he would go back to Hell. As horrible as it felt to be stuck in this walking corpse, barely feeling any physical sensation, it was immeasurably better than being a goddamn spook. It was torture beyond imagining to be nothing but spirit, the living world a faint tantalizing flicker on the horizon.

And if things worked out like he planned, the people pulling up in the jeep outside would help ensure that he stayed in the land of the living for a long, long time to come.

•••

"Your friends are here," he said. The guy still hadn't moved from his seat. He might be dumb, but he wasn't stupid. Carpenter knew he'd made Romeo curious enough about what he was up to that the little Chinese was restraining his urge to attack. Good. Carpenter had cleared away the chaff; he needed the rest of the group alive and in fighting trim.

Carpenter strolled over to the office door and opened it invitingly. As he made his way back across the room, he took one last look around to see that everything was in order.

It was just another old warehouse scattered through the neighborhood. Nothing distinctive about it on the outside; steel frame construction, brick and wood exterior, two loading doors and a regular door on the long front and another regular door to the side under the office. The interior was almost entirely bare. A trio of support beams ran down the center. A few crates sat in one corner and a 2001 Chrysler sedan crouched a few yards inside one of the loading doors (Carpenter bought American and paid in cash). The office was built above the floor, providing additional storage space underneath. A narrow staircase without a rail led up to it along the side wall. The office was ringed with windows, the two interior walls giving a commanding view of the interior except for the two hundred square feet directly underneath it. The other two walls overlooked the street corner. Aside from being bulletproof, the interior and exterior windows were also tinted. An ounce of prevention and all that.

The office was as Spartan as the rest of the warehouse, and as clean. A large wooden desk sat facing the door on the opposite wall, a plush leather chair standing behind it. The desk held a telephone, an ashtray, a humidor, and a small but finely crafted lamp. Two wing chairs faced the desk (Romeo sat in one), a small end table with an ashtray between them. A pair of leather couches with matching end tables faced one another across the room's width between the desk and the door. A portable wet bar rested against the wall to the right of the door. Hooded lamps sat

on the end tables by the couches, and a pair of large fans hung from the beams in the ceiling.

The whole place was nothing more than a front, of course. He'd planned on meeting these people for a while now, but he wanted to be sure it was on his terms. He wasn't the type to shit where he ate, though. Let them think this was his base of operations. The clever ones would know it wasn't and get a good look at the car downstairs, figuring they could track him down later. Let them think that. The Chrysler was just another prop. After the meeting, Carpenter would slip out the hidden panel he'd had installed against the back wall and drive back to his real hideout in the Lincoln he'd parked a couple blocks away. He felt embarrassed at times to be taking such extreme steps. Carpenter was playing a dangerous game, though. One misstep and the Mob would crush him without a second thought, or these self-styled hunters would be on him like a pack of dogs.

Carpenter grew impatient as the woman and three men bickered outside. He'd expected the jock and the little colored guy, but admitted surprise on seeing the fat one, the fag. By rights he should have been laid up in the hospital like the wallflower was.

They were trying to get up the nerve to come inside, wondering if it was a trap. Fucking amateurs. No sense getting frustrated with them; they *were* amateurs. But hopefully skilled enough that they could do what he needed them to. A good five minutes later the woman found some balls and stepped toward the door, disappearing from his line of sight. *Here we go*.

Romeo Zheng finally got up when the downstairs door opened. He walked over to the interior office windows to watch his friends approach, sparing a glance for Carpenter as if expecting him to lunge over the desk once the chink's back was turned.

Returning Romeo's look, Carpenter turned away like he couldn't give a shit what the punk thought. He sat down at the desk and took a cigar from the humidor. He made a show of lighting it — clipping the end with the straight razor he carried; using a wooden match instead of his silver cigarette lighter so lighter fumes wouldn't taint the taste; rolling the end around slowly over the flame as he puffed to get an even burn. It was like puffing on cardboard to his dead senses, but he wasn't smoking it for the taste.

Showing utter unconcern for the weapons they held as they walked in, occupying himself with a trivial bit of business while their friend stood nearby unrestrained, it all gave him the appearance of a man with nothing to fear. Didn't make them trust him any, but at least they weren't about to blast away first and ask questions after. Romeo met them in the doorway and exchanged hellos, looking none the worse for wear after a couple hours of captivity. Carpenter thought he noticed the black kid and the woman relax a little. Good; they'd be the ones to focus on. They might not be the soldiers of their group but they seemed to be the most savvy. If Carpenter fed them the right clues they'd end up talking themselves into this with only a minimum amount of effort by Carpenter.

Only the big shit-kicker type — Parker, his name was — kept his weapon pointed at Carpenter. One of those little box-like guns that fired an ungodly amount of ammunition in the time it took to blink. Carpenter had considered going with updated weaponry like that. Much like the suits he wore, he felt more comfortable with a .45 in his hand. And he didn't need a hundred bullets when one well-placed shot could do the job just as well.

Carpenter felt an almost overwhelming temptation to draw one of his automatics and put a round through the shit-kicker's skull — probably be doing the world a favor, really. That wasn't part of the plan, though. He needed these people.

Ostensibly enthralled with getting his cigar going, Carpenter watched through his lashes as they finished a quick reunion with their buddy. When he figured they'd had enough time to confirm that Romeo wasn't under some bizarre influence but before they started talking about maybe trying to take down the walking corpse, Carpenter cleared his throat. It sounded strange, more like a dry cough since he didn't exactly have a lot of fluid to move around for any throat clearing to begin with. It got their attention, though. The fat guy even jumped a little.

"Right. Like I said on the phone, I figure it's time we all met."

"Why?" The kid, Jake, asked, honestly curious. The rest looked offended he'd even bother having a conversation with the enemy.

"Because I have a proposition for you."

"An offer we can't refuse?" Parker said with a smirk and a glare.

What a moron. "Refuse all you like. That is, if you want to let the things you've been hunting keep churning out more and more critters just like them."

The woman, Thea, stepped forward and rested one hand on the back of one of the wing chairs. "Don't you qualify as one of those 'critters'? We can tell what you are, you know."

Carpenter sighed heavily, doing his best to act as human as possible. He knew they figured him for a walking corpse. No shit. With whatever unusual talents they had he couldn't have hid that from them if he'd wanted. But it was exactly *because* of those powers that he needed them. Otherwise, with a few grand and much less wasted time, he could've scrounged up a half-dozen goons to do the job.

It was tricky, though, dealing with people who knew what he was. It was safest to downplay it, of course. The more he acted like a living person, the tougher it'd end up being for them to label him as the enemy. He had to make them believe they were all on the same side.

"Like I said to you the other day, I don't go in for games. You know what I am, I know what you are. So what? That's not what this is about."

"So what *is* it about?" Jake inquired.

"Before we get into that," Carpenter said, "why don't you all have a seat? You look silly standing there all bunched up like that." He stood slowly and gestured toward the couches with one hand while putting out the cigar with the other. He still got satisfaction out of the lighting ritual, but after a few puffs he just couldn't take the shitty almost-taste. "Come on; I don't bite."

They all looked to Romeo. He looked at Thea, then at Carpenter, before nodding. The dame and the kid made for the couch on the left, the shit-kicker and the fag taking the one on the right. The chink stayed standing, as if that somehow proved something.

"Any of you want a drink, or a smoke?" Carpenter offered. "We could be here a while, so get comfortable." He was pretty sure none of them would take him up on the offer. Afraid of being poisoned, most likely. Romeo headed for the wet bar and fixed a little something. *Proving you're not afraid of me, but waiting till the rest of 'em were here to see it. Man after my own heart.*

Parker looked chagrined watching Romeo. It was clear he'd wished he'd thought to do that. *Goddamn, like a bunch of kids, they are. All about showing who's got the biggest pecker.* Carpenter smiled as he realized it wasn't too different from his days in the Syndicate, either. Gangsters were just as petty and childish any other snot nosed punks — most got in the life in their teens and just never grew up. Carpenter knew how to work that angle. "Everybody relaxed? Ready to—"

"Enough of this 'let's be pals' bullshit!" Already simmering, Parker came to a boil, lunging to his feet and waving his weapon. Carpenter barely checked the impulse to draw his heaters and ventilate the guy before the third word cleared his mouth. "Tell us what your big fucking 'secret' is before I blow you away."

"You go trying to piss me off just when I'm about to explain everything? What kind of asshole are you?" Carpenter looked around the room, his expression one of strained patience. "Give me five fucking minutes to explain. Then if you want to play shoot 'em up, go right ahead."

Dean nudged Parker's leg with his own to get his attention. "Come on; settle down a bit. If this… guy wanted to hurt us he would've done so already. Right?" Murmurs of agreement from the other couch.

Parker looked around, speechless. "You people are out of your fucking minds." He was trying to work himself up to something, but knowing his buddies weren't with him took the wind out of his sails. After a couple more seconds, his shoulders slumped and he dropped heavily back into the soft leather. "Fine. We'll give the fucking *undead monster* a couple minutes to tell us his sob story. But if I see anything the least bit goddamn funny, I'm blowing his head off!"

"That goes without saying," Thea said.

Carpenter shrugged. "Maybe this'll make you feel better." He held open the left side of his slate colored suit coat and gingerly removed the Colt from its shoulder holster. He hit the release and shook the clip loose, then slid the action to show there wasn't a round in the chamber. Then he tossed the empty pistol underhanded to the shit-kicker. Parker fumbled his own weapon, dropping it to his lap as he reflexively caught the .45. He clutched it suspiciously, like a contestant who still doesn't believe he just won the award.

"What about the other one?" The woman asked. Carpenter was mildly surprised. He was sure that after she'd fainted the other night he had successfully made her forget his intervention. Carpenter hadn't planned on stepping in to help her out. He needed to be sure these people could take care of themselves; dealing with a couple walking corpses was nothing compared to what he was sending them into. And she'd done fine with the first thing; might've even dealt with the other one, too. But sometimes, despite himself, he did things like that. Helping people. It was a part of him that hadn't been completely crushed by a life of pain and killing and an even longer death of more of the

same. If he could've taken that part of him out and shot it, he would've. He didn't have room for a conscience.

Best to come clean, though. Playing coy would lose him what little goodwill he'd gathered so far. "Pays to be cautious, you know?" he said, then repeated the procedure with the Colt holstered under his right armpit and hefted it to Thea. Adjusting his lapels, he asked, "Since we have that out of the way, can I get to it?"

"Please do," Dean said, waving a hand.

Carpenter paused to gather his thoughts. This was the tricky part: getting started. What he was going to tell them sounded pretty damn sketchy. If they didn't believe him, it was done before it'd started. He had to convince them of his sincerity with every word he said.

"Call me Carpenter. I've gone by a few other names, as I bet you know, but I'm Maxwell Carpenter now, so let's leave it at that. No need to introduce yourselves; I know who you are." He couldn't help but smile when he sensed them all tense. "That's not a threat; I'm just saying I've done my homework. I wouldn't be coming to you otherwise, right?

"And you've probably done a little checking yourself, so I won't bother telling you my whole sob story. Know anything about the 1930s and you've got it down. Let's talk about the here and now." He was somewhat startled that it was hard to get the next words out. Knowing what you are is one thing, admitting to it quite another. "So, first things, I'm dead. Let's get that in the open. I didn't choose it, but here I am, right? I'm sure some of you think I'm capital-E 'Evil.' I don't know that I'd disagree."

He leaned against the desk and crossed his arms. Five pairs of eyes watched him intently. "Next, don't go thinking I'm trying to cut some sort of deal with you, some kind of 'stay of execution.' I'm not going to feed you some line about how I've learned the error of my ways and deserve mercy. That's not it. I know what you do: you hunt monsters, things like me. You hunt them down and you take them out." There were a few aborted murmurs of protest.

"Hey, I have no problem with that. 'Cause it brings us to the third thing:

"I hunt them, too."

Emotions scurried across the hunters' faces — surprise, suspicion, anger, fear — and the one he'd been counting on. Hope. Carpenter still had a tough time ahead, but he'd laid the foundation. They might suspect his motivations, but they were at least curious to hear more. Time to take advantage of that willingness and convince them of what he said. "Hard to believe, I bet."

"You could say that," Dean replied.

"I could point out what I was doing at Klein's place as proof—"

"So you *were* there!" Parker crowed. Like that proved Carpenter was lying or something. Idiot.

Carpenter gave him a withering look. "You never would've gotten inside the estate if I hadn't been, shitbird. You get a look at his security setup? Jesus. I don't know what any of those electronic gewgaws do, but you were lit up like fucking Christmas trees."

Romeo frowned. "And if the estate was so well protected, how did you get in unseen?"

"Never said I wasn't seen," Carpenter said with a shark-like grin. "Just nobody who saw me had the chance to tell anyone."

"Including that guard inside," the dame said. "Icepick through the brain?"

"Him or me, baby. That's the way it goes sometimes."

"If you're so damn good, why didn't you take out the bloodsucker yourself?" Parker demanded.

Carpenter called up a heavy sigh. "You want to go over all this, that's fine. But we're burning daylight gabbing about shit don't really matter, right? So you mind if we stop the fucking coffee klatch and get back to it?" They exchanged looks, Parker obviously wanting to keep on with his inter-

rogation but the rest curious enough to overrule him for the time being.

"Okay? We good? Fine." Carpenter gestured at his midsection as he continued. "Like I say, I didn't chose this. When I first came back, I was hell-bent on getting back at the bitch responsible for putting me in the ground."

"Annabelle Sforza."

Carpenter nodded at Jake. "Right. You know her name, you know she died — *without* my help. I thought that'd be the end, finally. I'd be able to rest easy. Got to my final reward, you know?"

"Or punishment," Thea said with a crooked smile.

He couldn't help smiling in return. "Or punishment, yeah. But here I am still. I ain't the kind for thinking deep — what is it, now? Psychology? I don't much see the point of whining about how shitty your childhood was or how it made you feel when your fucking dog died. Get over it, get on with your life, I say." Carpenter straightened up, smoothing back his dark hair. "So I wasn't exactly staring at my navel trying to figure out why I was still walking around in this body. The bitch was gone, so what was keeping me here, right?" More nods. They were with him, every step of the way so far. "Took me a while, but I got it: Hate. I hated what I was, and I hated who did it to me. And I wanted payback."

Jake spoke up again. "You're saying that the... that what we hunt had something to do with your, uh, your death?"

"In so many words, kid. You ever find out just how I bought it?" Head shaking all around. Good. That'd make this next part easier. He knew it would be tough to get them to listen at the beginning, but he'd made it over that hurdle. Now he faced a new difficulty. He wasn't exactly lying about what he was telling them now, but he *was* playing a shell game with the truth. "It was one of them walking corpses. But it wasn't till now that I realized I had a hate on for them as much as for that bitch, Sforza. Took me a while, but once I—"

"Wait a minute." The dame. She was after something; he could tell by the look in her eye. "That's all you're going to tell us? 'I got killed by zombies, and in other news…'?" Thea shook her head. "If you expect us to even remotely believe what you're telling us, you'll have to be more forthcoming than that, mister."

"You want me to tell you how I fucking *died?*" Pain and anger surged up, threatening to overwhelm him. "You shitting me?"

"If you want us to keep sitting here, yeah. Think of it like that psychology you were just talking about. I want to know what makes you tick."

"Christ. I don't see the fucking point and I don't have time to dicker about it." Carpenter clenched his jaw tightly. He almost decided to hell with the plan right then. There was no fucking way Carpenter was going to tell these people what he'd gone through. Scanning their faces, he saw the others were just as interested as Thea, though. He would have to tell them *something*. Trying to avoid it would destroy everything he'd been working toward.

Only with supreme concentration, a force of will strengthened by decades of surviving in a spirit world of horror and devastation, did he refrain from lashing out at the hunters with the full preternatural forces at his disposal. His calm face a mask for the raging emotions inside his dead form, Carpenter told five strangers of his death.

•••

"You really want to know? Fucking fine." He took a deep breath. Not because he needed the air, but to focus his thoughts. "I didn't know a damn thing about zombies or vampires or any of that shit, back in the day. Big surprise, right? Who did? Even if I had known, probably wouldn't have cared. I had other things on my mind. One big thing, really: The Mob.

"It was huge back then, really starting to get its shit together. It'd been around awhile, sure; Torrio and O'Banion ran most everything in the early 1920s. By the mid-'20s,

those two were going at it like a couple rabid dogs. Seemed like every day somebody on one side or the other got whacked. Things even got too hot for Torrio. He retired after somebody almost got him and Capone took over." Carpenter almost laughed at their expressions. Even the shitkicker; he looked enthralled at the history lesson. "Yeah, now you know when I'm talking; old Scarface is still quite the name in organized crime around here. Funny, since he never looked like much. But that chubby little bastard was a crafty one, all right. He was one of the bosses part of what came to be called the Syndicate. In the '30s, Lucky Luciano and Buchalter took all the separate gangs — Capone's Mob here in Chicago, the Detroit Purple gang, Madden and Anastasia's rings in New York City, so on and so forth — and set up one big operation. Everybody did their own thing still, but now they shared information and resources and people, just like the government. Only more efficient. The whole thing's still around, too. Works a lot quieter nowadays, but they still got their fingers in about every pie you can name."

He started strolling around the room, the words coming easier as he warmed to the tale. "Anyway, back when Capone was taking charge of Chicago I was just a punk kid. I ran errands for the guys and waited for my big break. I got it February 14, 1929. Over seventy years ago; still remember it like yesterday. I was just a lookout, but it was the first time I'd been part of a real to do. And a helluva one it was, too. Bunch of Bugs Moran's guys perforated in a garage."

More nods of recognition. The St Valentine's Day Massacre was as infamous as Capone. Carpenter felt a surge of anger that his own name hadn't made it through to the modern era as others had. Fuck 'em. He might not have been among the most well-known, but he'd been among the best. And getting dead had only made him better. He smiled, the grin widening as he thought about the anniversary of the massacre, just two weeks ago. *Happy anniversary, you poor bastards*, he thought.

Anyway, back to the matter at hand. "I didn't do much but stand a block away keeping an eye out for trouble, but that's a big part of the life — standing around just in case. After I popped my cherry on the Valentine's Day job, I was in it all the way. When you're low man, you do a little of everything — bagman, collections, heavy lifting. You do good work, keep your head low, and don't get cocky, you start moving up. You get cocky, you rocket through the ranks or somebody takes you for a ride. Usually both, sooner or later."

He skipped over a few years then, even as he relived them in his mind. Those were days of wealth and violence. They held decadence Carpenter had first dreamed of when he was a 12-year-old Irish kid tugging on the coattails of O'Banion's men, begging for any kind of shit job just so he could bask in the glow of their dangerous celebrity. He'd become one of those guys, a thug with murder in his eyes and a wad of lettuce in his pocket. He got respect, from the neighborhood and from fellow gangsters. He was 22 and the future was wide open.

"We were hard back then. Had to be. The Syndicate was new, see, and trying to make order out of what'd been a big fucking mess for a long time. Capone wasn't afraid to make a big bloody example of somebody, but Lucky wanted rules. He wanted things a little more under control. Killings were contracted out; it was safer to bring somebody from out of town to make a hit — no ties to the victim, right? Slip in, do the job, slip out. That's when I hit the big time. You hear about Murder, Inc., those Brooklyn toughs who handled all kinds of hits. They took a lot of jobs, sure, but every town had a couple guys could be called on. I guess the Syndicate liked my heavy work, 'cause I got offered my first contract in 1932." Carpenter paused, savoring the memory.

"It was some guy in St. Louis. Crossed one of the bosses, skimmed off the top, talked to the Feds — who the hell knows? Wasn't my job to worry about what he'd done. I was there to kill him. Went off without a hitch, too, and by the next day I was back in Chicago on the corner with Cranky Joe and Danny P and Legs O'Dell and the rest of them."

"How'd you do it?" Parker asked. Shit. Looked like the guy might've turned around completely. Was he some kind of Mob nut? Fine by Carpenter; made his task that much easier.

"How'd I do what? Ice the guy?"

Parker nodded. "You still use a hammer? Make it look like an accident? Or just BAM!" He made a gun of his fingers and dropped the hammer.

Unbelievable. "Hammer's no good for killing a man. Messy, too. I never really used one much when I leaned on guys, either. But do something a couple times is all you need to get a reputation, right? I never much went in for signatures anyway; made it too easy for someone to connect you to the job." Even so, Carpenter's thoughts went naturally to the thing kept locked in a safe deposit box since his death. "But yeah, I just popped the guy. Took him for a ride and dumped him in a vacant lot after. They wanted a message sent is why, otherwise I'd've hidden the body.

"That doesn't matter now. It was just a job anyway, and I did a few more like them." He looked out the window. It was early, but in winter nightfall approached quickly.

"So where do the nasties come in?" Thea asked.

"'Nasties'? Haven't heard that one before. I like it." He shot her his quick, cold reptile smile. "Okay, yeah. You get the idea. I was a go-to guy, in the thick of it. Even had a sweetheart."

"Sforza."

"She married into the Sforzas, actually. That fucker Johnny, a lieutenant. She was a savvy one; ended up running his gig after he bought it." Carpenter shook his head bitterly. "This was before that, of course. It was the two of us supposed to be married. Then I did something... I told her." He sensed their puzzled looks. Glancing down, he saw his fingers were digging into the window sill, twisting the metal frame in his powerful undead grip. "Told her what, right?

"You know about Capone, you know about Ness. The Untouchables put Scarface away, on tax evasion of all things. That's because they couldn't make anything else stick. They tried their damnedest, though. The Feds leaned on a lot of us; almost got to me, too. They had dirt and they were gonna use it to get me to talk. They had somebody who was gonna spill about one of my hits. What could I do? I gave them a little — nothing, really; just enough to keep them busy while I tried to find out who squealed." He knew he should have gone to his pals, had them help track down the weasel. His pride hadn't let him, though. He'd been weak, scared even that he might take the rap for murder. After blurting minor details and promising more, he'd been ashamed. Ashamed and angry. But the damage was done; he couldn't enlist the help of the Mob to find the stool pigeon now. If he told them anything he'd end up as dead as the snitch. It didn't matter that Carpenter had given the Feds useless anecdotes. He'd *talked*, and that was enough to sign his death warrant. "The only thing to do was get rid of their witness. Then they wouldn't have the goods on me.

"I found him, too. Wally 'The Eye' Weiss. No relation to old Hymie Weiss. They had him holed up in a shitheel motor lodge in Rockford. Just one guard. I did them both and made it look like they killed each other when he tried to escape. Didn't matter whether that convinced them or not, really, but I figured it couldn't hurt." He chuckled, a cold grating sound. "Ended up the joke was on me, though. Their witness? He'd been in on the job with me. I didn't know till later that they'd need a corroborating witness. Somebody else, somebody who wasn't involved, right?"

"And you told Annabelle this?" Thea was looking at him with surprise mixed with disgust. At what he'd done and not that he'd told his fiancé, Carpenter was sure.

He busied himself with checking his suit for lint. What the fuck was he doing? Carpenter hadn't planned on giving them this much information. Just give them enough of the story to keep the momentum going, not this sob story. He couldn't stop himself, though. A part of him seemed to need to tell it. Same damnable part that'd felt the need to help the dame the other night. "The Feds contacted me again a few years later, around the time Capone was about to be set loose. I guess they were afraid he might try to come back to Chicago and start things up again. Anyway, they claimed they had more on me, wanted me to be their mole. I wasn't a big wheel yet, but I was around them a lot. Palled around with Gianni Sforza — Johnny the Stick, we called him, on account of how skinny he was. It gave me an inside track. Saw plenty of things that could put a lot of guys, not just Capone, in the big house for good.

"It was probably bullshit and I told the stinking Fed as much. He rattled me, though. I got drunk and ended up spilling some of it to An — to that bitch. Not much; I stopped just as soon as I realized the words were coming out of my mouth. It was enough to make her suspicious, though." Carpenter shook his head, knowing he shouldn't have been surprised by the betrayal — that was part of life in the Mob, after all. "She covered it at the time; I figured I had her buffaloed. And the next day I was so hung over I hoped it'd just been some kind of dream. Couldn't ask her, though. Might as well just shoot myself at that point and save them the trouble, right?

"A couple weeks go by and I figure I'm in the clear. That's usually the way it works. They wait till you relax. Easier when your guard's down, right?" He continued his circuit of the room, ending up behind the desk as he finished his story. "I came by her place one night — she had an apartment on Taylor Street. She wasn't there, but I could smell her perfume. Like she'd just left. In her place were a couple of the guys. One was Johnny, my good old buddy Johnny the Stick. I'd never seen the other guy before. So they knew. They didn't have to explain anything. Wanted to know what else I'd told the Feds, though. I wasn't going to tell *them* anything. Why bother? I knew I was dead, and I wasn't going to give them the satisfaction of squealing. I told them to do their worst.

"And they did."

The memory was vivid. It constantly overshadowed everything else he'd ever experienced, before or since. His death was the defining moment of his existence. "They took me to a place not far from here, in the Yards. Johnny did most all of the talking; the other guy watching me the whole time. I could tell something wasn't right with him. They started in, but I gave as good as I got. At first, anyway. Then the other guy had me tied up on some conveyer belt. Wasn't running; he just wanted me held still. He started with my left foot, holding it in his hands and crushing it." Almost through this. Carpenter wanted to stop, wanted to tell them all it was none of their business what the fuck had happened, but he couldn't. His spirit was not always his to command. "With his bare hands, you get me? He started up one leg then the other, pulverizing my body. He was good, though. I blacked out, but didn't die. I couldn't believe a body could stand such pain, then I noticed one time I came to that he was pouring something in my mouth. Just a few drops, but they were coming from his wrist. The fucker was dripping blood in my damn mouth, and it was somehow keeping me from dying."

There was silence as Carpenter choked back the rage at the vampire who'd tortured him, and the others processed another tidbit of information on the things they hunted. Finally, a tentative Jake asked, "So, what happened? Did you talk?"

A smile brilliant in its savagery flashed across Carpenter's lean face. "That's about the only satisfaction I got. The more he hurt me, the more determined I was that I was never going to give the fucker what he wanted.

"They worked me most of the night, I guess, 'cause I remember Johnny saying it was almost sunrise and they had to finish up before the workers got there. I remember the other guy was pissed. The look on his face was almost worth all the pain. He wasn't quite done, though. That shitbird tore a hole in my goddamn neck and sucked my blood. I was pretty out of it, hardly realized what he was doing. I noticed the Stick, though. He looked a little queasy but he wasn't surprised. Anyway, I was fading fast when the bastard stepped away. Then everything was shaking and I felt myself moving on the conveyer." He looked up, his eyes finding Thea's staring back without expression.

"They put me feet first through some kind of meat grinder," he said.

SEVEN

"We are to believe that because you died by a vampire's hand, you exact revenge on their kind?" Romeo asked. The guy didn't talk much, but he got to the point when he opened his pie hole.

"More or less." Carpenter leaned against the windows.

"I got a question about that," Parker said. "You tell us a vampire killed you for being a snitch? You saying there are vampires in the Mafia?"

Carpenter directed a glare at Parker that was as dark and cold as space. "…Yeah, I guess you could say there are bloodsuckers in the Syndicate. I never noticed them before that night, but I'm sure the families deal with them. Whether or not they know what the things really are, I dunno. But there are some pretty fucked up people in the organization. I bet most of them wouldn't give a shit."

"Hang on," Parker said when it was clear Carpenter was about to move on. "I got something else doesn't make sense. You said this all happened after Capone was released from prison? That was, what? In 1939? Didn't Lupe tell us you bought it, like, five years earlier?"

Carpenter was surprised they'd talked to that cab driver dame. He'd first considered using her for his little plan, but their last meeting had made him unaccountably nervous about her. He felt better about his chances with this crew. "I'm telling you what happened, pal. How the fuck I know what somebody told you? Maybe she got the year wrong."

Parker was shaking his head, sure he was onto something. "I don't buy it. I mean, come on. You turn state's

evidence on Al Capone and you only rated a footnote in *The Chicago Mob*? We're supposed to believe you're some hot shit hired killer who Capone personally has rubbed out — and by a vampire, no less? What's the deal with that?"

"Pay attention, buddy," Carpenter replied, ticking points off on his fingers. "First, I said the Feds *wanted* me to squeal. I never gave them anything and then they had dick to hold over me. The Untouchables were tight-lipped about everything. Those fucking Boy Scouts must never have breathed a word of it, so nobody ever knew about it to publish. I bet there were other guys pressured like that, too, and you never heard their stories either. The skinny never led anywhere anyway, so who cares, right?

"Second, Capone ordered hits all the time. Most of the time the Syndicate big boys met to give the go ahead, even. It was a business; couldn't just have some pissed off lieutenant taking somebody down. And I have no idea if the fucker knew the guy he sent was a bloodsucker. Probably, considering Johnny knew. But that ain't nothing new. They've been working with the living since forever."

He folded his index finger back down, flipping Parker off while he made his final point. "And third. 'Third' is that it doesn't matter. I didn't get you people here to argue about why I'm not a big name in some fucking history books."

"About that vampire, though," Jake interjected. "I have to wonder. Why don't you just hunt down the one who killed you? Why open season on all the walking dead?"

"Jesus Christ! You people and your questions! Fine. Okay. Partly because I never found out who he was. You know anything about what it's like on the other side?" He gestured with his off hand. "Hell, the afterlife, the shadowlands... whatever you want to call it. It's fucking chaos. Parts of it are a lot like the real world, the rest like living in a nightmare stirred up in a tornado. And it's separated from *this*... world, reality, whatever. So with all that shit, it's hard to find your own ass let alone track somebody down. Oh, sure, I did what I could when I was on the other side; how else do you think I learned all I did about these fuckers' habits? But it didn't help trying to find one particular bloodsucker. And it's not exactly like I could just ask somebody after I got back here." That wasn't quite true, but they didn't need to know that. And it was nothing to the whopper he was about to lay on them. "But that's only part of it. He's just one of many, and they're all out there doing the same kind of shit they did to me. They're monsters, and they need to be put down."

"You don't put yourself in the same category?" Dean asked. It was more of an accusation, really.

Carpenter laughed, a harsh, rasping sound. "Of course I do! Just look at me." He lifted his arms from his side in a loose parody of Jesus on the cross. He wasn't thinking, and he saw Thea's eyes narrow at the blur his arms made when they moved. *Got to watch that. Act slow. Act human.* "Like I said before, I'm not trying to get special treatment. I know what I am. But that doesn't mean I have to run around chewing on intestines and drinking blood like the rest of them.

"I don't know. A monster hunter who's undead himself?" Dean looked at his friends. "It sounds pretty farfetched."

"Yeah? But you have no trouble swallowing the general idea of... what'd your lady friend call them? 'Nasties'?" Carpenter shot back. That one got them thinking, all right.

After a moment, Jake inquired, "So've you been working with hunters before or what? How'd you get on hunternet and start doling out all kinds of information?"

"I been flying solo the whole time, kid. Getting on that, whaddayacallit, network, wasn't as hard to do as you might think. Thought it might help, but the way those people love to whine I'm glad I got kicked. And after the bitch died and I was still here, I didn't see much point in going back there. All those people do is yell at each other."

"You were trying to join the hunt then," Jake observed. "But if you gave up on that, why contact us now?"

Finally. They were to it. Carpenter hadn't been entirely sure he'd be able to steer things this way. "I've been watching you for a while. You're my best shot at taking something down I can't do on my own, even if you are a bunch of sloppy fucking amateurs."

"Gee, way to sweet talk us into helping you," Thea smirked.

Carpenter leaned forward, resting his palms on the desk to help convey the seriousness of what he was about to tell them. "You know you can't throw a rock without hitting something like me, right? One of the things I found when I was doing my digging before was that there didn't used to be so many of them."

Dean nodded. "That's why we're here. We are heralds of justice, driving back the darkness in His name."

Carpenter let that one go. "You ever wonder where that darkness is coming *from*? I haven't figured it out, not completely. I did find a joint that might have some answers." From the looks on their faces, he had them. Still a little doubt and mistrust, but considering they were ready to ventilate him a half hour ago, Carpenter thought he was doing pretty damn well. "There's a place near Lincoln Park. It's some kind of church — Temple of Akhenaton, it's called. I've seen lots of living people go in, but I haven't seen them coming out. But a couple times later some people I saw alive were walking around as bloodsuckers, or like me.

"You... think they're being transformed? Into undead?" Jake asked. The kid's eyes were about ready to fall right out of his skull.

"Fuck if I know, ya know? I don't even know why *I'm* up and walking around." Carpenter stood up straight and tugged at his cuffs. He'd always been a stickler for neatness. The harrowing night he spent being tortured to death amid the gore and the stench of the stockyard warehouse had kicked this into a full-blown phobia. He'd even burned his entire outfit from the other night dealing with the zombies and spent an hour scrubbing his cold skin to make sure no trace of blood remained. "But *something's* going on in that place. Haven't been able to get inside, though. There's some kind of, well, *force* in there. Something powerful that I don't think I can get past on my own. That's why I need you kids."

"You want us to help you break into a church and take down a bunch of nasties, all on your say-so?" Thea asked. Her tone was accusatory, but she looked faintly amused.

"Hey, I don't like asking for the help. And I'd love to give you all the time in the world to check the place out. Problem is, I think they're gearing up for something big. Just recently a bunch of towel-heads showed up there, and they've been coming and going at all hours. It's not their usual set up; they're up to something."

"You say there are normal people, living people, in there," Jake said. "We're not interested in some commando raid that ends up with innocent people dead."

Carpenter shrugged, turning his palms outward toward them to show he had nothing to hide. "The living ain't my concern. I just want to get in there and stop them from making any more things like me."

The hunters exchanged looks. He knew what they were thinking, but none of them wanted to say it. The woman finally bit the bullet. "Look, we're going to have to talk this over. Make sure you're not shitting us or anything."

"Go ahead; you'll see." Carpenter stepped around the desk and handed Thea a business card, blank except for a ten digit number. "Call me when you've made up your minds. But don't take too long. I think we might not have more than a couple weeks before they finish with whatever they've planned."

It was clear they were torn between wanting to ask more questions, run off and talk, and attack. Carpenter restrained a smile, knowing it must be killing the shit-kicker and the chink to walk away leaving him alive. Carpenter's

humor faded. Not "alive"; never again. And if his plan didn't work, these fools wouldn't have to worry about him for much longer anyway.

• • •

Carpenter left immediately after his guests shuffled out the front, looking quite baffled by the even stranger turn their already strange lives had taken. He didn't worry about the .45 that the shit-kicker had kept; he had another set in the Lincoln. Carpenter slipped out the hidden exit and walked briskly between the rows of warehouses to his car. The powder blue Lincoln sat sparkling unblemished amid the snowdrifts. He had the car washed every time he took it out and before he returned it to the parking garage. Carpenter couldn't stomach the idea of snow, grit, smog, road salt, and Lord knows what else marring the vehicle's finish.

He mulled things over as he made his way across snow-slick roads to the Dan Ryan Expressway, the heat cranked as high as it would go in a futile attempt to feel some warmth.

Carpenter had spent the years since his return following a plan. It was a plan based on revenge; a plan in which his enemies were his greatest resource. A plan that had allowed him to remain in the living world. Almost everything he'd told the hunters was true. He'd even given them more details than he'd intended, particularly regarding his death. Carpenter held close to the honest approach for two reasons: First, he knew these people had unusual abilities, and he wouldn't be surprised if that included the knack for sensing lies. Second, it was always best to lie through omission and qualification rather than give an outright falsehood. Either way, it made it that much less likely he'd be caught in a trap of words.

In the end, Carpenter didn't care what those people thought his motivations were just so long as they went along with his plan. A plan that focused on the world that had shaped him, the underworld to which he still felt an undeniable connection. Not the spirit world but the criminal underworld; the Mob. He may have been dead twice as long as he'd been alive, but the Syndicate had made him what he was. Six decades in hell had merely tempered that into something far stronger. The Mob was as much a part of Dennis "The Carpenter" Maxwell as the hate that kept him going. And at the center of it, at the core of his existence in more ways than one, was Annabelle Sforza.

She'd been Annabelle Maccioni back then. Italians and Irish worked in the Syndicate, of course, but marrying across ethnic lines was uncommon. Carpenter was always one to push the boundaries, though. He and Annabelle truly loved one another. Despite the grief he got, he was bound and determined to make her his wife. Besides, from hints here and there scattered down the Mob hierarchy, Carpenter got the idea that it might even give him a kind of cachet he lacked. Or if not him, maybe his kids. It could've been a bunch of bullshit, too; most Mob politics were, after all. In the end Carpenter and Annabelle didn't care what anyone else thought. They were young and in love and nothing could touch them.

Not until she turned on him.

Carpenter had kept an eye on Annabelle as best he could from the other side of the shroud. It was years before he'd torn himself free from the chaos of the shadowlands enough to try piercing the veil into the lands of the living. By that point, she'd married Johnny and become part of the Sforza family, a quiet but influential part of the Chicago underworld. To the outside world it seemed the family was just one of many involved in the interstate commercial transport game. And that was just the way they wanted it. With the eyes of government and the media looking elsewhere, the Sforzas had that much more room to operate.

Carpenter had discovered something more, thanks to his unique role as malevolent spirit. Much of the Sforzas' success through the years was due to their relationship with the creature that had killed him. Carpenter never did find out who the vampire was — by name, anyway. Nearest he came was that the bloodsucker was a relative of good ol'

Johnny the Stick. Carpenter had taken to calling the guy "Vlad Sforza." He knew the last name was right. The first simply helped him keep the vampiric Sforza separate in his own mind from the mortal ones.

The bloodsucker was hard to track from the afterlife; at best Carpenter had garnered only a rough idea of his habits. And the bastard had given Carpenter the slip right before he'd returned from the grave. It was only recently that Carpenter picked up the trail again, but he'd had to finish bringing these "monster hunters" on board before he could run off and tie up that particular loose end. While there was no guarantee that they'd go along with his idea, Carpenter couldn't do anything more to persuade them. So he headed for O'Hare. It was high time to take care of his bloodsucking buddy.

Those years tracking "Vlad" did show Carpenter the ties that gave the Sforzas much of their influence. Their vampire cousin was one of a whole group of the fuckers. They were related to the Mob only tangentially, it seemed, but they had a good amount of weight to throw around. He found it interesting that their structure wasn't too different. These vampires had families with heavies, button men, lieutenants, and bosses. They worked behind the scenes in big business, politics, the media — you name it. They operated on a scale more ambitious than the Syndicate did, but even more secretly. Carpenter hadn't learned much beyond that; the organization was too big and it was too good at maintaining secrecy, even from spooks. He knew enough to see the potential there, though. When he returned to the living world, Carpenter considered approaching the bloodsuckers, to see if they might be able to work out an arrangement appealing for both sides. He'd worry about the future some other time, though. For now, he stuck with the plan.

The plan called for the death of Annabelle Sforza and the destruction of her strange "cousin" — the two most responsible for killing him. But before they died, he wanted them to suffer at least as much as he had.

For Annabelle, he decided that meant destroying the life she'd built after tossing him aside. It meant killing everyone in her family. Not just her own kids and their kids, but everyone in her immediate family — her brothers and her hubby Johnny's siblings and all their offspring. He took his time, making most look like accidents, suicides, crimes of passion, or "business deals" gone sour. As an added level of security for himself, he left graffiti here and there that the hunters liked to use. The set ups certainly wouldn't stand to hard scrutiny, but that was never a major concern. The cops were as corrupt now as they'd been back in the Prohibition days. The Maccioni family had little Mob involvement by then aside from Annabelle, so the deaths sweeping through their lineage were a shock. The Sforzas got suspicious right off, of course, but their precautions did little to stop Carpenter. The abilities Carpenter picked up after his death were a tremendous help. And it was damn gratifying to give the bitch's own son, Peter, a mental shove and have the brat blow his own brains out than it was for Carpenter to pull the trigger himself.

He saved Peter Sforza for last not in the least to cast suspicion on him and his mom as he took down the others. Once the brat was in the ground, Carpenter started in on the grandkids. He'd leave the great-grandchildren alone... for the time being. Carpenter wasn't going to kill kids; he wasn't a monster, for chrissakes. Besides, keeping them around might help keep him here. Carpenter would stay in the living world until the last offspring of the Chicago Maccioni and Sforza families were dead.

Annabelle was supposed to be the last one, at least till Carpenter got through the remaining adults. She was to remain alive through it all, to figure out what was coming but not be able to do a damn thing about it. She died before that, though. Her death didn't change his original goal much overall, but it was galling.

HERALDS OF THE STORM

He'd since reached the point where there was only one adult left: Nicholas Sforza, the bitch's grandson. Carpenter saved him for last just like his dad. Something had happened, though, something Carpenter still hadn't figured out. He'd nudged little Nicky the same way he'd pushed Peter, liking the idea of the son "committing suicide" just like pops had. Carpenter had watched the whole thing from the garden of their estate. He stood twenty feet away in the darkness while Nicholas Sforza pulled the trigger of the pistol resting against his temple. He'd watched the man fall to the ground, blood and brain matter spraying from the wound. But the surge of emotion, of power that Carpenter normally felt when one of the Sforzas died, never came. Moving to the window, he'd seen the punk crawling to his feet, moving though half his head was blown away. Enraged, Carpenter had crashed through the window, determined to finish the little shit himself.

He'd grabbed Nicholas by the shirt front, ready to slice his fucking head off with his trusty straight razor. But the thing looking at him with Sforza's eyes wasn't Nicholas. Carpenter's deathsight showed Nicholas at the point of death, but with something else, something impossibly ancient, wrapped around him like a cloak. Carpenter didn't have a fucking clue what it was, but his razor cut spirit as easily as flesh. He was damned if he was going to let anything keep him from his task.

The surprise had been enough for Carpenter to pause. That moment's hesitation was all it took for the thing commanding Nicholas Sforza to act. With a strength equal to Carpenter's, it threw him bodily through the study's stone wall. It was a lucky shot; by the time Carpenter had recovered from the multiple breaks his spine had suffered, Nicholas Sforza was gone. He'd even scooped up the parts of his skull that had been blown out.

Carpenter still didn't have a clue what had happened. He guessed that he'd accidentally made Nicholas into another of the walking dead, but he'd never heard of it working like that. And it didn't explain the other presence that seemed tied to the guy. The mystery continued when he discovered that Nicholas vanished without a trace. The newspapers ran a story about a strange attack at the mansion, vanished director of a small security firm, latest in a series of tragedies plaguing a respected family, the whole bit.

Then, months later, Carpenter felt Nicholas Sforza in Chicago. He'd become so attuned to the family since his time as a spirit that he could concentrate and feel if any living members remained anywhere in the city. Carpenter sensed the five of Annabelle's nineteen great-grandkids still in the area, and he knew he could track down the others who'd been relocated to relatives. Nicholas' aura overshadowed them all. It was a beacon to Carpenter, but different than he'd sensed before. Something had changed Nicholas Sforza that night. Carpenter didn't know what it was, but it wasn't going to stop him from finishing what he'd started.

It took longer than Carpenter had expected to find out where Nicholas was staying. It appeared the guy hadn't told anyone he'd come back. Carpenter finally tracked him down to the Orthodox Temple of Akhenaton.

Carpenter was puzzled as to why a good Catholic would be hanging around some cult. That mystery was forgotten when Carpenter got his first and so far only look at Nicholas Sforza since that fateful night. Physically, he looked little the worse for wear aside from a nasty scar running from his right temple into his hairline. The deathsight revealed something far more surprising. Nicholas Sforza was alive, and his soul radiated a strength and vitality Carpenter had never before seen.

Carpenter had already been playing with the mortal hunters, and at first he thought Nicholas might be one of them. Although they had strong spirits, they were flickering candles compared to the halogen light of Nicholas Sforza's soul.

Further investigation showed that Sforza wasn't associating with any hunters, or with the vampires with whom his family was tied. In fact, he was making a point to keep a low profile, most of the time staying holed up in the temple. Carpenter could sense him leave, but never got there in time to catch him. Just as interesting were the foreigners. A bunch of camel jockeys they were, brown-skinned bastards like that Thea Ghandour. They were in and out of that temple like ants running around an anthill.

Carpenter was tempted to grab one of them for some in depth dialogue. Although they seemed just like any other mortals, he decided against it. He was sure he could squeeze out information and shellac over the hole, but Sforza was too much an unknown quantity. What if he somehow sensed one of his lackeys was fucked with? Carpenter thought it best if he let the guy think he was still operating in secret. At least until Carpenter was ready to make his move.

That's where these self-proclaimed "monster hunters" came in. They may be amateurs, but they had the skills he needed to get inside, to get to Nicholas Sforza.

Of course, it'd be easier if he could just push them mentally to go charging in there. But the very powers that he needed them for were also effective at blocking his own abilities. He'd tried to nudge their kind before. It worked when they weren't expecting it, but no dice when they were on their guard. Take removing Thea's memory of their meeting. He hadn't expected that would last forever, but he'd hoped it would have at least stuck until after the job was done. They were full of surprises, these hunters were. They puzzled him almost as much as Nicholas Sforza did. They seemed just like any other mortals, but their auras had a vibrancy he'd never seen before. They glowed with power, but nothing like the spiritual energy he saw in ghosts or zombies or vampires.

A lot of them thought, like that fag, Dean, did. They were warriors or heralds or crusaders — the label didn't much matter, really — chosen by a higher power to combat the forces of darkness. Carpenter wasn't much of one for theology. Even after being dead for a third of a century he didn't hold much truck with concepts of God or the devil. The ultimate pragmatist was he. There was no doubt they'd been given some kind of gift to take down things like him. Carpenter wasn't going to be another notch on their belts, though. If he handled this right, he'd use their own righteous cause to make them the tools of *his* vengeance.

•••

Maxwell Carpenter looked out the first class window of United Flight 2606 to Las Vegas and wondered how well he'd survive a fall from this height. This body had suffered traumatic damage in the past. Muscle tears and bone breaks healed like nobody's business, and even holes shot or poked into him closed up after a fashion. If something took an actual chunk out of his flesh, it healed but left a gouge. Such disfigurements offended Carpenter's esthetic sensibilities but he successfully ignored the damage as long as it remained hidden beneath one of his tailored suits. The physical repairs took a lot out of him to fix, temporarily weakening his spiritual strength. It also weakened his hold on the body itself. Battered enough, he imagined he'd lose his grip and plunge back into the tempest of the shadowlands. Falling a mile or however high they were might be enough to fuck him up permanently. A part of him was tempted to find out.

He idly contemplated pulling one of the .45s from his garment bag and blasting a slug through the window, just for the hell of it.

Carpenter remembered the minor complication of airport security. He could have blanked out security's memories of him carrying his weapons through the metal detectors, but he was saving his energy for later. Besides, it was easier to do things the old-fashioned way. He'd slipped a baggage handler one hundred dollars with the promise of another five hundred if he could "find" the bag that had been "misplaced" on his "connecting flight from Baltimore."

Carpenter acted properly surprised when the handler hustled up to the gate as the last stragglers boarded, the "lost" garment bag in hand and greed in his eyes. Carpenter got his bag, the handler got some extra spending money, and everyone was happy.

In the old days he'd have picked up a pair of heaters in the town he went to. He didn't know Las Vegas, though, and it was simpler to smuggle the guns than waste half the night hunting down a local dealer. Then there was his straight razor along with a couple other surprises he'd packed away. All told, it should be plenty to do the job.

Carpenter didn't plan on being in Vegas any longer than he had to. He felt uncomfortable being outside of Chicago, and he didn't want to leave the hunters alone for too long unsupervised. He knew full well that those punks could do something by design or by accident — most likely the latter — that would throw a wrench in the works if he wasn't there to keep them on course.

The lights of Las Vegas sprawled below like so many glittering jewels amid the black velvet of the desert night. This was his first time in Sin City. The town was nothing back in Carpenter's day, but he wasn't surprised at the size of the spectacle it had become. People were petty, greedy, and desperate. It was human nature. Las Vegas was the ultimate testament to that avarice and despair. Even from the air, Carpenter could feel the powerful emotions the city generated in its many residents, permanent and temporary alike.

He caught a cab to the Stardust, the nighttime chill that blanketed the air nothing to the cold in his bones. The cabbie tried being chatty, but one cold glare put a stop to that. Carpenter ogled in spite of himself at the decadence he saw along the way. On the ground, he found the corruption that permeated the city almost palpable.

Checking in was a breeze, the night clerk not giving a shit where Carpenter was from, what he was doing there, or how long he'd be around. It was Las Vegas; the guy only cared if Carpenter gave him a tip for all the hard work of punching some buttons and handing him the plastic card that functioned as a room key. Carpenter gave him a twenty for his trouble and took the elevators to the twenty-ninth floor. Twenty dollars, not to mention the hundreds spent on the guns, was nothing. He'd forked over easily ten times that tracking "Vlad" down after he'd got back to life. And it wasn't like it was his money anyway. He learned a lot of secrets when he was dead. It wasn't like mobsters were going to suspect that a ghost was watching them stash money or enter their secret computer codes for offshore accounts. Even if it had been his cash, Carpenter considered every cent well spent if this trip ended with his target a pile of ash.

After a minute or so of fucking around trying to figure out how the goddamn room key worked, Carpenter got in his suite, showered, changed into a blue suit, and headed for the casino. He was wandering the floor by 11 P.M.

The vampiric Sforza had shown an interest in his Chicago "cousins" through the years, so Carpenter thought the rash of Sforza family deaths would bring him running sooner or later. Certainly when combined with the hunter-related hints he'd planted. Vampires had to know about the monster hunters by now, and Carpenter doubted they were all that sanguine about the situation. "Vlad" wasn't obliging, so Carpenter decided on this plan when he finally had a solid lead on the vampire's location. It was simple, really: Pose as a bloodsucker himself. He'd done it before — in fact, he'd done it to visit Augustus Klein's estate, to get the layout before making his overture to the hunters.

He knew it was a risk; some vamps could tell what kind of dead thing you were (so could some of those hunters, too). But, like with anything else, Carpenter reasoned people only looked for something if they thought they had a reason to. It's not like he had to drink blood or show off a secret handshake as long as he could carry the basics like not breathing or having a heartbeat. The trick was the atti-

tude. It was like being a mobster or a cop; there was a way you carried yourself, others could peg you right off. And if there was one thing Carpenter had plenty of, it was attitude.

So he'd pull a Dracula routine enough to get some vampire's attention, then let it be known he was in from Chicago and knew something about recent trouble there. Their bloodsucking community was small enough they had to know each other, even in a town the size of Las Vegas. Then Carpenter just had to play along as need be till he had a chance to meet up with his killer and return the favor the bastard passed along so many years ago.

Carpenter felt he could leave the hunters on their own for a week or so before he needed to worry about them taking matters into their own hands and messing up his carefully laid plans. Gave him plenty of time to check out Vegas. After wandering the Stardust for a few hours Carpenter continued down the Strip. Before the first night was over, Carpenter could no longer tell one casino from another. The decor differed, but the people and their desperation were the same no matter where he went. The decay and despondency in the city almost overpowered his death-attuned senses.

He staggered back to his room before sunrise, his exhaustion only partly a sham of what he thought a vampire heading back to rest was like. Carpenter sustained himself on vibrant emotions. The dull anxiety and hopelessness that smothered Vegas seemed almost to leech the vitality from his soul. He spent the day in what passed for sleep, trying to regain energy. As when he was a ghost, Carpenter didn't actually need to sleep. Given enough time his spirit got worn out; just as with the living, rest was the best solution. He lay on the bed for a solid eight hours, .45 in one hand.

The second night was much like the first and blurred into the third which slid into the fourth. Carpenter didn't know the meaning of defeat, but by the fifth night he was willing to admit a minor setback. His luck at the tables was little better than his patrolling. He made some money, but the overall trend went in the opposite direction. Carpenter had only brought a half million in cash and he was halfway through it by the time he walked into Bally's. He was so deadened to his surroundings by then that he wandered twice past what he was looking for before he noticed it.

The floor boss in Bally's was a vampire. At least, he was dead and still moving around. Noticing the guy was making his way toward the blackjack table, Carpenter bellied up and started dropping chips. After finally spotting a damn corpse he didn't give a shit if he won or lost. For once, this seemed to help his game. He fluctuated a few hundred through the games but pretty much held steady to his starting amount. At least, he would have if he hadn't helped the pile of chips dwindle tossing handfuls to the dealer and the circulating hookers.

Within a half hour, the floor boss was looking at Carpenter fixedly. The guy, heavyset with narrow eyes too close together, finally sauntered up.

"Enjoying your evening, sir?" Squinty asked, trying to act nonchalant.

Carpenter looked at the stack of chips that was a third the size of his original pile. Down three grand in thirty minutes. "Sure am. Nice to be able to relax for a change, y'know?"

Squinty nodded. "Of course. Please let us know if there's anything we can do to make your stay more enjoyable."

The guy seemed like he was trying to give Carpenter a signal of some sort, but Carpenter had no clue what the hell it might be. Was one of the words or phrases some kind of code? *Fuck if I know,* Carpenter thought. He nodded slightly and tried to act like he got the hint, whatever the fuck it was.

The floor boss stared at him a second longer, then walked away, heading for an alcove. Carpenter wasn't sure if he should follow or what. Then he figured he sure as hell wasn't going to get any answers dicking around at the blackjack table all night. He finished the hand, a big win, and told the dealer to split the winnings amongst himself and other players.

Carpenter followed through the archway the floor boss had gone through. It was dark; looked like the lights had blown. It might have been a problem if Carpenter had needed the light to see. A hallway ran along about fifty feet and cut left. Two doors were set in the left hand corridor. Both were closed and lacked any identifying labels. Okay, so maybe he wasn't supposed to follow the guy. Carpenter decided to check around the corner. If that didn't pan out, he'd head back to the floor or maybe go back to his room. A peek around the corner showed no sign of his squinty-eyed friend. He turned to go and suddenly two hundred fifty pounds of ugly slammed him against the wall. Carpenter was surprised, but his dead reflexes reacted instantly. The guy was quick, too. His right hand held Carpenter's throat and his other hand caught Carpenter's right before it could pull the pistol from its shoulder holster.

"Okay, buddy," Squinty said, a hint of fang peeking out from his curled upper lip, "who the fuck are you?" He squeezed with both hands to show he meant business.

Carpenter wanted to know where the fuck this guy came from. It was like he'd popped right out of the shadows. That little mystery would have to wait, though. If Squinty wanted to play hard ass, Carpenter was willing to oblige. Flicking open the straight razor he'd grabbed from his coat pocket with his off hand, he held it next to the vampire's carotid. Staring coolly into the thug's eyes, he said, "I'm the guy you don't want to fuck with, asshole. Now you gonna let me go or do you want to be wearing a Colombian necktie?"

Squinty glanced down at the razor, keeping his head still. "You think I'm worried about some pansy fucking razor blade?"

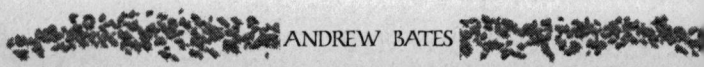

Carpenter grinned hugely, feeling alive for the first time in awhile. "Trust me, fucko. You don't want this thing to even nick your pasty neck."

Just like always, it came down to who had the bigger set of balls. Squinty spent a few seconds acting tough, but they both knew he was going to ease off. Finally, with one last squeeze at Carpenter's neck and wrist, the floor boss stepped back. Carpenter vanished the razor back into his pocket and made a show of straightening out his attire.

"Don't think I'm gonna just let you walk away, asshole," Squinty said, just as the lights came on.

"Yes you are," Carpenter replied. Somebody watching through one of those videocameras, messing with the lights? Carpenter realized he really didn't give a shit how Squinty did that trick with the lights. He was rapidly tiring of this game. He could tell the floor boss was the type to give him grief just because he could. "And you know why? Because you're not as dumb as you look. I'm here to relax a little and pass a message along to somebody. You want to bust my chops for that, you're gonna find yourself using your nuts for eyes."

Squinty thrust out his lower jaw belligerently. "Fuck you, shithead." Then the follow-up Carpenter was counting on. "What message you talking about? To who?"

"That's 'whom,' you fucking moron. Not that it's any of your business, but the guy's name's Sforza."

From the way his eyes narrowed even further, it was clear Squinty knew who Carpenter was referring to. "Uh huh. Why don't you give me the message, then. I'll make sure it gets to him."

"Do I look as stupid as you, you dumb fuck?" Carpenter noticed the guy relaxing as he fell into the old habits of standard Mob repartee. Parry insult with insult, sprinkle liberally with swearing, and toss in some useful information if you get the chance. "I'm supposed to give important details to some shitheel works the casino floor?"

"If your 'message' is so damn important, why are you blowing cash down here instead of talking to him?"

"Because none of your fucking business, that's why!"

"You know what I think? I think this is a load of bullshit."

"Funny, I was just thinking the same thing looking at you." Carpenter headed back to the casino floor, pausing at the archway. "You don't believe me, fine. I got nothing to hide. Now if you don't mind, I'm gonna get a bite to eat and be about my business."

With that, Carpenter strolled across the floor and out the front. That hadn't gone exactly to plan, but he didn't particularly care if the guy believed him or not as long as it resulted in "Vlad" coming to see him.

Carpenter realized his error as he made his way back to the Stardust. Even if Squinty figured him for a fellow vampire, their little tussle showed Carpenter wasn't exactly friendly. And although Carpenter was pretty sure the message would get relayed, "Vlad" Sforza would have to be a total fucking moron to check into it by himself. Carpenter was too used to working alone. Just because *he* did everything solo now didn't mean the other guys worked that way. *If it was me, I'd bring a couple of friends and take the guy for a ride. Everything checks out, no harm done. Otherwise, fuck him.*

Maxwell Carpenter saw he'd have to be pretty fucking clever to get out of this one.

EIGHT

A faint click of the lock was the only warning as the door to room 2901 slammed open a half hour later. Three figures rushed in, guns drawn, and were greeted by a grisly sight. The suite was trashed, the small table and chairs to the right smashed to kindling, the television screen blown out and the set ripped from the entertainment stand and thrown at the wet bar. The bedclothes were strewn about and sprayed with blood, the king-sized mattress yanked almost completely off the bed frame. Strange symbols and three words were scrawled on the wall in blood. A figure covered in gore sprawled on the mattress, facing the window and the Las Vegas skyline beyond. A table leg, the end sharpened roughly to a point, was shoved through the figure's chest.

Carpenter lay unmoving as the men approached cautiously. It had hurt like a sonofabitch when he'd first shoved the stake through his torso. Thanks to being dead, though, it caused him little more than minor discomfort now. And it looked like it was having the desired effect on his uninvited guests.

Resisting the urge to move his eyes, Carpenter saw only vague shapes in his peripheral vision as two figures approached the bed.

"Jesus Christ," one of them said. It sounded like Squinty. "This is unbe*fucking*lievable!"

"Buster, watch the hall," said another voice. Carpenter recognized that voice. He heard it every time he rested in what passed for sleep, a duet with the voice of the woman he once loved more than anything. "So this is the guy?"

Squinty moved closer, leaning in to look at Carpenter. "Yeah, it's him. You recognize him?"

The other figure — "Vlad", it could be no one else — resolved slowly in Carpenter's vision as he stepped forward. Sforza glanced down only briefly, then directed his gaze to the wall. "Never seen him before. Looks like he's not the only one who's heard of me, though."

Carpenter was gratified to see that they both looked rattled. They were spending more time checking out the room than looking him over. Desperation is the mother of invention, someone once said. Carpenter had to agree. He was pleased with his idea, hastily cobbled together as it was. Wrecking the suite and whittling the table leg to a point with his preternaturally sharp straight razor was a piece of cake. The tough part wasn't deciding to shove a big fucking piece of wood through his heart, it was working up the nerve to ruin his clothes. The stake looked good, very dramatic jammed through his middle. But there wasn't enough blood. Then he'd remembered one of the treats he'd packed. Carpenter had bought some pig's blood and poured it into a couple heavy duty Ziplock bags. Then he'd dumped all sorts of shit into it — rat poison, Drano, heroin, that kind of thing. He had thought it was best to be prepared in case the opportunity to torture "Vlad" presented itself. See how the bastard liked sucking down old blood choc-full of death. He'd opened the bags and squirted the contents around, also using some to inscribe on the wall a couple of the hunter symbols he knew. As the final touch, he wrote in blood a final warning to his intended victim:

YOU'RE NEXT SFORZA

Carpenter had learned that a staked vampire was paralyzed, no more a threat than a fucking wet rag. That was his role: Helpless victim. It was all he could do to lie there and wait. The wound around the stake throbbed dully. It was going to be tough to yank out, he knew, feeling his body starting to heal around the shape. Worse was the disgusting clammy sensation of the cold blood drying on his skin, staining his clothes, seeping into every pore and crevasse… Only the knowledge that he would soon face the man — the thing — who had killed him kept Carpenter lying still. But only barely.

And there he was. A being Carpenter hated almost as passionately as Annabelle Sforza. Maxwell Carpenter felt strength flow through his dead form and he almost moved, almost lunged for "Vlad" Sforza right then. It was too soon, though. The moment wasn't right.

"What do we do, Vin?" Squinty prompted the other vampire. "This guy's in no position to tell us anything."

Carpenter was so surprised he almost moved. No wonder "Vlad Sforza" had sounded like a good name to hang on the guy. "Vin" was Vincent Sforza. Carpenter *had* heard of him, just not as a vampire. He was a cleaner in the Mob back in the day. People fucked up, he got called in to clean up the mess. Carpenter bit back a cry of frustration. He so desperately wanted to take the fucker down right then and there. Not with two vampires standing over him, though. Wait until they split up, got distracted. Wait until the perfect moment.

Then Mister Big Shot Vincent "Vlad" Sforza as good as handed his ass over on a plate.

"Richie, don't be an asshole. Just because he's staked doesn't mean he can't talk. Pick him up. We'll take him to an out of the way place and see what he knows after we pull that kindling out of him."

Bingo.

Richie the Squint looked at Sforza, then down at Carpenter. "Oh, yeah. Hey. Good idea."

"Thanks for the vote of confidence, asshole." Vincent Sforza looked into Carpenter's eyes and shouted. "You catch that, shitheel? I know you can hear me; I can see it in your eyes. Better hope we like what you have to say, right, 'Mister Hammer'? What the fuck kind of dumbshit alias is that

to check in with, anyway? Christ." He straightened up and headed for the door. "Let's go. Buster! Get the car and bring it around back. Richie, we're taking the service elevator. Give us cover."

The burly vampire shuffled around, trying to figure out the best way to carry a man with a three-foot stake through his middle. He finally picked Carpenter up like he was a newlywed about to be carried over the threshold. Carpenter did his best to remain rigid, the table leg jutting up between them like a grotesque phallus.

"Hey, Vin," Richie said, adjusting his grip. "Something smells funny. Think it's his blood or somethin'."

"Yeah? You know what I think?"

"What's that?"

"I think you should shut the fuck up and get this piece of shit to the service elevator before I see what your blood smells like. *Capiche?*"

Richie hurried from the suite without another word, Sforza following behind after closing the door. Just as Carpenter witnessed in Bally's, darkness surrounded them when they entered the hall. His deathsight let him see the wall and ceiling pass by with their usual dim clarity. However, Richie became virtually invisible though he was right next to him.

Within five minutes they were through the service corridors and in the alley behind the Stardust Hotel. Richie's darkness hung about them like a haze, making it difficult for Carpenter to see the car approaching till it was almost on top of them. He wasn't the only one having trouble with his sight. The vehicle's murky shape rolled up and a new voice grumbled from the driver's side, "Goddamn it, Richie! Can't you drop the pea soup? I can't see a fucking thing."

"Don't smart off at me, asshole," Richie shot back. "Think somebody's gonna give a shit if I take your ass down? What's another ghoul, right?"

The two of them exchanged further insults, but Richie must have dropped the darkness because Carpenter could suddenly see again. Sort of. His natural vision was pretty much shot. His eyes had been open so long they'd dried out. Carpenter wasn't worried about that. His deathsight gave him enough of a guide to see by for the time being. Carpenter caught a sense of the third thug, Buster, and confirmed what Richie had said. The heavyset guy had an aura brighter than either vampire's, but not as steady. He was a ghoul all right, a mortal in the service of the undead.

"Would you two quit your bitching and get him in the goddamn car?" Sforza said, his voice cutting like a whip. As Richie turned, Carpenter saw Sforza dialing a cell phone. "Yeah, it's Sforza," he said after a second. "No, I don't recognize the guy. Look, the situation got fucked up real quick.... No, no we didn't. I'm not going to tell you on a goddamn cell phone! Jesus. Look, tell Rothstein that it looks like the ones giving us trouble recently just did a number on this asshole. And get someone to clean up room 2901, quiet like."

In the meantime, Buster and Richie continued their insults in a quieter tone of voice, punctuated by Richie ordering Buster to pop the trunk, then demanding Buster hold the damn staked guy while Richie made some room in the back.

This is it, Carpenter thought. His body felt warm for the first time since 1939.

•••

Thanks to his deadened nerves, Carpenter barely felt himself shifting around. He got a brief look at the car, a champagne colored Infiniti, then he was mostly upright facing toward the service exit they'd just come through. The thickset Buster stood before him, holding him gingerly by the shoulder and elbow. Carpenter sensed Sforza just to his right, and could hear faint swearing as Richie shoved things around in the trunk. Buster stared with uncomfortable fascination at the stake, his eyes flicking up to Carpenter's

face every so often. The third time Buster looked up, Carpenter nailed him.

Carpenter was filled to bursting with the raw power of hate and rage. He channeled the full force of it in the brief moment he locked eyes with the thug. His left eye flared an unnatural, vivid green. It lasted the barest fraction of a second, but that's all it took.

Buster flinched, almost letting Carpenter drop to the ground. His mouth worked like a fish gasping in air, then he found his voice. "Hey, Vin, come look at this," he said.

Vincent Sforza stepped into Carpenter's peripheral vision, slipping his phone back in his jacket. "Whatever it is can wait, Buster. Just throw him in the trunk and let's go."

"Look at this, Vin," Buster repeated. Then he pulled the Glock from his belt, jammed it under his chin, and pulled the trigger.

"Jesus fucking Christ!" Sforza yelled as the gunshot echoed down the alleyway. He lunging instinctively toward Buster, then jerked back, realizing his error almost immediately. Carpenter had anticipated Sforza, though. With speed equal to the vampire's, Carpenter grabbed his killer by the shoulders and pulled with his considerable undead strength while he fell backward to the concrete. The force of the impact drove the stake the rest of the way through his chest and skewered Vincent Sforza. Pain flared dully in Carpenter's chest, but he barely noticed. His eyes were riveted on his enemy's. He drank in Sforza's fury and agony, the emotions sweeter and more powerful than anything Carpenter ever experienced in his long unlife.

"Remember me yet, asshole?" he whispered to the paralyzed form. Carpenter gave a tremendous shove, pulling the stake entirely free from his chest and rolling the rigid Sforza to one side. Carpenter's body surged with power the likes of which he'd never felt before.

Not out of this yet. Lunging to his feet, Carpenter saw Richie wasn't as dumb as he looked. The alley was plunged in darkness again, the Infiniti's trunk lights the barest flicker amid the supernatural dusk. "Neat trick, Richie," Carpenter grinned into the gloom. "I got a few myself." He drew the straight razor from his left coat pocket and flicked the blade open from the well-worn handle. The metal shone unnaturally despite the darkness, its surface shimmering like an oil slick as Carpenter turned the blade. "Didn't take a good look at this when I had it out before, did you?" Carpenter slashed the razor in a wild arc, and watched with satisfaction as a chunk of darkness crumbled like ashes in a breeze.

"What the fuck?!" Richie blurted from the shadows. Carpenter whirled, but couldn't orient on the voice. His faded physical senses were too weak. "What the hell are you?" Richie continued. "A vampire who can move while staked? And what the fuck is *that*? Jesus!"

"That's right, shitbird," Carpenter said, moving to stand over Sforza in case Squinty tried to sneak up and yank the stake out. "I'm one old sonofabitch and you went and pissed me off. What d'you think of that?"

Carpenter was expecting Richie to try something, but he was nonetheless surprised when the vampire made his move. The darkness suddenly gained substance and wrapped around Carpenter's left hand, immobilizing the razor. He scrabbled at the bizarre substance with his other hand, but found no purchase on it before another ebon tendril grabbed his right wrist. Soon a half dozen tentacles curled around Carpenter, trussing him up tight.

"Yeah, some serious bastard, all right," Richie's voice rumbled from the darkness. "You got some big mojo, mister. Staked a vampire twice my age without even breaking a sweat." Still moving, Richie was, circling. Zeroing in. "I bet if Vin wasn't lying there like a raging hard-on he'd be draining you like a fucking Slurpee, man. He's done it before; got pretty goddamn powerful himself off it, too."

Richie had him cold. Powerful as Carpenter felt, he couldn't get any leverage against the darkness. Strong as his supernatural talents were, they were useless if he couldn't see his target. The smart thing for Richie at this point would be for him to get the stake out of his buddy and call for backup.

But Richie the Squint did something really fucking dumb.

"I bet I could mainline some major juice off you, buddy. And then maybe I'll tap Vinnie's vein, too. Survival of the fittest, right?"

Carpenter felt a presence at his back an instant before twin daggers bit into his neck. Richie sucked deeply at the tear he'd made, gulping down a double mouthful of Carpenter's old, dead blood. The vampire yelled in pain and disgust, shoving Carpenter away as he vomited up rancid, clumpy gore.

The tentacles of darkness around Carpenter dissipated and the faint streetlights regained their distant brilliance as Richie staggered, retching up gouts of blood. Not just the little he'd drained from Carpenter, either. The vampire's reaction was so severe he was vomiting huge amounts of his own vitae. Richie grabbed at the Infiniti's bumper for support. The vampire's grip was so strong the metal folded beneath his fingers. Distressed and disfigured, the Infiniti's bumper nonetheless held Richie upright as he literally puked his guts out.

Carpenter stepped up and patted Richie on the back. "Yeah, that's right, dipshit. I'm not a vampire." Then he shoved Richie forward and slammed the trunk down across the bloodsucker's neck with all his strength.

• • •

Carpenter knew he should finish destroying Sforza and get the hell out of there. Someone was sure to have heard the gunshot at least. He'd spent the better part of sixty years waiting for revenge; he wasn't going to rush it. He damn sure had to leave the immediate area, though.

He grabbed the keys from Buster's corpse and popped the trunk. He finally had to force it; he'd used enough strength slamming the lid that the edges had jammed.

Wrenching it open and destroying the lock in the process, Carpenter tossed Richie's head to the ground and stuffed Sforza inside. He paused to laugh at the expression of shock and outrage frozen on "Vlad's" face, then had to deal with the damn trunk again.

The piece of shit wouldn't close so Carpenter used the duct tape he saw in the trunk to tape the lid down. Carpenter figured he had maybe another minute or so before he was discovered. He could have driven off then, but only an idiot would drive around while covered in blood. Even in Vegas, someone would probably notice. More importantly for Carpenter, the disgusting state of his clothes (not to mention his body) was increasingly distracting. He was having trouble focusing on the business at hand. His mind kept returning to the blood covering him, sticking in his hair, caked on his face, running into the rude hole in his chest… it was too much to endure.

Furious at the dilemma, Carpenter tore off his shirt and jacket after stuffing the razor into his pants. He used the torn garments to wipe hastily at the blood Richie had gushed over the back of the Infiniti. Carpenter saw it was a waste of time; he'd have to make do. He grabbed Buster's jacket since it was mostly untouched by the gore strewn around the alley and slipped it on. Then in the car and down the alley, turn, get to a side street. Carpenter parked in a red zone, backing the Infiniti up so the rear bumped the panel truck sitting there. Seconds later he was sprinting back down the alley behind the Stardust, his legs churning with preternatural speed.

He saw the door was open, two figures standing there with flashlights pointing down at the bodies on the concrete. Carpenter's footsteps were so light and fast that he was less than ten feet from the door before the nearer security guard registered the sound. The man paused from speaking into the walkie talkie clipped to his shoulder and turned his head directly into Carpenter's fist. The combination of velocity and supernatural strength was enough that Car-

penter shattered the poor bastard's skull. The guy flew back, spraying blood and slamming into the other guard. The security guard staggered back, shoving his dead co-worker away. Carpenter followed up immediately, stepping around and delivering a sharp right hook to the jaw. He put considerably less force into it so the guy's jaw only cracked instead of shattering through the lower half of his face. The pain was enough to send him to the ground in a daze. Carpenter kicked the guard in the stomach just to be on the safe side. His dull ears caught the faint whine of sirens, but he paused long enough to unclip the first guard's walkie talkie and shove it in his jacket pocket. With the sounds of the surviving guard's pained retching acting as a counterpoint to the sirens' screams, Carpenter dashed back into the Stardust Hotel.

He got all the way from the back door to his room without having to brutalize anyone else. Carpenter was barely able to keep a coherent thought at this point. His normally dead nerves were burning under the sensation of dirt and gore that covered him. He knew it was all in his head but that didn't help the feeling go away. Then he realized he'd left his room key in his jacket. The jacket he'd had specially tailored, the jacket lying soaked in blood in the alley.

Carpenter straight-armed the door, snapping the lock and shuddering the thing almost completely off its hinges. He snarled at the bloody handprint he'd left and stalked inside, tearing the ruined clothes from his body. At this point he didn't care if the entire Las Vegas police department stormed in here; he had to get *clean*.

The blast of hot water from the shower did nothing to warm him, but it was an effective psychological slap in the face. Carpenter was embarrassed, to say the least. He couldn't understand how he'd let himself get so far out of control just because he wanted a shower and a change of clothes. Even as he realized what he was doing, he found he couldn't stop himself from scrubbing away. Clamping down with his will, Carpenter forced himself to step from the shower. How big an asshole was he, sudsing up when the cops were going to be there at any moment? Still he had to admit he felt a lot better, more focused.

Slicking back his wet hair, Carpenter grabbed another suit from his garment bag and dressed hurriedly. As he buttoned his shirt he remembered the hole in his chest and the chunk Richie took out of his shoulder. Another surge of concentration and he felt the wounds warm faintly as the flesh did its best to knit back together. A minute later he had everything he needed, including twin Colts in his shoulder rig and razor in his pocket. The walkie talkie squawked faintly as he shoved towels into his garment bag. Turning up the volume, Carpenter heard security being directed upstairs. Along with the rest of the blood he'd left in the service elevator, Carpenter had apparently smudged the button for the twenty-ninth floor. So the cops were heading for the room; fine. He hustled up to the next floor and called the elevator. So he'd left fingerprints all over; no problem. The body he possessed didn't have any prints on file.

An hour after he'd shoved a table leg through his own chest, Maxwell Carpenter sauntered out the front doors of the Stardust Hotel and into the Las Vegas night.

•••

Carpenter tossed the empty duct tape roll and watched it bounce down the incline, coming to rest amid some scrub in a dried out gully. The sky was a huge inverted bowl, a faint tracery of clouds scudding around the rim. To the east, the coming dawn was a light peach blending into a rich, royal blue. Turning around to face the Infiniti, Carpenter could still see countless stars glittering in the blackness. Scrub brush and small, lumpy cacti were all that marred the desert plain. The mountains were a black smudge on the horizon. He'd never been out west — in his day, the Mob was still breaking ground out here and what vacations he took were to the Catskills or down to Florida — and being Chicago born and raised, the wide open spaces took some getting used to. He found he liked the peacefulness of it, the bleak, broken terrain somehow soothing.

There wasn't a soul around for a hundred miles. Had Carpenter been the fanciful sort, he might have taken a moment to imagine what it was like to be the last thing on earth. Instead, Carpenter simply thought this was a fitting place for Vincent Sforza to meet his end.

Carpenter shifted his gaze from the horizon to look at the car. The Infiniti was pointed due west. The back, mostly cleaned of blood thanks to the towels he'd taken, glinted with faint reflections from the ambient dawn light. The trunk was propped open with the tire iron, its contents in full view. Carpenter had planned on driving out to some desolate spot in the desert and taking potshots at Sforza till he got bored, then slicing him up with the razor and leaving him for the sun. But seeing the duct tape in the trunk — a second brand new roll as well as the half-used one he'd used to tape the trunk shut — Carpenter had an epiphany.

Vincent Sforza, mobster, vampire, distant relative of the woman he loved and hated above everything else, was mummified beneath hundreds of feet of tape. Carpenter had spent over an hour wrapping Sforza, even drawing tape around where the stake protruded from either side of his chest to make sure it was securely anchored. Not an inch of the vampire was exposed to the sun.

If Carpenter had been alive, he would have been drenched in sweat after the labor of taping up a body. *Just another upside to being dead.* Carpenter moved to the side of the car and slipped back into his coat. Smoothing the lapels and adjusting his shirt cuffs, he stood by the Infiniti's left rear lights. Sforza's head lay below him, a dull silvery orb under its wrappings.

"Well, here we are," he said finally. They were the first words he'd spoken since the attack in the alley. He'd spent the drive out thinking of what to say. Then he'd spent the entire time he'd been wrapping rethinking everything. In the end, Carpenter decided to wing it. He did most of his best work that way. "So your name's Vin, eh? I don't like chopping a name up like that. Let's use your full name, how about. 'Vincent Sforza.'" He nodded to himself, leaning his hip on the car's fender. "That's good. Distinguished. You know I used to call you 'Vlad'? After 'Vlad the Impaler.' That's 'cause I didn't know your first name. Nice coincidence, them both starting with 'V', right? Took me about twenty years to even find out your last name. I feel a little stupid about that now. I mean, should've known to begin with. Sforzas brought you in, you look a bit like them — same weasely expression and everything. Nobody's perfect though, right?

"Want to know something else? For the longest time I didn't believe in vampires. It was just too fucking dumb, you know? I'd picture Bela Legosi or whoever the fuck was in *Dracula* and I'd just have to laugh. Don't get me wrong, he was good in that movie. I got a kick out of it. But that's all it was. A movie. A couple hours sitting in the dark with your girl, having a good scare. In the daylight, it just didn't make any sense." Carpenter reached over and gave the stake a good, solid shake. Sforza didn't move, didn't cry out even. Still, Carpenter figured it must hurt like a bastard. "The funny thing is, I still thought that even after I died. How fucked up is that, right? A fucking ghost not believing in vampires. We're in the same goddamn union, practically."

He squinted as he looked east. The first glimmers of the sun were finally peaking over the horizon. "So even after I saw the whole thing was real — spooks and bloodsuckers and all that — and I said, 'Okay, so these monsters exist,' I still didn't *believe*. Deep down in my heart, I mean." Carpenter thumped his chest for emphasis, then laughed. "There's some fucking irony. Ghosts don't have hearts, right? And what I got now ain't exactly helping me any.

"Doesn't make any sense, I know. When you got the proof right there, how can you think otherwise?" He shrugged. "I dunno, but that's what I thought. Anyway, the funny part, see, is what it took to make me believe. Deep down in whatever a ghost has instead of a heart."

Carpenter was slightly disappointed Sforza couldn't respond. He realized he wanted a dialogue with the fucker. But Carpenter would be nuts to even consider pulling that stake out. Even wrapped head to toe under a shitload of heavy-duty tape, Sforza could be dangerous. Who knew what kind of vampire hocus-pocus he could throw around? No, it was best to just let the asshole listen. Carpenter knew Sforza could hear him, too. Vampires had damn good senses to begin with — a shitload better than what a walking corpse like Carpenter had to work with, that's for sure — so layers of tape wouldn't matter much. But the big reason Carpenter knew the sorry sonofabitch was listening was because he could feel the rage and fear Vincent Sforza radiated. The emotions surged in time with Carpenter's monologue. Carpenter drank in the heady sensation, quite aware of the irony that he sucked up emotion like the vampire drank blood. *Not any longer; old Vincent's drinking days are done.*

"You ever see this movie, came out back in the silent days? Called *Nosferatu*? Story's not too different from *Dracula* — there's this vampire and he goes after this dame, and that ends up killing him. Even dead, the guy's a sucker for the ladies, right? Anyway, though I was on the other side I could still see, sort of, at least. And I caught this movie, shown I think at a college or a museum or something. It was for Halloween, projected up on the screen just like the old days, not on some goddamn television. I was just passing through, restless as usual. But then the guy, the nosferatu — it's some foreign word for vampire — he comes on screen. I was riveted, you know? Couldn't turn away. There was something so… well, to be honest, he fucking scared the shit out of me. And that's not easy to do, especially since I died." Carpenter shuddered mentally at the recollection. "He didn't look the least bit human. I swear, I was sure he was really a vampire. But from that point on, whenever I thought of vampires, I pictured the guy from that movie.

He was the… the *essence* of what I think you guys are. Some kind of monster, acting human.

"So the funny part is, it took a movie to convince me that vampires were real."

The sun was a sliver of fire in the distance, rising steadily as the minutes passed. The golden glow was almost to the car. It would hit the trunk before much longer.

"I know what you're thinking," Carpenter continued, waving his hands in surrender. "Who am I, shooting my mouth off, right? I can't argue with that. I'm a monster too, bad as any of you. Except I don't fucking drink blood. But that brings us to why we're here, enjoying the sunrise."

He turned to face Sforza directly, resting his hands on the car's flank. "You figured out who I am yet, shitbird? No? I bet I was just one more notch on your belt. And just like I didn't believe in things like you, I bet you didn't think there could be things like me. Ghosts coming back from the great beyond to wreak vengeance; about as lame as Bela Legosi in a cape, right? And even if you did remember clear back sixty years, you sure as hell wouldn't recognize me now. See, to come back I needed a body, but I couldn't use mine since you… you ground mine up." Anger welled up in an in a towering wave that crashed over Carpenter's reason. His fists slammed into Sforza's head and torso, the powerful blows cracking bone and pulping flesh beneath the dull silvered bindings. *"You ground me up into fucking hamburger while I was still alive!"* he shouted.

With a great effort he yanked himself away before he did any more damage. Sforza wasn't going to get off that easy. He had a lot more suffering to go through first. Reining in his temper, Carpenter focused his senses on the vampire. Pain was greater now and rage, too. And something else, a growing hunger. Carpenter saw the duct tape shift slightly as Sforza's face and chest moved slowly back into their proper shape.

"Can't move, but you can still heal yourself up, huh?" Carpenter said. "That's good to know."

HERALDS OF THE STORM

He stood silently for a minute, making sure he was completely in control. The desert exploded with color as the sun rose higher. Even with his veiled sight, Carpenter saw rich browns and tans, brilliant reds and yellows, striking greens and blues. He could only guess at how vibrant it all was to living senses. His scowl turned to a cold smile when he saw a leading edge of sunlight caressing Sforza's mummified form. The duct tape shown like burnished steel in the light.

"Sorry about that, buddy. As you can see, you made quite an impression on me the first time we met. And I guess I made one on you, too, just now!" He chuckled. "A little joke to lighten things up, right?

"Is it coming back to you, Vincent? Did I knock the old memory loose, there? I sure hope so. I want to make sure I offer you every courtesy you gave me, you know. You took your time that night, made sure I knew exactly why you were there, kept asking if there was anything I wanted to say. Remember? That night in the stockyards, fucking Johnny the goddamn Stick watching from the corner wishing he could be half the tough guy you were. He could've used a little toughening up, too. You know he didn't last much longer than me? By the time I got around to checking things on this side, he'd been pushing up the daisies for a couple years. Got caught banging Altieri's daughter, right? Kid was sixteen, old Johnny was, what? More than twice that, I bet. And married to the lovely Annabelle. Already had kids. And they'd been going at it for a while, too, him and that underage cunt. The old dog. Bet he never expected he'd end up fucking himself. Literally. Big Altieri was a dumb fucker for doing Johnny without the okay from on high, but shit. I'll give him a fucking A for style. Set Annabelle on track to run things after that, too. Surprised the shit out of a lot of people, her stepping in and taking over for Johnny. The bitch was good, though, no disputing that."

Wisps of smoke curled up from the shape in the trunk as the sun warmed the tape. The agony and the mindless fury pouring from Vincent Sforza created a pleasant throbbing hum in the center of Carpenter's being. "You look like a fucking baked potato, you know that, asshole? Throw you on the grill with a couple of steaks and have ourselves a cookout, right? I can't eat any more, though, you know? Tastes like cigarette butts and I end up puking it up or shitting it out the same damn way it went in." He drummed his fingers on the propped-up trunk. "You know what my last meal was? A goddamn ham sandwich and a beer. Wasn't even very good beer. Seemed like after Prohibition ended most of the booze turned to shit, you know? Maybe it just tasted better before 'cause it was illegal. Anyway, you can see, it's not like it was that great a meal. Not for your last one.

"What I wouldn't give to have a bite of a ham sandwich now, though. Or a sip, just *one sip*, of even the most watered down piss they make now." Carpenter poked the sizzling tape. "You ever feel like that, being what you are? Wishing you could trade it all in just for the chance to live again? Or are you one of those types who loves the power of being a fucking vampire? Living forever, stalking the night, preying on the weak. Must be like when you're a teenager, feeling like that, right? I remember back in the day, it was like nothing could stop me. All of us in the neighborhood were like that. We were fucking invincible. The world was our oyster, we'd crack the fucker and grab the goddamn pearls!" He saw he'd reached a hand out, the fingers curled so tightly around the stake in Sforza's chest that the wood was splintering.

Removing his hand, Carpenter took hold of the tire iron and grasped the trunk lid with his other hand. "Those days are past, my friend. Nobody lives forever, not even vampires." He looked down at the body virtually obscured by smoke, then eased the trunk closed. "But don't you worry, Vincent old pal. Your time's not up yet.

"We got a long day ahead of us."

• • •

Maxwell Carpenter looked out the first class window of United Flight 961 to Chicago and wondered how much time he had left. Taking his revenge of Vincent Sforza had infused Carpenter with a tremendous amount of spiritual energy. But when the vampire had finally exploded in a ball of actinic flame shortly before sunset, Carpenter had felt himself slipping away.

Only by clutching tightly to the straight razor and concentrating on his mystic connection to the hammer that gave rise to his alias did he maintain his hold on the body he wore. He'd stumbled across the razor during his time in the spirit world and brought it back with him when he emerged from death. It was infused with powerful supernatural energies, an artifact of death that straddled the boundary between the realms of the living and dead. Carpenter could draw upon it to give himself strength. Its darkness was so great that it had the danger of overwhelming him, though, so he channeled that energy only when absolutely necessary.

The hammer was a much stronger anchor to the living realm. As his strongest surviving link to the physical world, he'd tracked it down when he first returned to the land of the living and carried it with him wherever he went. Holding it was the closest Carpenter came to feeling at peace. When he learned about hunters and the other forces at work, Carpenter realized it was best if he stored the hammer out of harm's way. Carrying it meant there was a chance someone else might get hold of it, which meant they might destroy it, which would probably snap his link to the physical realm. He considered putting it in a safe deposit box, but then he found a more secure — and more poetic — hiding place.

After weathering the psychic storm of Vincent Sforza's passing, Carpenter arose full to bursting with power. He mainlined the rage and pain of decades, the charge like grabbing hold of the electrical cable on the El. But while he was suffused with the power of revenge, his ties to the physical world were eroding. Colors were washed out; a gray patina covered everything. Sounds had a tinny echo. While he could still feel, there was no real sensation; it was an abstract understanding. And he no longer had any perceptible sense of smell or taste.

Carpenter had never thought beyond his revenge on the Chicago Sforzas — in fact, it often seemed like he was physically unable to imagine anything past it. It was his sole reason for being. As Carpenter came closer to realizing his dark dream, something else grew in his comprehension. With every Sforza he killed, it became ever clearer that there was one thing greater than his rage; one thing that eclipsed the need to exact vengeance. Although he was dead, he was more alive now than he'd been for years.

More than anything else he could conceive, Maxwell Carpenter didn't want to die again.

PART III:
DRAWING BACK THE VEIL

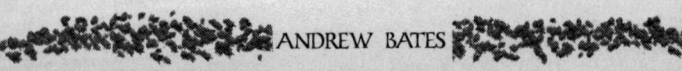

NINE

Almost immediately after they left Maxwell Carpenter's warehouse, Parker demanded they return and take the rot down. "He's playing with us!" he argued, turning in his seat to make his point to Thea, Romeo, and Jake in the back. "Trying to use us for something!"

Thea and Jake clamored for Parker to watch the damn road before he killed them all, leaving Romeo to reply. "I agree he is using us," Romeo said, "but it is possible that what he wants of us is something we would do anyway."

"You mean he might be on the level?" Dean asked.

"I am sure that he is not telling us everything, but he would be foolish to try lying to us. If he has been watching us as he claims, and I believe he has, he knows what we can do."

"Meaning we won't hesitate to nail him as soon as we find out he's playing us," Dean confirmed.

"Yeah, right," Parker scoffed. "I'd love to hook his ass up to a lie detector and find out just what he's up to."

"That wouldn't do much good," Jake observed.

"Why not?"

"Well, if he's actually dead, he's not going to have much in the way of a heartbeat or nervous response, right? So he could be lying through his teeth and you'd never know it."

Parker opened his mouth but Thea cut him off. "Sorry to derail the conversation, but where, exactly, are we going?" They were traveling aimlessly up Halsted Street, the Toyota skidding along the snow-slick streets.

"Uh, heading for the Stop n Go," Parker replied gamely. He focused more on driving than arguing and a few minutes later they were back at the hideout.

Thea piled out of the 4Runner with the rest and trudged through the snow blanketing the small unplowed lot. Watching the lowering sun while Parker fumbled with the store lock, she was again struck by the insanity of her situation. It was suddenly too much. "Look gang, much as I love hanging out in the clubhouse and arguing until dawn about what to do with this Carpenter, I need to get the hell out of here."

The four men looked at her, expressions ranging from the curious to the concerned. "What do you mean?" Jake asked tentatively.

She laughed, waving a placating hand. "Don't worry, I'm not throwing in my monster hunter badge. If I don't get a little down time, though, I'm going to scream." Thea looked around. "And it looks like you guys could use a break, too. Even you, Romeo. *Especially* you, Romeo."

The Asian frowned, appearing uncomfortable at the others' sudden scrutiny. "I am well enough. But rest might be good."

"I think so, too," Dean added. "I need to, well, finish up some things regarding Wayne's funeral. And then there's Carl's service the day after tomorrow. After dealing with all this, I could really use a few more days of recuperation."

Parker looked at the others, his face slack with surprise. "So, what? We all take a damn vacation while that fucker runs around loose?"

"Can't you ever relax, Parker?" Jake snapped, surprising everyone with his vehemence. "I think it's obvious from the way we've been going at each other lately that we could all use a rest. And so far we don't have any evidence Carpenter's doing anything other than what he's told us. I'm not saying I believe him, but I don't think he's an immediate threat. Seems like he's had the chance to take any one of us out whenever he's wanted, but he went out of his way to bring us together to talk. To *talk*, okay? So let's take a couple days, rest up and check out the guy's story before we string him up."

Thea slapped Jake on the shoulder. "Good plan, chief. I mean, it's not like Carpenter's going to go on some killing spree in the next week, right?"

•••

Thea tromped back to her apartment from the El, the mere idea of an evening without talk of monsters and mayhem a tonic to her nerves. Night came quickly to Chicago in the winter; it wasn't even five o'clock and darkness descended on Wicker Park. Thea almost didn't bother sensing for supernatural tagalongs, but one time of being sloppy was all it'd take to end up dead. Only tire tracks through the recently plowed street marred the dusky winter brilliance. Satisfied as to her safety, Thea went inside.

Margie Woleski lounged on the couch in UIC sweat pants and an old White Socks sweatshirt, drinking hot cider and watching a DVD of *While You Were Sleeping*. "It's a cute story," she said without preamble when Thea entered, "but I just can't get past the basic premise."

"The whole thing of her saying exactly the right thing for the nurse to think she was Peter Gallager's fiancé?" Thea shrugged awkwardly as she unlaced her wet boots and dropped them beside the door. "I thought they handled it pretty well, actually."

"No, I liked that. It's getting us to believe a woman like Sandra Bullock would have trouble meeting a man. I mean, look at her!" Margie pointed a finger in mock outrage. "I wish I looked half as good bumbling around the apartment in a sweater as she does."

"I'm sure if you had a personal trainer and a professional makeup artist, you would, hon." Thea crossed to the kitchen in her stocking feet, tossing her coat on a barstool. She poured a cup of cider, adding a liberal shot of applejack. It was nice to banter with Margie, especially after the past few weeks' intensity. But this wasn't the usual idle chatter. Margie was home in the afternoon, just hanging out. Thea hadn't witnessed that in months, even on weekends. And her roommate's voice had a brightness to it that meant she had something on her mind. Margie was just waiting for the right moment to bring it up. Thea had a pretty good idea what it was, but if she wasn't in the mood to talk monsters with her fellow hunters she damn sure wasn't up to spilling it to her friend.

"So not that it isn't great to see you," Thea said, shivering with pleasure as she sipped the hot liquid, "but what the hell you doing here?"

Margie chuckled, glancing at the movie while she spoke. "The storm knocked out power in the lab and there was a problem with the backup generator. I waited around a while hoping they'd get everything up and running, but by the time they did I was enjoying the sensation of not working for once. So I decided to play hookie."

"What's the world coming to? First you take most of Sunday off, and four days later here you are again!" Thea dropped into the loveseat and looked sidelong at her roommate. "Don't tell me my bad habits are rubbing off on you."

"Nope! Pure as the driven snow. I'm going to be a saint one day, you know." Margie waved a hand. "I think my brain didn't get enough of a break the other day is all."

"I know what that's like, believe me." Thea continued before Margie could broach the topic of strange men in their living room. "Since you're here and I'm here, what do you think about turning it into a night on the town?"

Margie looked nonplussed for a second, then her eyes lit up. "Say, that sounds good! Thursday night, Rush Street should be cranking up nicely."

"Yup, and I bet there are all kinds of guys looking to cut loose. Burn off the cabin fever from the storm."

"Can you get cabin fever in a day?" Margie wondered.

"I sure hope so," Thea said with a mischievous grin, "because I'm feeling frisky!"

The suggestion successfully derailed any serious talk Margie might have had lined up. Thea felt bad at first, knowing her friend deserved some answers. They were both excited by the idea of hitting the clubs for the first time in months, and it quickly eclipsed other issues for the time being. They started things off by making dinner, then discarded that idea when they saw their meal options ranged from Lean Cuisine to soup and grilled cheese. A call out for Chinese took care of that, and they spent the hour and a half wait digging through their closets and shouting out clothing suggestions for the evening. After Kung Pao, with some chardonnay Margie found in the lettuce crisper, they took turns making a mess of the bathroom. Thea won the rock-paper-scissors to see who got it first and left a minefield of wet towels and cosmetics.

They broke out the heavy artillery for their evening out. It may have been the middle of winter, but fashion trumped warmth when clubbing was concerned. They'd be inside sweating on the dance floor instead of scampering around in the snow anyway.

Thea wore a *Powerpuff Girls* T-shirt and a short skirt. The T fit snugly, accentuating her chest. It was also short enough to show a hint of the tattoo peeking above the top of her skirt and the short sleeves hugged her toned shoulders and let the tattoo on her right shoulder peek out. The skirt was a slick, faux snakeskin in a brilliant emerald color that picked up her striking eyes and was in no danger of covering her knees. Never much of one for jewelry, Thea stuck with her stainless-steel watch. A pair of strap sandals, small matching bag and a vintage black vinyl jacket completed the outfit. Thea knew she was tempting pneumonia wearing such impractical shoes in the Chicago snow, but she was feeling rebellious.

In contrast to Thea's more athletic shape, Margie was all curves. She'd originally had a fire engine red ensemble that accentuated her full red lips even further. After observing that the green-and-red made them look like walking Christmas decorations they'd done another rock-paper-scissors to see who would change. Thea won again, so Margie went for basic black — a spaghetti-strap tank top and a sheer skirt with black strap heels and a black leather clutch purse. With her full lips, short blond hair teased into a spikey tousle and healthy but judicious beefing up of her lashes, Margie was strikingly different from her normal wholesome look.

"Damn, Margie!" Thea exclaimed when her roommate stepped into the living room, fur-trimmed coat in hand, "you look ready to pop right out of that thing!"

Margie looked down at herself, suddenly mortified. "Is it too tight?"

Finished putting away the dolphin bong from which she'd taken a few pre-outing hits, Thea laughed. "No, no! I mean, it sure is hugging you, but the guys'll love it."

"You sure? I think I was skinnier when I bought these."

"Trust me, hon. You have a kind of Marilyn Monroe thing going on."

Margie frowned at her friend. "You mean I look fat?" She spun on her heel to head back to her room. "I'm changing!"

Thea grabbed Margie by the arm, still laughing. "*Skinny* Marilyn, Margie! Skinny Marilyn!" A honk from outside. "And the taxi's here anyway. Come on, you look hot! Let's go play with the boys."

Still dubious, Margie nonetheless let Thea drag her to the waiting cab.

• • •

Thea and Margie reached Rush Street early, so they hung out for an hour at the Starbuck's on Rush and Oak. They warmed themselves with coffee, getting jazzed on caffeine and indulging in their pastime of making up stories of passersby. When the nighttime crowd outside thickened up, the women tossed their go-cups and started on the clubs.

Thea had enjoyed their outing the previous Sunday; no plans, just two friends hanging out. Tonight was similar, but Thea was in a mood to really cut loose. She still had a lot of built up tension to release, and dancing and drinking was just what the doctor ordered. Really, the way she was feeling now Thea believed the only way to really burn off the stress was sex. She wasn't the casual fling type, but at the moment a good fuck would do wonders. *Hell, even a bad fuck*, she thought, snorting in amusement.

"What's so funny?" Margie asked, yelling to be heard over the music as they shouldered their way into a place called Flashpoint.

Angling for the bar, Thea said, "Just thinking about what my mom would say if she saw me whooping it up out here."

"You think *she'd* be the one surprised if you ran into each other in a place like this?"

It was still fairly early, about an hour till midnight, but there were a lot of people out. Looked like plenty of others were having post-blizzard celebrations. Thea and Margie camped out at one corner of the bar for a while, enjoying their drinks and the live band jamming on a raised stage the size of a postcard. Thea had the urge to dance but Flashpoint's dance floor was even smaller than the stage. Margie was ready to move along anyway, so they headed down a few doors to a dance club whose name was the street address. It had opened within the past year, but they'd missed it their last time through. The place catered heavily to the alternative lifestyle crowd, so the two friends were likely pegged as a couple. They didn't care, more interested in the eminently danceable tunes the DJ was cranking out. Thea cut loose for almost an hour, dancing to a mix that ran the gamut of old and new Madonna, Keoki, Depeche Mode, and beyond. Margie joined in every so often, but she was the type who enjoyed sitting and watching everyone else gyrate at least as much as jamming on the floor herself.

Thea finally collapsed next to Margie at the bar when the DJ took a turn to the horrendous with some bizarre Bangles-Tricky-Police medley. Sucking down her third plastic cup of water (the bartender gave her a look that said "the next thing you order had damn well better include alcohol, woman"), Thea looked over the crowd. Quite the collection of beautiful people, the women ranging from softly glamorous to hard-edged, the men almost uniformly in superb shape. She knew she was succumbing to a stereotype, but it seemed most straight guys lacked the same attention to their physical appearance that gay guys did. Thea decided she'd make a point of denying the stereotype by tracking down a properly fit heterosexual fella. *Not going to have much luck here, though.* The music had mercifully segued into something more dance-able, and Thea was sorely tempted to get back out there. If all she wanted was a night of dancing, she would be happy to stay there. But the wild part of her was on the make.

Turning to Margie to see if she wanted to head on down the street, Thea could have sworn she saw Romeo Zheng for a second. Was he actually out having fun for once? This was a strange place for him to be, unless he was exploring his feminine side. Thea wondered if he was following her for some reason. She looked around but couldn't catch sight of him — if it was Romeo even, and not some other Asian guy who looked similar in a dark club from thirty feet away. Thea was tempted to focus her sixth sense to scout the place for trouble. *No, this is fun time. Tonight, there are no such things as monsters.*

Still, she poked into her bag and checked her cell phone just in case one of the gang had left a message. Nothing.

Margie poked her on the shoulder then. "Ready to head out?"

"Yeah; let's try the Blue Velvet!" Thea yelled back. She pulled her hair away from her neck and dragged an ice cube across the skin to try cooling down a little so the February air wouldn't be too much of a shock.

ANDREW BATES

A nasty wind had picked up in the past hour, freezing their legs as they hustled the couple blocks from 981 Rush Street over to the Blue Velvet. Being attractive women, Thea and Margie didn't have to wait in the freezing cold before the bouncer waved them in. The place had been around ever since Thea could remember, undergoing a makeover every few years to keep up with the trends. Other places had more character and cheaper drinks, but the Blue Velvet usually had good music and a huge dance floor. It also catered to a middling-to-affluent trendy crowd, making it a good place to meet a guy and have a reasonable expectation that he wasn't a total creep. Or at least, if he was, that he was a big spender.

Thea wasn't normally the shallow type, but she was definitely indulging herself now. And when they entered the club, she saw it was a good place for it. The Blue Velvet was packed, a couple hundred people swarming the four bars and jostling one another on the dance floor.

The disc jockey segued into a heavily remixed ABBA medley when they got inside, giving Thea happy feet again. She dragged Margie to a corner of the dance floor and whirled to the beat. Britney Spears then Goldie followed, remixed into oblivion, so they escaped to one of the bars for drinks. In places like this, even women with hunchbacks and two heads got bought drinks by guys on the make, so the women weren't the least bit surprised when a couple with-it fellows swooped in. Thea gave them a chance but they were too much like Parker — big farmboy types one step removed from wearing coveralls and straw hats. A nice shirt and expensive haircut only went so far with a girl. The guys could tell they were getting nowhere after a little while and moved on, no harm, no foul.

The women spent the next hour or so following similar variations — dance, have a drink, chat with some guys, repeat. Margie was indeed a hit, projecting the right combination of sexuality and wholesomeness that drew men like kids to presents on Christmas morning. Thea's sensual

athleticism also attracted stares. Adding the contrast between the two physically — Margie full-figured to Thea's dusky beauty — and they were supplied with drinks and conversation through the night. Thea didn't find anyone who struck her fancy, though. She finally gave up on hooking up with someone for the night and indulged in dancing herself into exhaustion.

A while later, a figure dancing nearby caught her attention. With a start, she realized it was her ex, Archie. She hadn't seen him since last fall, when they'd broken up. It'd been a relatively low-key event, mainly because they'd each been so busy for the previous few weeks that they'd already built up some emotional distance from one another. Not without flares of conflict, though. Thea indulged in passionate outbursts, and Archie got condescendingly analytical. The worst part was that they didn't really have any problems with one another; it just seemed to be a case of seriously bad timing. Archie's DJ career was taking off and he was seeing some success doing white label remixes. Thea was coming to terms with her discovery of the things that lurked in the fringes of society. Despite their attraction and shared interests, they just didn't have the time or emotional resources to devote to a serious relationship. Rather than let it fade, they'd agreed to break it off clean — or as clean as a break-up could ever be. Thea went on with her life, but she never quite forgot him.

Watching Archie dance, lost in the music, Thea flushed. They'd had a visceral, animal attraction to one another from the moment they met. He still pushed her buttons, and why not? Archie was quite a specimen. He was young — barely drinking age when they'd met — with a wiry build and a graceful, almost feral, way of moving. His skin had a faint coppery tone even in the dead of winter that hinted at Native American ancestry, and close-cropped dark brown hair with a faint hint of curl from some indeterminate lineage. He wore a tight white T-shirt that showed off every muscle on his lean torso and a pair of shiny silver jeans that hung loosely in contrast. The impossibly expensive athletic shoes he wore battled it out with a skullcap to see which could be more wildly colorful. Three small gold hoops pierced his left eyebrow and a thin matching gold necklace was around his throat. An elaborate tattoo ran down the length of his right arm. His every move was masculine and powerful and lacking in self-consciousness or pretension.

He looked up when the Dubtribe transitioned into DJ Rap, noticing Thea's gaze instantly. A flicker of expression flowed across his face, surprise followed by his mercurial smile, then he was dancing next to her. Their movements complemented one another effortlessly. Thea gave herself over to the electricity sparking between them, lost herself to the warmth that blossomed in her loins.

They danced for an unknown time, adjusting to the changing songs as easily as they moved together. Thea marveled at his eyes, such a dark brown as to be almost black. He looked back at her with equal passion, drinking in her every movement with such intensity as if he was burning the memory into his brain. Thea noticed distractedly that they had moved to one side of the dance floor, brushing against one another in the darkness by the wall. Then they embraced, still moving, dancing in unison. Thea gasped at the heat she felt burning from his skin, her own body surging with warmth in response. As naturally as breathing, his left hand slipped around to the small of Thea's back and his right dropped to the curve above her thigh. Thea's hands caressed his shoulders, running lightly over his chest and arms in gentle counterpoint to their swaying hips. Archie was exactly her height, his face moving next to hers with only the barest hint of space between them. Her nose was filled with the bittersweet tang of alcohol on his breath and the musk of his sweat, pungent but not unpleasant. His eyes became huge, dark pools into which she fell without resistance.

Their noses bumped, that slight touch completing the circuit. Thea was kissing him then, gasps of urgent pleasure escaping her mouth as her tongue darted hungrily after his. Her hands fluttered over the smooth, sweat-dampened planes of his cheeks. She felt his strong hands move, his left drawing her to him even more tightly while his right cupped her jaw. Their bodies moved against one another more urgently, their passion becoming a frenzy. Thea felt a delicious emptiness in her center and her muscles tensed, trying to catch hold of the sensation flooding through her. A star exploded behind her eyes as the almost unbearable tension suddenly burst over her body in waves.

Thea gasped from surprise as much as delight. She broke their kiss, blinking rapidly as she tried to regain some measure of control. Her breathing was ragged and sounds came as if from a distance. Thea realized she was still leaning heavily against him. *Probably collapse if he wasn't holding me up*, was her first coherent thought in some time. A part of her was embarrassed at acting with such thoughtless abandon, but the rest was still busy trying to get systems back under control.

She realized he was still looking at her. Thea focused her attention on his face, still just inches away. He stared back, bemusement and mild concern evident on his long face. She gave him a crooked smile and rolled her eyes, playfully patting his chest with her hands. Archie grinned in return, and the way it changed his features from brooding to mischievous made her weak in the knees all over again. "Well, hey, Archie. How've you been?"

Strong white teeth flashed. "Pretty good. How 'bout yourself?"

Thea shrugged with a toss of her head. "Can't complain." They looked at one another and Thea decided to cut to the chase. "You do realize you're coming with me, right?"

He laughed, a healthy guffaw without a trace of smugness or innuendo. "Lead on, lady."

She pulled him through the crowd, heading for where she'd left Margie. Her friend had liked Archie, Thea remembered, so she wouldn't have to worry about any harsh looks or weird vibes if she brought him home. Although Margie was sure to have questions later, like *Are you two starting up again? What about those "friends" of yours from the other night?* and so on. Thea wasn't in any frame of mind to worry about the future; right now was giving her everything she wanted.

They got back to the table, but Margie wasn't there. They normally touched base with one another before going off to dance or get a drink or hit the bathroom to avoid losing one another in the crowd. And Margie was, if anything, overly responsible, not to mention frugal. It wasn't like her to leave the table, and a full drink, without giving Thea the high sign.

She felt a twinge of concern, then shook it off. Probably not a big deal. Their drinks hadn't been touched and no one else had snatched up the seats, so Thea figured her friend had just stepped away. Taking a look around, Thea spotted Margie's short blond hair in the throng. Sure enough, she was heading away through the crowd... except that she wasn't heading for the restroom. The crowd shifted then, showing that Margie was following a tall, rough-hewn linebacker kind of fella. *Guess I'm not the only one who's hooked up.* But it didn't look like they were simply going to the bar; were they heading for the exit? Margie could drink too much every so often, but she was definitely not the type to wander away with a stranger — and going off without telling the person she'd come with was unheard-of. It was rude, and Margie was always socially proper, even when she was bombed.

Still no big deal. Thea would just catch up to them and see what was what. "Let's catch up with Margie," she yelled to Archie. He nodded, taking her hand and giving it a squeeze. Thea led the way through the crowd, the two of them snaking around people as they headed toward the front of the club.

Margie was turned away, shrugging into her coat. The guy with her faced back, his eyes roaming constantly over the crowd. He flashed past Thea, then came back on target just as she poked Margie in the shoulder. "Hey, Miss M, what're you doing?"

Margie turned a distracted gaze to her friend. Thea took another step forward, concerned at the glazed look on Margie's face. She must be really drunk — or maybe drugged? What was that goddamn date-rape drug? Rohipnal? Something like that. Whatever the case, Thea was damned if she was going to let her best friend leave with some stranger like that. "Margie, you okay? Who's this guy?" She turned an accusing eye toward the linebacker, who smiled blandly.

"Oh, Thea," Margie said then. "We're just going. Leaving."

"Yeah, I can see that. I don't think you're in any condition to be going anyplace though, hon."

"Hey, she's okay," the side of beef said, the smile moving up a notch to cocky. "What are you, her mother?"

She felt Archie lean in close. "Stay cool, Thea," he said in her ear. "I've seen this guy around the place. Bit of a player, but I think an okay guy. Let me talk to him."

Thea frowned at Archie, but reined it in. She had no need of a knight in shining armor, but she knew it was probably for the best. The guy was rubbing her the wrong way, and she could tell she was about ten seconds from kicking that smug grin off his face. Instead, she talked quietly to Margie — or as quietly as the surging noise of the club would allow — trying to get her to focus.

Archie stepped around and turned his hands out in a can't-we-all-be-friends? gesture. "Hey, dude, looks like the lady's had a bit too much. What say you take a rain check. Plenty of fish in the sea, right?" He flashed his winning smile, one man of the world to another.

Focused on her friend, Thea almost missed it. Out of the corner of her eye, she saw the linebacker glare at Archie, his features — his entire bearing — promising immense violence. "Fuck off, pal," he said, "and take your woman with you." It lasted only an instant, but all the color drained from Archie's face. He flinched visibly and took a couple steps backward.

Thea found the linebacker looking directly at her, his smile now a cruel twist carved into his face. She felt a surge of fear and a desire to leave, to let the stranger go with Margie as long as he left her alone. She'd felt this sensation before, and suddenly she knew that Margie wasn't drunk or drugged.

Choking back her fear as best she could while stepping back involuntarily, Thea called upon her heightened senses. Although he looked no different physically, the stranger had a brutish, hulking quality that implied power out of proportion with even his well-developed physique. Her fear vanished, replaced with a sense of immediate danger. *Surprise, surprise.*

She felt Archie tugging at her arm, trying to lead her away. The stranger had already dismissed her and was guiding Margie toward the door. Thea shook off Archie's grip and barely noticed as he kept backing away without her. She lunged to grab the linebacker by the biceps. His muscles were rock-hard under his dark shirt, and strangely cold. "Get your fucking hand off her," she spat as the stranger turned.

"Excuse me?" the linebacker said, looking down at her with faint surprise.

"I said leave her the fuck alone," Thea repeated, thrusting her jaw forward aggressively to cover the fear she felt — this time a natural feeling, concern for her friend's safety. "I know what you are, asshole. I'm giving you one chance to get out of here with your skin intact."

The vampire frowned slightly, but seemed far from worried. "If you know what's good for you, you'll stick with your boyfriend and leave me alone."

Just a minute ago Thea was a raging mess of lust. Now she was overcome with fury toward this *thing* and fear for her friend. Thanks to the shift from one emotional extreme

to another, Thea had trouble thinking straight. She was ready to do whatever it took to get this monster away from Margie, even if that meant assaulting it in full view of the public.

Then Romeo Zheng was right there, facing down a monster twice his size as cool as you please. "She gave you one chance," he said, poking the linebacker forcefully in the chest. "I suggest you take it."

The vampire looked between the two of them, consternation evident on his face. "You have any idea the shit you just stepped in?" He jerked his head toward the exit. "Tell you what. *I'll* give *you* one chance to get out of here."

Thea saw bouncers converging on them. The vampire didn't seem the least perturbed by their approach. Romeo's solid presence helped Thea get back on track. This was not the time or the place to take on a vampire. Too many bystanders and she had no idea how many friends the thing had in the crowd. "It's a deal, ugly," Thea said, grabbing Margie and nodding for Romeo to follow. "But we're taking her with us. And don't think we won't fuck you up if you try anything, though."

They hustled outside, pausing only long enough for Thea to grab her jacket from the coat check. She felt badly for leaving Archie; a look back showed him standing pale by the bar. He nodded at her and smiled tentatively while making a shooing motion toward the door. And the vampire showed he seemed to have forgotten about Archie entirely. Instead, he stood with his thick arms crossed over his chest. Flanked by a couple bouncers, he looked for all the world like a conquering warrior watching his enemies flee before him. Which was pretty much the case, Thea admitted.

"Get us a cab," Thea told Romeo, leading Margie into the cold night. Taxis trolled the area constantly so they were on their way to Wicker Park in minutes. During the ride, Thea busied herself speaking softly to Margie and rubbing her friend's face and hands as if to restore warmth. It wasn't very long at all before Margie shook herself and her eyes came back into focus. Those five minutes scared the hell out of Thea, though.

"Oh, my God," Margie finally said in a small voice. "I think I had too much to drink."

•••

Thanks to being tipsy and suffering the aftereffects of some strange mesmerism, Margie was tucked into bed with a minimum of fuss. Thea walked into the living room and glared at Romeo. "What the fuck were you doing there? And don't tell me you just happened to be clubbing."

Romeo's normally stoic features reddened. "No, I was not. I was…" He shuffled like a kid in the principal's office. "The hidden, Carpenter. He had shown interest in you before. I was concerned for you… for your safety."

She was ready to yell some more, but then she realized how close it had all been. If she'd lingered with Archie just a little longer and Romeo hadn't been there… *Say it. Margie might be dead.* Delayed reaction finally hit. Thea felt a strange buzzing in her head and she had trouble focusing on her surroundings. A surprised sob burst from her mouth. Standing by the kitchen counter, Thea buried her face in her hands and cried.

Romeo was obviously startled. He stepped forward, raising a hand to pat Thea gingerly on the shoulder. "You… Everything… everything will be fine," he said lamely. "You did the right thing. It *was* a vampire. I could see it. In fact," a ghost of a smile crossed his face, "I marked it. We will track it down and make sure it harms no one else."

Thea nodded, then mumbled "I'm sorry" through her hands. Trying to recover her composure, she said, "I was so afraid for Margie. She's my best friend; if anything happened to her—" Tears overcame her again, Romeo's timid pats no real consolation as the sobs racked her body.

After another minute, Thea finally got some level of control. "I must seem like such a flake. Acting tough all the time, and here I am having a breakdown!" She lifted her head, wiping her nose with the back of her hand. "And now I'm a total mess, crap all over my face…." She reached for the dishtowel lying on the counter.

Romeo's hand, surprisingly gentle, wiped at the tears streaking the side of her face. "You are beautiful," he said, a hitch in his voice. "I have always thought so."

Thea looked at Romeo Zheng, for the first time seeing him without a mask shielding his emotions. *Oh, this is such a bad idea,* she thought, even as she returned the passion of his sudden kiss.

•••

Thea buried her face in a pillow while chaos played rugby with her emotions. She couldn't believe what a slut she'd been. Rubbing against her ex in a dance club, then screwing a guy who entertained serious paranoid tendencies.

At least the sex had been good. Better than good. Incredible. Mind-blowing. She'd probably wakened the whole building with her screams during the night. Helluva lot of stamina Romeo had. Thea supposed that Archie had primed her pretty well to begin with, and the encounter with the broad-shouldered nasty had gotten both their juices flowing. *Fuck, you never stop analyzing everything, woman!* Thea slapped herself around mentally, but it didn't stop her from thinking.

She couldn't just ignore the situation. If it was Archie in her bed the morning after, she'd have made coffee and some small talk. It might've been a simple, "It was great to see you again; talk to you sometime." Or, if the spark was bright enough, maybe even take the tentative steps of getting back together.

But it wasn't Archie Gerritt. She'd fucked Samuel Zheng. The evidence was right there behind her, taking up the other half of the bed and breathing with soothing regularity. Thea shivered. The idea of Romeo in her bed was equally welcome and unnerving.

She did all right doing the guy thing of taking sex for sex, no strings, no problems. But despite being a tomboy, Thea was definitely still a woman, and had different emotional wiring to go with her distinctive physical configuration. There was always some degree of feelings involved in her couplings. Even when she knew absolutely nothing about the guy aside from a physical connection, she had to at least get a sense that she liked him before she'd sleep with him. And there was no doubting she found Romeo attractive and interesting. Their relationship to this point was almost exclusively about violence and secrecy, though — definitely not something she wanted as the basis of a romantic relationship. And since they were involved in such an intense situation, neither could they easily shrug this off as a one time thing.

She wished last night could just be that. It happened, it's done, and that's it. But the gang's interactions were touch-and-go as it was, especially over the past week with all the trauma they'd suffered. She and Romeo could claim all they wanted that it didn't mean anything, that nothing had changed, but it was bullshit. Even if there weren't emotions involved — and Thea had to admit that there were — it totally changed the rules of their relationship. She wasn't naive enough to think they had any kind of future together; the guy was just too nuts for that to be possible. But Thea still had strong feelings for Romeo. Feelings easy enough to have kept out of sight before, but impossible to deal with now.

Then there was the rest of the gang. What circus *that* would be. Thea had no intention to tell any of them what had happened. It didn't matter, though. They would pick up on the vibe soon enough. Thea muffled a groan of frustration into the pillow.

"Are you all right?" Romeo said softly.

His breathing hadn't changed, nor did Thea feel him shift. It wouldn't have surprised her if he'd been awake at least as long as she had, mulling everything over in that mysterious little brain of his. She hoped he wasn't in the mood to have The Conversation, though; Thea didn't think she could take that on top of everything else that'd happened. She needed more time. They had to say *something* to one another, though.

She rolled onto her back, sighing heavily. "I'm fine. Just a strange situation, you know?"

Romeo's stubbled cheek scratched against the pillow as he nodded. She imagined him lying on his side, looking at her in the early morning light filtered through her bedroom drapes. Thea kept her gaze directed at the ceiling, her fingers unconsciously kneading the sheets she was hogging.

"I… This is not something I planned," Romeo said finally.

"Me neither." Thea grinned. "But we can't undo it, right?"

Another pause, then his voice, carefully neutral. "Do you wish that you could?"

Thea groaned again, rubbing her eyes with the heels of her hands. "Shit, Romeo. I don't know. It's a lot to take in right now, you know?"

"Yes, it is." The bed shook as he shifted position, sitting up to face the window. "I should go. The funeral for Dean's friend is today."

"You're going to that?" Thea eased open her eyes, seeing Romeo's taut back. It was covered in scars, scratches and gouges from God knew what. She'd felt them last night, over most of his body in fact, but they hadn't registered in the heat of passion. Another mystery to add to the Romeo Zheng file.

He shrugged. "I do not know. I feel responsible for… I think that it might comfort Dean."

You *feel responsible?* Shit. *Imagine how I feel.* And Thea knew their guilt was nothing compared to what Dean must be going through. He'd held up well through everything, but he was only human. "Yeah, I think it would. Look, we should talk, but maybe now isn't the best time?"

She watched his head bob in agreement. Romeo was on his feet then, dressing quickly but not as if he was in a hurry to get out. He simply did everything with rapid, economical movements. Then he turned and they finally looked at each other in the light of day. His face was as open and vulnerable as she'd seen last night, emotions flickering with the same degree of turmoil she felt herself. "I did not plan this," he said again, "but I do not regret it."

Then the old Romeo mask was in place once again. He left without a sound.

TEN

Thea lay in bed for a while longer, trying unsuccessfully to banish the thoughts and emotions running rampant within her. She finally got up, showered, made coffee, and called the number where Dean was staying. No one was in, but the answering machine relayed the time and place for the service, the funeral, and the wake to follow. Thea didn't think she could handle socializing, but finally decided to attend both. It was the least she could do for Dean, after all he'd been through.

Plus, she admitted to herself as she slipped out of the apartment before Margie got up, it would give her some time away from her best friend. She knew it was past the point where Margie deserved some answers, especially after last night. Thea needed time to process everything, get a better perspective. Revealing to Margie that monsters existed, that she'd been hunting them for the better part of a year now... well. It was just one too many things right now. It wouldn't be fair to dump this kind of revelation in Margie's lap and not be around to deal with the fallout. And with funerals and mysterious undead stringing them along and strange temples possibly churning out more monsters — no. Best to wait until things had settled a little first.

Thea knew that wasn't fair to Margie either, she was damned if she could think of a better alternative at the moment. The only thing she was sure of was that she needed a break. It was like her life was a Great Dane she'd taken for a walk. It was behaving itself, staying on the leash, then *BAM!* it took off running and dragged her along with. Now it was too damn big to get back under control no matter how much she dug in her heels and yanked on the leash.

Wrapped up in her own situation, Thea barely spared attention for Wayne's funeral. *Sorry, pal,* she'd thought as the coffin lowered into Rosehill Cemetery's frozen ground, *I'm topped out on self-pity. Got no room for anyone else in here right now.*

Although she felt awkward attending a funeral of someone she didn't even know, it wasn't as uncomfortable as it could have been. She didn't see hide nor hair of Romeo throughout the event. Giving Dean her condolences, Thea learned Romeo attended the service but ducked out immediately after, along with Jake. Dean mentioned it distractedly; the brave face he'd worn the past few days was cracking, and he had more on his mind than what his hunter friends were up to. He seemed honestly pleased to see Thea, which confirmed her decision to attend the wake.

It was at a sprawling house in Lakeview; Thea crammed into a car with some strangers to get there. The place was seemingly tailor-made for entertaining. It was a lively gathering despite the somber occasion, the people friendly to Thea though they didn't know her from Eve. She didn't feel too sociable at first, doing little other than chatting politely and deflecting a subtle come-on from a lesbian at one point. The food was good and the booze plentiful, and she finally became engrossed in watching the rest of the group. Despite being a stranger, Thea laughed along with many of the stories that got bandied around. It proved nice to be completely anonymous, to feel no obligation to others and have no expectations of her own.

The wake was still going strong when Thea left that evening. Dean appeared buoyed by the support of his friends and gave Thea a big smile and a hug when she made her good-byes. She lost the feeling of warmth and relaxation by the time she returned home, unfortunately. Approaching the apartment brought back the memories of everything that had happened recently. Margie wasn't in, thank heaven

for small blessings. Probably losing herself in work at the lab.

Thea went through her evening routine in a daze and awoke the next morning much the same way. The day passed with a kind of infinite timelessness. Margie wasn't in, and Thea was left feeling a constant, low-level dread that she might return from the lab at any moment. Thea needed someone to talk to, someone who would understand her impossible situation. That person was always Margie, though, and finding she was afraid of turning to her friend for support hurt even more. She was determined she wouldn't call Romeo. Instead, Thea called Jake, but got his machine. She hung up without leaving a message, and was immediately glad he hadn't been in. Night came finally, though Margie did not. Thea wasn't much surprised; her friend normally put in long hours and was likely in no hurry to head back home now. After lighting up a bowl in yet another unsuccessful attempt to relax, Thea finally drifted off to sleep early.

She slept completely through her alarm the next morning and had to hustle to get to the funeral ceremony for Carl Navatt. Having slept almost twelve hours straight, Thea was lethargic and her mind felt wrapped in an old wool blanket. She rushed through a shower, which did little to wake her up. Dashing back to her room to get dressed, she heard the clatter of Margie making coffee. The dance of avoidance continued when Thea emerged, dressed in mourning, to find Margie was already in the bathroom. Thea gulped down a cup of coffee and rushed out the door just as she heard the shower shut off. Her stomach clenched in self-disgust at the relief she felt in successfully avoiding Margie for a few more hours.

The grim spectacle of Carl's funeral did nothing to put her in a better mood. She didn't want to stereotype, but Dean's gay friends knew how to throw a party. Part of the problem was seeing the trappings of death for the second day in a row. Plus this time she got to look forward to a

drawn out ceremony, *then* a burial, *then* a wake. Not to mention trekking out to Wheaton for the whole thing. Thea was ready to cut and run when they filed out of the church. Then she noticed Lilly Belva, of all people.

Lilly was grim and pale, pushed out of the church in a wheelchair by Parker Moston. Surprised as Thea was to see Lilly out of the hospital, the expression on the woman's face was even more startling. Lilly had a look of such naked rage that Thea couldn't even look her in the eye when she rolled by. Thea noticed Dean and Jake in the crowd queuing up for the ride to the cemetery and sidled over.

"Hey, Thea," Jake said. He looked uncomfortable in the dark suit and tie that peeked out from the bulky parka he wore.

Thea was bundled in black slacks and a gray blouse and sweater under an overcoat her mother had given her for her birthday a few years previously. It was another bitterly cold day, and her outfit did little to keep her warm. "When did Lilly get released?"

"This morning," Dean said. He blew his nose into a handkerchief. Aside from that bit of business he looked dapper in a black pinstripe suit with matching vest and a red tie. Like Thea's own, the overcoat he wore fit the occasion of a funeral but not the Chicago winter. "I understand she can walk, but she's still a little weak so she's sticking with the wheelchair for now. Haven't had a chance to talk to her yet to see how she's doing otherwise."

Thea glanced at Jake, who shrugged. "Me either. All that we learned from Parker just before the service started. He's sort her appointed assistant for the day."

Thea wondered who'd appointed him. It would fit the soap opera her life had become if it turned out Parker had a thing for Lilly. "You notice how she looks?"

"You mean aside from tired and in a wheelchair?" They smiled briefly at Jake. "Yeah, we were just talking about that. I've never seen her look so angry. But then, I've only known her a few months."

Dean shook his head as he led them to a van piling in a few others. The crowd was smaller than Wayne's funeral, but it looked like the Navatts had a little money to throw around. *A fund saved for this very occasion*, Thea thought half-jokingly. The dour, downtrodden expressions Ma and Pa Navatt wore looked well-used. Glass half empty types.

"I've never seen her actually *angry* the whole time I've known her. Obviously losing Carl hit her pretty hard." Dean commented. He paused, looking down a moment before he stepped into the van. "I know how she feels."

The actual burial was blessedly brief, thanks mainly to the wind kicked up off the lake that sliced through even the warmest clothing like blades of ice. Thea felt comfortable enough flying in formation with Jake and Dean to tough out the wake at Carl's parents' place. Besides, she was curious to see if she could find out more about Lilly.

Nobody mentioned Romeo, which certainly made Thea breathe easier. His movements were mysterious enough the rest of the time that it was reasonable to assume he was off doing... whatever it was he did when he wandered off on his own. Probably more hunting. Samuel Zheng wasn't exactly the type to take in a movie.

They made small talk and snacked on healthy hors d'oeuvres like deviled eggs and bite-sized barbecued wieners, waiting for an appropriate lull in which to approach Lilly. She ended up coming to them first, Parker steering her through the subdued crowd to the corner of the living room they'd claimed for their own.

"So you know the... the thing that killed him?" Lilly snapped without preamble, looking right at Thea.

What the fuck? What Lilly had said was as disturbing as the vehemence with which she said it. Naked pain dripped from each word. Thea looked at the others in open puzzlement, then said, "Lilly, I'm not sure—"

"You know!" Lilly yelled. All eyes were on them in a heartbeat. "Parker told me! You all met him! It! Whatever it—"

HERALDS OF THE STORM

"Lilly," Jake broke in, kneeling and taking her trembling hands in his, "listen. This isn't the best time for this. Not here, not now."

While Jake tried to sooth Lilly, Thea looked at Dean and Parker uncomfortably, feeling the stares from the other guests boring into her back. Under her breath, she asked Parker, "Just what did you tell her? I never said Carpenter did anything to Carl. He was already… Carl was gone by the time he got there."

Parker shrugged. He looked strange wearing something besides camouflage or sports sweatshirts. "I know. But I've been doing some thinking. I think it was all a setup."

Thea and Dean stared at Parker. She sensed Dean was as angry with Parker as she was. "I'm not going to point out now why that doesn't make sense, not with all these people around. What really gets me is you spinning some half-baked theory to Lilly. You think she's in any kind of shape to hear your crap right now?"

Parker looked back at her coolly. "Look," he said softly, "I know you all think I'm just some hick with a gun fetish. Far as that goes, I don't see nothing wrong with being gung-ho about what we're doing. But that doesn't mean I'm stupid. We all know we're being set up for something, but I'm the only one willing to admit it. You're all being too trusting, and it's gonna get us killed." He looked down at Lilly, nodding to whatever Jake was murmuring. "Shit; it already has some of us."

Thea turned to Dean in appeal. He looked angry, but he didn't seem inclined to disagree with Parker. *This is too fucked for words.* "Fine, whatever. Obviously, we need to go over all this some more. But not right now."

"I agree," Jake said, standing straight. He patted Lilly's shoulder. "You need a little more rest, okay? This is a tough day, and we should all be thinking only of helping you through it."

Mollified but obviously no less furious, Lilly said, "Then help me track down every single one of these bastards and send them back to hell. *That's* what will help me through this. When you're ready to do that, you let me know."

Thea watched, jaw hanging open incredulously, as Lilly had Parker steer her away. Conversations resumed fitfully elsewhere in the room, but it was clear Thea and Jake and Dean were the subject of scrutiny and suspicion. "What the hell?" was all she could think to say.

"Good point, Thea," Dean observed. "But I think there's something to what Parker said."

"Sure, Carpenter's trying to use us for something. But that attack as a set-up? I don't know. Carpenter was following *me* that night; he couldn't have known where I was going beforehand."

Jake waggled a hand. "Let's save this for tomorrow or something. I don't think we should be saying anything more here."

Thea nodded, feeling a chill in the room that had nothing to do with the winter wind outside. Her Great Dane had run out of the park. It was hauling her through a forest choked with underbrush, tossing her back and forth on the end of the leash, smacking her against tree trunks and plunging her through briars. Just a matter of time before she lost hold of the leash entirely.

•••

Thea was getting tired of the continual bickering their group indulged in. They spent more time arguing amongst themselves than going after the things that were ostensibly supposed to be the enemy. Thea didn't think Carpenter was behind the attack on Dean's apartment, and the convoluted logic Parker presented when they all met at the clubhouse on Monday evening didn't make her any more inclined to change her mind. But if the hidden's plan was to throw them into divisive squabbling, it was going perfectly so far.

Jake finally cut things off before they could degenerate any further. "Parker, you may have a point," he said diplomatically. "I agree that Carpenter isn't telling us everything.

But I don't know if that necessarily means he's been manipulating us from the very beginning."

Jake held up both hands to forestall the assertions ready on everyone's lips. "Before we get into that again, listen to what Romeo and I found out on Saturday."

"Speaking of which, where is Romeo?" Parker asked.

Thea blushed reflexively. *Great spy you'd make*, she thought, trying to act nonchalant despite the burning she felt in her cheeks.

"I'm not sure exactly," Jake replied. "We did some digging on this Akhenaton place Carpenter told us about. He might be staking it out. Or patrolling, as usual. Anyway, he knows all this, so we won't be leaving him out of the loop."

Parker frowned. "I was more wanting to ask him about what he saw last Sunday night."

Thea blinked in surprise. So much had occurred, she found it hard to believe it had only been a week. "Why don't we see what Jake has before we go chasing Romeo down?" she offered.

Jake took the ball and ran with it. "Okay, like I said, we checked into this temple place. I know we talked about taking a break. It was just idle conversation at, um, Wayne's service. Not that we were bored or anything! I mean, you talk at these kinds of things, right, and it was on our minds and all…."

Dean waved a hand and gave Jake a smile mixed with equal parts humor and pain. "It's okay, Jake. I know what you mean."

"Right, well. Uh, sorry." Jake shuffled in embarrassment, busying himself with booting up his laptop on the counter. "Anyway, we decided to see what the place was all about. I lent Romeo my digital camera to take shots of the temple while I went online and hit the libraries for background."

He turned the Compaq to face the group. "These are some of the pictures Romeo took. You can look at the files I got, too, but for now let's just hit the high points.

"First off, 'Akhenaton' is another name for Amenhotep IV, who ruled Egypt way back in 1300-something B.C. Just before King Tut. There's a whole soap opera about how Akhenaton supplanted Amon, the sun god worshipped at the time, for Aton, an 'older' version. Really an abstraction of the sun and not technically a 'god' at all. Or something like that; it gets a little convoluted. Anyway, he was later considered heretical and the pharaohs who followed after him tried eradicating his memory when they restored the ancient cults." Jake paused, realizing he was getting off track. "It's a pretty cool story, but we don't really need to get into it now."

He leaned against the countertop and blew into his hands before continuing. "What's interesting is that part about him being a heretic — or a visionary, depending on whose history you read. Seems a little strange to dedicate a temple to the guy if he's a heretic, right? I didn't dig too deeply, but some historians seem to think he was innovative, going for a one-god-in-Aton thing instead of the previous pantheon… So this temple was maybe dedicated to Akhenaton as philosopher; I don't know. I can tell you the building was constructed in the 1920s, right around the time a lot of Westerners — by that I mean Americans and Europeans, not cowboys or whatever — were really into mysticism and funky magical pursuits."

"You don't mean that these people actually practiced magic, do you?" Thea asked.

"A few years ago I would've said no way," Jake replied. "But with everything I've seen lately, I wouldn't discount it. I don't think this is some wizard's stronghold like in *The Lord of the Rings*, though, if that's what you're asking. I don't know much about mystic stuff but I think a lot of it's like a philosophy, really. So with Akhenaton you have a bunch of regular folks who ponder the great questions of the universe, Tony Robbins style, instead of calling up demons or whatever."

"Wait," Parker said. "Built in the '20s? That Carpenter guy was alive then. Maybe there's a connection."

Jake nodded. "That's a good point. I don't think that's the main link, though. Let me spill the rest of this for you and you'll see what I mean."

He clicked open the first image and cycled through them as he spoke. "The Temple of Akhenaton doesn't take up much of the fronting, but it is pretty long; goes almost the whole block between North Halstead and Dayton. You have the main entrance in the front and another door in the back. Looks like all traffic is through the front, though. The place isn't too big, just two stories — or maybe one with really high ceilings — with one of those big onion-shaped roofs, a minaret. I think that was added later; the lower construction is all much more ancient Egyptian in style. This shot shows a wall going around a courtyard in the front. Here we can see through the front gate. That's a fountain there, covered for the winter, some Egyptian-style sculptures and columns along the front of the building. We don't know what it looks like on the inside. The gates were closed and we couldn't find any hours of operation or anything like that. So as far as it being private, even secretive, I wouldn't argue with Carpenter's assessment."

The name hadn't sounded familiar to Thea, aside from registering that "Akhenaton" was Egyptian. But the digital images tickled something in her memory. "I don't know why but that place looks familiar," she said. "It's not like I just happened to see it driving by or anything. Something else..." The memory was hazy, little more than brief, tattered flashes of insight. She rapped her knuckles against her temples as if to shake loose more cohesive images. Thea finally groaned in frustration and sprawled back in her chair.

"Not getting it," she admitted. She'd learned to trust her intuition; it had served her well in journalism and in the hunt. The fact that the place struck a chord with her meant there was *some* kind of link. But what was it? Why did she feel she knew this place? She cleared her throat and smiled brightly. "Anyway, something about it is familiar. I can't remember what, though; sorry."

Jake looked at her with equal parts surprise and concern. "You think you've been inside?"

"I think. With my mom maybe, when I was a kid? It's an Egyptian temple, we're Egyptian; maybe some sort of cultural festival or something?" She shrugged. "Who knows?"

"Well, your mom might," Lilly said. It wasn't intentional, but with all the anger she had bottled up, every word Lilly spoke lunged from her mouth like an accusation. "This is all too… what's the word? Coincidental? Maybe you should ask her."

Dean and Parker nodded while Jake looked thoughtful. "It might be a good idea. It does seem pretty convenient that Carpenter focused on you when he got in touch with us, and now it looks like your family has some kind of link to the place he wants us to raid."

Thea shook her head. "I just don't see what the connection would be. I mean, I never once heard my mom mention the place. And my dad… well, he left us before I was even born." But now she wondered. *Did* he walk out while her mom was still pregnant? "And I don't know how Carpenter could possibly know anything about me or my folks. There's nothing distinctive about us, no skeletons in the closet—"

"Wouldn't that be 'mummies'?" Parker sniped with a smile.

Thea shot him an icy look but smiled. The joke helped relieve the mounting tension and worry Thea felt. "As I was saying, we're just your average dysfunctional single-parent family. I couldn't imagine what the hook would be."

"Well, seems like a good reason to talk to your mom then, right?" Dean said.

Thea wanted to argue the point further, but they were right. It might turn out to be one of those coincidences.

She didn't really believe it, though. Her instincts said there was something here, something worth pursuing. That was the scary part. She and her mom had fallen into an uneasy truce years ago about her parentage. A gulf of unasked questions and unvoiced answers lay between them, swollen with the weight of twenty-five years' worth of secrets. Thea had enough secrets of her own now that she was acutely aware that her mother might think she had good reason to keep things hidden from her. But was now really the time to demand disclosure? Bringing this up was going to open a jumbo sized can of worms for them both. Added on top of everything else, Thea wasn't sure she could take the strain. But what the hell else was she supposed to do? Now that the memory was in her mind, tattered though it was, she couldn't ignore it. And they needed to learn whatever they could about this place. Simply going on Carpenter's word would probably end up getting them killed.

"I'm not going to explain how hard it's going to be, pursuing this, but I'll do what I can." She waved a hand at Jake. "In the meantime, what say you give us the rest of it?"

"Sounds good." Jake slipped easily back into his lecturing role. "I couldn't find out much of what the temple did in the way of services, classes, or anything else. Looked like it had a pretty insular setup; new people got in through references from current members, that kind of thing. There *is* a little detail you might find interesting. The temple underwent a change of ownership recently, bought by a company called S Securities."

"And what's 'S Securities'?" Parker asked.

Jake smiled. "Just a private security firm run by a guy named Nicholas Sforza."

Thea could have punched Jake for teasing them with that build-up. "Let me guess, you little weasel. Related to the late Annabelle Sforza."

"Grandson, as a matter of fact."

Parker swore. "What the fuck, Jake? Lupe said the woman wasn't even married, let alone had grandkids."

Thea quirked an eyebrow at Parker. "When did she say that?"

"Remember we were talking before about how that dead fucker got on hunter-net, which got Lupe to do some digging on him? Went back through and re-read those posts before we met with her the other day. Her last message on the subject talked about this Sforza woman's funeral, and how she overheard her fare say the dead lady had no husband or kids." Parker glared at Jake, as if he was somehow responsible for the discrepancies they were uncovering. "This doesn't make any sense. We got a guy says he's Carpenter but he doesn't look like the picture Lupe has on him, he claims he died, like, five years after Lupe said he did, and now she had a whole family when Lupe said she didn't?"

"So it's some other monster claiming to be Carpenter?" Lilly asked. "But why?"

Thea opened her mouth, then checked herself just before the words came out. Did she *really* want to voice her suspicion? She had nothing to back it up but her gut, and not even her extra-special sixth sense instinct. Just plain old women's intuition.

"Unless it's Lupe that's gotten these details wrong." Thea was startled, then realized someone else said the very thought she was having. It was Jake, his head canted forward in puzzlement and something else. Worry? He spoke slowly, as if feeling his way with the words. "I remember that post too, Parker. Got it here on the laptop. But Lupe's normally really thorough in her research. She's not perfect, but these kinds of details are too basic to get wrong with even the least effort."

"The only other thing that makes sense is that the corpse is impersonating this Maxwell Carpenter," Parker claimed.

"Well…" Thea felt the others' eyes upon her. She took a deep breath and a big leap of faith. "Maybe not. Maybe it wasn't an accident Lupe got that stuff wrong."

"What are you saying?" Lilly demanded.

"I'm not sure, just that... Okay, look. Something happened to me the night I met Carpenter at, uh, Dean's place. You know, how I didn't even remember he'd been there until Romeo mentioned that he'd seen Carpenter carrying us out?"

"It was a pretty traumatic situation, Thea," Jake observed. "You probably just blocked it out from shock."

Thea shrugged. "That's what I thought at first. But something bugged me when we were talking to Lupe. I'm still not sure why, but I just have this feeling she was hiding something."

"Like what? And what the hell for?"

"I don't know, Parker!" She rubbed her temples as a sudden headache struck. "I just said I wasn't sure. It's just a feeling, same as the feeling I have now that... that somehow Carpenter tried to make me forget we met that night."

Jake cleared his throat. "You know, I'd been thinking it was strange that Romeo tracked Carpenter down, but then got caught without any apparent injury to either one of them...."

Thea hadn't even considered that. She admitted she didn't *want* to consider it. "So... he can influence us somehow? Made Lupe misremember things about him, me forget we met, and, what? Made Romeo want to get caught or something?"

Jake nodded but held his hands up as if to deny any actual confirmation of the idea. "I don't know. Like you said, it's just a hunch. But even if he can exert some level of control, it must not be very strong."

"Why do you say that?" Dean asked.

"Because otherwise why didn't he just control all of you when you went to meet him, right?" Lilly said.

"Who's to say he didn't?" Jake replied. When they started looking at one another with mild panic he waved his hands frantically. "Whoah, gang, settle down! Joke, I was joking! Really, I'd say — if he *can* exert some kind of control — that it isn't very strong, and maybe it's only a one-on-one kind of thing. Think about it: if he really could mind read or whatever, why didn't he make Lupe just flat out forget about that funeral? It'd make things a lot easier for him than having details, even wrong ones, floating around. And Thea, if he did try to make you forget you met, it obviously didn't take. And Romeo— uh…"

Thea nodded. "We don't know if anything happened with Romeo, but at least he doesn't seem to have come to any harm when Carpenter had him under wraps."

"Though it does kinda make you wonder where he is now," Dean muttered.

"Okay, this is bad," Lilly said. "This is really bad. I don't mean that some monster might have the power to control us, either. Look, we're getting all suspicious of each other!" She gestured to encompass the room. "Maybe that's all it is, some kind of ability to make us all paranoid or something."

Jake nodded thoughtfully. "Hell, don't even need a supernatural power to do that. And I think it's pretty clear Carpenter likes to manipulate people."

"Whatever it is, he's obviously trying to use us, right?" Lilly looked at each of them. "I mean, that's been clear from right off, you know? Like Parker's been saying. So what do we do about it?"

"Fair question," Jake said. "I think that brings us right back to where we were before this idea reared its ugly head. Carpenter wants something from us, and it has something to do with this Akhenaton place. The thing is that he *could* be telling the truth about what he's been up to and what the temple is. We can't just take his word for it—"

"Never should've trusted a word he said, you ask me," Parker interjected.

"Okay, Parker, you're right. But we can't just treat him like another monster to drop. We have to know why he's doing what he's doing before we can put together an appropriate response. Agreed?"

They all nodded with varying degrees of enthusiasm. Thea added, "We'd be idiots to take anything he says at face value, you're right. And just in case he does have some kind of Jedi mind trick, probably be a good idea if we figure out all we can before he wants to meet again. He's been calling the shots so far; I'd really like to turn the tables on that."

"Meaning dig deeper into Carpenter's background and this temple and everything?" Dean clarified.

"You got it, big guy."

Jake gestured at his laptop. "Well, wouldn't you know I got scads of just that kind of information right here?"

"Yeah, but is it accurate?" Parker asked. "And if it's accurate, how do we know it's the right Carpenter we're dealing with? I mean, half the stuff we've found contradicts the other half."

"Because of Lupe, right?" Lilly said. "Shouldn't we should talk to Lupe again, see… well, see if she's, um, okay."

"Yeah," Jake sighed, rubbing at his temple. "I can try to get in touch with her. What it's worth, I don't think there's anything wrong with her. You're right, though, Parker, we need to confirm all this. Could be that the guy isn't really Dennis Maxwell or Maxwell Carpenter or whatever. For the record, I think it is. But even if it's somebody else posing as him, he's doing it for a reason. And even if we don't know precisely who 'Carpenter' is, I've dug up enough information on the Sforzas and the temple to feel comfortable that those details are accurate."

"Good," Thea said. "And whether it's really him or some other nasty, the only way we're going to get to the bottom of things is to follow up on the leads we got and see which ones pan out."

"Exactly."

There was a moment of silence as everyone thought about the implications of what they'd just discussed. Thea knew continuing along this line of thought wouldn't accomplish much of anything useful, so she tried to shove the conversation back on its original track. "So, Jake. You said Annabelle Sforza had grandkids, one of whom owns a security firm?"

Jake jerked slightly as he was roused from his thoughts. "Uh, yeah. And I'm pretty certain she's not some other Annabelle Sforza who just happens to be tied to organized crime. See, when I found out she had kids, I checked around to see how many other Sforzas are running around."

Parker was still irritated at the discrepancies they were looking at. Apparently hoping this line of inquiry might give him the chance to dig up the truth, he asked, "How many?"

"Of her sons, nieces and nephews, and all their grandkids? None. And yes, they all died within the past couple of years. Quite the rash of accidents, suicides and a couple of unsolved deaths, too."

They looked at Jake incredulously. "You serious?" Dean said. "The *entire* Sforza family's been killed off since Carpenter came back?"

"Well, every single adult, anyway," Jake admitted. "As far as I can tell, the great-grandchildren are still alive. I think."

"And how old are they, on average?" Thea asked.

Jake opened a folder on the laptop containing a series of obituaries and newspaper articles. After squirreling around the trackball for a few seconds, he said, "Looks like the oldest one is thirteen."

"So Carpenter's not a total monster. He'll bump off a bushel of adults, but he won't go after kids."

"Gee, that's a nice consolation," Dean muttered.

Parker laughed loudly. "Well, I told you so! The guy's a fucking psycho. If you had any doubt at all that he's been yanking our chain since day one, there you go! A serial killer rot and you all were thinking about helping him out? That's just fucking great!"

"Okay, okay. So Carpenter said he's hunting other monsters and it looks here like he's been taking out normal folks. That still doesn't tell us what he's really up to." Jake clicked back to the image of the snow-clad minaret topping the Temple of Akhenaton. "If all he wants is to kill off Sforzas, what's he care about this place for? And why's he been bothering us?"

Thea caught a tone in Jake's voice, and suspected it matched her own line of reasoning. "I think you know why, chief. Don't leave us in suspense."

"Right. First I'll recap: We have one of the walking dead, currently going by the name Maxwell Carpenter, who told us he's been going after monsters. It appears this Carpenter — whether or not he's actually the person he claims to be — has been knocking off every adult member of the Sforza family since he arose from the dead. He may or may not be going after other undead as well. Whatever the case, he claims he needs our help to check out the Orthodox Temple of Akhenaton. It's supposedly a source of supernatural badness that he can't deal with himself. From what I'll admit is a very limited investigation, the joint is really just the Egyptian equivalent of a Masonic temple. It was purchased recently by a company owned by a member of the Sforza family." Jake paused, making sure he hadn't forgotten anything. "Now, we don't know how Carpenter found us; maybe through Lupe, maybe we've been sloppy. We got bigger mysteries than that right now. We don't know why Carpenter needs us to help go after the temple. Nor do we know why S Securities bought the joint.

"I think we find our answers to both these questions in Nicholas Sforza."

"No kidding, I figured that much myself. But you said all the Sforzas were—" Thea interrupted herself. "Wait, Nicholas is still alive?"

Jake called up a new image, a newspaper article, and tapped keys until he had a close up of the accompanying picture featuring a dark haired man. "I honestly can't say. I know I said every adult Sforza was dead. Details suggest Nicholas Sforza is dead, too, but I can't actually confirm it. The newspapers comment on an attack at the family home, blood and signs of a struggle. But they didn't find a body. The authorities figured he might have been kidnapped — ironic, since he runs a security business — but there was never a ransom note or anything. And it's been months but he still hasn't appeared publicly, alive or dead."

"So... what? What *are* you saying?" Parker asked.

"I think — and this is only a guess, but Romeo agrees — I *think* that Carpenter might have gone to finish off the last adult Sforza and Nicholas got away. Makes sense if he's a security guy, right? I'd bet he knew someone was after the family for a while, and maybe *he* set up a trap but Carpenter got away. Anyway, for some reason I still haven't figured, Nicholas figured this temple was a safe place to hide. So he bought it and has been hiding there while he figures out a way to get Carpenter."

Lilly nodded, still puzzling some of it. "So he could still be alive and hiding in there? Why there? It can't really be some kind of monster factory, can it?"

"I don't think so, but there is most definitely something unusual about the temple. I'm not sure why Sforza picked it, though I think it'd be foolish to assume that he doesn't know there's something special about it. Romeo and I definitely got a sense of... power... when we checked it out. I couldn't tell much, but from Romeo's reaction I guess it's not surprising that Carpenter's kept his distance. It could be that there's some property to it that acts as a barrier to zombies." Jake shrugged. "Purely a guess, mind you."

"Wait, wait," Thea said, waving her hands in a "hold on" gesture. "You just said you couldn't confirm whether Nicholas Sforza's alive or dead. So his company bought the temple; what makes you think Nicholas Sforza is actually holed up in there?"

Jake grinned again. "Because although Romeo didn't get in the temple, he did get lucky. He told me he was com-

ing around from checking around the back when a bunch of guys showed up and hustled inside. He got a quick shot before they went in." Jake opened another file containing a color portrait. The newspaper image it was next to was hazy due to the low resolution of newsprint. This one looked muddy from having been blown up too far. Still, both images unmistakably showed the same dark-featured man.

"Ladies and gents, I give you Nicholas Sforza."

ELEVEN

The others, especially Parker and Lilly, were pretty spooked now that they all agreed Carpenter was running some game on them. Lilly had seized upon Thea's tenuous connection to the temple and kept pushing for her to confront her mother right away. Thea's observation that she wasn't even sure there was a connection made no difference. She understood Lilly's vehemence; Thea supposed that if the man she loved was killed she'd pursue any lead, no matter how slight, if there was the chance to exact retribution.

Thea agreed to think about the connection further, and if she felt there was a need, she'd talk to her mom about it. In the meantime, she felt it was best if they all took a little time to go over what they'd learned and see if any more details emerged for any of them. Once they'd all given Jake's information a thorough going-over, they could plan their next step.

She spent the rest of Monday night at the California Clipper on North California, mulling over everything from the past few weeks and considering the task before her. The old Prohibition-era speakeasy was refitted as a great modern joint with a great variety of live acts. Thea had found it a good place to relax and think.

Thea tried to go over Jake's synopsis of the Sforzas and the temple, but her thoughts kept turning to her mother. She couldn't deny that there was some kind of link between her family and the temple. Or maybe that wasn't even it. Perhaps the link was cultural, Egyptian, and not specific to

the Temple of Akhenaton. Thea couldn't say, but the more she thought about it the more certain she was her instincts were correct. Which meant she would have to confront her mother if she hoped to get any answers.

That presented its own particular difficulties. Theirs was a relationship built as much upon secrets as it was upon love. She'd long ago come to terms with the dissonance — born of Egypt and Islam, bred in Western thought and culture — and conveniently laid the blame for her mislaid culture at her mother's feet. She filed it away and got on with her life, always knowing that wasn't truly the case. Newa had tried showing her the richness of their heritage, but these attempts were clumsy, her mother as nervous about making the attempt as Thea was to be exposed to it. As a result, Thea had come to think her ancestry was some kind of guilty secret. That it was an unfortunate circumstance she could overcome with hard work and perseverance, as if it was a speech impediment or something.

If she grilled her mother on the temple issue, there was no telling what ugly secrets would be exposed, or how the whole thing would impact their relationship. Thea smiled humorlessly. It wasn't as if they had the healthiest relationship in the world to begin with. But it was, if nothing else, comfortable, established; a known quantity. To throw things in a turmoil based on scattered half-memories? It seemed a rash and misguided idea to say the least.

It came back to instinct. She was sure she'd been in that place, or one very much like it. She was sure there was some link to her family. And the only person who could give her any answers was Newa Ghandour.

She finally dragged herself home after hours of mental back-and-forth and saw that Margie was out again. Thea assumed her friend was staying at her parents' house. It was probably for the best; Thea certainly wasn't in any kind of shape to have a heart to heart right now. Ironic, considering she was planning to have one with her mother the next day.

• • •

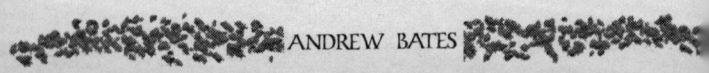

Thea stood outside her mother's condominium shortly after nightfall on Tuesday. The wind off Lake Michigan smashed against her, as if to push her up the front steps. She went grudgingly, the idea of freezing to death along the lake shore marginally more distasteful than the course laid out before her. *Can't avoid it, so you might as well suck it up and dive in.* Insha'Allah, *as Mom would say.*

Newa was surprised to see her, especially so soon after her visit upon leaving the hospital the week before. Despite living within a few miles of one another, the two women spent very little quality time together. Thea didn't have the nerve to start grilling her mother right away, so she stayed for a traditional meal of mezze and kebab with rice pudding for desert. The food was good but the dinner uncomfortable. Thea was nervous, and her agitation rubbed off on her mother who was already puzzled as to why she was there. Sitting with coffee afterward, Thea figured the time had come.

"The dinner was very good, Mom," she began. "I am sorry I haven't come by very often lately."

"You're always welcome," Newa said, shifting her cup nervously around on the saucer.

"Thanks." Sticking with politeness would make this take all night. Thea took a breath and blundered onward. Unable to look at her mother straight on, she directed her gaze at the fireplace. "I'm curious about something. What do you know about a place called the Temple of Akhenaton?"

Newa Ghandour was getting on in age, edging past the mid range of her 60s, but still in good shape. At least she was before Thea mentioned the temple. The older woman paled and almost knocked her cup over, a breathless gasp squeaking from her throat.

"I take it from your expression," Thea continued, "that you're familiar with it."

"Why do you want to know about that place?" Newa asked, her voice carefully neutral. "Is this for one of your stories?"

Thea had considered using that approach, but her mom wouldn't believe she'd come over personally just for story background when a phone call would have worked as effectively. Neither had she planned on telling her true motivation; one step at a time, thank you. Considering her mother's guarded tone, Thea thought a little bluffing might be in order. "I met a man recently, an Egyptian man. Well, Egyptian-American; he was like me, corrupted by the West." She smiled, the phrase directed at her years ago in family argument and since used only half-jokingly. "We got to talking, and he mentioned the temple. Said I should come by some time, that I might like to attend."

Newa leaned forward abruptly, her dark eyes, so different from Thea's own, dark and intense. "Do not go to that place!" She blurted, her voice almost a yell.

"Mom, I—"

Newa held up a hand, obviously choking on a further utterance. A deep breath calmed her visibly, and she continued in a more normal tone of voice. "I'm sorry. I… went to that place once, when you were still a baby. I was looking for community. But it was not the proper community for me. I hoped to find others who shared my culture. Instead, I found only a silly little collection of misguided souls."

Thea might have believed that if she hadn't already seen her mother's extreme reaction. Such a volatile response was very much out of character. Plus Chicago had a small but notable Islamic community that her mother had long associated with. Why try some obscure temple when there was a more established neighborhood on Devon Avenue? Not only that, but once she regained her composure, her mother had shot her words out with the smooth, controlled tone she took when she was handling someone. Thea's mom was handling her, like she was a misguided little girl again.

Confusion and discomfort turned to anger in Thea's belly. She was tempted to dive in all the way, to hammer away with questions and hound Newa till she got the full story right then and there. Her mother kept her at arm's length all their lives, compartmentalized her role in the family the same way she filed her job and friends and hobbies. Newa had no right to keep her shut out like this. *I'm your fucking daughter!* she wanted to yell.

But Newa had already retreated behind her emotional defenses. She was cool and collected as ever, as if her surprised yell from a minute ago had never happened. Thea knew it would be virtually impossible to break through that resolve. That's where she got her own willful personality from, after all. Thea was dealing with a master here. Best to retreat and figure out a subtler approach after she built up her own strength.

She had to make it look good, though. "If they're just some little church, why are you upset if I visit?"

Newa smiled. "I am concerned for your well-being. I do not think the place is dangerous, but I believe they might try to manipulate you to join. It is like many such groups that ask for 'donations' merely to gain your money and trust, not through any pursuit of spiritual enlightenment. For that, there is only Islam."

"So they're just some goofy cultists?" Thea asked, all naive confusion.

"That's right. I would not want you to waste your time. You have more important things to do."

Thea nodded dubiously, as if she was essentially convinced but retained her usual parental defiance. "The guy was really cute, though."

That was all she needed to have Newa bring up the son of some friends. A young lawyer, lots of promise. Within minutes they were down conversational paths worn to ruts from years of repetition. Through it all, the image of her mother's expression was burned in her mind. Newa's look of shock, fear, and suspicion.

• • •

Thea called Jake as soon as she left her mother's and asked him to assemble everyone. He was a little surprised at the excitement in her voice, and agreed that he'd gather the rest of the Van Helsing brigade by the time she got there. She arrived at the hideout to find them all sitting in Lilly's Suburban in the small lot, the heater cranked to full. Apparently one of the space heaters had given up the ghost, turning the already uncomfortable Stop n Go into a hypothermia-inducing hell. They spent a few minutes bickering about where to go; Lilly finally put the Chevy into gear and meandered toward Lincoln Park so they at least wouldn't be sitting suspiciously in a vacant lot.

Lilly looked measurably better than she had the day before, which itself had been a notable improvement over Sunday. Aside from the furrowed brow and narrowed eyes that added ten years to her age, Lilly looked almost as healthy as she had before the attack. Parker sat shotgun, literally, as always. Dean sat in the first bench seat, leaving a space for Thea to hop in. Jake and Romeo were in the second bench seat. By way of greeting, Jake said he'd tried to contact Lupe but hadn't heard anything back as yet. That line of inquiry cold for the moment, all eyes turned on Thea. They all shared expectant looks, though Thea suspected Romeo's might be for a different reason than the rest.

"I suppose you're all wondering why I called you here," she said with a smile. "But let's get something out of the way right off: it's not because my mom told me some amazing secret that's blown this whole deal wide open."

"Maybe you didn't ask the right questions," Lilly said, her hands white-knuckled as she gripped the wheel.

"Damn, Lil! What has gotten into you? This was a tenuous lead at best. Even if my mother did have useful information, she's not the type to just spill it. It's almost impossible to get her to tell me what she had for breakfast. It'd take more than a couple hours for me to get anything useful out of her. And even then I'm not sure I'll get the straight story."

"So why even bother, then?"

"To find out if there was anything worth pursuing. And I don't think there is. Instead, I think it's better if we—"

"Oh, *you* think?" Lilly glared over her shoulder for a beat before returning her focus to the road. "So suddenly you know what's best for all of us?"

"Cut the crap, Lilly. That's not what I'm saying at all. And if you weren't so blinded by revenge you'd see that!"

"Hey, take it easy, Thea," Parker said, twisted to face back over the seat. "She's been through hell, okay?"

"*She's* been through hell? What about the rest of us, huh? Dean lost someone he loved too, you know? And Jake got mangled all to shit by a nasty, and he's the most optimistic little cuss I know. And Romeo—" Thea stumbled for a second, remembering the scars upon scars laced across his flesh "—he's lost his whole family, right? You and I, Parker, we're the only ones who haven't been hit as hard, and I bet you it's only a matter of time. So forgive me if I'm not handling Lilly with kid gloves, okay?"

The air in the van crackled with tension. Parker frowned, preparing to respond, when Lilly spoke again. Her voice was softer this time, closer to how she'd sounded a week — a lifetime — ago. "You're right. We've all been through things no good person should ever have to experience. But that doesn't change things, you know? We're in a war, like Parker's said. We have to do everything we can to stop the... the enemy."

Thea looked the back of Lilly's head. "I don't disagree with that, Lil. But you need to give me half a chance to tell you what I have in mind before you jump down my throat about th—" The chirp of her cell phone startled everyone. She considered not answering it, but they could all use a minute or two to calm down. She dug the phone out of her pocket by the second ring and hit SEND.

"I hope you had a good weekend," Carpenter's voice said without preamble.

Thea rolled her eyes. Of course; who else would it be? "Well, as I live and breathe." *That makes one of us, anyway.* "If it isn't Maxwell Carpenter. Or should I call you Dennis Maxwell?"

"Carpenter's fine."

"I'm surprised you don't know how my weekend went, Carpenter. Seems like you've been pretty up on my habits recently."

There was a pause; Thea imagined the cold features twist in a smile. "I took a little vacation."

"Really? Where does a corpse go for rest and relaxation? Transylvania?"

"That's good. I get it." Another pause. "So have you and your friends come to a decision regarding our little talk the other day?"

Thea looked around the Suburban's interior. Everyone but Lilly stared right back with expressions ranging from excited to worried to angry. Covering the Motorola's tiny mouthpiece with her hand, she whispered, "I think he's watching us." That got the group darting glances outside, Jake digging in the back for night vision goggles while Lilly headed for Lakeshore Drive. Into the phone, Thea said, "I expect you know we're talking it over right now. This isn't exactly the kind of thing you decide in a heartbeat. Though I guess you don't do much of anything in a heartbeat anymore, do you?"

She supposed it wasn't a good idea to keep poking at him like this, but she was feeling cocky. For once it seemed they were in charge instead of being yanked this way and that by forces beyond their control.

It didn't seem to bother Carpenter, either. In fact he seemed to be enjoying himself. "You're quite the little spitfire tonight. You get some action while I was away?"

"Like I'd tell you."

"Yes, a lady never tells." He chuckled again. The guy was positively giddy. "So what do you have for me?"

"Nothing yet, pal. Like I said, we're still talking things over. That's the trouble with democracy, right? Everybody gets a say-so."

"Right. Well, don't take too long. I'm sure whatever's happening in that temple is going to reach a boil within a week. I expect you're the only ones who can keep a lid on it."

You got that right. "Thanks for the vote of confidence. You can bet we'll get ahold of you as soon as we have something for you." Thea ended the call and watched the faint glitter of ice on the lake in the distance as the Suburban headed north along the lake shore. They turned on Foster and wove their way along icy surface streets, heading gradually back downtown.

"So?" Jake prompted, the goggles strapped to his face making him look like some kind of cyborg raccoon.

"He was in a weird mood, like he was almost upbeat." She shrugged. "But I think he was honestly just checking in. He wants us to move, though, and soon. By the weekend."

"Who gives a fuck what that thing wants?" Parker growled, scanning the streets as if daring Carpenter to pop up.

"I hear you," Thea said. "But it's good to know what his time frame is. It means whatever we're going to do, we'd better do soon."

"And just what are we going to do?" Dean inquired.

"I thought you'd never ask."

• • •

Thea's plan was ostensibly a fact-finding mission, with backup in case things got ugly. It was simple, direct, and probably suicidal. Surprisingly, she faced little resistance when she offered it up. They'd all had enough of being led around by their noses. They had specifics hammered out within a half-hour. The toughest part was thinking of a believable cover for Romeo and making sure Parker could get

off work. A part of Thea worried that it was an indication of how flimsy the idea was. Instead, she chose to think that the simplest plans are always the best.

Besides, as she'd seen often enough in the recent past, even the best-laid plans went to hell five minutes into the execution.

•••

The next day was the last of February, and representative of the month. It was gray and overcast, a still coldness promising yet more snow sometime soon. In the Midwest, that could mean anywhere between the next five minutes and the next five days.

Thea, Jake and Romeo got out of a cab in front of the temple in mid-morning. She shivered in the chill wind, wishing that she could have dressed for warmth instead of for the role she was playing. She wore respectable reporter garb — tan slacks and pumps with a black sweater and the coat she wore to the funerals. The bandage on her forehead was gone; her hair was pulled back in a bun to make her look older and more serious (and stay out of the way in case she had to let loose with some whup-ass). Jake was playing photographer, so he didn't have to dress up; he had on his standard boots, jeans, sweater, and parka. He carried a Nikon with attachments they'd purchased earlier. It looked more like what a photographer would carry than his digital camera, and if all went well they'd simply return it later. If things didn't go as well, they wouldn't exactly be around to worry about it. Romeo wore a dark suit with a severe cut that matched his expression.

None of them were armed. This had occasioned quite a bit of debate. Everyone agreed marching into an unknown situation bold as you please was just this side of nuts. But going in without weapons? That was plain old stupid. Or so Parker claimed. Thea pointed out that this Sforza guy was supposed to be into the security trade. Since he'd bought the place, Thea bet he'd had all sorts of security installed along with metal detectors and stuff, or even a low-tech patdown. So going in supposedly undercover and getting busted for carrying unlicensed firearms was probably not the best idea. Besides, they had their edges; if they did end up facing a threat, it was probably supernatural, in which case their hunter abilities would come in handier than a bunch of bullets. Jake and Dean backed her up. Romeo even weighed in on her side, pointing out they had Parker's team standing by if they needed firepower.

Romeo. Thea shot him a sidelong glance as they walked up to the gate. They had exchanged hardly a word since they'd slept together. Of course, they seldom chatted it up, so that wasn't unusual. She knew Jake had already picked up on something, though he wasn't sure what yet. Romeo seemed content to wait for her to broach the subject. He had a long wait ahead of him; there was too much happening to bother with that soap opera. Despite the unresolved issues, Thea was glad he was there. The three of them had wildly different outlooks on life and the hunt, but they worked well together. And it was best to keep their two teams split equally. She just hoped the people inside bought their cover.

A small callbox was bolted to the outer wall; put in place recently, from the look of the freshly burnished metal. It was her show, so Thea moved to press the buzzer. She felt a hand on her arm as Romeo said, "We should take a look first."

He meant sense the place with their strange acuity. She and Romeo were the best ones for the job, another reason they were the obvious choices to go in. The three of them tightened their concentration to achieve that almost Zen-like state of awareness. A wedge of pain shot through Thea's temple almost instantly. "Damnit!" she yelped. "You guys pick this up?"

"I do not see anything unusual," Romeo said, "but I feel something. It was the same the other night."

Jake nodded. "Almost like a humming or pulsing. But it's real faint, like... well, I dunno what it's like."

"It's boring into my skull is what it's like," Thea said. "A swarm of bees or something. You really don't feel it that strongly?"

They shook their heads. "You have more acute senses for this kind of thing than we do, though," Jake pointed out. "So we can confirm that we have some serious mystical focus here. Carpenter said there was some kind of barrier around the place, back when he first laid his spiel on us. Any idea what it is?"

"Not a clue. I can only tell that it's strong. Romeo would be the one to give us the pedigree."

Romeo shook his head, indicating he had nothing useful. "The best I can say is that I do not think it is the building itself."

"Could be something inside the building, then, if it's not the actual place." Thea blinked and squinted through the gate to try getting her senses under control. "It's hard to tell for sure, but it doesn't feel like multiple, um, energy sources. If that's the right term. Just like a single big honkin' one. So it could be a barrier, just not tied to the building. Or it could be a major nasty. Or something else that'll end up surprising the bejeezus out of us at the worst possible moment."

"'Bejeezus'?" Jake asked.

"I'm trying to lighten the mood, okay?" She shrugged. "Whatever the case, there's *something* happening that is in a category completely different from normal. And from the feel of it, it's a seriously major-league something."

Jake frowned at the gate. "We're not equipped for things to get ugly. If you think this is dangerous, maybe we should just abort, right?"

"How cute, Jake. 'Abort.' You're like a little Parker when you talk like that." Thea smiled, shaking her head slightly. "I do sense power, but I *don't* sense any immediate danger from the place."

"No *immediate* danger?" Romeo frowned.

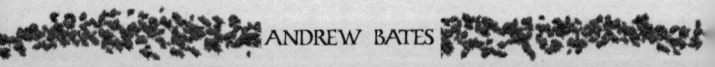

ANDREW BATES

"Well, the fact that I get a headache just standing here makes me want to cut and run. But my whole 'spider sense' deal isn't firing a red alert when I think about going inside."

Jake looked hopeful. "Well that's a good sign, right?"

"Let's hope so." They'd been standing outside the gates for a while. "We can't keep jawing out here. I say we keep on keeping on."

Thea pressed the callbox buzzer when Jake and Romeo nodded. A voice responded immediately. "We are closed. Undergoing renovations."

The man spoke only a few words, but Thea caught a definite hint of accent. She saw the little light on the callbox winked off after the voice stopped. "He cut the connection," Thea observed. "Guess he's not the chatty type."

"Maybe it's a recording," Jake said.

Thea hadn't considered that. Their plan was dead in the water if they couldn't get inside. Nothing to do but try again. She tapped the call button again and was rewarded with the voice sounding more abrupt than before. "I said that we are closed. There are—"

"I understand," Thea broke in. "I would like just a minute of your time, sir. I'm with the *Chicago Tribune* and—"

The voice cut her off in return. "We are not giving interviews," he said, and the light blinked out again. Thea expected that and punched the call button, holding it down in hopes that there was an irritating buzzing noise on the other end. The man's voice came on again, obviously at the end of its patience. "This is private property. If you do not leave immediately, we will call the police."

"I'm standing on the street, which is public property," Thea shot back, speaking rapidly to drop her depth charge before he could cut her off. "And I was planning on interviewing the police anyway. I'm sure they'd like to know where the supposedly missing Nicholas Sforza has been hiding."

The light glowed red a few seconds more, then the voice said, "One moment" before it clicked off again.

Thea felt a surge of excitement. Jake grinned and even Romeo looked pleased. She'd figured they hadn't anything to lose by playing the missing persons card right off. If they were wrong and it wasn't Sforza, no harm done. And it was possible whoever was inside might call her bluff, but Thea didn't think so. It looked like Nicholas Sforza wanted to keep a low profile. She expected the next step would be for the people in the temple to persuade Thea to tank her story.

The gate clicked open, each side folding back smoothly on hydraulics like large metal wings. The voice didn't give them any more instructions, but the intent seemed clear enough. "Here we go, fellas," she murmured.

Heart hammering in her throat, Thea Ghandour led Romeo Zheng and Jake Washington inside the Orthodox Temple of Akhenaton.

HERALDS OF THE STORM

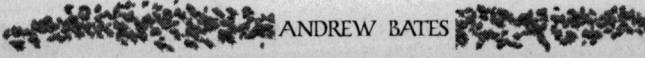

LIFE AND DEATH

TWELVE

Carpenter was willing to admit he might have made a mistake or two. Gratifying as destroying Vincent Sforza was, the whole venture ended up taking almost a full week. Even though he'd budgeted the time, he hadn't actually expected it to take that long. He'd felt he could safely leave the hunters to their own devices for a week without worrying they'd do something stupid. Now, of course, he saw leaving them unattended was a pretty stupid maneuver on *his* part. The need to exact revenge on his killer had been driving him more than the need to gain closure on the bitch's grandson. He'd been tracking Vincent Sforza for a long time, and the vampire hadn't even known it. Carpenter should have stayed in Chicago, shadowing the hunters, until he'd taken care of Nicholas Sforza. Then he could have gone after ol' Vinny at his leisure.

The fact was, Carpenter hadn't been able to resist going after Vincent Sforza any longer. His soul clamored for revenge, even as it feared the end of its unlife.

The second mistake involved the bugs he'd installed in their hideout and that big blue monster of a van. They came in damn handy in the beginning; the hunters were so nervous about monsters finding them they never bothered checking for mundane surveillance. Carpenter had miscalculated after the zombie attack. The hunters used the shitkicker's jeep after that, and Carpenter never got a chance to wire it up. Worse, they stopped using the abandoned convenience store as much. Maybe due to the cold; he wasn't sure.

And the hunters' meeting on Monday was a helluva thing. Listening to the tape he picked up from the Stop n Go after he got back Tuesday night, Carpenter was startled by how much they'd learned. They'd figured out practically everything he'd been up to for the past couple years. The nigger and the chink had learned pretty much everything about the Sforzas, all by getting on that damn Internet. As much as Carpenter had tried to learn about new technology since his return, as helpful as it had all been, quite a few things remained beyond his understanding. He knew the Internet was a great tool for communication and information. But it was so far beyond his own experience that he seldom thought about it. He thought in terms of physical contacts, bribes, rough stuff and the like to learn what he needed. It was vastly different from hitting a few keys and having the answer pop up on a screen.

The worst part was that they virtually confirmed he could influence them. That Thea had bucked his attempt to blank her memory. Plus, sounded like although the Latino woman, Lupe, wasn't free of the heavy-duty whammy he'd placed on her, she'd nonetheless been recalling strangely garbled details about him. Carpenter wondered if the chink had worked past the subtle tweaks he'd laid down, or maybe it was something about women that made it easier for them to shake off the effects?

Whatever the case, that talent was one of his most powerful tools. If they were on guard against it he'd have a much harder time nudging them in the proper direction. Carpenter wasn't panicked; a guy like him didn't get panicked, right? But he was certainly concerned. Time to make a move, get a clear idea of where the self-styled hunters were at and take stock of his plan.

He'd called Thea right after he heard the tape Tuesday night. He'd had to jam his ear against the receiver, his hearing was so fucking bad now. It was time to get the hunters back under control. They'd had too much time to themselves, were probably planning on something that would prove to be a pain in the ass for Carpenter. From the way she'd been full of piss and vinegar on the phone, actually *joking* with him, for Chrissakes, he figured he was right. Probably mouthing off at him to show off for her friends. So he rushed over to their hideout to catch them directly, bring some measure of focus back to his plans — and they weren't fucking there! The shit-kicker's jeep thing was parked just up the street, but nobody was inside the goddamn building. The new tape he'd slipped in the recorder hidden in the back room only had a couple minutes' worth of conversation. Some of them arriving, called together because Thea had something to tell them. Bitching about how one of the heaters broke, then deciding to wait in the Suburban, meet someplace else when everybody got there. He'd missed them by a half-hour.

They were in the van, so it wasn't a total wash. The bugs hooked up to the tape he'd secreted under the engine block would pick up anything they said. Even if they went someplace, he'd at least get tidbits of conversation during the ride. But just what were they talking about? What did the dame have to tell them? Just something about her mom, or had she figured his whole routine? Were they planning on coming after him? He'd drop their asses without a second thought if they tried. Carpenter forced himself to calm down, knowing what was really eating at him: The mere idea that a bunch of amateurs could puzzle him out.

And maybe that was the biggest mistake: Thinking these people would be of any use to him. They were a disorganized bunch. Even unruly and brutal as the Mob was, it had a clear chain of command, a straightforward arrangement of who did what. Carpenter thought, not for the first time, about hiring on some thugs instead. He knew that was trading one problem for another, though. Stupid and easily directed though gangsters were, they were next to useless against anything supernatural. Throw a vampire or a couple zombies at them and they screamed like little girls. At least the hunters would roll under their own power once

they were pointed in the right direction. It was just that getting them lined up was so much fucking *work*.

Parked across the street from the Stop n Go, Carpenter finally saw the big blue Suburban roll up. Only two auras inside: the wallflower and the shit-kicker. So everyone else was dropped off already? Fine. The van dropped the shit-kicker by his jeep, then moved on. Carpenter almost nailed Parker to work out some of the frustration he felt. That would be stupid, though. *Find out what the fuck they're doing first,* he commanded himself.

He waited till Parker left, then started his car and followed the Chevy.

Grabbing the tape from its hiding place was difficult only due to Carpenter's aversion to getting dirty. Playing it back in his hideout, he heard them sitting in the van for a long time, but the idiots kept talking while they waited for Thea to show up. Carpenter heard his phone conversation from her end and the first part of Thea's plan, then the tape ran out. He destroyed the cassette player and the table it sat on before calming down.

"Get it under control, shitbird," he snarled to himself. The room was utterly silent otherwise; he didn't even breathe heavily — hell, didn't breathe at all — from the exertion of shattering the wooden table.

Pacing the length of the hideout, Carpenter struggled to rein in his emotions. He didn't know everything they had planned, but he'd learned enough. They knew he had another agenda but they hadn't confirmed what it was. If they had balls they'd've come gunning for him. Instead, they were going to check out the temple. Reconnaissance.

Maxwell Carpenter's teeth gleamed in the light. It wasn't how he'd planned it, but it looked like the hunters would do the job he wanted them to after all.

•••

For Thea, walking through the entryway of the Orthodox Temple of Akhenaton was like stepping into the ancient past. The main doors were huge panels of shining bronze eight feet high, small series of hieroglyphs running in bands across the surface. A wiry dark-skinned man, looking more African than Arabian and dressed in simple white djellaba and turban, closed the doors behind them as silently as he'd pulled them open. Thea noted that each slab was at least three inches thick and proved to be wood on the interior. They found themselves in a front hall, a large space with a shallow arched ceiling ten feet high. The floor was of the same material as the rest of the building, some kind of slate or sandstone a rich gold in tone. A series of arches separated the entryway from the rest of the main temple space. Thea could see only a portion of it from where she stood. It didn't look that large for a place of worship, perhaps fifty feet deep by one hundred feet wide. From her recollections, the minaret was in the right spot to be above the main temple. Stepping forward, Thea saw the unmistakable angle of the inside of a pyramid rising above the temple. She realized the minaret had been constructed around the pyramid, as if to shield it from view. Lights were arranged in the space between the two structures, shining through the translucent material the pyramid was made of to create a warm, ethereal illumination throughout the temple below.

The rest of the decor was decidedly Egyptian rather than Arabic or Muslim. Egyptian statuary and hieroglyphs adorned the walls. The pillars looked like something transported directly from the Middle Kingdom. For all Thea knew, maybe they were — hell, the whole place might have been. Urns and bas reliefs could be seen around the temple's interior. Everything Thea looked at gave off a resonance she couldn't ignore. A part of her buried deep for years stirred at the sight.

Their silent doorman stood by the right hand wall, his gaze directed to the man standing in the center of the entry hall. Middle-aged and of Arabic descent, the man wore a simple gray suit and a dour expression. He was portly to say the least, but radiated strength and solidity that overshad-

owed any impression of being fat or sluggish. "What is it that you want?" he demanded, looking them over critically.

After taking a deep breath, Thea stepped forward and extended a hand in greeting. "Tina Grant, *Chicago Tribune*." When he continued staring at her coldly, ignoring her hand, Thea dug through her purse for a business card. It was the work of an hour that morning to scan the card from a reporter she'd once dated, plug in her own name and a new phone number, then print a few business cards on pre-cut Avery card sheets. The wonders of desktop publishing. The number was to her cell phone, which Dean had in the Suburban ready to play her editor in case these guys wanted to check her credentials. Poking into her purse also gave Thea the chance to check on the small walkie talkie she carried, the main component of the headsets they used on the estate raid. She'd set it at a low volume beforehand so that if it belched static it wouldn't carry through her purse. It meant the gang in the Suburban couldn't catch their conversation, but it should be enough to register yells or gunshots or any other signs of trouble. She caught the faint crackle of static as she dug around, in fact, so Thea turned down the volume a bit more.

She handed over the card as she continued her introductions. "That is my photographer, Jake Bookman, and this gentleman is Chow Li. He's with the *Hong Kong Times*, doing a piece on the differences between Eastern and Western news focus." She leaned forward to bring the man into her confidence. "He's been bugging us for almost a week now." It wasn't the greatest cover in the world, but she was counting on the fact these people would be more concerned about the fact they'd been found out than on checking backgrounds. And if it somehow did turn into a legitimate story, it wasn't like journalists had never fed someone lines just to get a scoop.

As it turned out, she probably needn't have bothered. The man took the card gingerly with an obvious expression of distaste, hardly looking over the information before pocketing it. "Again, what is it that you want?"

Tying together his ethnicity with the accent from the words he'd spoken, Thea felt confident pegging this guy as Egyptian. And probably not a naturalized American citizen, either, considering how he was obviously distressed to have a woman speaking to him as an equal. *Well, fuck him.* Maybe the culture clash would make it easier to run their game. "All right, I'll cut to the chase, Mister...?" He just looked at her coldly. "...Okay; I'll *really* cut to the chase. We have reason to believe that a man who disappeared under mysterious circumstances has been staying in this temple."

"And this is a concern of yours for what reason?"

She smiled. "It's *news*! A respected businessman whose family has a history of ties to organized crime vanishes — kidnapped or dead, no one knows. Especially curious since the rest of his family has been subject to a recent rash of bizarre suicides, accidents and otherwise suspicious deaths. Then it turns out he's hiding from public view, telling not one of his friends or relatives, let alone the authorities. The *Tribune* wants to know why, sir!"

The man exhaled heavily. "We do not care what you want, woman. This is a private facility and is not involved—"

"Don't bother feeding me the company line, sir," Thea's voice took on a steely tone. "We both know Nicholas Sforza is here, otherwise we'd still be outside talking to Chicago's finest right now. The only question is, do we get the full scoop or do I run with what I've already gathered from my sources?"

Anger was evident in the big man's eyes, but otherwise his composure was as cool as ever. He opened his mouth in a retort, then stopped short. His head turned slightly, as if he was listening to something. As the man looked over Thea and her companions, she saw a small flesh-colored device in her ear. Some kind of miniature radio, she guessed; easily the kind of thing a security firm would have access to. She

didn't see any transmitter, though. Maybe he had one at his wrist like the Secret Service.

The man looked displeased as he cleared his throat with a low guttural cough and nodded curtly. "You will follow me," he said, then marched down the aisle running along the main temple's right hand wall past a series of low stone benches. Thea had expected more back-and-forth; she wasn't sure what to make of this turn of events. They were in this far, though; no turning back now.

They trooped after the man, the darker skinned attendant bringing up the rear. Thea felt almost overwhelmed by the sense of great age and history in the place. Each step seemed to send her memories shaking, like her hazy memories of being in this place — or one very much like it — were contained inside a fragile shell. One good blow would break the shell wide open.

"You guys pick up anything?" Thea whispered as they walked.

"Both men are mortal," Romeo murmured. "Beyond that, nothing."

"Same here," Jake chimed in. "But doesn't it strike you as odd that these guys are foreign?"

"Why? It's a funky foreign cult, draws in foreigners," she hissed back.

"Maybe before, but Sforza bought the place. And he's Italian, right? Italian-American; whatever. So did he keep the old staff on board or did we just happen to meet the only Arabic guy on his payroll?"

The Egyptian paused before a simple wooden door at the far end of the main chamber. The attendant moved forward quickly and opened it, stepping back to let the heavyset man enter. Just before they followed, Thea shot Jake a look. "You know how far we are from figuring out even half of the coincidences and puzzles we've stumbled over the past few days?"

"Perhaps we should enter the room and see if any of these questions are answered," Romeo suggested with just a hint of sarcasm.

Thea rolled her eyes before stepping over the threshold.

• • •

Carpenter sat in the Lincoln, a parabolic mic directed at the Chevy Suburban half a block away. He didn't have the kind of gear to tap into the bugs he'd planted in the van, but the microphone did the job about as well. Unlike the Internet, Carpenter had little trouble recognizing the usefulness of a gadget like this, and had applied it to his monitoring of the hunters, and others, on any number of occasions.

The van was parked facing away from him, just up the street from the temple. The wallflower, the shit-kicker, and the queer sat in the vehicle. The idea of those three as backup brought a smile to Carpenter's face. Talk about a Mickey Mouse operation. Combining the conversation he overheard now with the partial plans he'd listened to the previous night, Carpenter determined that the three idiots outside were monitoring their friends via a walkie talkie in Thea's purse. If there was trouble, they were supposed to rush in like the cavalry and save the day. Carpenter could think of a half-dozen flaws in this plan, but at this point his agenda *counted* on something going wrong.

He watched as the other half of the brain trust got out of a cab in front of the temple, then stood around for a year and a day before finally getting buzzed in. Carpenter wondered what they'd said to get inside. The walkie talkie in the Suburban picked up only muffled sounds and it wasn't like the parabolic mic made noises any clearer. Add in Carpenter's hearing problems and it was pointless to even guess. As a result, it took him a little while to determine why the people in the van got excited. Adjusting the mic's position and volume, Carpenter finally figured it out. The

walkie talkie was spitting out static. They'd lost touch with their pals inside.

From the shouts and swearing, it was clear they were trying to decide if Thea and her boyfriends were in trouble or if the temple itself was somehow interfering with transmission. Carpenter didn't really care which. All he knew was this might be his only chance to act.

•••

Thea found the room jarringly Western after everything else she'd seen in the place. A perfectly-preserved sarcophagus stood in the near corner and small objects d'art stood on side tables and hung from the walls. The rest of the room was given over to traditional office furniture. A desk faced them from the near wall, supporting a hooded halogen lamp, a phone, and a computer with a slim flat screen monitor and compact hard drive. A pair of simple yet stylish wooden chairs stood on the near side of the desk. To the right, next to another door, a broad couch and two more wooden chairs framed a low circular coffee table.

Thea registered most of this as an afterthought. Her attention was focused on the man standing by their chaperone.

Perhaps six feet tall and solidly built, Nicholas Sforza avoided looking stocky thanks to his long face. His eyes were set deeply into his skull, giving him an intense, brooding look that casting directors love. He wasn't conventionally handsome, his nose a little too large and his jaw, though strong, not quite wide enough. He was very striking, though, drawing attention simply by standing there. Thea put him at his early 30s, give or take. Most distinctive next to his deep eyes was a large scar running from one temple into his hairline. His dark hair was cut short and brushed back from his forehead. It fell in a tousle over the scar line, the thatch of hair grown around it a startling white. He was dressed in black rubber-soled shoes, charcoal slacks and a dark blue crewneck shirt that fit him snugly about the chest, accentuating a well-developed physique. The sleeves were pushed up revealing hairy forearms braced akimbo as he looked over his visitors. He also wore an understated gold scarab necklace and an intricately wrought gold bracelet. Both were clearly of Egyptian design, but Thea didn't know if they were contemporary pieces or ancient jewelry.

There was an air about Sforza; a kind of regal, imperious quality that made Thea want to bow her head. She focused her vision to cut through the mystical interference she'd experienced since the temple gate, expecting Sforza to be the focal point of that energy. That proved not to be the case. He was a nexus of *something*, though; Thea got a clear sensation of impending trouble. Not for her, but for Sforza himself. Noting Romeo jerk in surprise, she found him almost completely obscured behind pulsing waves of focal energy, like a heat shimmer coming off a road in the desert. She'd never sensed anything like it, but it made her soul go cold. "Romeo!" Thea blurted, forgetting their flimsy ruse in her surprise and concern.

Romeo shook his head, indicating he was fine but obviously puzzled by something. Jake was looking around, trying to get a sense for what was happening on the rarified level of sensation that remained beyond him.

Nicholas Sforza spoke then, his voice strong and carrying a subtle resonance. "You're the guy from the other night," he said to Romeo. Then, looking at Thea and Jake, he stated, "And you are not from the *Tribune*. Or any other publication."

Need to focus; we're in a heap full of strangeness right now. Unsure of how to proceed, Thea stuck gamely with her cover. "Please, Mr. Sforza. Your man has my card; check with the paper if you like. You'll see—"

"Oh, come on," he said, "cut it out. You're not fooling anybody and you know it."

There was a tense pause, then Jake sighed. "Okay, okay. I like being straightforward anyway. I'm Jake, this is Thea and Sam. We call him Romeo, though; long story."

"A good start." Sforza's stern expression relaxed slightly into amusement. "Now what exactly are you doing here?"

"We're trying to figure that out ourselves," Thea admitted. Truth be told, she hadn't actually expected to meet the guy. If he was so cautious about being seen in town, why would he step right out and talk to some people who knocked on the front door? From the way Jake was acting, he was similarly nonplussed. Romeo continued staring intently at Sforza as if working through some kind of puzzle. "Okay, let's start with who — or perhaps I should say *what* — brought us around. You—"

Then, with perfect dramatic timing, they all heard a distant crash and the alarms went off.

• • •

In a heartbeat, Carpenter was out of his car and approaching the Suburban from along the sidewalk. When he reached the back of the van, Carpenter stepped over to the driver's side and moved forward until the whiney dame, Lilly, noticed the motion in her side view mirror. It took a couple seconds, but she finally turned from bitching at the other two to see what the dark shape was in her mirror.

Once Carpenter got eye contact through the reflection, he pushed his will into Lilly's mind just like he did with Buster in Vegas. His desire was different this time, though. He didn't want the bitch dead; at least, not before she did what he wanted. He knew he was taking a gamble. If she was on her guard against him, his mental trick wouldn't do a damn thing. She'd just see some guy in a black suit with his eye glowing a funny green color. And since they knew about his power, she would be on guard, given half the chance. Which meant Carpenter had to use the element of surprise.

Luck was on his side. Lilly Belva, distracted by the complication of the walkie-talkie, glanced in the mirror at the approaching shape. Carpenter's mental command hit her gray matter like a sucker punch to the kidney. He played on the woman's concern for her friends and hatred of the undead, boosting already active feelings into an overwhelming directive. Suddenly, more than anything else Lilly could conceive of, she wanted to get inside that temple.

Lilly's reflection shifted as she looked up the street. Then, instead of launching herself out the driver's side as Carpenter expected, she fired up the Suburban's engine. Even outside and with bad hearing, Carpenter caught the yells of surprise from inside the van as it squealed from the curb and roared across traffic at the Temple of Akhenaton.

The big Chevy barreled along at an angle toward the temple. A car swerved wildly as the Suburban lunged into traffic, forcing Carpenter to leap to one side. His preternatural reflexes were easily up to the challenge, though he was upset at dirtying his overcoat by rolling on the sidewalk. Tire squeals and honking split the mid-morning air, then a crash of metal and glass as a car in the oncoming lane clipped the Suburban's rear. Carpenter got to his feet in time to see the van, still building up a good head of steam despite the Mitsubishi that sheared off its rear bumper, crash into the temple's front gate.

The collision was tremendous, the sound painful even to Carpenter's dull ears. The van stopped dead, its rear lifting almost a foot from the ground as the momentum bled forward. Its front crumpled against the heavy steel gates and smoke billowed from under the hood. Carpenter knew Sforza reinforced the gates after he moved in, but the impact still did damage. The right gate buckled but held to its hinges as the left gate took the brunt of the collision. Its lower third tore loose from the hinge and folded inward, twisting down to slam heavily onto the front of the Suburban.

Incredible. Carpenter had wanted the temple's residents thrown into turmoil. He hadn't planned on a full-scale assault in broad daylight.

Nothing to be done about it; he'd simply have to adapt. Carpenter dashed across the street amid the chaos and leapt on the Suburban's roof. He sensed confusion and panic from

the van's occupants as he dashed across the metal. He launched himself over the temple wall, landing heavily on the tiled stones of the courtyard. If he was mortal, he'd probably have driven his knees through his pelvis on impact. Then again, if he was mortal he never would have been able to jump over twenty yards. Yanking his trusty Colts from their shoulder holsters, Carpenter sprinted forward.

•••

Thea couldn't believe how stupid they'd been. Marching into an unknown situation without weapons or a plan beyond "talk to the guy." Insanity! Then Romeo compounded the problem.

One second they were about to lay it all out for the mysterious Nicholas Sforza, the next he was accusing them of launching an attack. The big Egyptian guy, who Sforza called Gamal, pulled a huge damn pistol from someplace, commanded them to leave purse and camera on the desk, and seconds later was directing them through the office's other door and down a narrow corridor that led further into the temple. The silent attendant also produced a gun from someplace and led the way. Sforza stayed behind to coordinate things or whatever it is that strange guys with Mob ties and the focus of some bizarre mystic nexus do.

They followed the robed guy around a corner to see a door twenty feet ahead. As the attendant reached to open the door, Romeo gave her a look. Her eyes widened in dismay when she realized what he was about to do. If she just stood there, though, he'd get them all killed. So when Romeo grabbed for the robed guy's pistol, Thea lashed out at Gamal. The Egyptian turned reflexively to take aim on Romeo, so Thea's kick caught the guy squarely on the hand. The gun going off drowned the sound of Gamal's wrist snapping. Then man and pistol fell to the ground, the former writhing in pain and the latter smoking slightly.

Jake stood looking completely baffled, then snatched the Desert Eagle before the grimacing Egyptian could grab it with his good hand. Thea was focused on Romeo, sure he'd been nailed in the back by the stray shot. He looked none the worse for wear, crouched and smacking the robed guy's head against the unopened door.

"Romeo! Stop it!" She grabbed him by the arm and yanked. He swung at her, Thea blocking before she consciously registered what he'd done. They stared at one another in shock and anger for a second until Jake's voice roused them.

"Thea! Romeo!" He scowled, then looked apologetically at Gamal. "Sir, I'm really sorry. We didn't plan on attacking you, but this is a crazy situation. If you could just let us know what's happened, maybe we can clear everything up before anyone else gets hurt." Thea and Romeo looked at Jake just as incredulously as the Egyptian did, while the robed fellow dazedly tried to regain his senses.

• • •

Carpenter was a step from the temple doors when they swung inward. He knew Nicholas Sforza buffaloed his security firm into thinking he was away in hiding, handling all his business remotely. The guy's new lackeys were camel jockeys Sforza brought back with him from, well, wherever he went after Carpenter tried to have him kill himself. So Carpenter wasn't surprised when a pair of them rushed out of the temple. They looked a little ridiculous, wearing robes and turbans and holding compact machine pistols with some big round things on the ends. Carpenter had been in the ground too long to be able to identify guns the size of a pocketbook that could spit more lead in a second than a Tommy gun could in a minute. He knew the things wouldn't stop him, but they'd fuck him up and slow him down. Best to not give them a chance to begin with.

Carpenter barely slowed his forward momentum. He crossed his arms, fingers squeezing rapidly twice on the triggers just as he passed between the two men. He would have fired faster, but the triggers didn't spring back quickly enough. Besides, a pair of rounds for each would do the trick as well as a dozen. Bullets tore into the guards, knocking them back into the doors they'd just opened. Carpenter

didn't register the bloody smears the men left on the brass plating as they fell. His senses were devoted entirely to the spiritual pulse he felt emanating from Nicholas Sforza. Carpenter picked him up instantly, maybe a dozen yards ahead and to the right.

Carpenter's connection to Sforza, his spiritual need for the grandson who might otherwise have been his, operated on a mystical frequency all its own. His normal deathsight wasn't like X-ray vision. Carpenter had no idea if anyone else was with Sforza. For all he knew, the hunters could be beating the guy's ass right now. Or he could be down there with a dozen heavily armed thugs.

There were two reasons Carpenter wanted the hunters in on the job. The first was to break down the supernatural warding around the temple. The wallflower took care of that when she wrecked the gate, giving him entry to his target's sanctum.

The second, and more significant, reason had to do with the aura, the tremendous energy contained within the temple. He'd first noticed it weeks ago when he'd tracked Sforza there, but only when he'd come near the walls. His deathsight had picked up a staggering amount of life energy tied to something impossibly ancient. The wards around the temple hid its aura, otherwise anyone in the greater Chicago area with a degree of psychic sensitivity would have picked it up. Carpenter hadn't known what it was, only that it was more powerful than he. Probably some ancient vampire, maybe another Sforza like Vincent, in cahoots with young Nicholas.

The whatever-it-was became the deciding factor for why he went with the hunters instead of a bunch of greedy, slack-jawed gangsters. Carpenter wasn't worried about facing the supernatural; he had enough power and plain old nastiness to take on about anything. But he didn't like going in blind. Sforza was somehow changed, but that was an unknown he was willing to handle. Especially now, since destroying the undead Vincent Sforza had given him a tremendous spiritual charge. Carpenter was confident he could take whatever the bastard could dish out. But Sforza *and* a mysterious ancient entity? Carpenter wasn't a fucking moron. That's what cannon fodder like Thea and her pals were for.

But the current circumstances were not what Carpenter had in mind. He still had no idea what the other thing was, and he hadn't had a chance to position the hunters as an appropriately attractive target for it. He was going in blind, with no clue as to circumstances inside. Only an idiot would charge in with guns blazing in this situation. But this was probably the best chance Carpenter had… and besides, the hunger of revenge was upon him. His soul cried out for closure, to finish destroying the last of those who had killed him.

The rational, scheming part of him finally forced itself forward. Dashing in recklessly might destroy him, his vengeance unrealized. The fear returned then, the fear of death, of returning to Hell. There had to be another way. It was enough to bring him out of the bloodlust, at least partially.

Standing in the temple entryway with precious seconds ticking by, Carpenter saw it was time to re-evaluate his agenda. Now that he had access, he had a much clearer read on the entity, even though it was still some distance away. He sensed that it was quiescent. If it was a vampire, it was sleeping in the day; if it was something else, it seemed not at all perturbed by the chaos breaking loose in the temple. But, in fact, it didn't seem to have any awareness. Instinctive as Carpenter's paranormal senses were, he didn't even try to define what he perceived. In his dead gut, he felt that the source of this aura wasn't active; it felt like, for lack of a better concept, a battery. A power source. A tool or a weapon, not unlike his straight razor. This thing felt about a million times more powerful than that, though.

His decision made, Maxwell Carpenter ran through the temple down the left hand aisle.

•••

Thea glanced uncomfortably at Jake and Romeo, then down at Gamal. The large man had gotten his pain under control and looked at them expressionlessly. Then Thea realized his throat was moving irregularly and a faint muttering came from his parted lips.

"Hey!" she yelled, reaching forward to yank his collar down. The starched fabric almost cracked as it bent. And there against the coppery skin of his neck was a round black thing attached to a wire. "It's some kind of throat mic! You guys are state of the art all the way, huh?"

"Come on, man," Jake said, looking even more uncomfortable as he waved the pistol at Gamal, "I'm serious. We don't want any trouble. Tell your boss or whomever's on the other end of that."

Gamal glared down at Thea's hand, as if her very touch was an insult. "Your words are a lie. Others have broken the gate, they enter the temple with weapons."

"Oh, crap. What the hell were they thinking?"

"Perhaps it is not Parker and the others," Romeo said, shifting his attention between the corner they'd just come around and the closed door.

"Crashing the gate? Sounds like Parker to me," Thea said, letting go of the guy's collar and stepping out of arm's reach before he decided to get frisky.

"Carpenter's pretty violent, though. Likes blowing things up and all," Jake observed.

Romeo looked at Gamal and his dazed cohort. "I do not think it matters who it was. They believe we came to attack them. Our best option is to leave, quickly."

"Too late for that," Nicholas Sforza said as he stepped around the corner, the promise of death in his eyes.

• • •

Carpenter's supernatural radar gave him a general idea where Nicholas Sforza was even as he used it to track down the other aura. It seemed the bitch's grandson was ahead and to the right, heading further into the temple on pace with Carpenter. He wasn't sure if Sforza was coming around to meet him, if he was running away… or if he was heading for the mystic power source himself. Carpenter poured on the speed, rushing past the low benches and statuary heedless of any guards who might be hiding in the chamber. In fact, the main temple seemed completely empty. The alarms that blared when he first got inside were turned off almost immediately afterward, so the only sound was his wingtips clattering rapidly against the stone floor.

Carpenter reached the plain door at the end and kicked it in. The door tore loose and cracked against the room's far wall. Carpenter stepped into an office or cloakroom perhaps twelve feet on a side. A wooden table, some cabinets and boxes filled space along the walls, and some garments hung on hooks along the near wall. One door stood to his right while another was set in the opposite wall. Sensing the aura further on, Carpenter kicked open the second door, this time gently enough to pop it open without sending it flying down the corridor. Carpenter was greeted with a burst of automatic fire that staggered him back. The shock of surprise was infinitely more hurtful than the pinpricks of 9mm rounds. Carpenter collapsed immediately, playing dead — *really* dead — so these trigger happy fucks wouldn't keep ripping into his corpse. It worked. The two shitheels — wearing fatigues and boots instead of robes and sandals like the first pair — stopped firing, one stepping forward to check him out.

Carpenter blew out the guy's kneecap to keep him busy and to provide cover while he nailed the other guard with a double tap to the upper body. The asshole was still moving after that — fucking body armor; Christ he missed the old days! — so Carpenter dropped his aim eighteen inches and fired again. Carpenter looked over at the other guard holding his knee and staring in shock at his buddy. "At least you die with your dick in one piece," he said before planting a round in the poor bastard's brain pan.

He got to his feet and headed down the hall, slapping a new clip in the right-hand pistol as he went. It was only down half a clip, but it was best to go in fresh; nothing worse than running out of bullets in the middle of your entrance. The left was close to topped off, so he stuck with it for the time being. He paused at the corner, facing a door a few feet down. He tried to get a better idea of what lay ahead, but his deathsight was being overwhelmed by the power of the aura. Even Sforza was but a hazy blip on his awareness. Whatever this thing was, it came across as a helluva lot more powerful inside this temple than it had outside.

Looking down at his ruined suit made Carpenter furious. He prepared to charge forward, kick the door in and make someone else pay for ruining his outfit. His weakened hearing never registered the telltale *ka-chak!* of a shotgun being primed behind him a second before the hallway filled with thunder.

THIRTEEN

Thea felt like she was in some fucked up John Woo movie come to life. Sforza stood in profile in the middle of the hall, a blunt submachinegun with a sound suppressor pointed right at Thea. Romeo was in a traditional policeman's two-handed stance, the Desert Eagle he'd lifted from the attendant aimed at Sforza's clavicle. Jake, obviously unwilling to fire the gun he held, nonetheless kept shifting it between Sforza and the kneeling Gamal in front of him. And everyone was shouting at everyone else to drop their guns before someone got hurt.

Someone was going to get nervous and do something stupid. Then most likely Thea would end up getting shot. She had to diffuse things, but the chaos of the situation combined with her ongoing sensory overload made it difficult to focus.

Then the need to duck flared from deep in her reptile brain, her body following the command before she even realized what she was doing. The muted blast of a shotgun roared in the same instant she dropped down and forward in the narrow corridor. It tripped the switch on the tension in the hall and started the obligatory gunfire.

Sforza's weapon gouged a chunk of rock from the wall where Thea had stood a second before. Romeo fired three quick shots in rapid succession then another three, rocking Sforza back with impact even as he moved swiftly out of the way. Jake yelped as Gamal lunged forward, grabbing at the pistol with his good hand while swinging the elbow of his injured arm at Jake's face.

In dramatic echo of Romeo's shots, the air directly before Sforza cracked and popped like a live electrical wire. Sforza bounced off the far wall and tumbled back around the corner in a controlled fall. From where she lay, Thea could see Sforza roll to his feet. Blood flowed down his shirt front, but it looked like the six point blank shots had somehow only grazed him. *Okay, so he's not normal either.* Now that she knew to sense for it, Thea caught an aura surrounding Sforza and another, stronger energy around his heart. Instead of charging back around the corner, Sforza looked down at his chest with a grimace and began sketching quick symbols on his shirt with his own blood. *Right. Definitely not normal.*

Thea figured it was the perfect time to get the hell out of there, but Romeo and Jake were having trouble with Gamal. The big Egyptian was putting up a tremendous fight despite his broken wrist. There was hardly any room to maneuver in the narrow space, which helped even the odds in Gamal's favor. Then there were the gunshots and yelling she could still hear through the door. Okay, so try getting past the nigh-invulnerable Nicholas Sforza and run out the front to face the police who were bound to arrive any minute? Or head the other way into the middle of a firefight?

Thea had no real interest in fighting Sforza, but she doubted the guy was willing to listen to reason at the moment. And it was likely that if their friends *had* come charging in, they were the ones making the racket on the other side of the door. Thea reasoned it was best to get everyone together and retreat like nobody's business.

Thea rolled to her feet in the corner of the hallway behind Gamal. The guy knew he was in a bad way and tried turning to face the three of them. Thea used the corner to brace her arms and swept Gamal, knocking him back toward Sforza.

Then Sforza finished his bizarre writing in blood and Thea caught a sudden flare of energy from his chest. "Let's go!" she yelled, lunging toward Jake and Romeo. "Through the door! Come on!"

•••

Carpenter was sick of these fucking hunters. They'd gotten him past the physical and mystic security Sforza had put in place, but now they wouldn't leave him alone. The shit-kicker had nailed him in the back with a shotgun blast Carpenter hadn't even heard coming. Then the wallflower squeezed past and yelled at Carpenter to stop — and he found he couldn't fucking move! The dame just stood there, body rigid, glaring at him like she wished looks could kill. Well, thanks to whatever she was doing, they probably would. He tried forcing his will on her, but she was ready for it this time.

Then the shit-kicker held his hand out and heat shimmered for a second before flame burst right from his fist. What the hell?! The guy made a flaming sword out of friggin' nothing! He clearly wanted to stick the thing in Carpenter a couple dozen times, but the hallway was too narrow for him to just charge forward. He had to jostle past the wallflower; looked like it took all her concentration to keep Carpenter in place.

Then Carpenter faintly heard yells and gunfire from the other end of the corridor, with returning *pop! pop! pop!* and cries from the fat guy covering their backs. They all ducked, as if they could somehow move faster than bullets. Looked like nobody got hit except maybe the fat guy, but Carpenter didn't much care. The attack broke the wallflower's concentration for a second, but that's all Carpenter needed.

He brought up both pistols and fired furiously. She probably had a flak vest on, so Carpenter shot high. The rounds staggered her off the wall and into her fat buddy, then marched up to smash through her face like a bat bursting an overripe pumpkin. The shit-kicker charged, his face twisted with rage as he swung his flaming brand. Carpenter shifted aim, easy enough in the tight corridor, but the big

guy was too quick. He only got one shot off to the shit-kicker's midsection, into the damn vest, before the sword struck his left hand. The fire cleaved right through the automatic and sheared off Carpenter's first two fingers. The bullet in the chamber went off from the heat, which made the whole gun blow up. Shrapnel tore through Carpenter's hand and sliced across his torso. The shit-kicker screamed and recoiled as white-hot pieces of metal cut into him. Snarling against the dull pain, Carpenter kicked the guy in the nuts and rolled to the side around the L of the hallway.

Silence descended, the cries from around the corner a buzz Carpenter ignored as he looked over his ruined hand. He barely felt the injury, same as the shotgun blast he'd taken. It was clear his arm and his side were pretty fucked up, though. Good thing he was still charged from Vincent Sforza's death. He focused on channeling that energy to knit his damaged flesh while desperately changing clips one-handed on his other pistol.

Not a moment too soon. He caught a flicker of shadow as one of the hunters tried to get the jump on him. Feeling sluggish from forcing his wounds to heal, Carpenter still got a couple wild shots off. Didn't hit anything except the stone wall, but drove back whoever was coming. They were in a stand-off, the corner of the hall giving them each cover and leaving them trading blind volleys.

His wounds faded to a dull ache and he could flex his off hand, but the missing fingers were a bitch. Didn't know if he could get them to grow back. Now wasn't the time to see; he didn't want to blow all his energy on that when he might need it to face down Sforza.

Speaking of which, did he still want to bother with the fucking power source? He sensed Sforza was nearby; probably going for the whatever-it-was himself. Fuck it; he'd better just go after the bitch's grandson. Try and get him before he got to the whatsit. To hell with these hunters, too. He didn't have the time to waste trading bullets with morons. At least it seemed like they were hesitating to press the attack. Good; he'd get on the move before they found their balls again.

•••

Thea grabbed the gun from a grateful Jake and pushed him after Romeo. Romeo waved his off hand to get them behind him, then dragged the groggy attendant to his feet and shoved him through the door at gunpoint. They stepped into an antechamber. Immediately to their left were a pair of upright sarcophagi, their gold- and jewel-inlaid lids closed. A door faced them on the other side of the antechamber twenty feet away. To the right, the room opened into another temple space. It was difficult to tell this second temple's exact configuration. The only light came from the doorway they'd just run through, which Thea yanked closed behind her. In the brief glimpse the light offered, she saw some stone benches nearby and a low, blocky shape near the other end of the room. An altar, perhaps? The aura radiating throughout the temple was even stronger in here, and seemed to have its source on, in, or behind the low stone slab. It was strong enough that, along with everything else, Thea couldn't get a decent read on their best choice of action.

The four guards hiding under cover in the room helped decide that. They popped up as soon as the hunters burst into the room, yelling in Arabic and waving submachineguns. If not for the attendant Romeo held like a shield in front of them, Thea knew they'd be dead right now. This must have been where the gunfire from moments before had come from, but it was impossible to tell who they'd been shooting at. Wasn't like they had the luxury of investigating. Four agitated goons on the one hand and a pissed Sforza and sidekick ready to burst through the door Thea had slammed closed behind her meant they had only one decent option: the doorway opposite the alcove.

Romeo shouted back at the guards in Mandarin and English as he shoved the attendant along, Jake and Thea trying to stay behind them as they hustled for the door.

They were halfway across when the door they'd exited slammed back on its hinges. A second later, the opposite one opened.

Thea, Romeo, and Jake found themselves in between a bloody Nicholas Sforza and a livid Maxwell Carpenter, while the temple guards' shouts echoed around the chamber.

•••

Carpenter felt a surge of hate when he saw Nicholas Sforza. In that moment, he forgot about everything else. He barely registered the trio of hunters and their hostage standing before him. He didn't hear the shouts from the guards in the room or from the hunters behind him. The only thing that existed for him in that moment, the alpha and omega of his reality, was Nicholas Sforza.

Something moved in his way then, something kept him from realizing his revenge. Something else darkened his sight for a moment, stirring him to action. Carpenter's hand flashed up in a blur, firing his remaining .45 so fast and so forcefully that he broke the trigger. That was fine, the obstruction was gone. Moving forward, Carpenter dropped the gun and pulled the straight razor. He leaped at Sforza with strength fueled by sixty years of hate.

•••

Thea watched in shock as the strange dark swirls that surrounded Romeo since they entered the temple flared to dark brilliance. He reacted quickly when the doors opened, twisting so the attendant faced Sforza and bringing the Desert Eagle to point at Carpenter's face. Romeo didn't give any warning, just started firing. The first bullet tore through Carpenter's jaw, but the following rounds missed him completely. Moving faster than Thea's eyes could track, Carpenter ducked to one side and raised a pistol. The gun blazed inches from Romeo's chest, the bullets tearing vicious channels through his body. An implosion of spiritual energy rocked the Asian as he flew backward, gore trailing from him in hideous streamers.

Thea barely had time to register that Carpenter had just blown Romeo away. Other flashes of light and cracks of gunfire erupted from the darkened temple. Instinct kicked in, perhaps augmented by her strange new abilities; she wasn't exactly in a frame of mind to evaluate it at the time. Thea shoved Jake into the narrow space between the two sarcophagi and turned to go after Romeo. The attendant's head struck her on the shoulder, knocking her off balance and causing her to slip on the suddenly bloody floor. A silvery arc flashed above and to her right. Distractedly, she realized that Carpenter had sliced the attendant's head from his body with some kind of knife, and was now slashing at Sforza.

The fall cracked Thea's own head against the ground, knocking some degree of clear thought into her brain and inadvertently saving her life. The guards in the temple were running forward yelling wildly, obviously worried about firing in case they might hit Sforza or Gamal. With Thea lying senseless covered in blood, they ignored her in favor of attacking Carpenter as best they could.

Thea rolled away, heading to where Romeo lay sprawled and bleeding. She could sense more clearly now than she could a moment ago. Why, she didn't know and didn't care. The only thing in her awareness at present was Samuel Zheng.

• • •

Carpenter found more things hindering him now, and the object of his revenge was... running? He roared with inchoate rage, incensed that Sforza would try to escape him. Every portion of the energy Carpenter gained from destroying his own murderer was channeled through his body. The guards leaping on him were like fleas to an elephant; a minor irritation, nothing more. Carpenter flicked an arm and one of the distractions was gone. A few cuts of the razor and the others were gone also.

Advancing into the hallway, Carpenter faced one last obstacle. His deathsight showed a body with a strong life

force, someone that under other circumstances might have caused him some degree of distress. It mattered little now what this impediment might try. It was keeping him from retribution. Carpenter swung his arm so that the razor might quench its thirst.

• • •

Thea knew Romeo was dead. Her damned special senses told her as much. She scrambled to him no less quickly, as if she could somehow save him if only she could get to him in time. The dim light from the two doorways allowed shadows to disguise the worst of the damage. Still, there was no ignoring the ruin that was Romeo's chest. His torso was wet and black with blood, his face spattered with gore and twisted in naked shock.

Lifting his savaged form and holding it close, Thea barely noticed a body fly over her head and crash against the far wall as Carpenter flung a guard away with breathtaking strength. The screams of the other guards shook her slightly from her daze. Thea looked up to see the other three guards sprawled unnaturally at Carpenter's feet, the same gleaming blade dripping gore in his right hand. Intractable and unstoppable, Carpenter stepped into the opposite hall into which Sforza retreated. Thea caught yells in Arabic, then terrible screams.

Silence fell seconds later. Thea continued rocking on the blood-slick floor, holding Romeo's dead body in her lap.

• • •

Carpenter followed his target with the implacability of death itself. The power running through his body lent him tremendous speed. He overtook Sforza in the study as the man was in the act of scratching symbols into a bullet with a penknife.

"Shit!" Sforza cried, scrambling to chamber the round as Carpenter lunged across the room.

Then, just as he grabbed his prize in hands strong enough to powder marble, the gun roared. A blaze of agony, the first true physical sensation he'd felt in over half a century, tore through Maxwell Carpenter.

• • •

Thea didn't realize she'd slipped away from reality again until she felt someone shaking her. Looking up in a daze, she saw Jake Washington standing over her, his face ashen with nausea and sorrow. Past him she made out Parker Moston standing between the doorways with weapon ready. Turning in response to movement to her left, she saw Dean Sankowski, bloody hands covering his face as quiet sobs wracked his body. She noted with distant interest that he had blood spatters and what looked like bullet holes scattered across his midsection.

"Thea, he's gone," Jake said. "Dean tried to help him, but he was too... it was too late."

Thea nodded dumbly. She knew, she'd seen the life leave Romeo's body. Worse, she'd seen death embrace him an instant before it happened. If only she'd reacted more quickly, she might have saved him. She might have done *something*.

She was about to speak when a faint gunshot echoed down the hall Carpenter had disappeared after Sforza.

"Let's go, people!" Parker yelled.

"Come on, Thea. We have to go. We have to get out of here." Jake tugged gently at her arm.

Pain flared from her shoulder. She gasped and pulled away from Jake's grasp. Touching her collarbone, Thea cried out in pain and surprise. *I've been shot.* With the shock of Romeo's death fading somewhat, she became conscious of the aching throb in the meat above her right breast.

"Jesus!" Jake said. "Dean, look! Can you help her?"

Dean grimaced. "I don't know; tired from trying." He moved over, though, and placed his hand over the wound. Warmth and peace flowed through her body, then focused around the injury. When Dean took his hand away a few seconds later, the pain was reduced to a dull throb.

"Carpenter," she said then. "We have to get him."

"Fuckin' A," Parker said from the doorway. "Bastard killed Lilly, too. But if we're gonna do it, we'd better do it now. I think I hear sirens outside."

Jake looked like he might argue, then looked down at Romeo and nodded.

"Lilly also?" Thea lay Romeo flat and crossed his hands over his chest. "We can't take them with us, can we?"

"No," Dean said. "We're going to have a hard enough time getting out of here ourselves."

"Come on, people. Let's get him!" Parker waved from the doorway.

Thea picked up the Desert Eagle and followed the others. She paused at the doorway to look back at Romeo one last time. She felt hollow inside, a thousand possibilities now gone forever. Her gaze slid up from Romeo to take in the low slab further in the room. She still sensed tremendous potential there, a dynamo of mystic force. "Jake!" she said suddenly. "Why would Sforza run away from Carpenter like that, right in the middle of his stronghold?"

"Are you fucking kidding?" Parker retorted. "Take a look around. Why the fuck *wouldn't* he run away?"

Thea cast a cold look at the others. "You go after Carpenter. I need to check on something." Without waiting for an answer, she ran for the slab.

•••

Carpenter felt a swaying motion, like he was on a boat or something. No, that wasn't right. He was being dragged. Someone had him around the middle, their arm pressing into the gunshot as they manhandled him. Thing hurt like a sonofabitch, but the pain was bringing him back around to consciousness. Movement to the side, then Nicholas Sforza came into view, looking down as he grabbed Carpenter by the waist and shoved him back.

What the hell? He was inside a box now, upright. No, not a box; check out the shape of that lid, there. A sar-

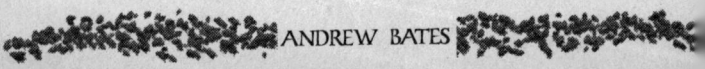

cophagus. Groggily, he asked, "What the fuck you shoot me with?"

Sforza's head snapped up in surprise, then shifted to look at something by Carpenter's right shoulder. "Didn't have time to make it as strong as I would've liked," he said, pulling something across Carpenter's chest. "You came 'round faster than I expected. Once I get this secure, though, only thing I'll have to worry about is taking care of your friends."

"What're you doing?" Carpenter felt stronger by the moment. Why was he just standing here? Take the guy out! He lunged forward, but his midsection felt frozen. Could still move his head and his legs, but his chest was... he looked down, seeing a gold band over his chest and secured to the sarcophagus. "What the fuck?"

"You have a limited vocabulary, you know?" Sforza said, smiling grimly as Carpenter thrashed his head around as if that would somehow get his arms to move. "You really don't know what's going on? Would've thought me walking away from blowing my own brains out would give you a clue. Or if not that, then this whole temple setup. Doesn't take a genius to figure out what happened."

Sforza stepped up, reaching for the band next to Carpenter's head. "You don't have a clue what you did to me, do you? You wanted me dead, right? Like you did the rest of the family, six feet under. Boy, did you screw up." He laughed with not a small amount of bitterness. "You made me immortal, you dumbshit!"

Carpenter narrowed his eyes and looked Sforza over closely. He radiated a vibrancy, a kind of dual vitality that Carpenter had never seen. "What the fuck? You some new kind of vampire or something?"

"You'll never know, buddy. Bet it's going to eat you up inside, wondering, while you finish rotting away in there."

"Yeah?" Carpenter said as Sforza pulled the gold band around. "I'm not the only one who screwed up."

Sforza smiled, eyes narrowing as he looked at Carpenter. "I spent long hours on those bands. You're not breaking out any time soon."

Carpenter grinned right back. "Who said I needed to touch you to fuck you up?" And he dug viciously into Sforza's mind, drawing forth the man's most painful memory.

• • •

Thea got a better look at the slab as she approached. It was a sarcophagus, not an altar. It lay horizontally, the surface weathered and almost devoid of detail. She sensed the energy came from within the stone casket. Grabbing hold of the lid's edge, she pushed with all her might. The stone barely scraped a fraction of an inch with her effort.

"Thea, we don't have time for this!" Jake called out, dashing back into the chamber with the others close behind. "I'm serious. We have to go now!"

"I… told… you," she grunted, lightheaded from blood loss and exertion, "there's… something… in here. I… need to… get it, okay?"

"Goddamn it," Parker scowled. "We're not splitting up again, I'll tell you that much." He stomped up to the sarcophagus with Dean and Jake. The four of them heaved to, moving the heavy lid to one side. "This is taking too fucking long, Thea! Better be worth it," Parker grunted between shoves.

"I think it is. Something about it feels really important."

After a couple minutes that seemed more like days, there was enough room to reach inside. They didn't have any lights, so Thea stretched her slender arm in and felt around till her fingers touched something. She got hold of something slender with a flared base and drew it forth. It was a small ceramic urn, covered in hieroglyphs and a patina of dust. "You guys feel that?" she asked, the pulsing from the urn throbbing like a toothache through her whole body.

"I feel... something, yeah," Dean said.

They marveled at the ancient container. Then a tremendous crash reverberated down the hallway, followed by a roar like a wounded beast.

"Fuck!" Parker yelled. "Come on!"

Thea gripped the urn by the neck and picked up the pistol before chasing after the others. This time she didn't look back before leaving the temple.

• • •

After sending Sforza into a hallucinatory nightmare of the time he blew his own brains out, Carpenter tried to get free. His torso was frozen in place, but he could still move his legs. Bracing his feet in the bottom, he shoved hard with his thighs and knees in a rocking motion. He didn't have the leverage to do much of anything, though. Still pumped from the surge of energy when he'd torn through Sforza's lackeys, he muscled through on brute force. Letting himself hang by the band across his chest, Carpenter swung his legs out and, tucking his knees on the backswing, slammed them into the back of the sarcophagus. The preternatural blow sent a shudder through the stone casket. A couple more of these and he heard cracking. Plus, the pendulum motion of his legs was starting to sway the thing forward and backward.

Chunks of stone crumbled under his kicks, spurring him on to greater effort. He figured he looked ridiculous, flailing around like this, but fuck it. If it got him loose, who cared what he looked like? Even his bloody and torn clothes didn't bother him compared to the rage at being restrained.

Sforza stirred on the floor just as Carpenter smashed a hole through the back of the sarcophagus. The blow carried through to hit the wall behind. Combined with the rocking, his kick was enough to tip the whole thing forward. Sforza was trying to come out of the fugue when the sarcophagus smashed down on him. He flung his arms out reflexively with such force that he shattered an entire side of the thing and knocked it off to the side.

Damn, he might be stronger than me, Carpenter thought. He wasn't complaining right then, though. The stone casket was riddled with cracks now; chunks fell to the floor and he felt the whole thing creaking. While Sforza struggled to his feet, Carpenter braced his legs and shoved as hard as he could. Since the lower part of the sarcophagus was rubble, the thing was seriously top heavy. He inadvertently flipped forward in a somersault and crashed to the ground with such force that the entire back of the casket cracked.

He thrashed around wildly, trying desperately to break free before Sforza collected himself enough to attack. Chunks of stone dug into his back, but then something snapped and feeding returned to his chest. The burning agony of the gunshot returned with a vengeance, tearing loose a scream of pain. Nicholas Sforza jumped on him then, scrambling with his tremendous strength to bend the golden bands around Carpenter.

Carpenter was having none of it, though. He headbutted Sforza with such force that they both felt their skulls fracture. Sforza was knocked back in a daze, while Carpenter registered the impact as little more than dull discomfort. *May be stronger, but getting hurt rattles him more than me. Good to know.*

Scrambling gracelessly to his feet, Carpenter kicked Sforza in the head so hard the guy spun into the wall. Carpenter sensed he was still alive, but pretty fucked up. Nothing like massive head trauma to ruin your day.

He was about to finish Sforza off when he remembered what the punk had told him just a minute before. Carpenter picked up one of the gold bands from the rubble. He could see how Sforza had bent it trying to wrap around him. "So these still work if they're not attached to that coffin, eh?"

A grin twisted Carpenter's ruined jaw. "I think we have more to talk about, you and me. A lot more."

• • •

Thea moved up behind Parker as they ran down the hall, leaving Dean and Jake to bring up the rear. She was acutely aware of Romeo's absence, and felt guilty that she didn't feel near as guilty about Lilly's death.

They all heard a heavy pounding sound up ahead. Thea tried sensing if it was dangerous but got nothing. There was a final loud smash, then the sound stopped. Parker looked back to make sure everyone was ready, then pointed the Spas-12 at waist height and blew the handle, lock plate, and anything beyond into a bunch of pulp.

They burst in immediately after, the echo of the blast deafening for a few seconds. A quick look around showed the room was trashed but empty. More striking than the sarcophagus wreckage or spatters of blood was the hole in the outside wall. A chill breeze blew through the opening, bringing a swirl of snowflakes with it.

"You have got to be kidding me," Parker said as he approached the hole cautiously.

Dean peeked through the other door and slammed it closed. "Police! They're sweeping the temple, coming this way!"

"Fuck!" Parker looked at the door, then the hole. "We're out of time. I say we split the same way this asshole did."

Thea felt the same fear and resignation she saw on the others. A part of her wanted to throw down the gun and let the police burst in and take them downtown. Then she thought of Carpenter. Nicholas Sforza might have destroyed Carpenter then fled, but Thea didn't think so. This rampage of destruction seemed better-suited to Carpenter. And since Sforza's body wasn't here either, she was willing to bet the thing had taken him hostage. No, she wasn't about to take all this lying down. Another look showed similar determination stealing over Jake, Parker and Dean.

When the police burst through the door a minute later after shouting for surrender and readying smoke grenades and other instruments of subdual, they found nothing among

the wreckage of the study aside from a small pile of snow blown in from the gathering storm.

• • •

Carpenter leaned back in the chair, flexing his ruined hand in contemplation. A few hours of concentration had repaired virtually all his injuries, even the trauma he'd suffered to his arms and shoulders when he'd battered through the temple wall. Only the loss of his fingers and the gunshot wound continued to pain him. For the fingers, the pain was metaphorical, at least. The wound was another matter. It remained a throbbing, burning ache in his midsection. As if that wasn't enough, it continued to leak curdled blood. No matter how hard he tried, he couldn't force the wound to close. Had to change the bandages every few hours or the damn thing stained through to his starched shirt.

He'd done what he could, and at least the rest of his body was in working order. The repairs, not to mention the entire conflict he'd just endured, had taken a lot out of him, though. Relaxing in the chair was welcome relief. And, all in all, he was happy with his results. He'd come through relatively unscathed, the hunters had ended up helping him more than they'd hurt him, and he'd come away with the prize he sought from the beginning.

Carpenter looked over Nicholas Sforza, a cold smile stretching the newly smooth skin of his face. Taking a page from his work on Sforza's vampiric cousin, Carpenter had wrapped Nicholas entirely in duct tape. Other than a slit cut for his mouth and two holes poked under his nostrils, Nicholas Sforza was completely buried under dull silver. The tape also wrapped the gold bands. Carpenter had no idea how effective they'd be long term, but they certainly seemed to work well enough to keep Sforza from doing little more than thrash around feebly.

Considering how into the whole Egyptian thing Sforza had become, Carpenter thought it especially funny that the guy was mummified in the tape. He didn't get tired pointing out that particular irony, either.

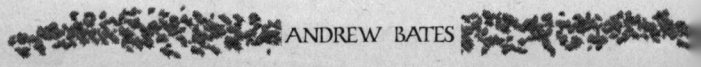

It was only a short term solution, though. Carpenter would need a permanent cage for Nicholas Sforza. Someplace he could be kept, safe and sound, for a very, very long time.

After all, as gratifying as killing Sforza would be, it would more than likely send Carpenter back to the shadowlands. A one-way ticket to Hell, mission accomplished. Alive, Sforza would provide Carpenter with endless hours of entertainment. More than the hammer that served as Carpenter's anchor to the living world, Nicholas Sforza would be his font of sustaining emotion. The anger, pain, and helplessness Carpenter could draw from the bitch's grandson would keep him going for a long time to come.

Maxwell Carpenter wasn't too sure Sforza was immortal as he'd claimed. But he now had eternity to find out.

The epic continues in **Lay Down With Lions**.

ABOUT THE AUTHOR

Andrew Bates was raised by monkeys on the frozen tundra of Wisconsin. **Heralds of the Storm** is his first novel. Visit www.devilbear.net to see what else he's been up to.

WHERE THERE IS LIFE, THERE IS HOPE

The price of immortality is high. But is there a path that leads to life eternal rather than damnation? The Undying know, and this new breed of mummies unleash their might in the Year of the Scarab!

Lay Down with Lions
Year of the Scarab Trilogy #2
AUGUST 2001

White Wolf is a registered trademark of White Wolf Publishing, Inc. Year of the Scarab is a trademark of White Wolf Publishing, Inc. All rights reserved.

THE RAGE RISES...

Garou — the werewolves of legend. Once they fostered humankind, once they hunted it. Now the Garou must choose their battles and their allies wisely, for the Red Star burns in the Umbral sky. Can the Apocalypse itself be far behind?

Will the tribes set aside their differences to confront an ancient enemy in Eastern Europe, or be consumed by their own Rage?

The seven-book Tribe Novel Series begins with:

Tribe Novels:
Shadow Lords
Get of Fenris

On Sale Now

WEREWOLF
THE APOCALYPSE

WHITE WOLF
Publishing

Vampire Clan Novel Trilogy Series

In the aftermath, a darkness before dawn.

Her most trusted ally is dead. Her hated sire has fallen to one she once called lover. Now, Lucita is on her own. And the next choice she makes will rock the world of Darkness

Clan Novel Trilogy: Lasombra initiates the Clan Novel Trilogies — and opens a chilling new chapter in the unlife of one of the World of Darkness's most recognizable characters — the beautiful and deadly Lucita.

The Clan Novel Trilogies continues with Lasombra in March 2001.

White Wolf and Vampire the Masquerade are registered trademarks of White Wolf Publishing, Inc. All rights reserved.